New (£19.99)

A Smell of Leaves and Summer

Nicholas Hagger is a philosopher, cultural historian, poet and former lecturer in Islam and Japan. He is a also a prolific author whose long-term project is to present the universe, world history and human life in terms of the mystic Fire or Light, the metaphysical vision that is central to his work.

By the same author

The Fire and the Stones
A Mystic Way
Overlord
Selected Poems
A Spade Fresh with Mud
The Universe and the Light
The Warlords
A White Radiance

"Shall I compare thee to a summer's day?
Thou art more lovely and more temperate.
Rough winds do shake the darling buds of May,
And summer's lease hath all too short a date."

Shakespeare, *sonnet 18*

"There are two sorts of talkative fellow whom it would be injurious to confound & I, S.T. Coleridge, am the latter. The first sort is of those who use five hundred words more than needs to express an idea – that is not my case – few men, I will be bold to say, put more meaning into their words than I or choose them more deliberately & discriminatingly. The second sort is of those who use five hundred more ideas, images, reasons &c than there is any need of to arrive at their object till the only object arrived at is that the mind's eye of the bye-stander is dazzled with colours succeeding so rapidly as to leave one vague impression that there has been a great Blaze of colours all about something. Now this is my case – & a grievous fault it is my illustrations swallow up my thesis – I feel too intensely the omnipresence of all in each, platonically speaking – or psychologically my brain-fibres, or the spiritual Light which abides in the brain marrow as visible Light appears to do in sundry rotten mackeral & other *smashy* matters, is of too general an affinity with all things and 'tho' it perceives the *difference* of things, yet is eternally pursuing the likeness, or rather that which is common."

Coleridge, *Notebooks, 25 December 1804*

"O nobly born, listen. Now you are experiencing the Radiance of the Clear Light of Pure Reality. Recognise it."

Tibetan Book of the Dead

A Smell of Leaves and Summer

Collected Stories

NICHOLAS HAGGER

ELEMENT
Shaftesbury, Dorset • Rockport, Massachusetts
Brisbane, Queensland

© Nicholas Hagger 1995

First published in Great Britain in 1995 by
Element Books Ltd
Shaftesbury, Dorset

Published in the USA in 1995 by
Element, Inc.
42 Broadway, Rockport, MA 01966

Published in Australia in 1995 by
Element Books Ltd
for Jacaranda Wiley Ltd
33 Park Road, Milton, Brisbane, 4064

All rights reserved.
No part of this book may be reproduced or utilized
in any form or by any means, electronic or mechanical,
without permission in writing from the Publisher.

Cover design by Max Fairbrother
Design by Alison Goldsmith
Typeset by Wendy Murdoch
Printed and bound in Great Britain by
Hartnolls, Bodmin, Cornwall

British Library Cataloguing in Publication
data available

Library of Congress Cataloging in Publication
data available

ISBN 1-85230-650-5

CONTENTS

INTRODUCTORY NOTE viii

PART 1
A SMELL OF LEAVES AND SUMMER

A Smell of Leaves and Summer	1
Castles in the Air	5
Radiator in the Snow	7
An Alternative Girl	9
This is the Way the Term Ends	11
A Ring and Horizontal Bars	13
Horses like Elves and Goblins	14
Waves across the Hedge	15
As Spanish as Lasagne	16
A Duchess in the Sun	18
Decca and Blue Flowers	19
The Manageress and the Pigeons	20
Woodcutter's Hut and Dolphin Square	20
Clubbing with Donald	22
Heart and Burning Night	25
A Vision in Winsor and Newton	26
Beehive and a Dahlia Horn	27
Cardboard instead of Bread	28
A Partridge in a Pear-tree	30
Folks Stoned	33
A Gasman Conned	35
A Blind Will and a Blunder	37
A Feathered Witch-Doctor and a Stranded Crab	42
Twinkling Hubert and a Hypocrite	45
A Castle like a Dazzling Girl	46
A Boutique behind a Mask	48
Of the Cannibalism of Mice and Shrews and Voles	51
Tyranny and Bad Luck	52
Nemesis at the Extraordinary General Meeting	55
Crabbe under Shingle	58
A Windmill and the Real Things	60
08.15 Horas and Fresh Fish	62
Flicking Fingers and Frayed Cloth	64
The Director is an Idiot	66
A Mother in Action	69
The Buses was Late	72
Friendship like a Potato Crisp	72
Breaths like Waves	73
Hoi Mate and the Water Music	74
Baby Belling	75
A Cherry-Blossomed Hell	76
Like a Burst Water-Main	78
A Standard like a Fluttering Pound	79
Politeness like a Split Canvas Chair	80
A Late Boy in the Sea	82
An Old Lady and a £40 Sack	82
Edward Thomas and the Swimming Gala	86
A Deck-Chair in the Sea	88
A Chanted Introduction and a Dig	91
Mean Time	94
Solitaire and a Nudge	96
A Harbour Creek and a Tiger Cowrie	98
Stone Cottages and a Teeming Sea	99
A Bonfire and a Village	100
Marinated Pilchards and Silver Lead	101
A Ladder and Quarrels at Church	102
A Christ in Hell	103
Like a Fish in a Storm-Tossed Sea	110
A Twelve-Year Dream and an Unsailed Boat	110
Lost Glasses and Clanging Seats	115
Shout to the Lord	116
A Nice Day for the Match and a Bottle of Optrex	118

CONTENTS

Crying Eyes and a Nearly Perfect Rose	119
A Situation like Nerve Gas	121
Three Cowherd Angels and a Cattle-Branding	125
Three Pure Chrysanthemums, or Faded Petals	132
Earth in the Way	139
April Fools and the Thirteenth Stream	140
Tattered Walls and a Gorgon's Scream	142
A Wag in Lyonesse	146
A Deathly White Boy and a Pact	149

PART 2
THE CLEAR, SHINING SUNLIGHT OF ETERNITY

The Clear, Shining Sunlight of Eternity	152
Bonhomie like an Oxbridge Smile	154
Eternity beside the Traffic Jam	157
A Bafflement like a Netted Fish	158
A Mouse under the Counter	159
A Body Fooled into Milk	160
A Zoo of Buffers	161
A Shermozzle and a Freudian Slip	162
An Orgy in the Churchyard	164
Two Smiling Buddhas and He Who Speaks	164
Spirits up the Spine and a Bucketful of Stones	171
A Hanged Man's Gift and a Mongol's Eyes	174
A Cobweb Christ and a Feather Duster	177
An Eagle and a Basking Shark	179
A Sandcastle and a Sun-Kite	181
The Waters of the Ocean, the Upper Reaches of the Air	183
Caravan People and a Fun-Hat	184
A Buzzing Bluebottle and a Frozen Fish	186
Toy Planes and Doggies, and a Merry-Go-Round	188
The Little Life and a Mirroring High Self	190
Lad's Love	192
A Grandfather among Ras Tafarian Hats	194
Like Bricks on Sand	196
Soda Water and a Scallop Shell	199
People Like Us and a Sash-Cord	200
An Archangel and Personal Responsibility	201
A Clown and a Volcanic Eruption	203
Chairman's Action and a Red-Eyed Comedy	204
A Spoon-Feeding Bully and a Pacifist	206
A Dotty Bard and a Cotton-Wool Ear	207
An Imperious Neo-Platonist, and a Genius's Volume of Verse	209
Laughter in the Dark	211
A Stumble and a Slammed Phone	212
A Flash in the Chemistry Lab	216
Irish Fishing and a Hurried Grave	220
Anarchic Laughter in the System	222
An Exile in Noyna Road	223
Yes Please to a Peeling House	224
A Chile Badge and a Lanced Boil	226
White Cars, Black Hands	227
A Boast and a Provoked Fate	229
A Bleary-Eyed Look and a Belly-Laugh	230
A Bird's Song and a Spreading Yew	232
A Poker Fork and a Bursting Bubble	234

CONTENTS

One of God's Chosen	235
French Howlers and Spilt Wine	236
The Ordinary in Pearly King Clothes	237
A Piggy-Eyed Broker and a Conniving Smile	239
Alison Bush, Eighteen, Wants Proof	242
A Rolls Royce Day-Dream and a Naiad's Chipped Nose	245
Subtle Bodies	247
The Mystery of the Great Pyramid	249
Across the Frontier	251
A Causeway of Light	255
Pinned Butterflies and African Carvings	257
Doorhandle for a Slammed Door	258
A Destiny in Hebrew Letters	260
Shahites in our Road	262
The Sweet Smell of Decay	263
Rôles like Fancy Dress	265
Providence like a Retribution	267
Mixed Metaphors and a Diamond Light	268
Like the Smell of Fresh Beans	270
Loyalty like a Company Label	272
White Globes and a Blood-Red Sun	275
Stagnant Eyes and a Vein	276
A Smile and Violent Streets	278
A Colonel in Civvy Street	280
Christmas-Tree Patterns on the Lunatic Fringe	281
Two Burps and Three Cheers	283
A Light on Dead Anemones	284
Stone Lions and Marble Veins	285
The Cold Heat of Alpha	288
Mulled Empire and a Hymn-Singing Flag-Planter	290
A Chauffeur for an Inspector	291
First Mate in the Coliseum	293
A Speaker like a Hurricane	294
An Imperial Egoist and a Car Wallah	296
Afternoons like Cinders	301
A Tide in the Cellar	302
A Run-Away's Stone and a Four-Knight Door	304
Loud Voices and the Long Silence of Christendom	306
A Pompous Fool and River Jordan Water	308
Mr Rubin's Fortune	310
A Red in the Surgery	312
Governors like Bowlers	313
Another Place	314
A Canon in his Dream House	315
Silk Apple-Blossom and Dried Greengages	317
Frothy Weirs and a Rising Sun	320
The Curtain Pulled Aside and Gamma Rays	324
INDEX	**327**

INTRODUCTORY NOTE

These 162 mini-stories were written between 1973 and 1981. They appear in thematic rather than chronological order. Whereas the stories in the first volume, *A Spade Fresh with Mud*, examined the horror of the materialist position and revealed Being as the way to meaning, the stories in this volume focus on knowledge of spiritual reality through illumination and enlightenment. The experience itself I presented in *A Mystic Way*, pp195-200, and these stories explore the peace the vision brings – the "peace that passeth understanding" – and a growing awareness of spiritual love through the Light, and of people who know spiritual love. Death is present in the opening stories of both Parts, but knowledge of the Light brings relief from the bleakness and finality of death and enables consciousness to move beyond materialism.

As with the stories in the first volume, these stories are visual prose-poems or paintings. Even when the subject matter is spiritual and inward, they go for the vivid, fresh, observed detail as would a painting, and often combine dissimilar ideas. Dr. Johnson defined the wit of the Metaphysical poets as when "the most heterogeneous ideas are yoked by violence together". When a Metaphysical sensibility replaces ideas with perceptions and observations, and presents "heterogeneous *images* yoked by violence together", then the ensuing *frisson* is akin to wit but distinct from it as the medium is not rational but observational, not ideas but things seen; heterogeneous impressions being associated or yoked together. Behind all multiplicity is a unity, and some phenomena of multiplicity correspond to each other within the unity in a way that surprises and delights.

In his *Ars Poetica* (c19-18BC or c12-8BC) Horace wrote: "A poet should instruct or please or both." In a letter to Pope (1725) Swift wrote: "The chief end in all I propose to myself in all my labours is to vex the world rather than divert it." My aim is not to vex mankind, though the bleak materialistic consciousness – whether proletarian, bourgeois or aristocratic – *needs* to be vexed into a change. It is not primarily to divert or please, to delight or entertain, though I hope these prose-poems or paintings are diverting, pleasing, delightful and entertaining. My aim is to reveal the Truth: which means showing that behind all Becoming and all surface beauty there is Being, reality, eternity; knowledge of which makes a difference to living as it cleanses, purifies and enhances consciousness and its appetite for life. To the extent that I reveal Truth I instruct. I show healthy, optimistic images of man and the universe despite an ever-present awareness of horror, suffering and death. I show images which present a vitality and zest for life that transcend bleakness and despair.

1st March 1995

PART ONE

A SMELL OF LEAVES AND SUMMER

STORIES OF PEACE

A SMELL OF LEAVES AND SUMMER
(OR: PEACE AFTER THE MORTUARY)

One Thursday in June I took the backward boys I taught to St. Nicholas's Hospital, Deptford, so they could see what it was like to work there. We were shown round the kitchens and the boiler-house, and then I ushered the dozen of them up to the Head Porter, who gave us a talk on wheeling porters' trolleys. He was a giant of a man, a full six foot seven inches tall and huge across the shoulders with a jutting jaw, and he wore a suit. He looked like someone out of a James Bond film, I could imagine whacking him in the solar plexus with an iron knuckleduster and he would not flinch.

He stepped aside as a trolley came out of the operating theatre, and I marshalled the boys against the wall so they wouldn't touch the pale unconscious patient who lay restlessly on it. "Anywhere else you'd like to go sir?" he asked me, and Trevor Varnalls said, "Mortuary, sir. Go on, ask for the mortuary."

"Do you want to go to the mortuary?" the giant asked.

"Yeah," chorused the boys.

"Have you any objection, sir?"

I had to make a quick decision. "I hadn't thought we'd be going," I said, surprised at the words that came out, "but if it's offered I think it might be a good thing. These boys have to be introduced to the idea of death some time, and I think it's good to do it in a controlled humane way. It's all part of education. They can't be sheltered indefinitely."

"Wait here a moment then."

The giant strode off. A few strides and he was round the end of the corridor. While we waited the boys asked me one after another, "Are we going?"

"I don't know," I said, wondering if I would get letters from their parents. I thought of my responsibility. I wandered away from them and looked into my heart, and I felt my heart telling me to go ahead.

The giant returned. "Follow me," he said, and we all piled into the lift.

The mortuary was in the hospital grounds. It was an old yellow brick building with wired glass windows. It could have been a Gents.

"Burke'll be sick," Trevor Varnells said. "What do you want to

A SMELL OF LEAVES AND SUMMER

bring a wally like that for? Show us up."

"No he won't. You will more likely."

"Go out, I ain't squeamish."

"Yes you are, you're a bottler."

"Go out."

The mortician came to the mortuary door. He was a beady-eyed man with rimless glasses, and he wore a white coat. For a moment he conferred with the giant. "If you're sure it's all right," I overheard him saying. While I waited I lectured the boys on respect for the dead. I told them they must keep silent – and no arguing. Then I realised Trevor was missing. He was bending head down at a nearby wall.

"Come on Trevor."

"I ain't going in there, what do you take me for."

Inside the door there was a unit of fridge doors with long handles. The giant peered at the names, which were stuck on the doors, and then opened a door to reveal the ends of three drawers. The giant pulled a drawer, and out slid – a man of around seventy. He was still in his clothes, there was no sheet over him. He had grey hair and a small clotted cut on his head. As the giant pulled the drawer right out the old man's elbow caught on the side, and it looked as though he moved his arm.

The shock ran through me. It was a shock of recognition, a strange disgust at his absence from his limp body. Then I smelt the sickly sweet smell of death.

There was a stunned silence. The boys stood in a semi-circle, absolutely still, every eye fascinated by the *thing*.

"Sir, is he dead sir?" Burke asked in an undertone next to me.

"Yes," I said, disapprovingly final.

"Sir, is he dead sir?"

"Yes."

Burke thought about it, his eyes darting madly from side to side.

"See," said the giant. "He died this morning. Fell. See the cut on his head? He's just asleep. Touch him."

My palms felt damp. My awe, like that of the boys, was a mixture of reverence and repulsion.

"Go on, touch him. He's only asleep."

The boys cowered back.

That *thing* was living that morning, I thought, what would he have thought if he'd known when he got out of bed that a dozen backward boys would be staring as if he were a gorilla at the zoo?

"What the Head Porter says is true," I said, to impose some sort of control on myself. "He's just asleep. He's asleep. There's nothing frightening in death." That last sentence was what my mother said when she showed me my father.

But *I* would not have touched him.

"He's looking at you," said the giant. "Let's close his eyes." And he put his finger and thumb over the old man's eyelids.

"Sir, is he dead sir?" Burke asked again.

"Yes," I said, more matter of fact now that the silence had been broken.

"You're a wally, Burke. Course he's bloody dead."

"Shhh."

"Sir, he *is* dead sir. Is he?"

"Yes," I said.

The giant slid the drawer back in. He pulled out the one beneath it.

This one had a sheet over it. The giant pulled it back to reveal a woman of about fifty-five, her skull bound with a bandage. She looked like a nun in a wimple, and her face was a waxy yellow-white.

The giant pushed her back and closed the fridge door. He opened another door and pulled out a frail woman in her seventies. She looked very peaceful, and all her wrinkles were gone.

"She was alive this morning," the giant said.

Burke had a weird smile on his lips. His eyes were darting madly. This was obviously the experience of his lifetime. These people were dead – you could see he was sure of it now. As the giant pulled out another drawer he clenched his fists and shook them up and down, as he always did when he got excited.

When I came out into the sunlight and walked back to the main hospital entrance and smelt the green leaves, I felt faintly sick. Yet what I remembered was not the repulsion so much as the peace. I had not been consciously aware of it, but I had felt a deep peace towards the end. The dead were – still; in another place. They had shocked my heart into discarding all its rubbish, they had purified my heart of all the wants and desires that enslaved it most of the time, and as a result I had felt a peace that now revelled in the smell of summer.

I was fully alive, I felt the blue sky and the blinding sun to be wonderfully good, and full of a rich meaning. I loved life, for I saw it through my heart. I could not think of those dead bodies as useless material, as rubbish waiting to be burned – all that mattered was to live intensely, to enjoy life to the full. I noticed things out of the coach window, and when I got back to school I lunched alone and watched the cricket on television. It was the first day of the first Test between England and New Zealand, and I concentrated on every ball that was bowled. It was important.

Then I turned off the television and just sat quietly. I just sat and felt the meaning of life outside the window; which the reason makes us forget.

CASTLES IN THE AIR

That Thursday I took my boys to Windsor Castle. The flag was up. "The Queen's here," I said to Burke. We walked round to see what we could find out and on the North Terrace, near the State Apartments, which were closed, there was a barrier that kept us away from the East Terrace garden. Burke stood against it and watched the sentry, who wore a red coat and a busby, and from behind him marched the changing of the guard: six more red-coated sentries with bayonets. When Burke saw them descending on him a look of horror crossed his face and he clutched his pockets, put down his head and ran as fast as his legs would carry him as if he thought he was about to be executed.

To get him out of everyone's way I took him up some nearby stairs to the courtyard that leads into the Quadrangle. Trevor Varnalls came too. "Look," he said, "there's me old man." I looked and saw one of the Royal chauffeurs dusting a large black car that carried the Queen's gold flag. "Oy," Trevor called, and to my shame he stuck two fingers between his lips and let out a piercing whistle. He wisely took to his heels while I pretended not to know him.

"Excuse me," I said to the glaring chauffeur, mainly to mollify him, "will the Queen be coming out?"

"The whole Family," the chauffeur said. "They're lunching here, and they're going to Ascot at one-forty-five."

There was a silence.

"Yes, but will the Queen?" Burke asked.

The chauffeur looked at me as if to ask 'Who *have* you got with you? What kind of a nut are you with?'

"The Queen," Burke mumbled madly, and as I tried to propel him away he put his fingers all over the Royal door, and the chauffeur said sharply, "Fingers off," and I knew that for a moment Burke thought he was going to have his fingers cut off.

I established that the Family were to leave from the back exit at Long Walk, and we returned in disarray. I collected the boys together and asked them, "Who wants to see the Queen?"

Trevor Varnalls said, "Nah, what do we want to see her for? What's she ever done for us? Why should we do anything for her? *She* doesn't earn her money. Good mind to pogger her, stupid wally."

"Er, you can go to the coach," I said hastily, looking round to see who had heard his treason and imagining beheaded bodies from Henry VIII's day turning in their graves. "And the same applies to anyone else who shares Trevor's Republican sentiments."

In the end I lost all of them except for Burke and a couple of meeker others. We walked round the outside of the Castle wall until we came to the Park, where a crowd was gathering in the sun. We took up a position near the magnificent back gates of the Castle. The drive across the grass to the brow of the hill was lined on both sides by colourfully dressed people. Around us, the crowd grew bigger and bigger, and I noticed several plainclothes policemen who were standing and waiting with rather too obvious nonchalance.

Eventually the first few black cars nosed round the distant corner of the Castle. Their windscreens glinted in the sun. They came down the steep hill, one under the other. The liveried gatekeeper opened the gates with the aid of the top brass from the Metropolitan Police, and they sped by. They contained confident young men in top hats whom I did not recognise. Very much the country cousins.

Then came the next fleet of cars. The second car bore the Queen's flag, and I saw, gliding past at speed, the Duke of Edinburgh in a topper, and the Queen, wearing green and looking strangely pale and unreal.

"There she is," I said to Burke, who immediately peered in the wrong direction.

Everyone waved, and there were a few cheers and she was gone.

And driving by in the cars behind were the Queen Mother and Princess Anne, Lord Snowdon and Princess Margaret, Sir Angus Ogilvie and Princess Alexandra, and the Duchess of Kent and a couple of others I did not have time to identify, all looking strangely smiley, like puppets: outline people without the faces properly drawn in. Empty stars.

As I came away, the image stuck. There was this family coming out of its Castle and driving through the Park, to be judged, ultimately, by their possession, or lack, of inner beauty like everyone else, and I pondered the meaning of privilege. *I* wouldn't have minded going to Ascot that afternoon. And how could I be sure that Burke had not a less humble heart that some of those men in top hats, how could I be sure they *deserved* it?

I got back to the coach late and counted my grubby boys. How could I be sure that their ignorance of the world disqualified them from all right to a seat in one of those cars? The driver grumbled because I was late, and on the way back I stayed in my own thoughts. We passed large company buildings near the M4: Siemens and Honeywells were two.

Suddenly I saw deep into Britain. Under the monarchy and the capitalist companies were the people – in Parliament, in local government, in houses. And the police were keeping the whole structure intact. They let you do what you wanted to do so long as you did not disturb the lofty Castles in the air. By looking at one of them, I had helped keep it up there. Perhaps there was something to be said for Trevor Varnalls after all?

RADIATOR IN THE SNOW

I was back in that seaside town and I looked in on the cinema on a cold day. I did not recognise the ticket-issuer so I asked her if Elsie still worked there, "Yes," she said, "she's in the well now. On the kiosk. Through there."

I went through some swing doors and there Elsie sat, long-haired and just the same after so long.

"Hello Elsie," I said. "How are you?"

Her eyes had widened with surprise.

"Quite a stranger," she said.

"Just passing though. Had to look in to say Hello."

She came out of the well, leaving rows of boxes of chocolates unattended. It did not matter, no one else was about. She went over to the radiator, all leggy and erotic, and we stood together.

"You haven't re-married?" I said.

"No."

"Divorced?"

"Yes."

"That's a step in the right direction. You know, I used to say I was your guardian, and that that would be a step in the right direction."

"Yes."

"So you're a free lady about town."

"Yes."

"Do you still go dancing?"

"No."

"Still living in the same place?"

"Yes."

"Among the fish-tanks?"

"No, we haven't had those for years."

"Those angel fish, with stripes...."

There was a silence.

"Is your mother all right?"

"Yes."

"And your father?"

"Yes."

"You know, I don't drink now."

"Not even orange juice?"

"Yes, I have orange juice. You remember when we went out I had beer and you had orange juice? It'd be the other way round now."

"No, I don't drink beer," she smiled.

I remembered walking with her in a cornfield, and in woods across the downs, and how we sat in a seaside car park.

"Well," I said, "I had to look in to say Hello."

Outside it was snowing.

We hugged the radiator.

"Thank you for looking in."

"Give my best wishes to your mother."

"She'll be surprised that I've seen you."

"I must be going now."

A man strode past the kiosk.

"Is he the manager?"
"Yes."
"I don't want to get you the sack."
She moved away from the radiator.
"Look me up next time you come down," she said.

An excitement leapt in my stomach, but I thought I probably wouldn't, as I walked out into the snow.

AN ALTERNATIVE GIRL
(OR: GANGSTER'S MOLL)

Mrs. Styles had a thirty-six inch chest and long black hair and brown eyes. She came into the staff room one day and was introduced as the new supply teacher, and I often saw her there and scampering round the upper hall playing football with her class of juniors. She sometimes wore a blue jean pinafore over a blouse, and she kicked the ball with a curious sideways scoop, and I did not think it odd that she was behaving like a man. It seemed a perfectly natural thing to do.

Once she described to the staff how one of her boys had brought her a foxglove. She dilated her eyes and threw her whole self into exaggerated gestures. For some reason – I thought principally because she was always surrounded by the male members on the staff – I never talked to her very much. I knew she lived in Tooting, that she was given a lift in by Miss Brisket, the weird middle-aged woman who looked foetal and who did not relate to anyone. I knew the boys fancied her: when she was on playground duty it was like looking at a hive swarming round the Queen bee. I did not know that the rest of the staff had warned her off me. She told me one Wednesday morning in the middle of June: "They've warned me off you, you're that Rawley man."

She said this as we left the staff room to return to our classes after break. I went on down the stairs with another teacher and said, "She's married?"

"Oh, but she's not living with her husband. She came to the British Queen with us the other day, and she told us she's not been living with him for a year or more."

I raised my eyebrows and said no more. At lunch-time I got a boy to bring my tray to my classroom as usual, and I might not have thought any more had he not said: "Shall I ask the girl with the sports car to come in?"

She taught nearby, and she sometimes joined me for lunch in my classroom.

"All right."

"Or shall I ask Mrs. Styles?"

He was joking, so I said as a joke, "Yes, go and ask her."

Bill Currant went straight up to the staff room. He threw open the door so it crashed against a chair, reducing the teachers to amazed silence, and barked in an authoritarian tone, "Mr Rawley wants Mrs. Styles to go down to his room immediately."

Most of the teachers were there at the time.

"Oh yes," said Mr Blair, the metalwork teacher, ironically.

"Here," said MacGregor, the woodwork man, "why can't he come up here?"

"What a cheek."

"Don't go," said MacGregor, who was a Communist.

"No, it's all right," she said, apparently wondering what she had done wrong. "I'd better go and see what he wants."

I was eating shepherd's pie. I said as she opened the door and squeezed in, awkwardly turning to close it: "It was Bill Currant's idea. I'm surprised you came after being warned off me. Sit down."

She sat down, rather startled that I did not want her for any reason except to make a point to the staff. We talked, and she told me about her last boy-friend.

"I left him. He hit me. He was called Beau. I've been living with two girls I know since then.

"I'm an orphan," she said. "I've got no parents. In fact I have a very shady background." I stiffened. My upbringing made me cautious about things like that, I did not want to hear about that. "I was illegitimate," she went on, "and I was in homes until I was fostered. My foster-father was a Communist, like MacGregor. I don't see so much of him now, he used to try and grope me and I'd rather stay away. Yeah, grope me. Yeah, I generally did what he asked. So you see, I had no moral standards, no one ever expected anything of me, so I did what I liked. I got onto drugs, I was Suzie the junkie, and I got in a bad way. Then I got mixed up with some Hell's Angels and with the police – I don't want to go into that – and then there were suicide attempts in front of cars.

"Then I went to college in Canterbury to do my Teacher Training, and I was in the same year as the man who became my husband. He acted as my psychiatrist, for I was in a very bad way. We married in our first year. It was a terrific event, he was terrifically attractive. I should never have married him, for by the end of college we weren't lovers properly, I started having affairs. And I'd had gay experiences before – as I say I had no moral standards when I was young and I thought everything was natural – and after that I carried on and I still go to the Gateway sometimes, that's a gay club in London. I go with Janie, the girl I share with, or else with my friend Donald, who's also from Canterbury. He's gay, he's like a brother to me. I worked a lot in cafés and offices and places like that, you know, making tea, and after I left my husband I lived with several men, for I'm impetuous and erratic, and then I met Beau. I've met rotten people, he turned out to be a gangster, he knew the Kray twins. He was always involved in fights, and he was always chucking bottles through windows. So I was a gangster's moll. You see, I've a terrible background. It's really an alternative background. I'm an alternative girl. Isn't it fabulous?"

I had listened with barely an interruption. She had a common face – no eyebrows and a snub nose – and I saw how she would tempt someone into an infatuation from the body rather than a love from the heart.

I was content in the evenings, living through the spring of my creativity. I should not neglect it; if I did I knew from experience that it would sulk like a jealous woman. I was complete. I had peace, and I should not lose it by wanting.

THIS IS THE WAY THE TERM ENDS
(OR: A WOOD AND A SACRED COW)

On the last day of the summer term the teachers who were leaving were given a Parker biro at assembly. The Head apologised to us. "Sorry, he said to me, "it's not very imaginative I'm afraid."

At lunch we all went to the British Queen. I had half a pint of lime juice because I had given up drink. Ken Barnes bought it. "You're still writing then," he said. "I've decided it makes for unhappiness. You know Yeats's lines, 'The intellect of man is forced to choose/Perfection of the life or of the work?' I've come to the conclusion that unless you're good, and demonstrably good, it's better not to do it, because it messes up your life." He had brought his two year old son for sports day, and he had a beautiful wife, and I knew how he felt.

Then Jones started talking about teaching. He said, "You're a credit to the school, you've turned out some very decent boys."

And, thinking what drop-outs we teachers were, and what hooligans the boys had been on the streets of Deptford for the last two months, I said, "Everybody has some good in them. The secret is to find it and nurture it." And Mathur, the Indian left-winger, nodded with approval.

In the afternoon, the boys went home and the teachers drank some alcohol the Head had dumped in the staff-room. Suzie came to my classroom, where I was writing a story, and said, "I don't want to drink with them. I can't bear Mr Mackenzie going on about Communism or Jones about teaching. I've been invited to the Barneses for dinner tonight. Could you drop me there?"

She went out through the kitchens. I went out the front way and ran into the Head.

"Coming up for a drink?" he asked, beaming through his spectacles.

"No," I said, "I'm just going to check my car battery."

"Oh, what's wrong with it?"

He frowned suspiciously as he did when my boys told him, 'It wasn't me sir.'

I said, "Oh, nothing. It's just part of the usual Friday routine. Water, oil, tyres and battery."

Suzie joined me at the garage. We drove past Eltham wood. I said, "I can see the trees in your eyes, I can see the sky in your eyes."

She said, "But no babies?"

I said, "This is the way the term ends/This is the way the term ends/This is the way the term ends,/With a whimper, not with a bang."

She laughed and then she said suddenly, "I can see what sort of a wife you need. A wife must believe in you."

Then the sun went in, and there were spots of rain.

The Barneses lived on the edge of Blackheath, down in a dip. Ken's wife came out. She was very attractive with long hair and a long dress, and she held the little boy. Ken was with her. "Come in for coffee," he said.

In the kitchen, his wife (who had been on school journey with Suzie and Ken) said, "You know, Jones offered me a job at his new school. He came up today when I fetched Ken and asked me if I was accepting, and I said No, I wanted something less remedial and more advanced. He said, 'You might have told me sooner. Arrangements have to be made.' Silly old fool." I smiled my agreement. "And earlier he rang up and said, 'It's Stan here, you can call me Stan.'"

I said, "He's Bob, isn't he? Not Stan?"

"Oh yes," she giggled, putting her hand in front of her mouth, it is, it's Bob. I've been calling him Stan."

The house was a palace of art. Ken had done everything. He had built the kitchen out of wood and painted the walls and done the paintings and sculptures. There were some abstract bronzes he had cut on the metal-room lathe, and there was a picture he had painted after he and his wife had hitch-hiked round India. In front of some erotic lovers from the temple of Konarak stood a dodo and a sacred cow.

"It has a Stanley...I was going to say Jones. It has a Stanley Spencerian quality," I said.

He smiled. "That's my writing," he said. "Dead as a dodo."

Then I looked at him. Dodo and cow, life and work. I looked at Suzie. I had to make my work into a sacred cow, I had to choose work.

A RING AND HORIZONTAL BARS

That afternoon I took my daughter to buy a second beanbag frog. We got it from a shop near South Kensington station. She was very pleased with it. "Thank you Daddy," she said. "I'll call it....Now let me see...."

"Who always keeps his promises?" I teased.

"I wish I had my tape-recorder here," Pippa said as we crossed the road.

My daughter said, "The one I've got's called Jeremy after Jeremy Fisher, so this one will be Humphrey."

We went on to the Victoria and Albert museum. There was a notice saying that samples of the Beatrix Potter competition were on display on the Library landing. They were in a glass case – neat children's writing in ink and drawings of frogs and mice – and nearby there was an exhibition of jewellery.

"Oh, can we go in?" my daughter asked.

You had to go through a turnstile of horizontal bars. A notice said "No Handbags Allowed", and Pippa held a small collapsible umbrella that looked like a truncheon. I looked doubtful.

"Please," my daughter pleaded, so we creaked through to the other side.

We slowly walked through Celtic gold and medieval necklaces and nineteenth century lockets. Pippa walked behind.

In the last room there was nothing but rings: Papal rings, signet rings and wedding rings.

Pippa stopped in front of a large ruby wedding ring.

"Pippa," my daughter said, taking her hand, "nice, sweet Pippa." But she would not budge.

I wanted to get out and away from the stupid things, but the two of them stood there. I looked at Pippa.

"Let's go," I said.

The exit turnstile was operated by an attendant who pressed a button. The released mechanism made a buzzing noise. I went through with my daughter and found myself near an exhibition of Constable paintings. Looking back, I saw Pippa still standing in front of the rings. She was cut off from us by horizontal bars.

"Come on," I said to my daughter, "we'll look at the Constables. I'll show you where I want to buy a cottage in Suffolk."

HORSES LIKE ELVES AND GOBLINS

While Pippa was in Cheshire I took my daughter to stay in a Hall. The Hall is like a Gothic castle, and it is supposed to be haunted by a Black Abbot, and she loved to explore the turrets and the woods. I left her there, and I drove on to Worthing. I tried a guest-house with a swimming-pool. I asked Jack, the writer of children's stories about elves and goblins, if he had a room for me. He rang the Major and fixed me up.

"How's the writing?" I asked.

He wrinkled his nose. "I've just had a couple of X-rays," he said, tugging his spade beard, "and I've been told I've got a couple of patches, one on either side. It it's what I think it is I shall sell up and go to Devonshire and sit on the edge of my bed and say, 'At least I've lived.'" In the next room his black-haired wife looked worn out as she lay with her feet up.

After dinner I went to the TV room. The colour TV was

showing the Royal Horse Show, and there was just one other person watching: a silken-haired old man with a hunched back and glasses. "Thank goodness someone else's come in," he said.

"Been here long?" I asked after a while, getting bored with horses knocking down poles and planks and gates. I had to repeat the question.

"Oh, I live here," he said, turning deafly. "Yes, my wife died last year, and so there's nothing for it but to live here. There are twelve of us who do."

I went to the bar. I asked for a soft drink and the Major made me a sunshiner, which is Angostura bitter and lime and fizzy lemonade. I took my sunshiner back to the TV room. The widower turned deafly.

"Don't come down much," he said. "I stay upstairs and read or listen to the radio. I can't bear to watch TV normally – you see I always looked at it with my wife. I find it depressing. But I'm interested in horses. I used to ride in the First World War."

"Cavalry?" I asked.

"Royal Engineers. I never rode after the war. I was one of the luckiest fellows of that time. I was drafted abroad the day the war ended. No, I normally don't come down. This is the first time this year."

Then I knew why he was so pleased I'd gone into his room. Like the horses, I had helped him escape his reality. He and Jack were two of a kind. The whole guest-house was a place where ageing people came to terms with the pain of their reality. I shuddered slightly in recoiling admiration.

WAVES ACROSS THE HEDGE
(OR: YOU SHOULDN'T THINK IN THE OLD CURRENCY)

In the morning I did my exercises. They ended with three hundred and seventy-five runs on the spot, and every seventy-five steps I did ten scissor jumps, which made me feel like a leaping Nureyev.

I went down the stairs to breakfast and as I picked my way past folded wheelchairs and wizened old folk, imagining I was still doing my scissor jumps and smirking, an old lady smiled sympathetically at me. She had bad arthritis and she had enormous varicose veins in her arms, and she looked rather like the aged Colette. I sensed a wistful nostalgia as she sat in the window.

From my breakfast-table I had a view of the sea. I could see a sparkling of waves across the hedge. When I reached the toast Colette asked the widower from the TV room, "How much is seven and a half in the old currency?"

"It's one and six," he said, standing up to go. He was still used to his wife, and he did not want to talk to Colette for long. "You shouldn't think in the old currency."

Then one of the waitresses was standing in the window. She was blonde and middle-aged. "Wave to him, wave," she called to the ginger Irish waitress.

"Who's that?" asked Colette. "Your boy-friend?"

"Yes. We share him. He stayed here two weeks. He sat just there. See him? Beyond the hedge."

I craned my neck, but he was out of sight.

Colette peered. "Ah yes," she said. "I thought he was that one over there." She pointed to where the widower had sat. "*He* lost his wife too. They both lost their wife. I can't tell them apart." She waved an arthritic hand.

Later Colette looked at me. "Staying long?" she asked.

"A few days," I said. "Are you?"

"Oh I live here," she said.

She was one of the twelve, and I realised that for her, too, life was sad and empty. She, too, knew about the hedge that separated her from her youth and from the vitality across the road and on the pebbly beach.

AS SPANISH AS LASAGNE

That evening I ordered lasagne. The French waitress looked amazed and then shifty, and I thought it was on the menu for show and that no one else had asked for it.

In the window sat the Beetle. He was bald with a big vein down his horny head and I could almost see his feelers. He grumbled through every meal and now complained that his glass was dirty.

The hoary Head Waiter shuffled up. He walked on tiptoe with great slurpy shuffles as if dancing a Spanish tango. He looked like a tortoise, his neck protruded from his white coat. "This glass isn't clean," the shuffler gruffly told the French waitress, "and go and get two forks and a knife."

She came back and said in her English, "There is not any," and he said, "Wash some up."

While she disappeared again he dusted the white table-cloth on the side-table, and I felt he was the only one who kept up the standards in the place.

One of the guests stooped badly over his soup. The collar of his jacket was halfway up the back of his head, it needed turning down. He looked like a clothes-hanger.

At the table next to me, President Hindenberg (I call him that because he looked like the portrait of Hindenberg in 1930s German stamps) got untypically mischievous. He had a basket of bread on his table, but he asked the French waitress, "Can I have some more bread?"

She said "Yes," and disappeared again.

"I didn't mean it," he giggled, "I thought she knew it was a joke."

"Don't confuse her," said a tall greying man from a nearby table, "she's confused enough as it is."

Colette looked as if she was dining with the Queen. She was wearing enormous rings and ear-rings and several necklaces and brooches, and she was in a suit that would have flattered a woman forty years her junior. She was very interested in my lasagne when it arrived. "What is it, is it Spanish?" she asked.

"Italian," I said.

"Oh, has it got onions in it, and potatoes?"

"No, it's mainly pasta."

Colette had lived in France for nineteen years. "Italian," she said. "Oh, have you been in Italy?"

"Yes," I said, having once been there on holiday.

Colette's table partner looked like a mottled trout. She stood up and left without a word and Colette said, "She's deaf, you know. We never speak. I have to shout, and I don't like that in the dinner hall. And she never speaks to me. I'm going upstairs now. I'm going to visit the woman with the bad heart. She can't get down the stairs you know. I've got a dicky heart, but I'm on the ground floor. I only stay here when it gets bad."

She stood up to pass me and she gave me a long, nostalgic look. "You look Spanish," she said. "You remind me of someone I once knew who was Spanish. He was very handsome."

I looked back at the table behind me to borrow the water-jug. The tiny old lady with the scalded face who looked like a boiled lobster was nodding and smiling.

A DUCHESS IN THE SUN
(OR: POTATO FIELD AND GUNPOWDER TEA)

Back in London I went into the gardens. I unlocked the gate with a long key and lay on a rug and sunbathed, wearing swimming-trunks. The sun streamed over the tall plane-tree and was warm on my back. I dozed.

Out of the corner of my eye I squinted at a nearby body in a bikini. I thought of Beckett's mutilated thalidomide creature unnameable in its jam-jar and wondered how he could write of such pygmies when human beings had beauty and greatness.

The body sat up. Improbably it was Suzie.

"The Barneses were driving me, and we thought you might be sunbathing," she said. "I didn't want to wake you. I'm returning your Browning."

"How's the Duchess?" I murmured, thinking of Browning's poem *My Last Duchess*.

She smiled. "My nose isn't very Duchess-like," she said, screwing up her eyes for the sun. "It's more likely come from a potato field."

"Duchess of the potato fields," I said.

Then a very bombastic couple came up. They had loud voices and sounded as though they had come from a country house with rolling lawns where they could spread themselves as they liked. They sat too near, invading my vital space, so that I didn't want to talk any more.

I lay in the hot sun and my front tingled warm. I gazed at the green leaves under the blue sky. The sun shone through them. Then I heard a noise like a lawn-mower. I turned. The man near me was snoring. He had a beard and three-quarter length trousers and being naked from the waist up he looked like one of the pirates of Penzance.

Later the sun got caught in the branches of the tall plane tree and the shadows stole up and crept over my legs, and I felt a sudden chill as if I were experiencing the early numb of death. A child ran behind me, humming like a bee. I looked back. An enormous horse-fly had settled on the Pirate's big toe. I wondered if it would sting him.

Then Suzie laughed. I thought of the Pirate's snores amid all this wonder, and I thought of *her* response to the sun. Then I no longer thought about the tall plane-tree or no-good Beckett or the shadows, the Pirate could keep his rolling lawns, I would settle for the sun and the potato fields any day.

Soon I would make some gunpowder tea, from a boiling kettle.

DECCA AND BLUE FLOWERS

I dreamt someone wrote a long article attacking my view of *The Waste Land*. I found a copy, and then the author was in front of me, and I gave him a long ticking off, wagging my finger, until he realised his mistake and admitted it.

Then I was visiting my ex-wife and daughter in a large Hall. It was a great country house, and there was a concert in progress. On one of the corridor walls there was a mural of a beautiful red-haired girl who had a balloon out of her mouth that said, 'I don't go to parties any more.'

"That's Decca Oshwez," said someone. I remember the name because I asked her to spell it several times. She took me to the two rooms Decca had occupied until she died in 1915. They were both originally part of the upper circle of an opera house – you could see the iced-cake columns and ceiling – and one room had gold foil on the walls, the other silver foil.

Later I met my ex-wife. She had been in Canada, helping with some educational or welfare project. She looked like Decca. She sat by the bed where I had been sleeping and we talked. I quoted *The Waste Land* at her: "The barge she sat in, like a burnished throne...." Whether we got together again depended on whether some blue flowers came out. They were in clumps, like hyacinths, on the lawn outside.

Then I was in the grounds with her. The blue flowers were out near my feet, they were everywhere. We saw her husband walking down one of the paths. I had to greet him, and thinking of *The Waste Land* again I said, for her benefit, instead of 'Hello': "Co-co-ri-co."

I woke to hear a growl of thunder, and it occurred to me that I must have heard thunder in my sleep, for the cock in *The Waste Land* crowed when thunder was due. It was raining very hard so I got up and put the bucket and bowls to catch the drips and then I lay in bed and listened to the music of the stairs: a high drip, then a low drip into the bowls.

In my concert I looked out at the dark sky. I had no blue flowers round my feet, but I did not want Decca any longer.

THE MANAGERESS AND THE PIGEONS

"Your laundry's ready, love," said the elderly, spectacled woman at the Knightsbridge laundry. "I saw it last night when the van delivered."

"Been feeding the pigeons?" I said. For outside a dozen grey pigeons were pecking crumbs below the kerb.

"Oh yes," she said in her sing-song South-country accent, "I *shouldn't* you know, but I do. It's only because some have no legs."

I looked again. Two of the pigeons had stumps where their right legs should have been.

"They wait for me on that ledge over the road and when I walk home with my bag, you know my shopping-bag, they recognise me and they gather into a flock and fly low. I pretend not to know them, for people would think I'm mad. Yes, I give them a loaf a day. It's not cheap, eleven p a day I spend on them. Couldn't do that if I didn't work, could I? Yes, I shouldn't do it, but it's always the gutter, I don't believe in crumbs on the pavement, and I do sweep up after them. I feel sorry for them. You know, they sit up there on that ledge, and I'm here managing the shop, and, and....They've got just as much right to live as I have, haven't they? Yes, I just feel sorry for them, that's all."

WOODCUTTER'S HUT AND DOLPHIN SQUARE

Suzie lived in a street of terraced villas. She still wore her cheese-cloth smock, and she took me up some stairs past a bicycle and a pair of crutches to a landing of cats and discarded mattresses. There she introduced me to Janie, a boyish young woman in a man's shirt who was typing through an open door.

"It's my 'A' level notes on *King Lear*, Janie said. "I've just been disturbed by Mrs. Big Gob. That's what we call our neighbour, in fact her husband's sitting in the garden down there." I peered out of the window and saw a man with a hairy chest sitting in a deck-chair. There was a heat wave and the temperature was in the 90s. "You must hear Mrs. Big Gob," she went on. "When she tells her children off it's deafening. 'Get out the f—g way you f—g herberts.'"

As I smiled at this "separatist" independence of language, Suzie added, "And the other day the Ceylonese swinger had a row with her husband, and the whole street came out to watch, and the police sent a panda. The next night they had a worse one, and the police sent two squad cars."

We went to Suzie's room. On the door a label said "Yes Please." "That was my predecessor Marion," Suzie said a trifle smartly.

The room was tiny: a bed, a few pots on a chest, and airy-fairy postcards on the walls – all nymphs and contorted nudes in pseudo-Beardsley styles.

She handed me my anthology of twentieth century poets and, sitting on her bed while I perched on a chair, prattled on about her neighbours. There was something tarty about her, and I looked critically at the way she wrinkled her nose, at her plucked eyebrows. I listened to her diction. It was elusively unclassifiable. Sometimes she sounded Cockney ("Sor' of", "lo' of", "bo'les") but her vowels were very well pronounced. She acted out what she said, putting her eyes into everything, and gesturing. Looking at an old photograph of her *with* eyebrows and with longer hair, and at a photograph of her "first bird", I wondered if she wasn't just a very good actress.

"That's a fairy princess on the wall," I said.

"Mmm. The Princess in her woodcutter's hut, as she really is."

She had a copy of Silvia Plath's *Ariel* by her bed.

"Which is your favourite poem?" I asked.

"*Poppies*," she said. "But *Lady Lazarus* is good, for it tells you what it's really like to wake up and hate the doctors when you try to kill yourself."

I began to tell her about the revolution in the arts that was needed. She interrupted with: "Oh, Donald was here last night. He's got this new boy-friend, a solicitor who lives in Dolphin Square in a fabulous flat above Shirley Bassey. There are chutes for laundry, and he throws a bundle down and it comes back a couple of minutes later all washed and ironed." (Her talent for cartoonising, I thought with some disparagement.) "The solicitor has an estate outside London, and Donald's invited me on Sunday. I'll go and have a look at it. Donald was here last night. He was terribly upset. He feels patronised and treated as a country bumpkin by these men in suits. He said, 'Oh Suzie, I can't talk as well as they can, and I haven't got anything to wear, and they go to the best clubs, where you normally can't get near people like them.' So we all went through our wardrobes and gave him shirts and things to wear – Janie too – and he was nearly in tears. Oh I'm so close to Donald, I adore Donald."

Then I remembered how she had tried to get me to meet Donald, and how she had said, "Donald and I have a pact, one always helps the other. If I have somewhere to live, he can always come and sleep on my floor, for really he's very poor." And I remembered how she had said, "I'm going to grab every penny I can get." And: "I'm fascinated by conning." Suddenly I felt that the pair of them were on the con. I had no evidence, but it was there in the atmosphere.

CLUBBING WITH DONALD
(OR: HEART AND GAY ROCKINGHAM)

"Can I see you?" Suzie asked me over the phone. "Otherwise I'll only start clubbing with Donald again, and that'll be bad for me."

So I met her round the corner. She had come straight from Dolphin Square.

We had a drink in the Stanhope across the road. It was hot, and she had a lager, I had a coca cola. Next to us a group of filthy-haired youngsters were munching steak sandwiches they'd brought in from outside, and the landlord asked them to leave, and they retired, still munching, to the Gents. She wore a flowery smock and jeans.

I told her how I'd been thinking about the heart. "Everything must come from the heart," I said, "not the head. The heart of the tree outside my window or my dahlia is in the roots, and it flows upwards from there through the trunk or stalk to the head."

She said "I haven't got a heart."

And I recoiled slightly from her. She was a head-woman. We talked about abstract art, and I saw it in terms of the heart, and she argued for movement. I said the movement had to be seen from a still heart, otherwise it was not seen truly.

A woman who looked like a buxom whore stepped across me and nearly sat in my lap. She was with a mop-haired man, but ten seconds later she put her fingers round my elbow and asked for a light. Afterwards her foot touched mine.

"Donald was so happy in Dolphin Square this afternoon," Suzie said. "His bloke's good-looking, which is good for him. He's soooo-per. And he spends a lot of money on Donald, which is nice. He took quite a shine to me."

I asked, "Did you and Donald ever plan to con people together?"

"Not really."

"But sometimes?"

"It's hard for you to understand because you've had a different background," she said, "you've *had* the good things in life. But I haven't, and nor has Donald. We made a pact we'd grab them, we'd *make* it. That was two years ago. This afternoon I stood with Donald in Dolphin Square, in this fabulous flat with a swimming-pool and laundry-chutes and porters. We were alone because his bloke was at work and he said, 'Suzie, we've *made* it.' We'd dreamt of it so often I could hardly believe it."

With scathing contempt I said, "How unreal to want vulgar material things like that, and to believe they're going to last. You know the solicitor will chuck him, and if he doesn't, you said yourself Donald's got an in-built defect in his character that makes him opt out of his relationships in a week or two."

"Yes, but it's because of our background."

"But don't you realise that when you get material success, it's empty?"

"It's easy for you to say that when you've got it."

"Donald's values are false if he doesn't know that now. They're artificial and superficial. You're crazy if you listen to Donald."

She turned urgently to me. "I've never had any parents," she said, "and I've got no one else save Donald. I'm always washed up every so often, probably because I've met rotten people, and because I plunge in quickly and don't think things out deeply. In between there's Donald. He's there, he's everything to me. We have a joke that at ninety we'll still both be walking down the Earl's Court Road. We'll still have each other."

"Yes, maybe," I said, "but he gets you into a mess. You get confused, and you go to him and he says, 'Let's go clubbing.' You go to a club, and there you meet rotten people who wash you up more and get you into more of a mess, and a few days later you go to Donald again, and he says, 'Let's go clubbing.' The people at clubs are worthless, so why search among them? Your Donald's a bad influence."

"Yes I know, you *are* right."

"Take my advice, and I hope you'll always remember this as long as you live. Steer a straight course. Don't get distracted by worthless people. Otherwise you're like a rowing-boat trying to get upstream. People shout to you from the banks and you zigzag backwards and forwards across the river, and never get on with your direction. In fact you end up further behind than when you started. You should be in a boat with a worthwhile man and steer straight ahead."

She fell silent. The woman next to me was rubbing the sole of her shoe against my ankle.

"Donald's friends asked me out tomorrow evening," she said. "They're going to the Rockingham. That's a club we never dreamt we'd ever get near, let alone inside. It's the top gay club, you have to wear hundred pound suits to get in there. I said I'd go. I *am* curious."

"And you asked me if you could see me this evening so you *couldn't* go clubbing."

"I know. I'm sorry. I feel very unsettled inside. I feel very insecure. And there's nobody except Donald and his friends. And Janie. I really like being with you."

"That's because I'm at peace," I said. "You share my peace."

She looked restlessly down.

"Come on," I said, "I must go."

I stood up. The woman who had rubbed her shoe against my ankle did not look up. Outside in the street I bumped into a friend from Libya. I had not seen him for two years. He looked terrible. He had hundreds of small boils under his yellowy jaundiced skin, and he wore dark glasses to conceal a congealed cut.

"I have orders from Col Gaddafi to place you under arrest," I joked.

He looked drugged. "You," he said, "hey I've just got back from Saudi Arabia and in three weeks I'm off to the Yemen. Give me your telephone number."

"For me too," said his revoltingly made-up companion who held his arm.

I wrote a number on a matchbox and threw off his companion's hand.

"I'll ring you tomorrow," he said.

After he'd gone I said to Suzie, "When I knew him he was married. He looks as though he's gone queer and on drugs. He's a bad influence, he's in a mess."

She smiled sadly. "I may not go clubbing tonight. When shall I see you?"

"I don't know."

"Shall I give you a ring?"

"All right."

"When? Tomorrow?"

"Make it the next day," I said.

We crossed the road to the station. I'd seen through her. I felt sorry for her of course – she couldn't help being an orphan. She was a girl lost among gays, she needed someone to sort her out and give her a direction. She was in too much of a mess. At present she had no heart, she was by her own admission only out for what she could grab. 'Look at me, this is what I've got' – that was her attitude, and she would do anything and pretend anything to get what she wanted.

I watched her walk sadly off. Tomorrow, when she was at the Rockingham, I would be watching football on the television. I would have unity of being. And peace.

HEART AND BURNING NIGHT

After Pippa had gone to bed I read Teresa a poem from St. John of the Cross. I came to the third stanza: "Upon that lucky night/In secrecy, inscrutable to sight,/I went without discerning/And with no other light/Except for that which in my heart was burning."

"Heart?" I queried softly. "Shouldn't it be behind the eyes?"

"No, murmured Teresa serenely, "it all comes from the heart. First you discard all that clutters the heart, get rid of all the rubbish and the wants, and then, when it's peaceful, the heart starts burning and it steals up to the head and becomes the light in the head, the spirit. 'Heart' is right, 'burning heart'. I've had so much experience of that in St. Ives. When I pray I discard and feel at peace and I go deep, so deep I'm not aware of my body or my hands, and I *see* what I'm thinking, yes, *see* it. If it's Mary, I *see* her, looking frontwards and at a distance, it's always the same. If it's God, I *see* the presence."

I said, "I can see St. John of the Cross now. He's a white-haired man with a white beard, and he's looking to the right in profile, his eyes down, and I see a sinister, hooded man near him. Aren't they just day-dreams?"

"They are visions," she murmured dreamily. "It's your religion coming out from your childhood perhaps. It's the heart that starts them: love. If you are humble, you are at peace. When I pray I don't speak to anyone, I don't talk. I had a vision of truth, the best I have ever had. I don't want you to tell anyone. Do you promise?

"It was last October. I had been so peaceful. It was dark in my room at St. Ives, and…suddenly I saw Jesus Christ. He was life-size, dressed in white. Black hair, no beard or moustache. He looked straight at me, and I could have touched him he was so near."

There was a silence.

"I thought only the saints have had that," I said quietly.

A lovely smile crossed her middle-aged face.

"Don't tell anyone," she said.

There was a great peace in the room, a deep silence underneath the distant traffic sounds.

"You see, I don't need proof," she said. "I didn't ask for it, I didn't want it, but it came to me. Last time we were together, I was all confusion, it was a Dark Night of the Soul. But now I'm all right."

A VISION IN WINSOR AND NEWTON

The next morning Teresa brought a small pottery figurine to the breakfast-table. It was a tall triangle, and the third side surprisingly revealed a floating vision of the Virgin Mary. I picked it up and turned it round, puzzled.

"I know your work requires a lot of looking," I said. "Where do you start looking at this?"

She took the figurine and turned it over so that I could only see the two blank sides. "It's about angles," she said. "Most people have angles, they look along the line and see nothing, whereas if they change their way of looking and peep round the corner, there is this vision. You see, if you don't peer round the edge, you never see it."

"It's beautifully simple," I marvelled.

"Life should be simple. The heart discarding mess and flowing up to the head."

"It's a triangle," I mused.

"I have no triangles any more. That's one of a serial." (She spoke English with an Austrian accent, and she meant "series".) "The latest I've done has just two sides."

I did not follow.

"One side was perhaps Father Charles. One side was me. Between us perhaps we protected this important vision. Now I don't need Father Charles."

"Mmm," I said. "I shall call this *Vision*."

"It has to be mysterious."

"It's done in clay?"

"Yes, white Winsor and Newton clay."

Winsor and Newton, I thought, looking at the two blank sides, the social and the rational. I knew what hid the visions from me. My Light was beyond both, wasn't it?

BEEHIVE AND A DAHLIA HORN

"I'm going to get my three million pounds from my husband and finish with business," Teresa said. "I've been thinking, I don't want to have any more to do with his business. I've given him two years to pay me my share, I just haven't thought about it, for money is so unimportant. They've done nothing, out of greed, they've lied and evaded, so I'll have to go ahead. I need the money now, not for myself, for I won't spend a penny on myself. I need it to finance artists. That is right. You told me that I should do that and I was not ready. I thought I would be doing it for myself. But Father Charles has told me, 'You have a talent, it must be shared, you must not keep it to yourself.' Remember the beehive pot I made? The base fell out, and then I dropped it and it smashed into three pieces."

That afternoon we walked in the gardens. We went to the Cupid fountain.

"Look," I said, "he's holding a *cornucopia*, a horn of plenty. It's like a spring, only it's always overflowing with flowers and fruit and corn. It's a goat's horn, it suckled Zeus."

"Yes," Teresa said quietly, "not a beehive now, a horn."

In the evening, Pippa threw out the dahlias that had died. She left one good dahlia in the vase, and some stems with buds on them.

Teresa sat at the table and stared at them.

"Yes," she said dreamily, "I will not say 'That is a good bud, the rest out.' That would be aggressive and ruthless, *destructive*. With a little care that small bud there can develop into a better flower than that good one. I shall build a beehive that everyone can enjoy, a beehive of dahlia flowers shaped like a *cornucopia*."

CARDBOARD INSTEAD OF BREAD

That Christmas Eve we went to Midnight Mass at St. Augustine's, Queen's Gate. It was only a short walk, and as we approached the porch a young coal black man with darting eyes came out in an important-looking surplice. A notice on the door said: VISITORS ARE ADVISED NOT TO SIT UNDER THE SCAFFOLDING. There was, in fact, so much scaffolding that it looked as though it were holding up the roof of the church, and it is quite impossible to avoid sitting under it. The church was empty, save for a sprinkling of elderly men and women in coats, and then another black man appeared with a smoking censer. He had a great mop of woolly hair, and I began to wish I had not turned out at 11.45p.m. after all.

Eventually the service got under way. It was conducted by a white Father. It was very high Church, with a lot of incense and candles, and everything went smoothly enough until the collection. This was taken by a boyish, undergraduatish man in his early sixties, and –

"Christ," I whispered to Pippa, "it's Eric Ashby from Japan. I haven't seen him since Japan, though he tried to get me to give some lectures over the phone recently."

As he came level with the money-bag, I whispered, "Hello Eric," and he looked startled and then winked.

There was a very short sermon, and we got through to Communion despite some desperately slow organ-playing. Pippa edged past me in the pew, and I found myself going too. We were the first, along with an old lady who limped resolutely on a stick. Eric Ashby seemed to be a churchwarden, for he was in the aisle pointing us up to the rail. We knelt at the rail beside the old lady and one of the priest's entourage.

It was so long since my last Communion that I had forgotten what I had to do. I held out my hands, and then the priest was on us, shouting, "The Body of Christ." He dropped a wafer in my cupped hands. I put it on my tongue. It tasted awful, it was very hard. The priest was taking the silver chalice, and I bit. But nothing happened. It was impossible to swallow it. Then I suddenly had the thought that it was cardboard, like one of the round cardboard discs I wore at school receptions that said, idiotically, "English". Convinced I had been given cardboard instead of bread, and having to free my mouth for the wine, I quickly put the wafer out into my left hand, which I clenched shut so that the priest did not see.

"The Blood of Christ," the priest shouted, thrusting the silver chalice under my chin and tilting it, and I gulped the first wine I had allowed myself to taste for a year and a half. Immediately the old lady and Pippa were standing up, and I was obliged to stand up too. I walked back past a winking Eric Ashby to our pew, my left fist clenched over a sticky, gooey, doughy mess. I was condemned to keeping my left hand closed until the end of the Mass, for which I now fervently prayed.

It was the most ridiculous situation I had found myself in since the day I made my first visit to my main Japanese University. I had gone to the Gents, and washed my hands. There was no towel, and outside the door, my right hand dripping wet, I encountered the President of the University who was advancing with his right hand extended. I had to shake it, and he went off wiping his hand.

The last hymn presented a problem. I had to find the place with one hand, and in the middle there was a blessing of the crib. Then we knelt. Eric Ashby came up the tiled aisle and I introduced my wife under the scaffolding. He looked more undergraduatish than ever.

As we followed the congregation to the door he said he normally went to church in Brighton, where he lived. He did not say why he was not at home for Christmas. "I'm now a grandfather," he told me, "my grandson's five." Then he introduced me to the priest as "one of my old cronies from Japan," and the balding priest pumped my unclenched hand, and then we were outside on the kerb and walking towards Brompton Road.

"You'll be retiring soon," I said, as something to say.

"Yes, this year."

"Are you hoping to move somewhere? Saint-Tropez maybe?"

"No, I shall live here in London. I've got a scheme lined up. I'll be in touch with you about it."

"Oh, what is it, in a few words?"

He looked evasive for a few moments. "Japanese and literary houses over here. I'm going to arrange for them to come over and do a tour. I'll be in touch with you. Thanks to you I've just been back to Japan for two weeks, for a 'businessman's conference'."

"Through...."

"Yes," he said, "your contact, the one you sent along to me."

A year earlier I had been taken to Hiroko's by a Japanese of great age and wisdom. Indeed, his first appointment in the U.K. was as far back as 1912, when he was an attaché to the Imperial Navy. He was in his nineties, and he had told me he had a private air company. He wanted some English teachers to address some Japanese visitors, and as Eric Ashby was in the British Council I had sent him along to see him.

"Well, well, well," I said. "Isn't life strange?"

"I'm going to get them over on his planes," he said. "It's a private venture. I'll be in touch with you."

"Good," I said. "Dish it out among the old gang."

"Yes, that's what I want to do. Get the old gang in on it."

We laughed on the corner of the Old Brompton Road, and he invited me to his local some time. It was the Zetland. "When it's not cordoned off by the bomb squad," he added, "for you know they've had it cordoned off for the last two days."

"We must go," I said, turning to Pippa. "I must play Santa now. I must creep into my daughter's room and leave her stocking by her bed."

I watched him walk up the Old Brompton Road. He had a sprightly boyish step for a man who was on the verge of retiring. Perhaps a life abroad had kept his mind curious and open, perhaps that was why I never thought of him as being older than I was. He stepped it out with the same undergraduatish neatness with which he had taken the collection up the aisle to the priest before the high altar, and I realised I did not take his scheme seriously, there was something about it I could not swallow. There was something strangely cardboard about him.

Yet, like the dough that was sticking to my clammy, clenched left palm, perhaps my feeling was a deceptive one? Perhaps the cardboard would dissolve into clinging yeast after all?

A PARTRIDGE IN A PEAR-TREE
(OR: A GAME OLD BIRD)

That year Mrs. Marsh sent me a Christmas card of a pear-tree with concentric rings that contained the menagerie of the carol. The top ring showed a partridge. I interpreted it as a view of our Department, with me in lonely isolation at the top.

She also invited us to dinner. She had invited us once before, and I could not go, so we made sure that at 7.30 that Monday after Christmas we arrived with our baby at Mrs. Marsh's Wandsworth house. It was in the fashionable district near the Common, where there are networks of roads of semi-detacheds, and we were shown into a back room by one of the five children. Then Mrs. Marsh appeared, dressed up for her Head of Department, and Mr Marsh entered behind her. He was forty-six and much smaller than she was. He was in his shirt sleeves.

"I'm terribly sorry I'm like this," he said in his French-lecturer's well-enunciated diction, "but the central heating went wrong and I've had to repair it so the room will be warm enough for your son." He indicated the carry-cot inside which the little mite was sleeping, and he launched into a long technical explanation of what he had done, assuming that I had a plumber's knowledge.

At his sweeping invitation I flopped back on the sofa – and nearly skidded out of the room for it was on castors and the floor was parquet. We chatted until he went and changed. He returned in a suit. Now he was like a waiter – he was a dapper little man. He made quick neat strides to the drinks and brought the nuts round in the palm of each hand, clearly revelling in the asthetic movements he was making. He was the perfect humble servant.

"John did the parquet floor too," Mrs. Marsh said in her fierce examiner's manner – she had the open face of the good soul, she helped the Samaritans every other week – "and the marble slab in the grate. We were given it by an old lady, and we took it to the local undertakers to get the edges chipped straight."

It was soon time to eat. Mr Marsh did the organising. He made sure the children were settled in another back room, and then he quickly fixed a dimmer switch in the dining-room to hide all the places where he had been stripping wallpaper. He told us this with great pride. Then he took us all to the enormous dining-table, and took Pippa round to her seat, elaborately pushing her chair in. He then did the same for me, and for Mrs. Marsh. Then he was off out into the kitchen to bring in the soup. After he had served it he sat down himself, and was immediately up again to look for the salt and pepper, which were also in the kitchen. At the end of the soup it was he who served the main course – chops done in a sauce – and he who bustled round pouring wine for everyone.

"John's a perfectionist," Mrs. Marsh said on what must have been his tenth expedition to the kitchen. "He was always going round behind me, correcting everything I did, so now I let him do it, and he does it well." And I began to wonder why this lecturer in French, who was such a do-it-yourself fiend, was such a perfectionist.

As I wondered, the conversation proceeded in the English manner, with everyone taking the topic under discussion and adding something to it, as if they were adding morsels of food to an elaborate dish. There was no possibility of asking anyone anything so direct as a question.

Mrs. Marsh was talking about how teachers find out the home situations of their children. "I had one child who wrote an essay about how her parents quarrelled," she said, and she elaborated this point at some length.

"*We've* never quarrelled, that's not true," said Mr Marsh, misunderstanding.

"No, not us, the Palmers."

"Oh."

Later Mrs. Marsh described how after the fire they had had at an earlier house "the entire Women's Institute came and fed the children."

"No, not the entire WI," said Mr Marsh. "That's a bit exaggerated, there were only two of them."

His perfectionism required a pedantic accuracy of facts.

Mr Marsh carried all the plates and dishes round for second helpings. He really was giving us royal treatment. To make conversation I had waffled about the teaching of French: how some expert had said it was "useless" to teach French at a comprehensive school, and how the French mind worked.

"John comes from a family of Francophiles," Mrs. Marsh said, "but John isn't terribly Francophile himself."

And then I wondered if *that* had something to do with it? Perhaps he was very attached to his mother. But would that lead him to wait on everybody so enthusiastically? Through the pudding and the cheese and biscuits – which saw him cut a large round cheese with the most elaborate care – and while he went off to find his coffee-grinder, I racked my brains, but I still could not understand him.

We adjourned to the next room for coffee, and I saw, among the Christmas cards, my card to Mrs. Marsh: a scholar being visited by an angel while an academic God swung a pendulum over his head that was marked with the Greek letters alpha-omega. I was reminded of the card she had sent me: the partridge in a pear-tree. A partridge; I remembered the OED definition I had once, for some reason, looked up: "a game-bird." And that was what he was: a game old bird. I could not fathom how or why without asking inappropriately inquisitorial questions. As Mr Marsh handed me coffee, and brought me cream and sugar in the palm of each hand, I decided I had to accept the surface he presented to me. He was a partridge in a pear tree.

FOLKS STONED
(OR: THE IMMIGRATION WAITER)

That year we went to Canterbury and we spent the night in Folkestone. We put up at the first guest-house we found on the front because it was nearly time for our son's bottle.

"Winter season," I said to the young wife who ran the premises for her husband, "how many have you got staying here?"

"Oh, seven before you came," she said. "They're from Immigration." I was not sure whether they were officials or a group of Pakistanis discovered rowing across the Channel.

We camped in the front room on the first floor, overlooking the deserted roller-skating ground and the swimming-pool, where, as a boy, I used to watch the Channel swimmers train. That was in the days of Mari Hassan Hamad and Eileen Fenton, when the Channel race was front page news in all the papers and a Channel swimmer's autograph evoked admiration at school. We huddled over the fire, which worked from a meter, for it was bitterly cold, we fed our son, and then we went out to look for a place to eat.

We found that at 7 o'clock on a Thursday evening in February, Folkestone was deserted. Every street sign said "Town Centre" and some said "All Directions", and after much driving round in circles we stopped at a Chinese restaurant, where we were the only customers. The one Chinese waiter served us well, stage-managing a selection of Beatle records. The frail songs came from echoing rustles out of sight – it was very much the atmosphere you encountered behind the Iron Curtain – and they sounded doubly sad, and I thought with sorrow how all life was a filling-in of silence. TV and records on the radio kept us Westerners from feeling the loneliness and silence as a dentist's injection kept us from feeling pain, and I was sad that my children would be deluded by the Western soporific. Yet I did not want them to feel the pain.

There is nothing to do in Folkestone at night if you do not drink, and after driving round the town, following one "Town Centre" sign after another, we returned to our guest-house. Downstairs the colour television played loud, exciting music, and there was loud laughter from the bar, and a hacking cough that was repeated every ten seconds.

"The Immigration people," I said to my wife, looking at the Visitors Book. It gave a name from Leicester and a name from Scotland, and for the address: "Immigration, Terminal 3, Heathrow Airport. Jan 6-Feb 21." "On a tour," I said. "God, what a life."

I had seen through Western civilisation too much to be deluded by the make-believe danger on the colour television – they weren't going to take me out of myself that easily – and so we went to bed, even though it was only 8.40, and snuggled together to keep warm.

I awoke very early and lay for a long time, half-paralysed by the sea air but wide awake. This was why we had come to the sea. The first day wiped out the city cobwebs, the second day filled the lungs with health. It was a ritual I observed religiously at least twice a year. Our baby was quiet, and it was a very long time before the wife who ran the house knocked on the door and called "Eight o'clock."

Breakfast was in the basement. As I approached the door I heard the loud aggressive cough I had heard in the bar the previous evening. It was repeated every ten seconds, and punctuated by a long noisy nose-blow which – I swear it – made the windows rattle. The perpetrator of these accompaniments was, I soon saw, a young man in a white bow-tie. He was dressed as a waiter, and he sat with another youngish white man and a rather dumpy woman. We sat at a table at the other end of the dining-room, having laid our son on the floor by a storage heater, and every ten seconds there was a deafening cough that would have held its own against the slipstream of any Jumbo jet at Heathrow Airport.

Between coughs and nose-blows, the Immigration waiter said, "You were staggering last night too, weren't you?"

"Not as much as you," said the other man.

"I wasn't too bad," said the dumpy woman.

"I wasn't staggering," said the Immigration waiter after the most enormous cough and nose-blow that made our son jump off the floor and curl his lips in an early frightened cry. (How on earth did the man carry food to a table with such a chronic habit? Did he have to put his tray down when he was overtaken with his itch?) "I was just stoned."

He coughed tensely, aggressively, loudly, nervously.

For a moment there was actually a silence, and I tried to imagine him seeking peace; though of course his own body would sabotage any fragile spiritual calm he might achieve. Then:

"You know that man from Customs, he's coming to Immigration now," said the Immigration waiter. And I thought: poor fellow, what he will have to put up with. He, too, would go on six week tours and find nothing to do in Folkestone save join the folks and get stoned.

A GASMAN CONNED

In Margate we slept in a guest-house that overlooked the Winter Gardens. We were down to breakfast just after nine. The only other guest was a large man with silvery hair, probably around sixty, who was eating egg and bacon. Every so often he raised the tip of his knife to his lips and licked it.

"Morning," he said after we had settled down. "Staying for a day or two?"

I explained that we had come from Folkestone.

"Oh, Folkestone," he said. "It's got a good harbour. Have you been to Broadstairs?"

"Yes, we passed through it."

"It's got a good harbour." There was a silence. "Ramsgate?"

"Yes," I said madly, determined to be in first, "but there were a lot of cars on *its* harbour."

"Yes," he said, "Volkswagen have an agreement, there's a lot of exporting that goes on there. But," he said, not to be outdone, "it's got a good harbour, has Ramsgate."

There was an absurd silence while I digested this remark and pondered the logic of our conversation so far.

"You evidently like harbours," I said.

"Oh yes," he said, "I like a good harbour. But it's nice here in

Margate as well. Nice place here. Got central heating too. *Gas* central heating at that. Fellow who owns it is doing very well. Only been here since July. He was a car worker in Oxford before that, and he got fed up and he came down here and bought this. He's the chef now you know."

Through the kitchen door there was the sound of sizzling, and absurdly I pictured the car worker with his spanners and grimy hands holding a palate knife in the same elbowy way.

"How long are you down for?" I said, to fill the silence while my wife bent over my son.

"Oh just a day or two. I come down once a fortnight. I've got a business down here, and just come down to keep an eye on it."

"Oh? What kind of business may I ask?"

"Holiday flats," he said.

We all ate in silence.

"There must be a big demand for them in the summer," I said, leading him on.

"Oh, there is. I've converted a large house into four flats. It's very good you know. It cost me three thousand five hundred six years ago, and you can get thirty-five pounds a week for each flat. That's a hundred and forty pounds a week." I calculated. Between May and September he must have been pulling in over £2,500; a very good return for such an outlay.

"And I've made a lot of friends down here," he said. "I'm in the Conservative Club, and I eat at some good places. There's the Castle Key in Kingsgate and the Captain Digby before Broadstairs, just near the North Fordham golf course. They're big places with their own grounds."

We chatted on and eventually he left the breakfast room. The woman who was married to the chef came in from the kitchen with her three children. She looked rather intense and theatrical, and the youngest was a boy of two who clambered everywhere. Within ten seconds he had put his fingers in some marmalade, upended a pepper-pot, and flung an empty glass to the carpeted floor.

"Clive," the woman shrieked, and she apologised: "He's into everything. I overheard what Jack was telling you. You know, I wouldn't pay too much attention to what he says. We did at first, but he goes around telling everyone his business is marvellous, whereas in fact he's in financial trouble. He had to pay out a hundred and fifty pounds last week to get rid of a tenant who hadn't paid any rent since last May. And now it's February. Just think, nine months. He's too soft-hearted. He tells everyone how ruthless he is, but he gets conned. And he will save on solicitors. It's a false economy, and so he has to pay out in the end. You know this tenant was subletting. He was supposed to pay thirty-five pounds a week, and he was subletting for forty-five pounds a week, and keeping the lot! I don't think it works to have holiday flats unless you're living on the spot. He's a gas worker who lives in Croydon, you know, he's on the Gas Board, and he's too tied up to give his full attention to what's happening down here, and so he's conned."

Towards the end of her intense, impassioned monologue, her husband came through and lolled at the bar. He had longish hair and the face and unconcerned manner of a car-worker on a tea break.

"I mean," his wife was saying while the three children swarmed round our son, "I went to grammar school and my husband didn't, but he's got a sense of when he's being conned. You have to have that, don't you."

The chef had the mouth and vacant eyes of a very early school-leaver indeed, and he nodded slowly without saying a word.

A BLIND WILL AND A BLUNDER
(OR: HOW THE EXTREMISTS TOOK OVER)

The challenge from the extremists began after the Head decided the staff were not doing enough at tutor-group time. She decided to call the houses in one by one, beginning with our house. We were summoned at 9 o'clock and some fifteen or twenty of us filed into her study where chairs had been placed round the wall. I felt as I did when, a small boy, I entered the Head's room to be told off for kicking a football too near the library windows.

The Head started by humiliating Mrs. Parkinson in front of her house. She told her to go and find a list of the staff in her house so that she could check their attendance. Then followed a very direct talk. She appealed to us to do more duties. The resentment mounted, and I could have cut the atmosphere. It was a complete miscalculation: confrontation when she should have been winning co-operation. Clumsy handling gave her talk the appearance of an unnecessary display of power.

The house staff came out seething. Some went to Mrs. Marzeki, who had the strident manner and politics of a militant trade union leader.

Mrs. Marzeki was married to a Persian anarchist who had been exiled or imprisoned for trying to assassinate the Shah, no one was quite sure which. She was an International Socialist and a self-professed Marxist of great militancy, who, it was rumoured, attended meetings at which she was advised how best she could disrupt the school. She had brought the school to a standstill only three weeks before when she persuaded fourteen NUT teachers to go on a day's unofficial strike against the Houghton Report.

Mrs. Marzeki immediately engineered the calling of a Staff Association meeting, at which she read a motion objecting to the Head's use of house divisions to meet the staff, and resenting "the unprofessional manner in which we are being reprimanded for inadequacies relating to the tutor system."

It was a stormy meeting, with a vote being insisted on. Mrs. Mitchell, the Madam Chairman of the Staff Association, was a small woman who was known to be close to the Head. She held strong Conservative views which, working at a comprehensive, she wisely kept quiet about, and she clashed with Mrs. Marzeki. She allowed her a vote on one matter. Mrs. Marzeki was defeated, but immediately protested it was not fair. "You say you want a vote and we have it and now you say you don't want a vote. What do you want?" Mrs. Mitchell snapped, to which one of the Deputy Heads called out, "A mess."

After that there were mutters against Mrs. Mitchell, especially in the Modern Languages Department, where Mrs. Marzeki worked. "It was disgraceful," the Head of that Department said to me. She was a French woman with a very Latin temperament.

"She can't chair a meeting," said Mrs. Kestrel, a spiky housemistress who wore spectacles, and who would shortly be leaving the school.

As a result a motion of no confidence in the Staff Association appeared on the noticeboard of the staff room. The motion said that the Staff Association should not be formed on a house basis but by secret ballot from the whole staff. It also said, "It will be necessary to declare a vote of no confidence in the present Committee," and it demanded a review of the Constitution.

The motion was proposed by Mrs. Kestrel and seconded by

A SMELL OF LEAVES AND SUMMER

Mrs. Marzeki. Everyone said it was strange that Mrs. Kestrel, who was known as a right-winger, should team up with such a blatant left-winger as Mrs. Marzeki, and no one could understand why she was activating such a campaign when she would not be in the school to enjoy the fruits of her victory, if she won. There were mutters that Mrs. Kestrel had become jumpy and over-critical recently, and there were suggestions that this had something to do with her marriage and her childlessness. Rumour had it that her husband was about to run away.

A few days later, Mrs. Mitchell asked me to accompany her to the Constitution Club, where the Shadow Secretary of Education – a Conservative – was making a speech. We drove there on a rainy night. Mrs. Mitchell had ambitions of becoming an MP, and she kept pointing out people from Central Office, where she sat on an education committee. After the speech during which we were advised to struggle against left-wing ideas in the schools, there were questions. When she put up her hand to ask a question the Chairman, a former Minister for Energy, said, "Sue Mitchell," and she winced, for her name was Jane. Later she wrote the Chairman a note about a woman in the front row who wanted to ask a question: "The woman at the end in the front row caused trouble at a recent meeting by asking a question about a racialist subject." The note was passed to the Chairman, and then to the Shadow Secretary for Education, who then said, "I want to hear this woman's question," and Mrs. Mitchell looked down.

I could see now how Mrs. Mitchell had come to put herself forward for the rôle of Chairman of the Staff Association.

On the way home she said, "I'm worried about the next meeting of the Staff Association. I'm going to be voted out unless someone puts a counter-motion. I think I ought to fight them, just so that the left-wingers don't get their way."

"Mrs. Marzeki," I said.

"Yes."

"I dare say something can be arranged," I said. I knew two members of my Department who were anti-Marzeki. Next day I spoke to them, and sure enough they drafted a counter-motion that included a vote of confidence in the Committee of the Staff Association and a proposal that the choice of the Committee should be discussed at a later date. There was a brief meeting among the Mitchellites. Mrs. Mitchell agreed to take the two motions together.

Unfortunately, this was procedurally out of order, as Mrs. Mitchell learned to her cost at the crucial meeting of the Staff Association. It took place in the staff room after school – never a popular time with the more indifferent of the moderates – and there were barely half the staff present when the supporters of the Kestrel-Marzeki Axis objected to the two motions being taken together. The first motion had to be taken first, there could be speakers against it, then it had to be voted on. Only after that could the second motion be considered.

Mrs. Mitchell looked very small and frail. She was barely taller than some of the high-backed armchairs the staff sat in, and the chiffon scarf thrown over her shoulders gave her performance a false, social ring. Mrs. Kestrel spoke, emphasising that there was nothing personal in the vote of no confidence in the Committee, although everyone knew there was something personal in it. Mrs. Marzeki spoke, her voice for once a husky whisper due to laryngitis.

"Now speakers against," Mrs. Mitchell said. She was losing her grip. She had trouble in identifying raised hands, the meeting became messy, teachers began to drift home.

"Now we come to the vote on the motion," she said. "Those for." It was ambiguous, and about forty hands raised and were counted. "Right," she said, "now those against the motion."

"No, those against voting," chorused a group of anti-Marzeki-ites.

There was a pause. We had all voted on the wrong motion.

"Oh, sorry," said Mrs. Mitchell. "Some of you were voting for voting just now. We'll take it again. This time it'll be on the motion."

Her supporters looked stunned. At the meeting they had agreed to press for a secret ballot, which the Marzeki-ites also wanted. Why now an open vote on the motion? She had been panicked by her loss of control into self-destruction.

"On the motion," she said, and she read it out. "Those in favour, but before you vote I would like to say that some people may feel it is politically motivated."

She looked at Mrs. Marzeki.

This personal intrusion was a total miscalculation. It was the wrong thing to say, it was a complete blunder. There was an immediate storm of indignation from all quarters of the thinned staff room. Several members of the staff jumped up and said, "I object," or "I must protest." The temperamental Head of Languages called out, "Really, this is disgraceful. This just shows the way this Committee is carrying on. We want a vote now to vote the present Committee out immediately and clear the air and start again."

Mrs. Mitchell appeared unabashed. She grinned, but all her sympathy had gone. She could do nothing else but read the motion again for a vote. A forest of hands went up for the Kestrel-Marzeki motion, and I noticed a member of Mrs. Mitchell's Department who had had words with her voting against her now.

The vote against was negligible: some eight teachers who felt that this was not the way to bundle out the Committee, and who suspected the proposers' motives.

"I have resigned," said Mrs. Mitchell, "as of now. I have been collecting for the staff party at the end of term. I will hand what I have collected over to whoever is carrying on. What about the rest of the Committee? Is anyone staying on after this vote of no confidence?" No one was.

Mrs. Kestrel looked amazed, as if she had not envisaged the collapse of the structure of the Staff Association. Then someone proposed that there should be a Steering Committee until elections had taken place, and with lightning speed the names of Mrs. Kestrel and Mrs. Marzeki were proposed and seconded for this Steering Committee.

After that Mrs. Kestrel became more and more fanatical. She was always hurrying to meetings to rewrite the Constitution of the Staff Association. One of her former friends rang her up and in the course of conversation asked her if she felt she was not being used by Mrs. Marzeki and her political advisors. "Oh no," Mrs. Kestrel said, shocked. "We are keeping her in check. No, the boot's on the other foot." It did not seem to occur to her that after she left Mrs. Marzeki would be left in an unchallengeable position. She was absent from the end of term party. "No fear," I heard her say to the librarian when asked if she was going, "that's not *my* idea of how the term should end."

And that was what she had done: imposed *her* idea of how the Staff Association should run, or rather, Mrs. Marzeki's idea. She was all sharp and spiky, she was everyone's idea of a schoolmistress in her spectacles, she was strict and prim-looking, and she had imposed her idea on the staff, even though she was leaving. What her motive was did not matter – whether she genuinely felt she was improving things, or whether she was stirring, or whether she was getting her own back on the Head for some obscure feud which, gossip said, she had been pursuing all the year. The point was, that the extremists took power through the blindness of self-important people who imposed their wrong ideas, as much as through the inept blunders of those already in office.

A FEATHERED WITCH-DOCTOR
AND A STRANDED CRAB

Mrs. Brown did not get on with Mrs. Parkinson. she was given her orders in an unusually peremptory manner. Whenever Mrs. Parkinson lost some demerits or the late list or a key, which happened frequently, she blamed her number 2 as if *she* had mislaid it. It had something to do with her divorce, I think, and the early death of her ex-husband; and with the school-phobia her eleven year old son apparently felt, for she brought her son to school with her every day, even though it was a girls' school. I certainly felt that Mrs. Parkinson could not cope properly, and so turned aggressive and humiliated Mrs. Brown in a kind of panic.

Mrs. Brown did not see it that way, as I discovered at the end of term Christmas party our house threw for the girls. Mrs. Parkinson had apparently done all the organising, but Mrs. Brown had her own ideas for helping, and had started pouring orange juice too early. Mrs. Parkinson came to me on the verge of tears, her whitish hair as always in a mannish style, and said "She's impossible." She disappeared to her room, locked the door, and took no further interest in her house's party. Mrs. Brown passed shortly afterwards, a fat Indian woman – or was she West Indian? – and in reply to my sympathetic enquiry sniffed and wept, "Please don't say anything, I can't bear it, she's irrational." She disappeared into another room and shut the door. I was left to go into the house-room and set about entertaining the three hundred girls who were lolling on chairs listening to indifferent records, and clearly in no mood to turn the compulsory occasion into a real party.

Next term Mrs. Brown was away with "mumps". Her absence grew longer and longer. She was away the entire first half of term, and as her attendance record was not good, the hierarchy decided that she should lose her classes and cover for absentees, like a run-of-the-mill supply. When she returned I had to break the news to her.

She said she was not surprised. "You know," she said in her elusive, Asian accent, "I thought I would be moved from being number two in the house." It was as though she had wanted it, and expected it. "In fact," she went on while girls drifted by us like a stream in the corridor, "it wasn't mumps I had. You know, the doctor thought it was cancer at first, because that was what I had last year when I had my hysterectomy. But it wasn't. It's when I'm upset, the swelling comes up. It's emotional, I'm sure of it. I'm allergic to Mrs. Parkinson."

Mrs. Brown was very enthusiastic. Within a week of being back she had taken up an idea of mine: she started a sponsored spell throughout the house. She put it to the house at a house assembly she had to take in Mrs. Parkinson's absence. Mrs. Parkinson heard about it and two days later she vetoed it. She announced to the next house assembly that she was having a sponsored poetry learn instead, which not one girl was interested enough to do.

"I don't think I can take any more," Mrs. Brown told me the next day. Then Mrs. Parkinson came up, and I heard her give Mrs. Brown her orders: "Go to my room and work your way through these. And write this down...."

Two days later I was drinking coffee in the staff room when one of the teachers in my Department thrust a petition in my hand. It expressed opposition to Mrs. Parkinson's bringing her son to school. I was asked to sign. I said, "I can't sign this, but I'll have a word with the hierarchy."

The hierarchy were the three-strong team who ran the school, the Head, and the two Deputy Heads. My contact for such delicate matters was Mr Reynolds, the only male member of the trinity. We had a discreet word, and Mrs. Parkinson was called to the office over the tannoy. I later heard that she would not be bringing the boy in any more – and the petition had been dropped.

The next day was the last day of the spring term. I saw Mrs. Brown as I was signing in (one of the strange customs at that school). She said, "I've got to see the Head at nine o'clock. I wonder what I have done. Have you reported me for anything?" To my amazement she meant it, so I assured her I hadn't.

In fact Mrs. Parkinson was summoned along with Mrs. Brown. The Head told them both, apparently, that they must put aside their differences and work together from now on.

An hour later Mrs. Brown encountered me at the entrance to the staff room. She was in tears, and she said, "Have you got a Scale post in your Department? I have been scolded in front of the Head, and Mrs. Parkinson said I was spoiling the atmosphere in the house, and I want to leave."

I told her we were waiting to see how the Houghton Recommendations would apply to our school, and so we just did not know yet what the position would be about Scale posts.

The Steering Committee of the Staff Association put on a lunch for the staff after the girls had gone home. It was a fork buffet with wine, and Mrs. Parkinson had wanted to go to it. She had not got a ticket, and the female Deputy Head asked me if I would let her have one. "No," I said, "but I can work the dodge the girls use on the tiled gate, and hand mine through the window." Mrs. Parkinson laughed, and both she and the Deputy Head applauded.

At the lunch the Head sat in the centre of the room at the long table on which the buffet dishes were spread. A councillor sat beside her, and various Governors sat nearby with Mrs. Parkinson. The staff sat round the walls, so the hierarchy seemed strangely isolated. I was just having a word with Mr Reynolds when there was a great whoop and totally unexpectedly, leaping up and down, dressed as a witch-doctor with a bone stick, with coloured feathers hanging down behind her, came Mrs. Brown, followed by three women with ape masks over their heads.

Mrs. Brown pranced from one foot to the other letting out savage noises. It was embarrassing, first because she was as coloured as the savage she was playing, and secondly because she was throwing too much of herself into the part, and it was not really getting across to the startled audience. She was striving after effect. Mrs. Brown pranced up behind the Head and the councillor, who were totally unaware of what was happening in the hubbub. The Head turned, fork in mouth, peering through her bifocals, and a look of horror flitted across her face as Mrs. Brown shouted, from a foot away, "Bingle, bangle, bungle, we're from the jungle...." She shouted and chanted her way through several dozens lines of inaudible verse, all the while prancing from foot to foot.

There was a titter round the room. The Head looked grim, and for a moment she and the councillor looked like a crab and a jellyfish left stranded on a beach by a receding tide.

Now Mrs. Brown was shouting her incomprehensible, savage words at Mrs. Parkinson, and when she finished there was the

A SMELL OF LEAVES AND SUMMER 45

thunderous applause that always signifies relief when someone has made a bit of a fool of themselves. Then songsheets were handed round, and the piano struck up, and the staff sang:

"Pack up your roubles in the Houghton bag
And leave, leave, leave!
While you've a tutor group it's such a fag,
Now you need not grieve,
No more hash or hurrying,
The holidays are here!
So pack up your roubles – you might just afford
A half of beer.
Oh, how I hate to get up in the morning!...."

The staff sang their way through the second verse while the Head looked grim, and then came the third verse:

"When this lovely term is over,
No more break duty for me!
No more covering in a house-room,
(No work set, and it's 3E!)
No more credits or demerits!
No reports or yellow slips!
No more meetings! No more marking!
No more tannoy! No more pips!"

It was a good rollicking song, and Mrs. Brown sang it with more gusto than most. From time to time she looked at the Head and Mrs. Parkinson, and as she sang "No more pips" she had a faint smile on her face. In some obscure way, I could tell, she had got something off her chest.

TWINKLING HUBERT AND A HYPOCRITE

I knew Mr Cuthbert was leaving, but I did not know why until I sat opposite him one lunch and he asked me if I knew. For once his eyes were not twinkling in his bald Chaucerian head, and he looked rather sad.

"It was 3D," he said. "I was teaching them and the Head came in and found a bit of noise. They fell silent when she stood there, of course, and she turned to me and said in front of the girls, 'You see, Mr Cuthbert, they *can* be quiet.' And I felt so humiliated I wrote a letter of resignation that evening, and I handed it in the next morning. I never heard anything. I know it's gone through, because I've heard from County Hall, but the Head hasn't referred to it. When I see her she says 'Good morning' perfectly normally. And I could have been persuaded to stay."

I thought the Head probably did not realise what she had done – she was not renowned for having that seventh sense of sensitivity and was better at confrontation than conciliation – but I did not say so. And he told me how, now that he was retiring, he was selling his house, and how the estate agent had valued it at £15,000 instead of the £18,000 he had hoped for, and he was so lovably impractical that it had not occurred to him that the estate agent might have been understating the price so that he could make a quick sale and pocket the commission before a rival moved in.

On the last day of term the Head came to the staff lunch. She stood up and made a presentation to Mr Cuthbert on behalf of the staff. She thanked him for all that he had done for the school.

Mr Cuthbert stood up to reply, looking rather red. He looked just like Chaucer's Hubert, with his eyes twinkling in his head like stars on a frosty night. He thanked the Head, and said: "You know, I shall be sorry to leave. I shall miss the girls – not all of them, but some of them. They are not hypocritical." He looked at the Head. "Most people say nice things to your face and unkind things behind your back. They say unkind things to your face and nice things behind your back. I prefer it that way."

The Head stared in front of her with the tough look of a woman dedicated to her job.

A CASTLE LIKE A DAZZLING GIRL
(OR: A MIRACLE AT EASTER)

We left London in snow. Snow at Easter! I had broken the indicator lever in my car – it hung trailing by my knee from a wire – so I drove carefully to the road in the Forest where the Mansion for sale was situated.

It was set back among trees, it was in a clearing in the Forest. It was a large, square gabled building with balconies all round. It had eight bedrooms, five attics and a long ballroom. It was an empty echo of the vanished, grand Edwardian life, and it captivated my heart. The four-acre lawn overlooked the Forest, and though the Mansion had been neglected and needed a lot doing to it, and though it was priced out of my reach, surely I could find a way of buying it and putting it in order little by little? Surely, if someone went halves with me and lived in the other wing....

We drove to my mother's for the Good Friday reunion. She lived less than a mile from the Mansion, and she had already been offered nearly as much for her house, because of its convenient position for a developer. Before lunch I put it to her that if she put up half and I threw in the rest we could share it. Of course, everything would have to be tied up legally, I said. My solicitor-brother looked at the particulars and put them down, my mother mumbled something about the bank manager pressing her as it was, since her Chingford house was still unsold.

Good Friday lunch was a chaotic occasion. I carved an enormous turkey and then we sat and ate in a hurry as my mother had to show a prospective buyer over the Chingford house at 2.15. My two brothers talked business conditions. To me, all their business jargon was not worth one vivid simile in a poem. I sat among the three small children, retrieving rattles and avoiding having soggy rusks wiped down my new suit from the high chair, and I thought: an artist is only interested in opinions in so far as they reveal character.

After lunch my solicitor-brother took my mother to the Chingford house. I washed up. My other brother and his wife were anxious to return home and do some decorating, and the conversation was desultory.

I prepared to go for a walk in the Forest. My mother returned and said she would like to see the Mansion, so we drove her there first. We got out and, since it was empty with some windows boarded up, we had a closer look at the splendid wide staircase through the wide glass front doors, and we walked round the back on the springy hoof-marked turf on which a shrinking frozen snowman stood forlorn, the only touch of white in all this greenery. It was like a small castle, it was a dream. This was my estate, and the view across the Forest....

"It would be very expensive to maintain," my mother said. "And the rates would be colossal. And I wouldn't like to live so far away from the shops. I would need a car to go everywhere."

My dream was slipping away. I dropped my mother back home, and then we drove to the pond. The sticky buds were out, and we looked for frogspawn, but it was too early. Last year's bullrushes were still standing, a withered ghostly white in the brown water.

When we returned, my mother was accompanying my solicitor-brother on the violin. They were playing a violin sonata. My other brother and his wife had gone. My wife talked to my solicitor-brother's wife by the coal fire, the babies were all asleep.

I went to the sitting-room and sat alone and listened to the music. It was like a music from a never-never land. I had fallen in love with that Mansion, it looked as though I would have to forget about her, like a dazzling girl who passed by in the night.

"O God," I prayed, "please help me to live in the Mansion, if it is for the good of my family. I can't see how it will be done, and it will take a miracle, but please, if it is for the good of my children."

Next day the telephone went. It was my mother. "I've had to go to Chingford today," she said, "and on the way back I stopped and had another look at the Mansion. I couldn't do anything now, but July or August would be a different matter. And I might do it for five years, say, and pull out. My share would have to be sold leasehold."

Had a miracle begun to happen?

A BOUTIQUE BEHIND A MASK

It turned five as we arrived in Worthing. The sea was rough and stormy green with white sea-horses, but the sun shone. We put in at the first guest-house we liked the look of. The room had central heating and a television. Then we went to Shoreham to find Teresa's new boutique.

It was a quaint little shop that previously sold antiques. It was one room, round which were spread various French garments, and Teresa sat on a chair at the back, among her paintings and her pottery. I was accustomed to see her meditating peacefully, and the business setting struck me as incongruous, for her peace would be disturbed each time any stranger took it into her head to push the door open and look round.

We went in and sat with her and talked while our six month old son kicked on the floor. We soon moved on to religion, and though a customer came in, a tall gangling woman who thumbed all the French dresses, Teresa talked on, ignoring her.

She talked about the power of prayer. "My father was ill three weeks ago," she said, "and I prayed for him to get well, and a week later he rang me from Austria and said, 'I have had a miraculous recovery. I can talk again.' You know, even my niece, who is five, said, 'Oh, I must pray for grandpapa to get well.'" We talked about Uri Geller and how his fork-bending had knocked the bottom out of science. "These scientists should just go and sit in a field and take their lunch with them," she said, "and watch the flowers for two days. They would soon see who looks after the flowers and waters them and makes them grow year after year. They would soon see there is someone bigger than us."

It was time to feed our son, so we made an arrangement to call back for her and we drove into Worthing. It was nearly seven when we returned and I knocked on the shop window. She was sitting in the chair, absolutely still, and she came and unlocked the door.

We rang the new restaurant, "It's all to do with business," she said, "I have their cards. Are you open?" she asked. "Do you mind if I bring two friends and their baby?"

We had the restaurant to ourselves. It was locked, and the manager opened specially for us. We put our son, who was in his carry-cot, by the radiator, and sat at a table. The two men who ran the place stood and talked – one said he was a nuclear physicist – and the waitress stood by. We had pâté and prawn cocktail and then Aylesbury Duck. Teresa had wine and we talked about Jesperson the writer, who Teresa was always hearing about, though they had never met.

"I think he will be rude when I meet him, *if* I meet him," Teresa said. "But I don't care about that. I know it's a defence against something. He is aggressive in what you call his 'waistcoat-and-glasses' mood because he is trapped in his literary reputation. He shouldn't care twopence about it, but he does." We talked about his Eliotian reluctance to write anything autobiographical. "Of course, it's ridiculous," Teresa said. "I can paint that girl if I want to. It's the Catholic in him. Not 'I' but God. Do you see? Only the trouble is, God has been left out. When I meet that man I will tell him what he is missing by turning his back on his Catholic background. That is the key to him, and to his ulcers. God, that awful flat of his. I said so when you were staying there last summer, when he was away. It had nothing on the walls, though there's enough to pull down. I shall give him such a shock. I shall pull down that horrible mask and destroy it. It's horrible."

"That's because you think he's hiding behind a persona," I said.

"From the point of view of his being a Catholic at heart, perhaps you are right, but in fairness to him I must point out that a mask is allowed in art. When Eliot writes in the first person he holds up the mask of Prufrock between himself and the reader, just as Pound holds up Mauberley. That is allowed. They both write as 'I', as did Wyatt, Shakespeare, and Tennyson, who all managed masks. My criticism of Jesperson is that he wears a mask on top of that mask, which is why he won't write about himself. He has an outer mask over his inner mask."

"I suppose a writer *is* more exposed that a painter," Teresa said. "I can just say 'This picture is not for sale.' A writer can't do that and has to put up more defences."

Some musicians arrived, together with some customers. When the musicians had seated themselves and started singing, the wine went to Teresa's head, and she talked about her boutique. "I like it," she said. "I know I haven't painted for four months, but I'm getting it off the ground. I might sell it in two years' time, as a thriving business. I'm going to talk to the manager of this restaurant when he comes over. He can dress his waitresses in French clothes."

The bearded manager came over. He sat down on the empty chair and talked about his new venture. "I've just got the licence," he said. "The other publicans didn't like it, they were in court today, but I've got it, that's the main thing. There's trouble over the lighting and the fire station aren't pleased with the sign over that door." He had a very East End accent, and he talked on about the place, seeking to catch someone's eye as if he needed to be reassured that he was being listened to. He talked about how he served what *he* wanted to serve and how he would not serve chips and how he had thrown some rowdies out. I switched off and talked to Pippa, and later I heard Teresa saying, "Send your wife in and I will look her out a nice dress."

He was called to the telephone. He retired, taking his drink with him.

"Oh, I do like my boutique," Teresa said happily. "You know, I had the chance to paint all the time, but it wasn't enough. Now people come in. I can be myself."

"Yes," I said to my own surprise, "but which self? For you are a mystic painter."

She hesitated. I saw that my point had gone home.

"Yes," she said. "But that's private."

Then she said of our son, "Hasn't he been good down there? He hasn't made a sound. You have a family, that's more important than any work."

Soon afterwards she paid the bill and we left. She was going to sleep in the boutique to avoid going back to her sister's, for her niece had chicken-pox and she did not want our son to catch it.

We drove back to Worthing, and I went for a last walk on the dark shingle. The stars were very bright, lights flashed beyond the horizon and the waves crashed and foamed round the breakwaters, throwing froth in the air.

Which self? I had asked. Suddenly I thought I knew. There was the private self, the mystic painter, and there was her public self, the boutique-owner and business woman, from which she liked to meet the people of Shoreham. And I thought I knew what *her* mask was now. Her painting was not enough, and so she had adopted a mask and was playing at being a boutique-owner.

But, as always with this ambivalent woman, I had only achieved a partial view of the truth. She had the last word when we visited her next morning. She was sitting serenely at the back of her shop, and I asked her about one of her paintings: arches across an alleyway down to a tranquil sea.

"I have discarded everything," she said, "I am not involved in anything, I am free of everything. I don't want to be taken over by anything, not that" – she pointed to her paintings and her pottery – "not people, not anything. Do you see, I am free, at peace. So don't worry about self-glory, don't be cluttered by your work."

And I realised why she had been so outspoken against Jesperson. She was living out the ideal of her religion, which put God first. In comparison her art was irrelevant, a mere mask. She was living out an ideal of simplicity among simple people, sitting in her shop and waiting for the occasional customer. I wondered how long it would last.

OF THE CANNIBALISM
OF MICE AND SHREWS AND VOLES

We breakfasted in a room overlooking the sea. Our son lay on the floor in his orange Union Jack cap and squawked, and the radio blared a discussion on the cannibalism of mice and shrews and voles, and the two old ladies sat in the window.

"We have fresh fruit," said one, who, I gathered from listening in, was married to the Deputy Head of an ESN school in Darlington. She was down for a few days only.

"I'm sorry?" said the white-haired old lady who was resident.

"We have fresh fruit."

"Oh, fresh fruit."

"Yes, fresh fruit."

The discussion on the radio was heaping up examples of the cannibalism of mice and shrews and voles.

"Some of this bought pastry is atrocious," said the Darlington lady.

"I'm sorry?" said the resident.

"Some of this bought pastry is atrocious."

"Bought pastry."

"Yes, it's atrocious. I always bake my own."

The radio babbled on and our son was lying on his back pulling golly's hair, kicking his legs and chanting, and I saw the two old ladies as a couple of mice or shrews or voles, and I felt how much their eating habits told me about their lives.

TYRANNY AND BAD LUCK

Miss Endersby was Head of Drama. She was a spiky, prickly, lean woman, and she kept very much to herself. She was good at wriggling out of work. In the staff room she kept her nose in her *Times* crossword. She was supposed to be producing *The Boy-Friend*. She cancelled the production. I was Head of Department over her, but I was not informed until after the cancellation.

After that the Indian drama teacher, Mrs. Brown, started *Oliver*. Her long absence had to be atoned for, and this was her atonement. But now a dangerous situation had been created. Miss Endersby, on Scale 4 for Head of Drama, had produced nothing, and Mrs. Brown, on Scale 2 only for her House responsibility, was doing all the work. So the male Deputy Head, a tall bespectacled fellow, and I summoned Miss Endersby to the room we shared with Sister Moore, the other Senior Teacher. There we confronted her with her "lack of leadership" (a criticism she had sweepingly made against all Scale 5 staff at a public meeting with the Head) and generally turned the screws, hoping she would resign.

At the end I said, "*Oliver* should seem to be coming from the

Drama Department, not from the private endeavours of Mrs. Brown, so I want you to start some diplomacy with Mrs. Brown to make it look as if you are both involved in the Drama Department."

Mrs. Brown's difficulties with her Housemistress, Mrs. Parkinson, were well-known, but after the Head called them together and read the riot act, there was "an armed truce." The words were Mrs. Brown's. The truce was broken one disastrous Tuesday, the day after Mrs. Brown had a fall and twisted her ankle.

Tuesday was house assembly day, and Mrs. Parkinson was late. She had known she would be late and had told everybody except Mrs. Brown. Mrs. Brown, faced with two hundred girls, started the assembly. I should have been there, but just as I was leaving my room my deputy asked me to explain a poem he was setting his sixth form. My answer involved metonymy and synecdoche. He staggered me by saying he had never heard of them – *he*, an English teacher of fifty-five – so I had to show him the dictionary definitions, and by the time I had finished assembly was in progress, so I stayed away.

Mrs. Parkinson arrived and publicly told off three girls who were late. Her staff looked amazed. Then she took over from Mrs. Brown, and at the end of assembly she apparently shouted at Mrs. Brown: "I knew I was going to be late, and if I had wanted you to take the assembly I would have asked you to. I *chose* not to tell you. You did the wrong thing by taking assembly."

It was strange that someone so liberal in her views who evidently believed in democratic discussion so much as Mrs. Parkinson did – the Minutes of our house meetings always expressed some form of dissent from the Head with her spoken approval – should have so Nazi a conception of authority. Not for her the casual "Would you mind...?" which is a feature of so much of the British way of work. I had often seen Mrs. Brown standing before her, and Mrs. Parkinson saying, "Now send a DO12 to Mrs. So-and-so...." and Mrs. Brown would nod her head as if she were in Colditz or Ravensbruck, and I half expected her to say, "Yes, Frau Commandant." I wondered if Mrs. Parkinson was so frightened of not doing her job properly that she was exceptionally tense. Perhaps that was why she shouted at girls who were late even though she was blatantly late herself?

After this particular episode Mrs. Brown spent the morning in tears. "Is Mrs. Brown suffering from hay fever or has something happened?" Mrs. Marsh asked me discreetly in the staff room at coffee time. I shrugged. I knew she cried easily. I had often seen Mrs. Brown in tears, and besides, Miss Endersby was sitting with her. It was Miss Endersby who later told me what had happened as we walked to our classes together, my criticisms of her "lack of leadership" apparently forgotten, or being proved groundless by her "concern" for Mrs. Brown. "She shouldn't allow herself to be upset so easily," I said, referring to our clash earlier, "it's only a work situation." And Miss Endersby agreed.

Towards the end of the lunch hour the tannoy blared: "Would Mrs. Brown please contact the office for a telephone call. This is very urgent."

The next I knew was that Mrs. Brown was sitting in the staff room utterly distraught, very red-eyed, her mouth open, her head sprawling, her expression as tragic as if it had been sculpted by Michelangelo or Rodin. Then Mrs. Pye, the small, frizzy-haired and bespectacled Classics woman, was by my side. "We'll have to cover for Mrs. Brown for this afternoon," she whispered, "she's just heard that her son has been run over in a car accident. It's not known how seriously he is injured."

My first thought was: so this is how it comes, the supreme test. In public. And who was to say how anyone should react in the teeth of such appalling news? After making sympathetic noises I said: "Trouble always comes in threes. Her fall, Mrs. Parkinson, and now this."

"I think it's the diabetic son," Mrs. Pye said. "Her husband's got a heart condition and can't work, you know. He can't stand a shock like this. And she's the bread-winner."

Appalled at her run of bad luck – her six week absence with "mumps" was in fact a suspected recurrence of her cancer, for which she had had an allegedly successful operation the previous year, and on her first day back she had seen a child knocked down by a car and killed – I went over to her. But her grief was too deep, her tears too uncontrollable despite the four teachers who were consoling her, for her to gasp more than:

"I...I can't take any more...."

"He's in hospital in Croydon," Mrs. Pye said in my ear. "I don't think she can drive."

"I'll find someone to drive her," I said, sickened at her understandable loss of control, while her consolers contradicted her

A SMELL OF LEAVES AND SUMMER

and told her to get a grip on herself, and forced her to gulp a cup of tea.

Then Miss Endersby came into the staff room.

"I'll drive her," she said. "I'll just set my fifth years some work, if that's all right. They won't need covering."

I thought of the diplomatic move I had initiated, and I saw how Miss Endersby could twist this act of kindness to her own end, and I felt faintly sick.

In fact Mrs. Brown's son only broke his patella – his kneecap – and he was allowed home that same evening.

On my way home I saw Mrs. Parkinson's eleven year old son. I recognised him from the time when Mrs. Parkinson had brought him with her every day, as he was supposed to be suffering from "school-phobia". He had now been placed in a local comprehensive, and he was slouching home in his school uniform, which was black, clutching a large bottle of red pop and talking to himself, and his mouth was bright red all round his lips like a circus clown's. I thought of Mrs. Parkinson's tyranny and her son, and of Mrs. Brown's bad luck and *her* son, and I thought of their troubled home lives, which, like luggage, they should leave at home and not bring into school, and the contrast between mother and son on the one hand, and mother and son on the other hand lodged inscrutably and hauntingly and utterly inexplicably in my mind.

It wasn't a distinction between a survivor and one who had gone under, for with such outbursts, who was to say that Mrs. Parkinson had survived? Might she not yet go down? On further inspection the contrast looked strangely like a parallel. It had something to do with the way they lived. Both of them suffered from a chronic lack of peace, and so they attracted their circumstances: Mrs. Parkinson the worried lack of harmony which was the consequence of her panics, and Mrs. Brown her back luck.

NEMESIS AT THE EXTRAORDINARY GENERAL MEETING

Mrs. Kestrel's rewriting of the Staff Association Constitution culminated in her calling, as Chairman of the Steering Committee, a meeting after school to discuss the draft. Great posters went up throughout the school attesting to the importance of the event. I could not help having the image of an old crock of a car after some appalling accident, all crashed up with the steering column bent and buckled, having been steered into a ditch by an incompetent driver.

The meeting was a desultory affair. Mrs. Kestrel's inexpert Chairmanship immediately ran into problems, and when I left an hour had been spent on the first ten lines of the draft, and nothing had been achieved. An Extraordinary General Meeting was to be called after school the following week to ratify the new Constitution.

Mrs. Kestrel was undismayed. All that week she was much fuller of herself than usual. She talked throughout the next Head of Departments and Housemistresses Meeting, referring everything to herself while others sat in respectful silence of the Head, and I thought: arté, how hubris has become arté.

The Extraordinary General Meeting was equally desultorily attended. Whether bored by politicking or suspicious of Mrs. Marzeki's presence on the Steering Committee – freshly back from taking a party of girls to the Communist splendours of Romania – two thirds of the staff stayed away, including Mrs. Mitchell, who was on a course. There were only some forty teachers sitting opposite the Committee of seven. "It's like the Armed Forces Movement in Portugal," I said to Mrs. Marsh, referring to the previous night's news. "The junta is going to explain to us why the elections did not mean what they really meant." And she laughed and went on drawing fire-engines for her two year old son, for whom she had not been able to find a baby-minder.

Mrs. Kestrel opened the meeting as if everything was going to proceed smoothly. A two-thirds vote was necessary to change the Constitution, and as it was important that all present should be subscribers, would everybody please pay 1p so that they could vote. A dish was solemnly taken round.

The first article had an amendment which defined the Staff Association as "Common Room Association" to exclude the cleaners. This was carried. Then we came to the question of eligibility. The draft Constitution here had a complicated system of A or B, with options (i), (ii) and (iii) within each. It looked exactly like a straight multiple choice comprehension, and invited the traditional school pupil's approach of pressing a pin.

The crucial paragraph allowed all staff to be members, including the Head, Deputy Heads, and Senior Housemistress, OR it excluded these senior dignitaries, OR it excluded only the Head. There were speakers from the floor on the rival merits of including or excluding these members of the staff. Basically it came down to whether problems were to be solved by discussion in a unified way, with the Head being present, or through protest, with the Committee representing the staff. Mrs. Marzeki spoke at length of how the younger members of the staff needed to be represented so that their complaints could be put, and it was clear that she favoured representational democracy so that, like an MP, she could speak her own views about the necessity for strike action and claim to be representing the staff.

It came to a vote. Mrs. Kestrel asked us to vote first on A or B. It was A. Then on A (i). 22 for, 21 against, 6 abstentions. She went on to A (ii) and A (iii), which likewise failed to obtain a two-thirds majority.

There was a silence when this position was announced. Sister Moore, the only moderate influence on the Committee, stood up and said: "In this case we are forced back to the relevant article in the original Constitution." And, to the discomforture of the Committee, this was read out and found to contain nothing about eligibility, though there was a paragraph headed "Forfeiture of property", which gave an appropriately feudal slant to the proceedings.

There was now a long silence. Neither Mrs. Kestrel nor her Committee had expected this stalemate, and they just did not know how to cope. Procedure broke down, and several times Mrs. Kestrel made suggestions which were called out of order. Meanwhile Mrs. Marzeki made the diabolical suggestion that as (ii) and (iii) had the absence of the Head in common, they should be adopted, even though they came second and third in the poll.

After an hour and twenty minutes of random discussion against a general exodus of the small section of the staff that had attended the meeting, Mrs. Kestrel had no alternative but to say:

"We must now adjourn our Extraordinary General Meeting."

"Extraordinary," someone said, changing the intonation to change the meaning.

"But first I want to ask you if you would like us to resign?"

"No," the Head of Home Economics called, "you're adjourning, you can't resign now."

But it was clear that Mrs. Kestrel had been delivered a slap in the face, as had all those on the Committee who had engineered the removal of Mrs. Mitchell. Their Constitution had been rebuffed, their attempt to exclude the hierarchy had gone wrong, and it was a more humble Mrs. Kestrel who sat in the staff room the next day. Nemesis had cut her down to size, just as it had reduced the over-reachers of Aeschylus, Sophocles and Euripides.

CRABBE UNDER SHINGLE
(OR: A QUIET THAT MIRRORS THE HEART)

That August Bank Holiday I took Pippa down into Suffolk as I was thinking of going to live there. We went through Kersey, which I had visited five years previously with my ex-wife. There is a beautiful water-splash in the middle of the village, and I remembered how she and I watched a red admiral flutter and settle on the lilac of "Woodbine Cottage", and how we went into the pub and somehow stood in a kitchen full of wasps. I couldn't find "Woodbine Cottage" or the lilac, and the pub had been modernised inside, and there were no windows at all in the kitchen now. I left Kersey feeling sad at heart with a nostalgia for the days that could not come again.

After that we headed for the coast. It got misty and dark, and Aldeburgh was a few lights by a dark sea. We tried several places, and in the end we found a double room at the White Lion, which is on the front.

It was nearly 9.30, and the hotel had stopped serving dinner. So we went out to look for something to eat. It was the same with the other hotels, and there was no restaurant in town, so we ended up eating fish and chips, on the shingle.

We had a drink at the Cross Keys Inn in Crabbe Street, and then wandered slowly back along the front. The lighting was very dim, and hardly any of the houses had their curtains drawn, and looking in at people sitting alone, working or reading or watching colour television, I felt a great sadness. There was a great quiet, as I wandered up into Crabbe Street I couldn't hear the sea, there was only a rustle in the trees and the clack-clack-clack of Pippa's heels. The town was deserted, it was as quiet as a graveyard, and I thought of all these people frittering away their lives. There was a great nothingness around me and I thought it must have been what Crabbe felt when he described the people of Aldeburgh as they really were – and left the place because of their ensuing hostility.

The quiet disturbed me, and I pondered it down by the reassuring, susurrating waves. It seemed to me there was good quiet and bad quiet. Good quiet was when you were by yourself and at peace, bad quiet was when you looked in on other people's loneliness, which living in London somehow helped you forget. Perhaps they were two parts of the same quiet, two sides of the heart. And perhaps Crabbe had known them both: the good quiet in his poems and the bad quiet when he, too, looked in on the people of the borough.

I suddenly felt I wouldn't like to live in this disturbing quiet, amid sad old buildings with lights in the windows. I would rather live in London.

I took Pippa back to the hotel room. We put the fire on and turned on the soft music on the radio in the wall, and Pippa said, "I want to gather you up in my arms and protect you from sad things." I fell asleep in a soft bed.

I woke to a thunderstorm. After it had passed I lay awake and I listened to the clanking of scaffolding and a whistling builder. Then I got up and did my exercises: they included three hundred and seventy-five runs on the spot. We had breakfast in the old part of the White Lion, and then I visited an estate agent who was a friend of a friend. He advised me to look for cottages in an arc from Framlingham to Otley: North of there the clay was heavy, and nearer the sea the railway connection to Ipswich was poor, and west of there ran into development and the new road to Norwich. He gave me a lot of good advice, and I came away more or less resolved not to live in Suffolk after all.

Afterwards I went up to the church where Crabbe was curate before he was driven out of the town. I stood in the pulpit where he preached in 1781. On it there were dragons that looked like dolphins, and arches and grapes in the manner of the English Renaissance. Nearby there was a bust of Crabbe. It made him look cold and remote, and I knew the sculptor was on the side of the people of Aldeburgh. We went down to the Moot Hall, one of the few houses of the old town that had not been washed away. We went in and I studied a map of 1790 which showed P. C. Crespigny Esq. as owning the house next to it and some land near the church. Perhaps he was Crabbe's chief persecutor? I walked back along

Crabbe Street to see if I could find a house where he lived or practised as an apothecary, but the sea had taken it.

I walked back along the beach. The breakwaters were sunk under encroaching shingle, and the tops peeped through the stones – like Crabbe's Aldeburgh. The quiet he had felt then was still present in the quiet I felt that day, like the pulpit in the church. Then I understood. I had felt it through a troubled heart. When the heart is troubled, so is the quiet. When the heart is at peace, so is the quiet.

I had come with the sadness of Kersey. Whether I lived in Aldeburgh or in London depended not on the quiet but on my own heart and how peaceful it was: the quiet mirrored the heart.

A WINDMILL AND THE REAL THINGS
(OR: LIVING IN THE COUNTRY)

We checked out of the White Lion and left Aldeburgh to tour the Framlingham-Otley area. We intended to spend the night in Sudbury. We went first of all to a cottage in Middleton that the estate agent had on his books. It was a tiny doll's house with a tiny garden of dahlias and humming bees. There was a thatched pub nearby, but it wasn't worth the asking price of £9,500. We drove on to Saxtead Green Post Mill, and we stopped and had a look. Its four great sails were faced into the wind by a contraption round the back that had a propellor on it; the wind blew the propellor and the contraption moved round on a wheel, angling the sails with it.

"It's like an artist," I said to Pippa. "Ponder the mystery of sails turned by the wind, grinding corn. Fresh moments, like ears of ripe corn."

We drove on and passed a hedgerow of red poppies, and later we saw a field on fire. They were burning the stubble round Earl Soham, and the earth was scorched into black furrows that acted like peat.

"How can people paint abstract art and distort nature, when so much here is real?" Pippa asked.

"I quite agree. If you break down a cornfield with analysis, you show it – through the reason – as something abstract or linear. If you don't, you don't. To me, it's a cornfield, as it is. It isn't ugly, not to my heart, so it shouldn't be uglified."

"It's restlessness, to change what's there."

"Yes, the Age of Analytical Restlessness is coming to an end. The artist should be content to grind his corn and forget about the stubble. The stubble should be burned."

We passed apple-trees. A yellowhammer flew up from the side of the road.

"In the country you see things as they are – real," I said. "Distortion begins in a city room. Who'd want to be here now and distort the dahlias in that garden over there?"

I wanted to live in the country now.

We found ourselves near Wickham Market. "We can go to Orford," Pippa said, looking at the map. I knew she wanted to go to Orford.

The road went through Scotch pines and bracken and heather. I stopped and smelt the musky smell of pine. There was a twittering quiet. I felt strangely back in myself, and I picked a sprig of heather to commemorate the moment, and gave it to Pippa.

"Oh, isn't that nice," she said, touched.

"Towns take you away from yourself and distract you. The country is simple and uncluttered, it brings you back to your heart."

Orford was a decayed redbrick Georgian sailing village. I stood on the quay and looked at anchors and rusty chains and bladderwrack waving in the water. A boy had a crab on a fishing line, its legs clawing at the air. Away to our left were the masts of Orfordness, the American early warning system which the Russians had jammed, and which the Americans had now left.

It was overcast, it would not be long before dark approached.

"We're not going to make Sudbury," I said, "and Aldeburgh's only a few miles. Let's stay there again tonight, and I'll get to the bottom of that quiet."

We couldn't very well book in again at the White Lion, not after leaving so ceremoniously that morning. So we put in at another hotel opposite Crabbe's church. It used to be the house of Elizabeth Garrett Anderson, and it was run by a retired Colonel with a monocle and an ex-military staff. I noticed that all the guests wore a collar and tie. I hadn't brought mine.

We walked down the hill to an Inn on the front that advertised "Evening Grills". "Have you ordered?" the barman asked, and I gathered you couldn't have a beer unless you ordered it twelve hours in advance. Remembering the previous night's fish and chips, I took Pippa back to the hotel, put on my most acceptable clothes (a black sweater) and went in search of the Colonel. He was in Reception, wearing a dark suit. I asked if we could eat. He gave me a glare and called his wife, the Manageress, who gave me a glance of haughty contempt and showed us through a sumptuous dining-room of old wood and candles and dark suits to the table next to the kitchen.

We had Aylesbury duckling. It was good, and all the better for my being wrongly dressed. Afterwards we walked back down to the front and again wandered along the dark Crag Path towards where the lighthouses flashed from Orford. The street-lamps were incredibly dim; the bulbs looked five-watters, it was as though the Suffolk ratepayers couldn't afford more, it was like being in East Germany.

I peered into all the curtainless windows and listened hard for the breathless sadness I had heard in the sea. It was no good. I was trying to recover what I had felt too consciously. I was explaining everything to myself from my head, whereas the previous night, my heart had opened.

Perhaps it was the duckling, but I felt a solid sense of well-being and an inclination to rational ridicule. It was better that I should come and live here for a while, if I could work it, rather than experience the country from the loneliness of a hotel. It was like the visit I made to that boring town in Lincolnshire. If I had lived in the vicinity, it would have been much less of a lonely ordeal. I needed quiet and the real things as the propeller on that windmill needed the wind to direct the sails; I needed bagfuls of corn.

I was ready to live in the country. I had left behind the pubs of the King's Road and the girls, the great drunken whirl into which I'd fled the agony of my heart. Now I was teetotal and aware of my purpose, yes, despite that vastation of the lights in windows. I could face up to myself. Another aim had thrown itself up and chosen me.

08.15 HORAS AND FRESH FISH

The next morning I felt good. I felt relaxed through and through. It was very quiet – a wood-pigeon in the garden and the church clock were the only sounds – and the bed was very comfortable. I lay and thought of the temptations I had avoided. I recalled *The Enemies of Promise* and the temptation of journalism, which Cyril Connolly had seen in terms of Crabbe's blue bugloss: "There the blue bugloss paints the sterile soil." Eventually I got up, did my exercises, and then went downstairs for the morning papers, which were in a pile near the Reception.

The silver-haired Colonel was writing with his monocle in his right eye. "Ah," he said, "I've got you down for a call at 08.15 hours."

"I won't be needing it now," I said.

"Mmm." He was a little disconcerted by this variation in regulations for the day. He made a note.

To get him talking I asked, "Do many of your guests ask you questions about Crabbe?"

"Eh?" he barked. "Crabbe? No. They haven't heard of him. I hadn't either till I came here. I don't read anthologies. My eruditity (sic) doesn't go that far."

And abruptly he returned to his writing. There was a heavily disapproving silence.

Breakfast was at 08.30 hours. Now everyone wore open-necked shirts, and we were given a pleasant table in the window. On the mat in my place there was a chit. It listed the menu, and I had to put ticks in boxes to order. At the top it said : HELP YOURSELF TO CEREALS. The Colonel's ex-RSM thundered over and snatched the chit and bore it off to the kitchen, and I stood up and went to a table and ladled out, mess-style, a plate full of rice krispies. The RSM reappeared, and an elderly woman asked for a packed lunch and the RSM boomed, "You can pick it up before nine-thirty. The staff's out at ten for a funeral." The voice echoed all round the hall.

A blonde woman sat down at the next table, together with her husband. She looked at the marmalade, which was rather chunky and dark, and asked the waiter, "Could I have some ordinary marmalade please?"

The waiter went to the RSM, who grabbed a jar. "I don't know what you mean by ordinary marmalade," he boomed from the kitchen door, advancing on the wretched, blushing woman. "There's this, if that's any good." And he gave her the jar from which the dark marmalade had been taken: Old English thick-cut marmalade. That sums it up, I thought. They are tasteful, and if you question it they sling it aggressively in your face.

Afterwards we went up to our room to finish reading the papers. There was a knock on the door, and a rather nice chambermaid opened up, looked flustered, and said, "Sorry."

"We'll be going out in a few minutes," I said.

She closed the door. A minute later there was a great crash and the door burst open. The Manageress stood there.

"Oh, sorry to burst in," she said with aggressive insincerity. "The staff are going to a funeral, and we'd like to do your room."

"We're just going out," I said.

"Oh, are you? Oh, good." She went out, leaving the door open.

We walked down the hill to the sea. The fishermen were winching in their boats. Outside their huts, near drying nets, there were tubs of fresh fish and small queues of local people. I wandered from one to another. They had caught plaice and whiting mostly. They had died with their mouths open. There was a large cod, a skate and a couple of lobsters.

As I watched, one of the fishermen, a ginger-haired man in a sweater who had rings in his ears, opened the window of his hut, picked off a bumble-bee, nipped it, and lazily dropped it among the lobsters. He seemed indifferently aware that the thing could sting him, he looked too strong for the sting to make any impact. The bee lay, crippled on its side, making feeble movements with its legs to get on its feet. I felt a strange peace. It was good to watch the fish, it was exciting, there was a law that was being worked out quite blindly. It was natural that the fishermen should kill the fish, even the fate of the bee was part of the working of a great plan.

On the way back I passed the Moot Hall. On the back wall there was a sundial, and for the first time I read the gold inscription: HORAS NON NUMERO NISI SERENAS. 1650. "I do not count the hours unless they are peaceful."

This was put up in the Civil War, of course, and it had a poignant political meaning, but to me it had a profound personal significance. I thought of the military hotel staff and their obsession with "horas", I thought of them at their funeral in the church on the hill. Somehow, their outlook didn't count. Ten years of their aggression wasn't worth one moment of standing in delicious idleness and watching those tubs of fish.

FLICKING FINGERS AND FRAYED CLOTH

I changed jobs. Now I worked at a comprehensive for boys in South London. That morning there was a Year Assembly. It was held in the Theatre. Three hundred second year boys sang "All Glory be to God", reading the words from a screen. When the Headmaster left, striding slowly out, his shoulders hunched in his stoop, the Head of the Year called from the stage: "File out quietly. If anyone talks, keep them behind will you, Mr Rawley."

The boys filed out in dead silence. Over the far side Mr Bronco, the Latin and Greek specialist called, "Burns, fetch the cane from my room will you." He held out his keys, and a shudder swept through the remaining boys.

Two boys whispered to each other as they passed me. It was too blatant to ignore. Bedsides, the Head of the Year had seen. I indicated that they were to sit down. A coloured boy bounced down between them and said, "What are you sitting here for?" This was Simms.

"Stay where you're sitting," I said.

"Me? Why? What have I done? I wasn't talking."

"Talking?" the Head of the Year asked behind me. "All right, thank you Mr Rawley." He held Mr Bronco's cane in his hand. "Come on, up the steps to the top. Then hand out."

I watched from the well. The three boys lined unwillingly up. One after another they put out a hand, the cane swished, and they returned down the gangway flicking their fingers as if they had touched a very hot oven. Groups of fascinated, uniformed boys gathered to greet them at the theatre door.

I looked on, unmoved. I felt tough and uninvolved. Justice had been done, it was not a thing to emote about. I felt like a judge who has passed a sentence required by the law.

At lunch-time I went out to make a phone call. (It was rumoured that the Head had bugged all school phones and took a dim view of personal phone calls.) I had to make my call by the Clapham clock. One of the kiosk panes had been smashed, there was glass on the floor. Through the jagged spider's web the cold October air chilled my legs.

As I dialled I felt a great tugging at the back of my suit jacket and the fray of cloth against sharp glass, and a coloured woman outside the kiosk said nastily, "Hurry up."

I turned indignantly. But as I was about to say 'You've got a nerve' the pips were going, and I turned back to insert my coin.

She interrupted twice more: "Hurry up, I said 'Hurry up'." I ignored her, gentleman that I am; I merely scowled and finished my conversation.

As I came out she pushed into me. Then she was inside the kiosk.

I opened the door, boiling with rage at her aggression. "Next time you make a call," I said, "you have some manners."

As I came away I saw Simms lurking near the Ladies with Hoborough.

"Into school," I called.

"Go away."

Simms ran off.

"Sir," said Hoborough, "that's Simms's mum in that telephone box. And Simms has gone home."

That afternoon the Inspector was supposed to visit us. The Head of our Department had put on tea in the staff room. I went in at 3.50 and was told:

"He's not coming. His child's had an accident. We'd better drink the tea. Join the mad hatter's tea-party."

One by one the English Department came in and sat round and drank tea and ate biscuits.

Then the bearded Geography teacher strode in.

"I hope you lot know there's a bomb scare," he said. "You're supposed to be out of here."

"That's all right," I said. "The boys are out, it doesn't matter if we get blown up."

We carried on drinking tea.

We left at 5. As we came away, I bumped into Hoborough.

"You haven't got Simms with you," I said.

"No sir. You know the bomb scare? Sir, it was Simms's mum. She was talking about you before you went into the telephone-box. It was because Simms got the cane. She said, 'I'm going to telephone the school.' Sir, it *was* her, I know it was. Simmsy told me."

THE DIRECTOR IS AN IDIOT
(OR: TOY SOLDIERS AND YOU SHOULDN'T
WRITE A THESIS ON A MILITARY SUBJECT)

Christine got married very suddenly to Anthony. He was her boss at the Museum Foundation, and no one knew there was anything between them until they announced it. They had kept their relationship quiet ever since Christine gave a party at her Greenwich flat and invited Anthony, not expecting him to come.

They held a reception some weeks after their wedding. It was at the Old Kitchen, Kenwood, and it took place on a fine Saturday in October. The great white house, the rolling green lawn, the lake shimmering among the golden-red leaves – all provided an ideal setting. I arrived three-quarters of an hour late with Pippa, having encountered a traffic jam near St. John's Wood.

"Sorry," I said to Christine.

Seventy guests were sitting at separate tables eating melon with forks. Christine, smiling and in a long dress, showed us to a table in a corner.

"Hello," said Jean beside me, "how are you?"

She was a friend of Pippa's. She had shared Pippa's old flat. I had not seen her since her wedding. She had been living in Paris.

"Perhaps we'll have a speech from you about how Christine had to come through your room to get to the loo," I suggested.

"This is a family affair, remember," she laughed.

"Do you know Anthony? Which is another way of asking, which is Anthony?"

"Yes, that's him over there in the black shirt and red tie."

She pointed to a gaunt, long-haired, thin man and I immediately saw he was ill at ease.

"His Director's here," Jean said. "That wiry man over there. Honour Marchant. Comes from Cumberland, large country house, wrote the official book on the First World War. Anthony's smiling up to him, hoping for promotion, see?"

As I watched, Anthony fawned up to a silky, grey-haired man with a face that was distinguished and strangely gross at the same time.

"Have you met Delia?" Jean said of a girl near me.

I found myself talking to a squirrelly brown woman who sat next to her husband.

"Are you working?"

"I'm writing a thesis for a PhD."

"Oh? What on?"

"Hardy."

We discussed this briefly. She was interested in the relation between fictitious places in Hardy's work and the real places – in how Hardy put real social communities into his novels.

"Are you ready for your next course?" a waitress asked. "Will you go up and help yourself?"

On my way I came across Anthony, and introduced myself.

"I gather we share an interest in T. E. Lawrence," I said.

"Oh yes," he said, "Christine's told me about you. I've edited the photos we've got in the museum and I've–"

At that moment the Director accosted him, and he was all ears. Then Delia was beside me.

"You remember Delia, don't you," Anthony said to the Director.

"You used to work in the museum," he said.

"Yes, that's right."

"And this is your husband?" he said of me.

"No," I said, and I introduced myself.

The Director did not want to talk to a man.

"And you're writing a thesis on Hardy," he said. "What on earth are you doing that for?"

Anthony told me more about his book on T. E. Lawrence, and the next time I listened to the Director he was saying:

"Yes, but only military subjects are worth writing about. It's like toy soldiers in front of you, you give your interpretation of what they have done. Whereas everyone who's intelligent knows what Hardy is on about."

"But there's the economic and social side," Delia said.

"Sounds very sinister to me," the Director said to Anthony. "Communist."

"Yes," Anthony fawned, simpering.

"Literature is a waste of time. You shouldn't write a thesis on a literary subject. You should write one on a military subject."

I was indignant. He stood for false values, pomposity, and the confidence of a large country house. Yet behind it all he was just a boy playing with toy soldiers. I wanted to put him right. But then I looked at Anthony and thought how desperately he wanted promotion, and how I would spoil the atmosphere. The Director was too old to change, I wouldn't achieve everything. And besides, I *had* been invited, and it was a bit off for a guest to make a scene. I went off to fetch my lunch.

When Delia had returned with her plate I said: "What do you think of the Director?"

"He's a twit," she said. "I used to work with him. He thinks women are there to smile at him."

"I think he's an idiot," I said. "He sees everything in simple black and white military terms and has no appreciation of subjectivity at all. He's at the level of toy soldiers. He needs one pound of air deflating from his self-importance."

She smiled appreciatively. "I'm surprised you saw that so quickly," she said.

I looked back to where Anthony was fawning on the Director. He would go on intriguing and in thirty years' time he would have a high position, and then others would do the same to him, and then he would die. That was his life. I felt sad, and suddenly the party lost its meaning. You came in and you went out, and what happened in between was a waste: me saying things I didn't want to say and learning things I didn't want to know. I thought of Omar Khayyam's lines, as translated by Fitzgerald:

"Myself when young did eagerly frequent
Doctor and Saint, and had great Argument
About it and about: but evermore
Came out by the same Door as in I went."

I wished I hadn't given up drinking.

A MOTHER IN ACTION
(OR: ITALIAN WINE)

Sam and I went to the 007 at the Hilton. We had drinks at the bar and Sam danced with a couple of girls. One was called Sheila and the other was Irish. She was very striking and independent. She did not look at him at all. When the music stopped she left him and returned to her girl-friend, and a man who had been sitting alone went and joined her at her table, as if to let him know that he owned her.

"That's strange," Sam said at the bar. "He must be their controller, they must be business girls. Yet I thought they weren't, because she was singing to the music."

I said I thought they were connected with the IRA – I recognised the fanatical independence in her dark eyes – and I was glad he was away from her.

"I don't want to get mixed up in politics," Sam said. "Look, that woman over there. She's sitting alone, she looks sophisticated and interesting. Believe me she is good. I'll ask her to have a drink with me in Chelsea Cloisters. I'll tell her I have some Italian wine."

He walked in front of the band to ask her. She was sitting in virtual darkness, and he did not see her face until he was talking to her. She looked frightful: she was gnarled and hoary, like a hawthorn tree. She smiled with pleasure and nudged her friend, who had just sat down beside her after dancing.

I heard her ask: "What about my friend?"

"You can bring her too."

"All right, but I must have a word with her first."

"What's your name?" Sam asked above the music, not looking at her frizzled fair hair.

"My name's Deborah," she said in a very upper class voice.

"Do you work?"

"Yes, in an insurance company. I handle the VAT. It's not what I'm really interested in, it brings in some money."

Sam returned to the bar. "She'll come," he said. "With her friend. Brilliant. Less than five minutes, and it cost me nothing."

"And she's not a politician," I said. "She's just a girl."

"You can be very successful tonight. Believe me, all the girls have been looking at you. I have been watching them. They are crying out for *you* to go over and ask them."

I went over to Deborah's table.

"It'll be all right," she said. "But I'm not sure about Juliana. She's dancing with Ali. I've got a drink to finish. Come and sit down and meet Juliana."

Juliana came over with a Pakistani. She was tall and dark and attractive. 'A divorcée going through a difficult time' Deborah had said.

"I'll stay," Juliana said. "Ali will look after me. You can go so long as I know where you're going," she laughed.

"A good question. Where am I going. I'm going to drink some Italian wine with his friend."

"In Chelsea Cloisters," I said.

Juliana gave me a sharp look. She was impressed by the opulence of Sam's address.

"All right," she said.

"You'll feed Maria will you?" Deborah asked. "I've got a six year old daughter," she explained to me. "So you'll give Maria her breakfast will you?" she asked Juliana. "There's a bicky under her pillow, she's sure to sleep late."

As we crossed over to Sam, Deborah said to me: "We came here on Wednesday, and Juliana met Ali then. This is only our second time here, and I'm not sure what she thinks of him."

To Sam, I said: "Deborah's friend can't come."

"I'll stay," Sam said, having looked at her close up in brighter light. He was clearly more interested in Juliana.

"We won't be able to drink Italian wine," I said to Deborah.

"We can have a drink downstairs."

So we left Sam and collected her coat and found a corner downstairs. She had soda water; she didn't want anything stronger.

"Tell me about your daughter," I said.

"I had her illegitimately. That's all there is to tell. I'd rather tell you about what I really like doing."

"Tell me that then."

"I helped found Mothers in Action," she said. "Do you know it? It's a pressure-group. We campaign for better rights for women who have illegitimate children." She talked at some length about what she told the press and TV, how she lobbied MPs and got up research projects. "We've just been given a grant by Rowntrees," she said.

"Like FRELIMO."

"Yes."

"So you're really a politician," I said, thinking of the Irish girl and my feeling that she was in the IRA.

"I have strong feelings about this sort of situation," she went on. "Everyone thinks that women who have had illegitimate children must be promiscuous. I'm fighting that image, that's part of what Mothers in Action is about. I admit that I'm no angel, but I don't sleep with anyone until I know them."

Soon afterwards she said, "I'd better be making a move. I told Juliana I would get back to my daughter, remember?"

I did not remind her about the bicky under the pillow. Outside the Hilton I put her in a cab.

As I drove home I thought of how she had sat alone in the 007 waiting to be asked to dance, of how she had gone downstairs to appear daring to Juliana and then run back to her daughter with her principles. There was a contradiction in the way this mother lived. The contradiction was between what she wanted Juliana to think of her and her politician's feelings, and I resented the way that particular mother in action had involved me in her private mess.

THE BUSES WAS LATE

"Come on," yelled Thomas, the Welsh teacher in the centre of the new comprehensive, with mock severity, "get up to your year room."

The Head of English mimicked a boy running. He was fifty-seven with grey hair and glasses, and he had recently been passed over for the post of Senior Teacher, though he had taught fifteen years at the grammar school across the playgrounds.

"I'm sorry sir," he called. "I'm doing my best, the buses were late. No," he said, "the buses *was* late."

I smirked. That summed up his attitude to his Department all right, and to the lousy stinking dump of a school. The only trouble was, he was the one who was late. He had missed the bus, like all his generation. He did not know it, but I, who was twenty years his junior, I was a Senior Teacher now.

FRIENDSHIP LIKE A POTATO CRISP

I went to a farewell for Ahmed Mbakwe at the High Commission. Ahmed was standing in the window. He was a very black, wiry African, and after shaking hands with the High Commissioner I went over and joined him. He greeted me with an enthusiastic shout, pumped my hand, held on to it – and then left me abruptly. The next three-quarters of an hour I hardly saw him.

I sipped bitter lemons and spoke to the High Commissioner. I asked him if he knew the Budget details, and he said, "Oh yes, it's Budget Day today isn't it. What's happened, do you know?" I made conversation with the First Secretary of the Chinese Legation and with various trading contacts of Ahmed's. Then I saw my deadly enemy, the Horror, a Communist female of appalling character. She had once rung up a newspaper I freelanced for and made false accusations against me. She had had her hair chopped.

"I didn't recognise you with your short hair," I said.

I wished I had said, 'You look as if you've been cropped for fraternising with the enemy.'

"Oh, what are you doing now"

"I'm in education. Academic cloisters. But I miss being involved."

"Where are you?"

"In Clapham. I'm a reasonable man. You know the song."

At that moment the chubby High Commissioner called for silence. The seventy guests clustered round. He coughed self-importantly, produced a thick wad of typewritten notes, and began to read.

It was all there – all the usual guff about Ahmed and his absent wife, and an embarrassing bit about their handicapped son. Then he told a long and irrelevant story about a foreign diplomat in London who wanted to be sent home. He got drunk and assaulted a Senior Minister, but no matter what he did he received commendations from his own superiors back at home. "I don't say that this is true of Ahmed and his wife," the High Commissioner said, beaming chubbily like a teenager, and Ahmed was handed his presents to applause – two giftwrapped boxes large enough to contain bombs.

As he stepped forward I noticed he had a potato crisp sticking to the bottom of his jacket.

He made a good, spontaneous reply. It began, "I am full of emotion...." It was totally unprepared. It went down well and drew profuse applause.

He stood back and well-wishers surrounded him. His sleeve caught a glass on the table beside him and spilt Scotch over the table-cloth and carpet.

"Sorry," one of the African well-wishers apologised, though it blatantly was not his fault.

I had not realised Ahmed was so drunk. Then he turned to me, his coal black forehead glinting in the electric light, and said, "You can come to Stockholm, I will be there alone. My wife and children are staying here for four months, you can come and stay with me."

I was staggered by his warmth. Then I saw the crisp which still clung, absurdly, to his jacket. Suddenly I saw deep into him. I felt I was on his emotion like that crisp – I would soon drop off.

BREATHS LIKE WAVES

I married Pippa on a rainy day. She wore a pretty dress with roses on it. I was happy. I am a tenant of my body, I will move on when its lease comes to an end, and I know outer things are transient, and yet it was with some heaviness that I finally committed myself against sophistication, glamour, social chatter, and all the emptiness and shallowness of the outer beauty that had wrecked me once; and opted for the quiet life of the fruits of work, sincerity and inner beauty.

We drove to Hastings. We stayed at the Royal Victoria Hotel, where Queen Victoria stopped in 1875. We looked out of our fourth floor window onto a wrinkled sea, sand and rocks, and there was a constant cry of gulls. The sea panted slightly and washed gently, shhhing the shingle, and as we lay together it seemed that each soft wave and backsuck was a breath in and a breath out from a full body, and I was a part of the unity of a loving universe.

Later the breaths turned to sighs, and I felt a sadness, for I would have to release the old, let it go: a gull did not cling to its old plumage, nor did a tree cling to its fruit. Soon we would be moving out of my flat, which was sold, and we would be moving into our new flat, and I would have to move out of my old life and into a new one. I, a tenant of my body and possibly of other bodies in different lifetimes, had already discarded the past for this new joint-soul, which we would make into a home.

HOI MATE AND THE WATER MUSIC
(OR: AN OAK-APPLE BY THE GRAVES)

That Saturday afternoon was glorious. All the buds were coming out. I went up to the Strawberry Hill pond. It was full of young frogs. I counted twenty near one cluster of weeds. They were packed together and making ripples, big brown ones. Then four horses came up and the riders took them down the bank and they stood with slightly cocked necks waist deep in brown water. They churned the pond up and I lost sight of the frogs.

Pippa was with me, and we drove on up to the church. A robin was hopping over the mounds, and the water music of the birds trickled through the silver birches near the copper beech. I sat on the black rail, my feet on the spot where I would be buried. Pippa sat beside me. In the mossy churchyard I felt I could see every tree and flower that had ever been. It was very peaceful. From far off inside the church the organ started, and I listened to Handel's water music on the wind.

A car went by. A young tough in a tee shirt was standing in the open roof. He whistled and called, "Hoi mate, give her one from me."

The car slowed down and stopped. A motorcyclist thundered to a halt behind him through the trees.

"You park down that lane at night, mate," the tee-shirted tough shouted to the motorcyclist, "and it's pitch dark. It ain' arf good to take a girl there."

I was disgusted by his noise. I did not like to feel I belonged to the same humanity as this yob.

I stood up, and Pippa followed me into the church porch. The organ swelled loud.

By the church door a gnarled old woodland man beckoned me in. He winked.

The organist was a youngish man with red hair and a ruddy complexion. I could see him clearly from the door. Half a dozen locals were sitting in the back pews, listening to him. The organ drowned the coarse voices and the revving machine outside, and I wandered down the aisle and sat in a pew down the front. Somewhere outside the tough in the tee shirt was pouring his voice out into the woods in an egoistic, unself-critical dream, and the motorcyclist was racing his engine. That was different from the birds, and this joyful organ.

Sitting in the pew I was at peace. I followed the variations of the clever organist. In my pocket was an oak-apple I had picked up near my own grave. It was round and knobbly like a skull, and I thought the moment was as indestructible and hard as it felt in my hand.

BABY BELLING
(OR: IF YOU TOUCH IT YOU'LL BE SATISFIED)

"Come in sir," said old Mr Cullen in Ravenscourt Road. I went through a peeling door that had naked wires trailing from the inside of the bell and found myself in a room that was cluttered with Catholic pictures. "I'll just get the Belling," he said in an Irish brogue. He shuffled off in his slippers and came back, seventyish, balding head bowed, and plugged in a quite presentable baby Belling, which we needed for our new tenant. He put the palm of one hand on the hotplate, and I heard voices in the next room. Nothing happened.

"Oh, must be that plug," he said, getting on all fours and switching the switch up and down. "Must have blown the fuse. I tried it when I got it and it worked perfectly then."

"It's probably just the fuse," I agreed, trying to be helpful.

He padded out and returned with another plug and a screwdriver, and laboriously switched fuses. "It's a fifteen amp," he said, showing me a thirteen-amp fuse, and I wondered how he came to be there, this old man fumbling with fridges and cookers – he had more outside, he said; for what? A pound or two for himself, I thought. It couldn't be more.

He got the fuse off and padded through into the kitchen. He beckoned me.

"Sorry to disturb you on a Sunday afternoon," I said instinctively as an elderly Irishman and an equally elderly woman stood unsteadily up. The woman had a bun and yellow stockings.

"Just testing it at this switch," Mr Cullen said. I sat in front of a stove and waited. The other two had gone. "Yes," he said on hands and knees, "it's coming up. Put your hand there." I held my hand near the plate. "No, right on it." He forced my finger on to the plate and I winced away. A steady heat was rising.

"That's fine," I said.

"No," he said commandingly, "I'm not going to let you go till you've tried the oven. I want you to be fully satisfied."

He turned on the oven and put his hand inside. "There, this is redding up. Put your hand on that."

"I – er – I believe you," I said.

"No, I want you to touch it. If you touch it you'll be satisfied." He seized my hand and forced it on to the reddening bar, and pain seared at my finger. I wanted to howl out loud, but I controlled myself and said, "Yes, you're right. How much?"

I took out my cheque-book, but he had not heard me. He was still on hands and knees, touching the bar with his old hands and babbling on about how good the stove was. He was like a baby with his obsessive desire to please. In some strange way his mind worked like the Belling: when it came on he came on too, his head was glowing in its own way just as much as the hotplate or the oven bar, and he was as oblivious of my cheque-book as if he had just bought it himself. There was a wonderful peace in that cluttered room.

A CHERRY-BLOSSOMED HELL
(OR: TEA AND SCRIBBLING TORMENT,
SAUCER ON A STEAMING CUP)

That sad April day the pink cherry-blossom looked ragged in New Square, and there were faded petals on the wet ground. In the waiting-room I read *Country Life*. Then my solicitor came, a trim

A SMELL OF LEAVES AND SUMMER 77

man with a chubby face, well-parted hair and glasses. He was called Mr Torment: if this was a Last Judgement, he could not have been better named. He told me he had been away. His back was troubling him again. It didn't warrant the neck brace this time, but he would have to go for heat treatment.

As we left the waiting-room we ran into my ex-wife and her moustached, bald husband. She looked very beautiful: all sad and golden and ravaged. I introduced her to Mr Torment, and then Mr Torment and I went upstairs to a Georgian room that overlooked the pink blossom. There we discussed an agreement he had drawn up until he left the room to fetch Sibyl.

When they came in, Mr Torment said: "Sibyl's husband insists that it's very important that he should attend the meeting. But I've said it's not worth my job to say Yes."

"He should be here," Sibyl said, "After all, he is paying half Susan's school fees."

"Taking account of what has happened," I said, all bubbled up inside of a sudden, "I think he ought to pay them as a fine for what he's done to Susan's life. He has a moral obligation to do so."

Soon we were arguing out the agreement. Mr Torment umpired. He sat, head bowed over his bow-tie during the worst parts, and came up with suggestions that were acceptable to the two of us: his art was an art of compromise, and his tactic was to keep us both happy. On the subject of her husband's parents hogging half-terms I was adamant.

Quietly Sibyl started to cry. Detached, I observed her. Had I hurt her? Did she feel remorse? I thought of all the situations in the past when I hadn't wanted her to cry. We were in a cosseted Hell.

Eventually we reached agreement, and Sibyl left to join her husband in the waiting-room. There she would sit and wait while Mr Torment scribbled out a revised document which he would then photocopy for us to take away.

Tea was brought in: three cups. The secretary put the saucer on Sibyl's cup to keep it warm.

"She's beautiful," Mr Torment said of Sibyl as he scribbled.

"Yes," I said, "a writer-friend of mine says she's the most beautiful woman he's ever seen. After you've been round the world a bit and looked at Vietnamese women and Cambodian women, you get an eye for beauty."

Mr Torment scribbled on, and I thought of how he had advised me, just under four years ago, to end my marriage. We had been in a different room, it had a green table-cloth like a billiard table surface.

"She hasn't got over it," I reminisced from my thoughts. "She still gets upset. She didn't cry for a year, she told me. She can cry now."

Mr Torment scribbled away.

I sipped my tea. Steam had gathered round Sibyl's saucer.

"It's an uncanny feeling I have, a premonition....I feel she'll be left. I suppose you find that hard to understand...."

Mr Torment stopped writing.

"It's all right," he said, "I know how you feel, I've been through it myself."

I gaped at him. "When?" I blurted.

"Four years ago. The same time as you. I haven't seen my younger boy of fourteen for three years. My wife won't let me see him. She writes me letters but I don't read them, they're unpleasant."

"Are you divorced?"

"No, just separated. I know what it's like. I wake up in the night in a cold sweat. Sometimes I'm watching a film and I burst into tears. Then I feel a certain amount of self-pity, and remorse."

Like a greenjacket in Belfast, I had stumbled into an Inferno of pain. I had not suspected it was there, and I was appalled. Then I realised that this man who had so confidently advised me to apply for a divorce had been going through the same himself, and I felt a clammy sense of what might have been creeping up the side of the saucer that lay on the steaming cup.

LIKE A BURST WATER-MAIN
(OR: ENTERTAINING LIKE A FLAMING GASPIPE)

That Sunday morning, Pippa woke up first. She went to the Essex window. "There's a burst water-main outside," she said. "It's...." She made a fountain with her hands.

I got up later and walked round the block for the Sunday papers. It was misty, and a dozen men stood round a hole they had drilled. They were having their tea break on double time. As I read my papers the phone rang. A friend's fiancée invited us up to have a pre-lunch drink with her parents.

The Whittles lived on the edge of the crater. They had a view across the urbanised village. They entertained a lot. With two daughters and no hobbies they passed the time in talk, and as soon as one evening finished, they repeated it on the next. Jane, the second daughter, was there when we arrived. She was doing "O" level.

Mrs. Whittle was a Celt with reddish hair and a ruddy complexion, and he was a bald-headed businessman who dealt in bathroom equipment. To my surprise he was not too sure about London leaseholds, and I soon found conversation difficult. They were not interested in us, and they expected us to be interested in their boring, narrow experiences. We discussed the wedding that was a month ahead, and I thought of the burst water-main.

As if by telepathy Pippa mentioned the flood, and Mr Whittle added inconsequentially, "You might have a bath in it."

Everyone laughed.

Mrs. Whittle said, "I prefer a bath to having a shower."

I thought this an interesting statement of preference.

"Oh yes," said Jane, the bibliophile, "You can read a book in the bath."

"The book gets wet in a shower," said Mr Whittle.

"You can't lie back in a shower," said Mrs. Whittle.

"You don't lie in your own dirt in a shower," said Sue, who suffered from a dose of glandular fever and a sore spleen.

"You get wet and warm in a shower, and when you go to soap yourself you turn it off and get cold," said Mr Whittle.

"That's because you're supposed to soap yourself when the shower's working," said Sue.

I had had enough of this blather. The expense of spirit was like water foaming across the road. I remembered walking past Clapham Common station and passing a gaspipe that stood as high as a bus stop. There was a hissing flame at the top. Their notion of entertaining was like that flaming gaspipe: burning off excessive gas.

A STANDARD LIKE A FLUTTERING POUND

The night before the wedding my brother had the family to dinner at a large hotel at the top of a Forest hill. We all ate in a room that looked out on Scotch pines and a sunset, and a herd of cows nosed round the cars under the window. We sat at a long table and my aunt described the dinner she was going to attend the next day.

"It's at the Methodist church," she said. "The men of the church are going to give the women dinner, and they say they're cooking it themselves. But I've found out from my latest boy-friend, Sir Hugh Dukes, that three of them have ordered it from the Chinese restaurant next door but one. Talk about deceitful! I've been reading my *Bible* to see if I can find a proverb I can quote at them, but I think I'll have to say, 'Solomon with all his wives never thought of that.'"

And I thought, Yes, how typical. That is what happens when a rural community becomes urbanised. There is money to spend, services replace your own efforts, everything becomes that bit more meaningless. And honesty is eroded another chunk.

After dinner we went to the lounge and sat at a reserved table for coffee. My brother and I discussed politics. I said I was a Conservative because I stood for standards. As I spoke, a pound note fluttered through the air and fell on the expensive carpet.

"Did you see that?" I said, pointing to the new piece of litter. "A pound, I wonder who dropped it."

"Where?" my brother said urgently. "Did you see where it came from? Can you identify the owner?"

"I think it was the young Pakistani who's just left the room."

He jumped up, picked up the pound, and chased out after the Pakistani. I sat back. I knew my brother would find the owner, and I admired his action. He stood for a standard of honesty which had decayed. Like our family. The urbanised countryside we lived in now had made the pound its standard, but we stood for an ideal that was in the fluttering of that note.

POLITENESS LIKE A SPLIT CANVAS CHAIR
(OR: CROQUET AND COULD I MOVE?)

I went down into Kent to attend a christening. It was a squally day and when we arrived at the house I was introduced to a middle-aged woman. I did not know her from Adam.

"I'm Mrs. Latham," she said.

"Oh," I said brightly, "the relative who's the Inspector?"

"No," she said, "that's my sister-in-law." And the conversation was temporarily killed. Everyone stood around awkwardly admiring the baby. It was all very polite.

We drove to the church in a convoy. It was a ninth century Saxon church with a long, steep graveyard and a fine view over hills and fields. I led the way up the lich path. I held an umbrella over Pippa's head. Some girls from Fosse Bank school came out of the porch – they had yellow crosses on the tops of their berets – and we all stood near an old yew and eyed the gathering strangers, nodding politely. Then we went into the church and sat at the back near the Font.

It was a variation on the usual christening service. The vicar introduced it, explained it, and went through the glossy card line by line, response by response. The rehearsal over, the five godparents stood in a line, opposite the parents, and then we had the performance, including a profession of the Christian faith on the part of each of the godparents. There were no hitches, though I was disappointed that no lighted candles were handed out. I love the symbolism of the lighted candle. I thought of how rooted this life was: you lived in a huge house and you had five godparents to look after your children, the only snag was that you had to work your life away to achieve it. Soon we were all standing together by the yew among the graves, and then we were heading back to the house for lunch.

It was quiche Lorraine and strawberries and champagne, and soon everyone was pleasantly merry. I ate standing up and talked to a property developer and a solicitor, both of whom were only making conversation to pass the time.

"When did you come back from the Lebanon?" the solicitor asking, having forgotten what I had told him a few minutes previously.

Soon afterwards I went out and played croquet on the enormous lawn. The rules were variant ones. They seemed to favour anyone who got a hit, and there was an enormous penalty of missed gos for being put out of bounds.

As I came belatedly in I saw Mrs. Latham. She was sitting in a line of deck-chairs.

"It's like Brighton beach," someone said.

"No," she said as snootily as she could, "it's at least Bognor Regis," and everyone laughed. Then I realised she was sinking rather deep into her upright canvas chair.

"I don't like to be rude," she said, "but this chair is collapsing. Could I move?"

It was said straight, and it was meant straight, and I thought: that's about it. She's so polite she would rather go through and sit on the ground than make a fuss.

I thought I would go to Chartwell and see where Churchill had lived. At least the Golden Rose garden and the pond of golden orfe were settings where a man of genius found peace.

A LATE BOY IN THE SEA

"Snell is a puzzling boy," said the ex-vicar, Mr Bragg, on Hastings beach. "He's quite good at maths, but his reading is very poor. He's supposed to be dyslexic, but I wonder if he isn't putting it on? To get attention or something? Because sometimes he reads quite well. He's always late for school, and it doesn't matter what you do to him. Cane him, offer him ten p to come early for three days, it doesn't make a blind bit of difference. It's always, 'Sir, the hare got out' or some such excuse. His mother came up to the second year parents' meeting a few days ago. Her first words were, 'I'd like to apologise, I'm Mrs. Snell.' She's a teacher. She's bought him loads of Ladybird books, which she can't really afford for there are five children and not a lot coming in. But he won't read them. He's an enigma."

I looked at Snell. The boys of his form were building an enormous sandcastle to resist the tide. Snell was standing apart, in blazer and trousers, his long blond hair blowing in the wind. Quite deliberately he ran up and methodically began kicking down the sand walls.

"You see?" Mr Bragg said. "Destructive behaviour. He's outside all the others."

"Go away," one of the numerous coloured boys shouted, and a troop turned and rushed at Snell, swept him up onto their shoulders, surged forward and dumped him, kicking wildly into the sea.

When the class cleared, Snell was standing with the sea swirling round his trouser legs. A large wave washed up and poured through the hole he had made in the castle's fortifications, and I had the feeling that in some strange way Snell belonged to the sea.

AN OLD LADY AND A £40 SACK

I was invited to a fund-raising reception at the Guyanian High Commission. It was for a liberation movement, and knowing the people who regarded it with liberal benevolence, I put on a well-cut suit.

Two rooms were packed when I arrived. I fought my way to the table of drinks, and there were cheery greetings from Africans I had dealt with a few years previously: a South African black, a Rhodesian black, and a Namibian. As I hunted for a glass I realised a very old lady was standing beside me. She looked at least a hundred – she was very wrinkled – and she was bent over a stick. She was completely alone, and was trying to get through the crush. No one paid her the slightest attention, everyone was too busy talking about faraway injustices that were happening to distant Africans whom nobody had met.

"Here," I said, "let me pour you a drink."

I held out the glass.

"Orange juice, thank you," she said.

There was little else on the table, actually. The beer had already run out. I poured her an orange juice, which she took gravely, and I watched her shuffle off to be buffeted by people standing, turning, stepping back.

I poured myself an orange and pushed my way to the other room. There I was greeted by some whites I used to see: a couple of South African women, a journalist who had just married an Egyptian, and a man called Kim who used to be an Opposition Leader in South Africa. I had not seen him for nearly two years.

"Hello," he said, "can you come to a UN meeting tomorrow at noon? It will be a good discussion."

"Tomorrow might be a little difficult," I said tactfully, wondering at the immediate invitation. Perhaps that was how he saw people: as political counters to be moved around some draughts-board in his mind.

"The Lisbon coup has given us all heart."

"Good."

It was an oak-panelled room. I surveyed the scene, wondering what motives had brought all these well-fed, elegantly dressed people together, and then Kim banged the mantelpiece and announced the Ambassador for Guyana, who made a short speech about Guyana and Guyana's support for liberation movements: he might have been advertising his country for a travel agent.

He was followed by the leader of the liberation movement, for whom funds were being raised: an intense young African who stuttered. Try as hard as he could, each sentence led unavoidably to one word which he could not pronounce at all, and there was a tense embarrassed silence as everybody pretended not to notice. What he said was utterly confused, and there were excruciating pauses, but somehow the total effect was one of strange, fumbling sincerity. There was relief as he finally stumbled to a conclusion, and thunderous applause when he finished.

I was behind Lord Winston, the distinguished elder statesman. Applauding hysterically hard he stepped back onto my toe. Half-recognising me he smiled.

"The last time we met," I whispered, "was in Brussels. We had a chat together."

A BBC friend of mine had been doing an imitation of the good Lord in the lift, when the lift stopped at a higher floor and in walked the old boy himself.

"Oh, oh yes," he said in the tone of the perfect buffer, "I knew it was somewhere. We had fun and games then, ay what?"

Then he caught sight of a flamboyantly dressed Junior Minister in the Foreign Office. She was standing in the doorway.

"Oh, I think Tessa ought to be down here," he said. He made a curious flapping movement.

The woman looked pleased and came and stood in front of me.

The important guest from the UN was speaking now.

"I should like to pay tribute to several people who are here tonight," he said. "First of all, to Tessa Marchant. This is, I believe, the first time the British Foreign Office has been represented at one of our gatherings."

There were "hear-hears" and applause for this snub against South Africa.

The woman beamed. She had a common smile. It was the smile of the saloon barmaid.

A Liberal MP whispered something in her ear.

"Ay?" she said in the new language of the Labour Foreign Office. "Whatcha sie?"

The UN man spoke on. He was of indeterminate nationality – he spoke English with a thick accent – and he was about thirty years out of date in his dress. He draped himself over the end of the mantelpiece in his too large shabby jacket and baggy trousers, and spoke of the timetable to independence. In the middle there was a commotion.

I could not see what had happened, but there was a pool of space in the audience, and the window was opened.

Soon afterwards I caught a glimpse of someone sitting in a chair. It was the old lady. She was gasping for air, supported by two Africans.

The UN man talked on about faraway struggles, and ended to respectful applause. Kim now started the fund-raising.

"This is where I want everyone to come in," he said. "Will you tell everybody out there there's free champagne going? This is where I ask for money. Girls will be coming round with plates, and I want everyone to take an envelope, dig deep and put money in, preferably paper money. And if you have left your wallet behind, I want you to write how much you *will* give, and leave your name and address." Laughter. "As to where it will go, we've held a meeting and we've decided it should go directly to the movement we have been talking about, as no one else has done as much to bring independence to their country."

There was applause. The money would go to buy guns so that blacks could kill whites in Africa, it was a case for very benevolent approval.

"Now while you're doing that," Kim said, "I have a sack...." He unfolded a sack and held it up like an eiderdown. "It's a very good sack, it might even adorn a High Commission." Laughter. "Indeed, it is a most excellent sack. I want you to bid for it. Who'll start off with fifteen pounds?"

"Twenty-five," said a man near me.

"Thirty," someone else bid.

Lord Winston started shuffling uncomfortably towards the door.

"Thirty-five," someone else called.

"Forty pounds," called the man near me. He was chubby, between thirty and forty, and he beamed, and I thought: does £40 mean so little to you? Do know what the money will do to other whites not in this room? Or is this just an attention-catching moment, a chance for all these celebrities to turn and look at you?

Again the audience parted.

The old lady was being carried out. She was upright between the two Africans, and her legs were together, her shoes dragged along the floor. She was just conscious, she seemed paralysed from the waist down. She looked like a sack of vegetables at a Covent Garden auction, and as she was dragged by, she muttered ridiculous breathless apologies to everyone she passed.

There were glares and vexatious looks. She did not belong to any colonial conflict, she was not interesting.

"Forty pounds," Kim called in an auctioneer's voice, "who'll give me more than forty pounds for this very fine Smithfield sack?"

EDWARD THOMAS AND THE SWIMMING GALA (OR: ISN'T IT MARVELLOUS?)

I took my daughter to a school swimming gala at the local swimming-pool. The parents sat several deep on ribbed wooden benches in the spectators' gallery, and the girls sat beside the pool. The twenty-six events began at 7 o'clock with infants jumping in and doing widths in inflated amulets.

There were cheers of encouragement and the race ended to tumultuous applause.

Mrs. Tambling was in charge, and it was soon clear that the organisation was not going to be very effective. The second event was announced through a microphone on the Headmistress's table, and Mrs. Tambling then ran from one side of the bath to the other and organised the finish. She then ran back to the start, and after five minutes of negotiations with five teachers who were standing doing nothing she started the second event without blowing the whistle which hung round her neck. Not all the infants heard her, and there were several separate splashes as the race got under way.

At that point I saw Jocelyn. She was sitting with her mother looking very dressed-up. I had had a letter from her that morning – she asked if I would write her an essay on Edward Thomas as she had to do a project on Thomas for her college course, which she somehow fitted into her busy married life – and I beckoned to her to come and sit with Pippa and me.

"I can't," she called, and then she apologised for her long dress. "We're going to a party in Hertfordshire. We're supposed to be there at eight-thirty so we'll be leaving before the end." I did not see her husband but gathered he would be joining her to watch their daughter.

Event followed event with dreary monotony. My daughter was up against some strong competition. I caught her eye from time to time to reassure her: she had come on no end as a swimmer – could her confident crawl and backstroke belong to the same girl who was desperately dog-paddling two years ago? I reflected how the chilly open-air pool of my schooldays reduced my inclination to swim, and wondered whether I would have swum more than I did if I had had today's amenities.

Behind me, one of the teachers crouched beside her father, who was quibbling over the wording on the front of the programme. "'As you will appreciate,'" he read, "'this event requires considerable preparation, for which we are indebted to Mrs. Tambling and her helpers.' That's bad English. It makes it appear that Mrs. Tambling is responsible for there having to be considerable preparation instead of just preparation."

"Well," his daughter said, "I couldn't do better myself so I don't criticise."

It was obviously not the done thing to be so critical.

The organisation really was atrocious. The events dragged on, and by 9.30 it was almost dark outside, and there was a causeway of amoebic puddles of gold light on the blue water. When Event No. 26 was announced I muttered to Pippa, "Never again."

Then Jocelyn came over.

"What do you think of it?" she asked.

"The organisation," I began, looking at my watch, for there were a lot of people sitting all round us.

"Isn't it marvellous."

"Oh marvellous," I said quickly with a trace of irony, surprised at her sincerity. "It's just gone on too long, that's all."

"You old cynic, I think it's marvellous. And the children all look so happy." And she asked how my daughter was getting on.

As I replied, aware that everyone was listening in, I wondered why she was contradicting the truth of the situation so blatantly. The gulf between what was evident before her eyes – and after all she had bargained on being in Hertfordshire at 8.30 – and what she had said was amazing. Was it a social thing? Did she feel it was bad form to criticise, did she feel it was not the done thing? Or was she trying to show the right spirit? Which amounted to the same thing.

As she left me to return to her husband, who had just arrived, I thought of her request for an essay on Edward Thomas. Perhaps she was writing her essay in the same spirit? Perhaps it would be bad form to tell the truth about him, too? Perhaps judgements that to me (being involved in an objective vision) were a matter of life and death, were to her just the social distractions of dinner-party gossip? Whether on account of social politeness or some other reason, veracity, which is so important to the critic and to the artist, did not accompany her attitude to what she had seen.

A DECK-CHAIR IN THE SEA
(OR: A CANUTE STAYS PUT)

Edward MacGregor was an elegant Head of English. He was in his fifties, and he looked like George Devine, the late director of the Royal Court. He had distinguished and abundant grey hair, bushy eyebrows and sideburns, and black-rimmed spectacles which hid a scar from a war wound, which he suffered when he crashed a plane into the sea. He always wore a bow-tie. He was Scottish by origin, and for twenty years he had been a conscientious grammar school master. He had seen two generations of boys to Oxford and Cambridge. He was everyone's idea of what an English master should be: he was scholarly, witty, profound, and it was a measure of his intelligence that he did the *Times* crossword in ten minutes every lunch-time.

Then his school turned comprehensive. Its intake was increased to 1,400 boys, sixty per cent of whom were now coloured immigrants. Windows started to be broken. Graffiti appeared on all the walls and desks, many of a highly undesirable nature. Gangs of boys now rushed fiercely to and fro in the remoter corridors, and the playground was filled with the tinkling of coins as threes and fours tossed at the end of their "penny-up-the-wall". Respect for the staff plummeted. Staff were regarded as annoyances, to be jostled and threatened if any dared lay a hand on a boy. The Head left, and a new Head was appointed. He was a scientist in his forties whose thought echoed all the things that were said about comprehensives in the speeches of Labour Ministers. One day, he said, we will reap the benefit.

There was a vacancy for a Senior Teacher, and Edward MacGregor was an obvious choice, after his years of service. His main rival was a man who had been just as long as he had at the old grammar school. He sportingly stood down so that MacGregor would get the job.

The Head appointed a young history teacher who had been at the school just a year.

Edward MacGregor was away from school for a week. When he came back he was full of bitter and hostile feelings towards the Head. "That is a man I despise," he told me, "I have no respect for him."

A year later, during which time the school became even more of a dump and MacGregor had numerous conflicts with the Head, I was with him in Room 129, where all the examination books were kept. Here from time to time great parcels were delivered from publishers, and it was my responsibility to unpack them. For the most part they comprised books of glossy photographs with a few poems or passages interspersed, with titles that began *The Experience of* and with a voluminous appendix of acknowledgements at the back. It was the feeling of the staff that there should be nothing too difficult for the culturally deprived immigrant boys.

"You've got this shelf for 'O' level Literature," I said, indicating the books that had come in.

"I've been thinking," he said, "now that you're leaving I'm not going to do Literature any more. We can't get the staff, let alone qualified staff. And we did it with seventy boys this year, and so few were really interested. It's only a handful really. And it took up three of their five periods a week, which meant they neglected their Language. If I stop the Literature, they'll only have one exam in the fifth year."

"Certainly those who are good at Literature have got there in spite of this school," I said. "It's sad that standards are dropping, but it was a miracle that Jenkins liked *Macbeth* after all the loutishness he had to come through."

"Oh, absolutely," said Edward MacGregor. "And one of the louts has just been expelled, as you know." He mentioned an 'O' level student who had thumped a teacher – an ex-commando from D-Day – in the eye in Sloane Square while out on a visit. "Yes, I think we'll do just Language in future in the fifth year, and have a small Literature group in the Lower Sixth. I know it's a lowering of standards, but what can you do? There was a time when everyone read Shakespeare in the first year – you did, you told me – but now they don't even know who Shakespeare is in the fourth year, and the Inspectorate supports them in their ignorance. It's terrible. You know, I met Randall the other day. He was Gloucester in my *Lear* probably fifteen years ago, and I walked straight into him outside the station. He looks very distinguished now – he must be over thirty – and he immediately said, 'Can I talk English Literature with you sir?' and I thought 'It makes a change to hear someone saying that,' so I said, 'Yes, of course.'

"And you know what he said? He said, 'Sir, you made us read Hopkins, and you made us write something on Sprung Rhythm. I didn't understand him properly at the time, and though I did the work and learned what you asked us to learn, it was beyond me. I've gone back to Hopkins recently, and everything I learned came back, *only now I understand it*. I suppose you need a bit of experience to understand what you learn at school. You learn by rote, and then later, when you've had the experience, you understand it. I suppose that's the justification for a good education – that you understand it in later life.' And I thought, 'My God, you're so right.' He said, 'I expect the school has deteriorated since I was there,' and he said it must be very difficult for me....I'm fed up with this place. That last paragraph I wrote in my letter to the Inspectorate sums up what I feel: 'I'm disheartened by it all.' I wish I were leaving, like you."

There was a silence. He looked terribly vulnerable with his bow-tie and his twitching war wound under his eye. This was not the tough Chairman of the Common Room who ruled the heated discussions of the staff.

"You should move," I said gently. "You have a lot to give an academic boy. If the tide of mindlessness and ignorance is coming in – and I'm sure it is coming in – then you should move your deck-chair further up the beach."

He looked sharply at me. For a moment he clearly savoured the image. Then he said:

"I can't. I'm fifty-six. I retire in four years' time. Who will have me? Not a Grammar School Head. I'm too old. Would you, if you were a Head and you had a choice between a man of fifty-six and a man in his thirties and you wanted a Department organised – would you give it to the man who's only got four years to do? And if I became a lecturer I'd take a steep drop in salary. And I'm not prepared to do that. What else is there? Go abroad? That would disrupt my wife's life. You know she acts in rep round the country. She wouldn't want to leave this country. Besides, I'd lose my pension. No, I'm stuck. I've got to stay here."

There was another silence. I saw him sitting like Canute in a deck-chair with the sea swirling round his waist. He could not move. And it might be the same with me one day. We were kindred spirits. Two of a kind. We both embodied a respect for learning in an unacademic society. I vowed that, somehow, I at least would escape.

The next day I left that school. During coffee time he came and sat beside me and presented me with a second-hand copy of *The Tempest* which he had had on his shelves for some years. It was his favourite book, and it fell open at the last speech of Prospero's: "I'll deliver all;/And promise you calm seas…." As he paddled off I realised that we had shared more than a high tide.

A CHANTED INTRODUCTION AND A DIG
(OR: A MAN WHO SERVED A USEFUL PURPOSE)

We were invited to the Montgomerys for drinks that Sunday lunchtime. It meant I had to hurry through the Sunday papers by 12 and forfeit a poem I felt like writing, because an ageing man in the business of book distribution and his ex-hotel manageress wife had nothing better to do with their Sunday than distract themselves with other people and put themselves into an alcoholic haze.

The Montgomerys lived a floor below our London flat. I put on a suit and we duly rapped on their front door and Selina opened up. She was all dark hair and wrinkles and heavy make-up, and she wore trousers, and she led us into a room of books and quality furniture, which had a strangely garish carpet. There her husband Humphrey awaited us. He was all chubby-cheeked and oiled hair and spectacles, like a fifty year old fifth former, and he was sprucely smart in a suit. He beamed and chanted the introductions. The other guests looked unpromising: a Market Research couple of around fifty, a bald man in spectacles, and Mrs. Dupont from downstairs, and her son.

Humphrey had mixed a punch – sanguine – and he was rather pleased with himself. He fussed to and fro, trying it out on the gathering with the enthusiasm of a little boy. He bustled with a quick, puppety walk, the walk I had seen him execute regularly every Saturday morning as he hurried back from the shops with half a dozen bulging shopping-bags, while Selina stopped and chatted to acquaintances on the way. "Selina's been to Barbados, you know," he said once as he passed, and "Selina's also just spent two weeks in Kent looking after a dog." Needless to say, no one had looked after *him*.

Pippa sat next to Selina and they were soon talking about the fire two doors away. I overheard Selina say, in answer to a question, "It was last Easter, wasn't it, it started from the top, didn't it." As Pippa had no means of knowing, I identified this turn of speech as a demotic one, and I grasped that there was less to Selina than this room of expensive furniture might suggest.

I was on the wagon, and I stood and drank my Shloer next to Mrs. Dupont's son, who, alone of the company, was in an open necked sweat-shirt. He was fortyish and had black hair and a furrowed brow. I had earlier been intrigued by a card he had written his mother from Brussels. It was in the hall, and the handwriting was an elaborate copperplate in Indian ink. It was fussy. Now he told me he had been in films. He had not got out into television when everyone else had, and he was now in microfilms. He told me he was going to ask for a rise, even though the government had asked everyone to curb their wage demands. He seemed to have a complex about his low salary. "Still," he said, "it's not as though I've ever married or had children." He kept referring to food, and his principal hobby seemed to be gastronomy. He sipped tonic water because he had something wrong with his pancreas. He told me about his visit to the doctor – who was a Knight of the Realm – at such length that I howled within in boredom. I thought of a pot I had on my mantelpiece: snails crawled towards the rim – inessential people getting into my personality when all I wanted to do was write my poem.

The bald man in spectacles took a piece of cheese on a stick. It fell off the stick into his lap, and he picked it off his trousers with a curious dabbing movement of his fingers, as though he had something sticky on them. Humphrey fussed around filling everybody's glasses.

Mrs. Dupont's son told me about his holiday in Brussels. "Actually," he said, looking across the room to where his mother sat regal and grey-haired in a Regency chair, "I went to see a girl. I was rather fond of her, and...." I thought: he is telling me this because he does not want me to think he dislikes women. Does he?

The girl, it turned out, worked in a cabaret. She had been asked to design the clothes for the next show, so he had stayed on for ten weeks and helped her. The motif had been Winter Sports. "It was hard to do," he said, "I mean, they had to be scantily clad."

Then he asked me about Japan. I had been hoarding my energy for the poem that was ahead, and I thought: why should I tell him? Why should I let virtue go out of me? He means nothing to me. Why should I squander the energy I have reserved on these inessential people? So I talked vaguely about Japanese gastronomy, knowing that that was sure to interest him. I told him how I had been invited out and how I had been given a live plaice, which blinked and squinted dolefully at me as I ate the raw flesh off its back. I told how when I had finished it "blinked twice and then died", and then I told him about eating raw tuna fish with soy sauce and horse-radish, though you had to watch out for the mercury in the tunafish these days, and then I told him about the delicacy of delicacies. "You sit in front of an aquarium and catch shrimps in a net. Then you break their heads off with a nip of the fingers and swallow the bodies, raw and still wriggling, and feel them gyrate inside you like dead bodies of decapitated wasps." To my satisfaction he turned slightly green.

Then I got on to the subject of a writer who was out there. "He was terribly unpopular with the British community there," I said. "He was always on about how snobbish the British are, and how everything comes down to class. He attacked the Ambassador and he called the British Council the Brutish Council. When T. S. Eliot died he wrote about what a good thing it was that Eliot was dead, and what a Jew-hater he was. I suppose it was good that the British community should have had an Opposition, as it were, to make it think about itself, but the trouble was, the Japanese don't really understand that sort of thing. They expect a foreigner to be an Ambassador for his country. Consequently he was always out of favour, though I suppose he served a useful purpose."

Humphrey had sidled up to pour me some more Shloer. "Oh," he said, turning in the middle of his room to Selina, and as everyone fell silent he said: "Do you hear that dear? There's a person we're talking about in Japan who's 'always out of favour, but who served a useful purpose.'"

There was a deathly silence. Suddenly the whole company saw deep into the relationship of the host and hostess. Those very words had obviously been uttered, and recently. I guessed that very morning. And I guessed that she had used them of him. I looked again at Selina's black hair and her wrinkles and her heavy make-up. She had spread a travel brochure of Barbados on the coffee table, and I wondered about her two weeks of looking after that dog.

And as I wondered, Mrs. Dupont's son went across to Mrs. Dupont, drew up a chair, and sat very very near. He rested one bare elbow on the head of her Regency chair. She did not move or even incline her head. She did not appear to have noticed him, though she could not have failed to notice such closeness, such an invasion of her vital space. Sitting there in his sweat shirt he looked strangely like a little boy, and he looked strangely happy, and I thought I knew the answer to my question about him, too. And looking at the aloof mother, I felt that he, too, served a useful purpose.

MEAN TIME
(OR: THE 14.55 GOES TO LE TOUQUET)

My eleven year old daughter was flying unaccompanied to visit her mother in Germany. Her mother lived on the German border and did her shopping in Holland, and her husband, who was in the RAF, had sent a ticket from Gatwick to Wildenrath. With it there was an official piece of paper signed by two Flight-Lieutenants saying that the flight left at 14.55, that my daughter would be allowed 30lbs luggage and 9lbs hand baggage, and that we should check in half an hour before the departure time.

"It's quite safe," he had told me two months previously. "The RAF escort parties of children. She'll be with lots of other children. The RAF are very efficient. We'll meet her the other end." Thinking of the way he had managed to mess up every meeting we had ever fixed, somehow or other, I was not exactly encouraged by this confident statement. I thought of a remark one of the elderly teachers had made at school. "The new Deputy Head," he said, "is a typical young RAF officer: brash; abrasive; cocksure; and ignorant." I hoped that this time the last epithet at least would not apply.

We drove to Gatwick through deep countryside and quaint villages. We reported at the British Caledonian desk at 14.15. We weighed in the 30lb case and surrendered it. "You go to desk seventeen for the escort," the receptionist smiled.

We went to desk 17 with the hand baggage and checked in.

"Wildenrath," I said.

"Yes, yes," said the girl impatiently. "How do you spell her name?"

"It's on the passport."

"Yes, yes. The escort will be here in two minutes."

A woman was waiting nearby with two girls. "Is she going to Le Touquet?" she asked.

"No," I said, "Wildenrath."

"Oh," she said, "We're going to Le Touquet."

I turned to the girl at the desk.

"She *is* going to Wildenrath?" I said, indicating my daughter.

"No, Le Touquet," the girl said.

The escort had arrived and was talking to my daughter.

"Ah," I said, intrigued at being overruled. "The thing is, she's supposed to be going to Wildenrath."

"Fourteen fifty-five? The fourteen fifty-five goes to Le Touquet."

"Well, she's still supposed to be going to Wildenrath," I said patiently.

She hunted down a list.

"*Fifteen* fifty-five", she said.

"But this is the RAF form, and it says fourteen fifty-five."

"No, it's fourteen fifty-five GMT. Greenwich Mean Time. We're on British Summer Time. Fifteen fifty-five. You'd better come back in an hour. Will you wait with her?"

"Yes," I said hastily, snatching her away from the propelling domination of the escort who seemed equally determined to escort her to Le Touquet.

"Oh, that's *great*," my daughter said when I broke the news. "A whole hour?"

"We'll go and sit on the grassy bank outside," I suggested, for the sun was warm. "And we'll have a choc ice."

How could the RAF have made such an elementary blunder? I wondered as we went out. Then I remembered that Welsh teacher's words again: "a typical young RAF officer: brash; abrasive; cocksure; and ignorant." Yes, I thought, that's it. Everything is from *their* point of view. They worked by a mean time – it was all regulations – and they didn't think how it affected you. That required imagination, thinking themselves into other people's shoes. They were trained to be egotists. They lived in a monstrous dream of self, the self which the mystic made his starting-point to dismantle.

I was glad I had nothing to do with their self-centred life – and I was angry that I had been caught up in the incompetence of their bungling administrators.

SOLITAIRE AND A NUDGE
(OR: FARAWAY EYES AND A FIDGET)

I had to wait thirty-five minutes for a tube, and I only just made it to Paddington. The train was in. I found my reserved seat, H28. A woman was sitting in it, and she had the same ticket I had. It had been double-booked. So I went back on to the platform and found the Reservations clerk, who had a red stripe round his cap. He took me further up the train to carriage J and pointed to a window-seat, and a squat elderly man in a blue shirt and braces leapt up to let me in.

"You want to sit here?" he said, and he quite needlessly gave me a hand with my typewriter. He was much smaller than me, and he could only just get it onto the rack over the window. Then he sat outside me while I spread my files out on the table.

His wife, I soon gathered, was saying goodbye to a bevy of young people on the platform. She was thin and quiet, and she dabbed at her eyes with a handkerchief.

"Going far?" the man in braces asked in a West Country accent.

"St. Austell."

"Oh, I'm going right down to Penzance. I live in Newlyn. Going on holiday?"

"Yes, my wife's down there."

"Ah, I've been visiting my three daughters. They live up here. They're out there on the platform."

One of them came and waved through the window. She looked at least thirty-five and had two sons. He flapped back across me and then looked away.

"What time does the train leave?" he asked.

"One-thirty," I said.

"Oh, I thought it was one-thirty-five." He made important adjustments to his watch. "Going for long?"

"A week."

"I'm glad to get away from London," he said.

There was a silence in the carriage, and I was aware that a dozen or more people were listening in. He had got me into conversation about all the subjects that fascinate people on impersonal train journeys, and I had work to do. I buried myself in a file. Soon the train started moving, and after more flapping across me on his part, his wife came and sat opposite him, dabbing at her eyes with her handkerchief. She dabbed while the train pulled out of the station. The seat opposite me was empty. It had a Reserved ticket on it.

I read.

"What time does it get into St. Austell?" asked the man. He had not spoken to his wife.

"Six-eleven," I said, and I returned to my reading.

He looked at his watch.

I read on.

"Want a sweet?" the man asked. He thrust a packet of sparkling fruit pastilles under my nose.

"It's very kind of you," I said, "but I don't eat sweets."

"Oh."

I read on.

A woman came by with a case. The man leapt up, showing his white pants above his braced trousers. He snatched the case from her hand and with much puffing, heaved it two yards to the connection between the carriages. He waved aside the puzzled thanks of the case's owner, and returned to his seat. His wife was still.

But even then he had to fidget. He rolled a cigarette and lit it. Then, realising he was in a Non-Smoker, he stood up and went and puffed at the window round the corner.

I worked on.

His wife sat motionless with her handkerchief.

A young girl came by with a case. The man swooped. There was a swoosh as she was brushed off it. She staggered back, reeling against a seat, and he transported it two yards for her, then put it triumphantly down, his face and neck flushed red. Still reeling, she recovered her balance, and, mystified, carried on.

The man produced a beer can.

"Six bob these are, on the train," he said, sitting down.

He had waited until I looked up from my work, and he had caught my eye to speak.

I mumbled something and got on with my reading.

He drank his beer noisily. Then he stood up above me and –

A shower sprinkled my typed page. The empty can lobbed over my head and out of the open ventilator window onto the track outside.

I dabbed at the page with my sleeve, and read on.

He turned his attention to the woman at the next table.

"What's that you're playing?" he asked.

"Solitaire. I'm trying to get left with one in the middle."

"Have you done it?"

"I've got it down to two."

There was a pause.

"Throw one away," he said in his West Country accent, and he threw back his head and gave a great, cackling laugh.

The daughter of the solitaire-player began to giggle. She bit her lip and looked down.

"Hey," said the man in braces, showing his pants, and he nudged the daughter accidentally-on-purpose and said, "Oh – sorry," as though it had been an accident, and he winked, and I looked at his wife. She was sitting still, dreaming with faraway eyes of the three daughters she had left behind in London, and I wondered how she could be so still – and how he could be so restless that, though he had not said goodbye to his family and though he ignored his wife, he had to disturb the solitaire consciousnesses of all his fellow-travellers.

A HARBOUR CREEK AND A TIGER COWRIE

That evening Pippa drove me by the blue hydrangeas of Carlyon, and then we went to Charlestown. We stopped at the shell shop. It had a lot of shells with exotic names like Red Moon and Green Turk's Cap and Orange Spider. I picked up a Tiger Cowrie. It was polished and had a cleft slit down the middle, like fingers clenched in a fist.

I bought it, and we wandered down to the harbour. There was an old sailing-boat in the creek. It was the Marques of Palma, and in the shop I had seen a yellowing newspaper cutting which said it used to run almonds off Majorca. "It's a traditional boat," I said to Pippa, thinking of the Cutty Sark, and watching a boy swing in the rigging.

It was misty, and from the harbour wall under the Japanese-looking headland we peered across the bay. We could not see

Fowey point, but the Black Head of Trenarren was there, a dark outline plunging to the skyline of the sea.

There was a large boat coming in. It was manoeuvring outside the tiny harbour wall. It was a long china clay cargo boat with masts at either end. We waited among the fishermen, hoping to see it enter the harbour, but it stopped and turned and appeared to go away. And at that moment it came on to rain very hard.

We returned to the car and sat for a while by the creek. I thought of the long tradition of Mysticism, which some contacted through the Church.

"It's not coming into the harbour," I said, staring at the still rigging of the Marques.

In some strange way the harbour was a haven of peace under the china clay shoot and the Harbour-master's pink house on the hill.

"Yes it is," Pippa said. "Look, they've taken the creek bridge down."

And sure enough the big cargo boat was backing into the harbour. It looked as though it must smash against the old stone walls, but they had hung old car tyres at strategic places, and it squeaked and squealed and bounced off. Then the boat stopped and swung round so that it pointed up the creek, and, tying lines round capstans to increase their control, and hanging more car tyres over the side, the sailors on the front deck marshalled her up the narrow creek until it came to rest alongside the old sailing-boat with the rigging, under the china clay shoot. On the back of the large cargo boat I read "Cumulus".

I thought of my religion again, and I looked at Pippa, and holding the Tiger Cowrie in my fist I knew I belonged to them both. I had been blind and indecisive, like that boat. My individual "abiding alone" had come to an end, and I had come to rest in a tradition as old and real and peaceful as that harbour creek.

STONE COTTAGES AND A TEEMING SEA

It was cloudy, so we drove to Mevagissey and walked in the narrow streets. There was a shark shop. The sun came out, and we walked along the inner harbour wall. The tide was out, and the gulls screamed on the green weed. We wandered along to the end of the outer harbour. Several men passed holding clusters of green mackerel. We stood among the anglers and felt the warm sun on our cheeks and arms. The sea lapped against the stone wall, and trailing bladderwrack swayed to and fro.

Then we walked back to the shops. We sauntered past the cockles shop, and I turned and looked up at the hill. The tiny stone cottages were set one above the other, some were pink and blue and yellow, and the gulls were wheeling and screaming below, and someone was carrying a boxful of mackerel from a boat. And suddenly I had an image of a whole community living off the sea. The waters contained God's plenty, and the men went out in boats and cast their nets. There was an ample supply as they made their journey through the simple life, and the sea was teeming with good things.

A BONFIRE AND A VILLAGE

That Saturday night was Gala night in Porthleven. Constance and June were on the hot-dog stall in the field. At dusk we drove the car to where they were and watched the Cornish wrestling. Bare-footed men in Cornish jackets gripped each other's sleeves in holds and tried to trip each other while a man commentated desultorily over a loudspeaker.

It was dark now, and the torch lights were just visible on the hill. We walked to the front and waited for the procession. They came, following a band: flaming brands in the air, orange-yellow fires leaping, children and grown-ups, with the rest of the village lining the roads. They passed us, and we sat on a boat by the shimmering water while the cascade of lights passed up the hill, disappeared, then reappeared lower down by the harbour water. We watched them flow along the road to the field, and we followed them.

There was a big heap of furniture and rubbish in the car-park: old chairs and tables, old boxes. It was covered with petrol, and as the leaders of the march arrived they threw on their brands. The flames shot into the air, leapt and darted against the night. And seeing the village gathered round, avoiding the sparks, I thought: this is the heart of the religious artist, roaring away, reducing what it consumes to a new shape, giving off brilliant sparks while all stand admiring its brightness and enjoying its heat.

The artist was a special kind of human being, and he should be recognised for what he was: more than the President of the United States, and Watergate, he was the leader of the human race.

MARINATED PILCHARDS AND SILVER LEAD
(OR: TWO WIDOWS)

We sat in the Porthleven parlour. It was a Sunday morning. June sat in the window and Constance stood by the stove. They had finished arranging exotic dahlias, which they would take to their husbands' graves.

I asked questions about the local tin-mines. "There are two chimneys," I said, "and a kind of ivied arch. We saw several yesterday on the hills."

"Yes," Constance said, "Tom was interested in them, I remember him asking about them. Oh we had such good times when our husbands were alive, didn't we June. I used to come here with Tom, and our mother looked after the children, and the four of us would go out. Hayle we often went to. We'd have a drink, remember? And sometimes we'd dance, though Bill didn't like to dance at the beginning. Then we'd go for a walk to the end of the pier in the moonlight. We always did that. Then we'd come back, and we never went to bed before four. We were just laughing and talking. Tom had an infectious laugh and he'd get me going and we'd just laugh. My ribs would be sore with so much laughing. Remember, June?"

June sat in the window. "Yeah," she said in her trouser-suit, and stone necklace, staring ahead of her.

"Yes, we had such good times."

There was a scraping on the door. A man stood in the parlour. He looked weather-beaten and earthy, and strangely like a coalman.

"I'm collecting for next Sunday's fête," he said, taking a teddy bear out of a hold-all and showing it round.

June stood up and found him a tin. They chatted.

"You don't know anything about old Porthleven I suppose?" Constance asked him. "The tin-mines? You haven't any old photos? Only Philip here is interested."

"No," he said. "But I've got something from the old lead-mine near Looe Bar. It goes down under the sea. I've got a lump of silver lead. Would you like it?"

"It sounds valuable," I said in the tone which declines.

"A man made three hundred pounds selling precious stones like that. Yes, it's valuable."

"Perhaps you'd better keep it."

"Oh no, I've got four. You can have one."

He left.

"He's such a dear," said June. "I remember when I was living with my mother. He lived opposite me, and he came round and said, 'I'm just going home for marinated pilchards.' And my mother said, 'Oh, I haven't had them for a long time.' And do you know, he said, 'Come back, all three of you.' And we went. Just imagine, bringing three unexpected guests back. These Cornish have got a heart of gold. And they did so much for me when I lost Bill."

"Yes," said Constance, "they're not…." She paused, aware that she was describing me. "Educated or anything like that, but they've got a heart of – "

"Silver lead," I said.

"Yes, a heart of silver lead," June smiled.

And I looked at the fresh dahlias they would take to their husbands' graves. The two widows were like two disused tin-mine chimneys, and their past was like my lump of once-mined silver lead.

A LADDER AND QUARRELS AT CHURCH
(OR: WHERE HAS ALL THE MEANING GONE?)

Vincent Mullright was the local solicitor. He was stout with enormous jowls and he wore a black pinstripe suit and a bowler hat. He had lived a most conventional life as one of the most respected members of the community. He was a JP and he was on all the local boards and committees, he had climbed to the top of the social ladder before he moved out of the district. He threw himself into property – he had a dozen firms connected with it – and he was massively remote from anything personal. I once spent a week in his office room, to see if I liked the idea of being an articled clerk, and the only personal remark he made was, "What's that book you've got with you?" It was Chester Wilmot's *Struggle for Europe*, and he nodded gravely and said, "Not bad. You won't get much time for reading in the Law. Or for anything that has much meaning." It struck me as a curiously bitter remark for a man of his standing.

He was enormously good at making money, and after he left our town he lived on a rural Essex village green. One day he went to his son's cottage. His son was also a solicitor, but they did not get on, and he worked outside the family firms. Vincent Mullright did some restoration. He propped a ladder against a beam and climbed to the top. The beam broke, he crashed to the ground and broke his arm.

The consequences of that fall were not apparent till some while later. He took to sitting morosely in his study at home. "The Law has been a waste of time," he would mutter to his uncomprehending wife. "I've wasted my life on things I didn't want to do: cases, documents, work for other people, inessential things. Dinners and committees. Skeletons, that's all they are. Skeletons." He was on all the church committees, and it was disgraceful but this man of blameless reputation began quarrelling with everyone, from members of the congregation to the churchwardens and the vicar. The quarrels were over footling, trivial things. It was all totally unworthy. In addition he stopped answering letters. The following winter he had a nervous breakdown.

"The Church should have meaning but hasn't," he said as he was taken to hospital. "The Law should have meaning but hasn't. My home should have meaning but hasn't. Where has all the meaning gone?"

He lived in silence after that. He was always so solid in the old days, and I still sometimes imagine that I can see his portly frame turning the corner in our town, dressed in a pinstripe suit and a bowler hat.

A CHRIST IN HELL
(OR: A HANDKERCHIEF AND FALSE EYELASHES)

I was now teaching in a girls' comprehensive. I was Head of English. There were two thousand girls and I had a Department of twenty-eight teachers. Senior Prize Day was in October, and Lotte Strawberg, the actress, was invited as guest of honour to distribute the prizes. There was a rehearsal all morning, with the Hall packed, and the Senior School was dismissed at lunch-time.

It was supposed to reconvene at 6.30 p.m. That was when I arrived at our classroom for registration. Only a dozen of the hundred and fifty senior girls in our house had turned up, and they and we teachers – the women all dressed up – sat and killed time.

"I wasn't going to come this evening," one of the West Indian girls said. "It's boring, this day. Why don't I get a prize?"

Someone mentioned the National Anthem, which would be played.

"I don't know it," said one of the white girls. "I know God Save the Queen, that's all. Just the first line, God Save the Queen."

I was sitting next to our Housemistress, Mrs. Parkinson. She had whitish hair in a mannish style.

"They don't know the Lord's Prayer," I said, "and they don't know the National Anthem. What hope *have* they got?"

Mrs. Parkinson smiled. She had been strangely quiet for her, and she said to me in a quiet voice that the others could not hear:

"I shan't be here tomorrow, I'm afraid. On Monday my former husband died and the funeral is tomorrow."

Shocked, I made sympathetic noises.

"It *is* terrible," she continued. "It threw me for three days. I felt numb. We have a twelve year old boy who lives with me." ('*Have*', I thought.) "You see, if *he* had lived with us, his death would be part of the natural process of things. But the boy's father having lived away...."

Then one of the teachers was offering Mrs. Parkinson a sweet, and she was putting a brave face on her grief.

"There's an art in eating sweets at functions like these," she announced to everyone with a rather desperate cheerfulness. "You have to be very elegant and lady-like and use your handkerchief, like this." And she gave a demonstration of unwrapping a barleymint behind her handkerchief, disposing of the paper without anybody seeing.

Eventually we were sent for by the Senior Housemistress and we filed down to the Hall.

The attendance of the other houses was just as bad as ours, and in contrast with the morning's rehearsal, the body of girls had shrunk so that they only filled half the Hall. Parents filled some of the empty seats.

We sat and looked at the stage, which was tumbling with flowers. I was sitting next to Mrs. Parkinson again.

"Prize days are out of date," she said, clutching her handkerchief in the palm of her right hand. "They used to be to encourage work that would result in passing the Indian Civil Service exams – but you know the history of education as well as I do. Now all that's gone, and by keeping this, we're imposing values on our society. We should be finding out what values society has, we've no right to expect all these parents to make their daughters go through this. That's my view, at least."

Knowing I would be taking her away from her grief I said: "I disagree. We are living in the breakdown of Western civilisation – the oil crisis is just one symptom of what happens when a civilisation weakens and loses the will and the power to defend its own interests – and in any time of disintegration there are two scales of values: the traditional ones, which are hard, and an easier alternative. Prizes belong to the old set of values, along with grammar schools and the concept of a poor boy working his way up to a high position through qualifications. What you're saying is that we should find out what the easier values are and confine our education to encouraging them. They're decayed values, the collapse of the spiritual for a vulgar materialism."

"Yes," she said sadly, "the spiritual has gone."

"But we should be proclaiming it," I said. "*It* hasn't failed, families fail it."

"Hmm."

From the platform the Senior Housemistress said, "School stand," into the microphone.

On to the stage filed the Governors and the many guests of honour: the Mayor and Mayoress, the MP and his wife, the Chairman of the ILEA, and numerous other figures whose names were known in the London educational world, and whose opinions had been heard in the press and on television. With them was Lotte Strawberg. She wore a long dress and had her fair hair done up into a cottage loaf.

The Chairman of the Governors had a bald head. He had an accomplished manner at the microphone, and when the school was seated again he introduced the distinguished guests. He got two names wrong, including a national figure. Then he introduced the Governors, who were sitting behind him. Each Governor mentioned stood up. They were all sitting on different parts of the stage, and as each stood the effect was of a head coming over a wall, sometimes in the middle, sometimes to the right, sometimes to the left, and soon the Senior girls had the giggles.

At length the Chairman announced: "Now we come to the verse-speaking, which has been arranged by Miss Firley."

In fact, the name was Miss Farley.

The sixth form verse-speakers duly stood and chanted their poem and then sat down again.

The Chairman of the Governors introduced the Headmistress, who stood and read her report on the year. It was straightforward and factual, and when she had finished the House Captains gave reports on all the extra-curricular activities in the school, all the various clubs and societies and options that sound so impressive to those who have never had to enforce options on unwilling pupils.

At last it was time for the presentation of the prizes.

Miss Chadwick, the Deputy Head, stood at a microphone and read out a batch of some twenty or thirty names, and then, one by one, the girls filed to the centre of the stage to receive their books from Lotte Strawberg, who snatched at each girl, pumped her hand, bent and gushed words, holding the book ostentatiously up to read the title.

Behind her handkerchief Mrs. Parkinson whispered to me, "*She's* obviously not given prizes before."

"How can you tell an experienced prize-giver?" I asked, knowing the answer but wanting to bring her out of herself.

"A quick shake of the hand and a slip of the book, and 'Next please'," said Mrs. Parkinson.

"It's very unstuffy," one of the teachers behind me said. "Here, have a sweet."

The teachers were, in fact, making more noise than the girls.

At the end of each batch there was applause. Then Miss Chadwick read out the next batch of names. It would have had meaning if the prizes had been earned or won, but no Heads of Department had been consulted, and no tests or examinations had been used as a basis for the awards, in keeping with the best socialist philosophy, and a lot of the prizes seemed to be going for general usefulness around the school.

"I'm not Julia," one of the girls said indignantly to Lotte Strawberg, returning her book in some disgust.

"Oh," said Lotte Strawberg, seizing on the muddling-up of the prizes to play a part to its full effect and get through to the audience, "she says she's not Julia. Where's her book? It's most important. Quick, quick, where is it?"

The audience laughed.

"You're supposed to keep things like that a secret," Miss Chadwick said from her microphone.

There was another laugh.

"Oh," said Lotte Strawberg, put out by the reprimand, "I've always done what I wanted."

There was another laugh and applause. Miss Chadwick looked angry.

At last the file of prize-winners came to an end. It seemed as though every girl in the Senior School had received a prize for something. There had been true equality of opportunity when it came to collecting a prize.

Now Lotte Strawberg began her speech. "Gals," she began. "I say it again: 'Gals.'"

The speech was rambling and, at times, so incoherent, that I wondered whether she was boozed. It was all about her reminiscences of her life at an expensive school in Hampstead. "It's a wonder I learnt anything," she said, "for I spent most of my time out in the corridor for being naughty or for mimicking the teachers." All the girls laughed, and she went on to give some impersonations of various girls in her class, one of whom she detested. "She's now sewing umbrellas in Selfridges," she said. There were hoots from the girls, and each sentence she intoned in now a German, now an ultra-posh accent, brought bigger and bigger gales of laughter.

She exaggerated every word she spoke – she was a bit like a female Kenneth Williams – and then she became political. "I really envy you the opportunities you have here," she said. "In fact, I'm jealous....I'm a member of the Labour Party, and I've been on marches, and I support the comprehensive idea." There were one or two raised eyebrows among the staff, many of whom were Conservative, and many of whom had written a letter of complaint to the Chairman of the Governors about the excessive Labour propaganda at the Junior Prize Day a few months previously. But it was hard to take exception to this frank statement, even though the Chairman of the ILEA raised her hands and applauded, for it was said in the tone she would have used if she had said, 'I like cheese.'

The rest of her speech was a pandering to the passive values in our society. "I suppose I should be 'giving you advice'," she said, mimicking a pompous prize-giver, "but the only advice I can think of is that everybody I know has agreed that success is five per cent inspiration, and ninety-five per cent perspiration. And you don't want to know about perspiration." Otherwise there was no appeal to the hard-working values that Prize Days (according to Mrs.

Parkinson) are trying to impose. At the end she offered to come and help with the school's drama as she would be living near us fairly soon – "I will be big sister" – and there was thunderous applause. Mrs. Parkinson clapped one handclap every ten seconds.

I clapped politely and then refrained. Lotte Strawberg had got on the same wave-length as the girls, and she had been unstuffy, and she had given them what they wanted like a true performer. But it was totally unedifying, and she had failed to appreciate how seriously schools take themselves on such formal occasions, and there were glum looks on the stage.

After that there were votes of thanks: from the Chairman of the ILEA, a weird-looking woman in spectacles with mannish curly grey hair who confessed to being "a working-class girl from Hammersmith who lost my accent"; from the Head Girl; and from the two Deputy Head Girls. In fact, I thought we were going to have equality of opportunity in votes of thanks, with perhaps every senior girl being given an equal opportunity to express her appreciation.

We had three brief songs from the sixth form choir, and we sang the National Anthem, with a notable tailing off after the first line, and then the Chairman of the Governors spoke his farewell. But even then he could not avoid making a mistake:

"And now," he said, "I understand there is something to eat and drink in the house-rooms. I invite all present to join us there, and I hope we will all meet and talk, as we Governors want to get to know you."

The Headmistress looked appalled. Mrs. Parkinson was dabbing her nose with her handkerchief, and she said, "No, *not* the girls."

It was too late. The doors were open, and the girls of the fourth, fifth and sixth years who had turned up were pouring across to the house-rooms where trays of mulled red wine stood waiting for the distinguished visitors. Young hands greedily reached out. I could see it all happening as I came up the path. Where three hundred were expected, a thousand fought and the red wine was gone within five minutes.

I found Lotte Strawberg besieged by autograph hunters, the young girls I had been teaching earlier in the day. She had not managed to find one glass of red wine, though the West Indian girls evidently had.

I had put on a badge. It gave my name and it said, ridiculously, as though it were my nationality, "English". I introduced myself, holding the badge on my lapel, and said: "Did you mean what you said about coming to help with our drama?"

She snatched at my sleeve. "Sure, yes, I meant it, I mean it," she said, exaggerating every vowel, rolling out every consonant on her tongue. In close-up she was even more gargantuan that I had supposed. Her false curly eyelashes were fully four inches long – I swear it – and her ear-rings rivalled the Mayor's two chains in the complexity of gold that dangled. She was made up as if for television – she was currently appearing nightly in a soap-powder commercial – and with her hooked Jewish nose she was utterly preposterous. I marvelled at her strong personality, and her mannered self-assurance. Had she never thought to ask herself how *real* it all was?

She prattled on, lilting and diving, lobbing her voice round the crowded house-rooms, intoning, emphasising, converting what was a highly inarticulate mind into one that seemed to be far weightier than it was. She talked about the house she was buying up the road, and how she would love to help us produce *The Boy-Friend*, and her delivery became so exaggerated that before my very eyes she turned into a caricature. She was a false persona, but she had that star quality that goes with a magnetic personality. She had cultivated an exaggerated falseness, and it accorded with the values of our time, and it was fitting that she should be surrounded by her semi-tipsy admirers.

Near her stood Mrs. Parkinson. She was laughing stridently and waving her hands in a desperately hysterical forgetting of her grief. Her handkerchief fluttered briefly, as if she were waving a white flag in surrender. The Headmistress was saying, "I put down my glass of wine and a fourth-former took it and drank it," and she looked accusingly at the bald Chairman of the Governors. Miss Chadwick was standing in disapproving silence, glaring at Lotte Strawberg who was blatantly ignoring her, even though, as Deputy Head, it was her task to keep the distinguished prize-giver entertained. And as Lotte Strawberg ogled me from round her Jewish nose and under her false eyelashes and said, "You know, Albee originally wrote the part of Martha for a man, the play's a male counterpoint of *Sister George*," I detected something almost diabolical about her, and I suddenly felt very lonely in that crowd, as if I were Christ before the harrowing, standing in Hell.

LIKE A FISH IN A STORM-TOSSED SEA

Pippa rang from the hospital at 5 a.m. "I'm starting," she said, "can you come along?" When I arrived she was in the Labour Ward, on a high-up bed with machines on either side of her. I put on a surgical coat which tied at the back of the neck and a shower-cap, and sat beside her. She had had an epidural, and the lead trailed into her, and her feet were tied up to bed-posts. The contractions were coming at quicker and quicker intervals – I watched the needle measure them – and on another machine I watched the "Fetal Heart Beat" register as a green wavy line.

Suddenly it went dead, registered zero. Sister saw it even as I did, and ushered me outside. I waited in the corridor for about five minutes while a doctor and two more nurses hurried in. Then I was called back in, and the Fetal Heart Beat was registering again. There were several nurses round the bed, and one said, "This baby is very tired, he's struggling to get out the wrong way," and I thought of the tiny thing as a fish in a great rolling ocean, swimming against the currents of the tide, not knowing that air was near at hand. Someone said "Vantoosh", and the young doctor who was doing the delivery tried to draw it out with a suction "plunger" to the head. "It'll have to be forceps," he said in the end, "your wife's got high blood pressure and that makes the baby very tired," and he slit Pippa so that dark red blood splashed into a pail at the end of the bed, and I sensed that there might be a stillbirth and felt shaky inside.

The baby emerged: a fish, covered in marine blood and slime, exhausted from a storm-tossed sea, and looking terribly stillborn. "It's a little boy," the young doctor said, holding the thing up. A nurse snipped the cord, another whisked him over to a trolley at the end of the room, and the team fell upon it and soon it was crying. He was crying. A new life had begun. I felt a great surge of awe in my relief, at this new being that had swum its way into the world, and who would grow and know me and attend my funeral.

A TWELVE-YEAR DREAM AND AN UNSAILED BOAT (OR: A ROMANTIC OUT IN THE SUN)

For the twelve years before his retirement – from the time his daughter was eleven – Gregory Davidson lived for a dream: to retire to Minorca. "I'll be out there in the sun," he used to say to his friends on winter evenings, "and I'll be sailing my boat on that blue water, and I shall be happier than I have ever been as a company director or financier."

When retirement time came, the Davidsons went to Minorca and bought a lovely villa near the sea. They returned to London and put their flat on the market. It was rather a splendid flat – it had two floors and a roof garden – and it was probably worth that, but for a year there were no takers, largely because there was no central heating. While he waited, Gregory Davidson took a part-time job in a car sales firm. Then the three day week took over, and no one was interested in buying, and the price dropped. That was when I went along to view it.

The appointment was rather against my will, for I wanted a flat in a garden square. I only turned up because the estate agent who sent me insisted it was a bargain. As Sheila, Gregory's wife, showed me round I thought it was all too luxurious and outside my price range, but right at the end I fell in love with the place. I told Sheila, who was a blonde fourteen years younger than Gregory, and who looked little more than thirty, that I would come back and view it again.

In fact I viewed it another twice and established quite an understanding with Sheila. She told me about the twelve years she had spent there, and about her daughter. "I'd like it to go to someone who's going to treat it in the same way, for I'm very attached to it," she told me. "I don't want to go to Minorca. Gregory knows that. I work at Harrods and I don't want to leave."

I saw her out near Gloucester Road station after that – I was living round the corner – and then I visited the estate agent, another blonde, and made an offer for £8,000 less than the original asking price.

The estate agent communicated this offer to Sheila, who said, "What? Oh Gregory would never accept that."

I waited a week. Then Sheila rang and invited me round for a drink "to meet Gregory".

Gregory had a moustache, and slightly longish hair. He looked like an arty version of Albert Schweitzer, and he had a very husky, deep voice. "I'm itching to go to Minorca," he told me, sitting in his tasteful drawing-room of fine antique furniture, "I just can't wait to shake the dust of this country off my feet." We discussed the three-day week and eventually he asked if I would go up £2,000.

I refused, politely, but offered £200 for various items of furniture, to include the carpets and curtains.

"All right," he said at length.

I made him promise that he would not sell to anyone else while I went ahead and sold my flat, and then he showed me round again. When he opened the door of the enormous bathroom, Sheila was sitting on the loo behind all the tropical vegetation. She was dabbing at her eyes, and it was then, flushed with exhilaration as I was at having chosen my future, that I realised how much Sheila was going to miss her home.

I saw the Davidsons several times during the next few months while we worked out what they would be taking with them, and what they would be leaving behind. Gregory was usually tinkering with his car when I arrived. He was mad about cars.

As the day for departure approached, Sheila became more and more tearful.

I sold my flat and I had to move out quickly as the condition of the sale. The Davidsons were not ready to move, so my furniture went into the flat below theirs, which was empty. Sheila came down in tears. "I'm so upset at going," she sobbed in front of the startled removal men. "We've been here eleven years and had a daughter. I hope you'll be as happy as we were."

The removal men stood and looked at her in amazement.

I stayed in a hotel in Onslow Gardens until they moved out. After that I saw nothing of the Davidsons, though from their friends in a lower flat, the Montgomerys, I heard that Gregory had crashed his car in Onslow Gardens, that they had gone out to Minorca in May, and that Sheila had come back in June in tears. "I don't like it out there," she wept. She carried on living in Minorca, but she came back to London in July, in August, and in September.

Selina Montgomery had asked to see my new son, so one October afternoon my wife and I rang their bell and I hauled the carry-cot in, and there was Sheila, blonde and attractive and expensively dressed, drinking wine from a silver goblet and smoking a cigarette. She smiled, and I thought I detected tears behind her heavily mascara-ed, beautiful eyes.

I sat down beside her while Selina (who was in trousers) held my son and talked to my wife. Humphrey was sorting book

A SMELL OF LEAVES AND SUMMER

catalogues, which were on piles on the carpet.

"You know, the first month I couldn't stop thinking about you in our flat," Sheila said. "I kept having to get up in the night and have a drink and a cigarette. I've been dreadfully unhappy."

Embarrassed, I said, "I'm sorry."

"I don't like it out there," she said, her eyes flashing briefly with tears. "Minorca's full of young people. The cost of living's gone up, and it's as expensive as it is here now, so we haven't gained on that as we thought we would. We can't afford to buy great rounds of drinks, and that just leaves the gin and the cigarettes. We've no television, and there's nothing to do."

Nauseated by her self-pity, but sorry for her nonetheless, I said, "But I expect you've been on the beach a lot."

"Do you know, we've only had six days in the sun since I've been there? Gregory has decided he doesn't like the sun, and the sand gets between his toes, and he made a mistake about his car. I told him, but he wouldn't listen. We're so bored there. There's nowhere to work. We go to the pictures and see old films, that's all. We've been back a fortnight, and I'm back at Harrods more or less indefinitely. Gregory's going back to Minorca but I'm not going with him. He'll come back to London soon. We'll have to find somewhere to live, we can't go on staying with our daughter. We made a mistake to sell our flat to you. You see, we should have put the furniture in store and let the place and given Minorca a three-month trial period to see if we liked it. And now, all our furniture's out there in Minorca. That cost a thousand pounds to send alone."

Soon afterwards she stood up and went, with exaggerated hugs and kisses for Humphrey and a handclasp for me. My wife and I stayed on, and we discussed the Davidsons with the Montgomerys.

I said, "I was involved with them at the beginning of their venture, and I'm sorry they don't like it."

Selina said, "Gregory's been in a terrible state. We saw him a week ago. He was near to tears. He was gulping them back."

"Yes," said Humphrey, "I couldn't get one laugh out of him the whole evening. He was always good for a laugh, old Gregory. He's been depressed."

"He's been to the doctor," Selina said over my son, whom she was nursing, "and been given pills. He just sits around in Minorca and does nothing. He has a boat. He's been too depressed to go out and sail in it once."

I frowned. I said: "I don't think they've given Minorca a chance. Sheila certainly hasn't, coming over here every month. I've lived abroad, and I know you have to give it six months or more to take root – and no visits anywhere in the meantime. If I'd left Libya every month for the first four months, I'd never have settled."

"I quite agree with you," Humphrey said. "They haven't chosen it properly. You see, Gregory is a romantic at heart, that's the trouble. As long as we've known him, for twelve years, it's been his dream. We've heard him say a thousand times, 'I'll be out in Minorca in the sun....' It was a romantic idea, he didn't think it out properly. It never occurred to him that he wouldn't like it."

"They should give it a fixed time with no visits back here," I said, "and they should improve their attitude towards the place and really make an effort to like it and to sail that boat. And if they don't like it by the end of that fixed time, they should sell up and come back to London."

"I quite agree," Humphrey said.

I sat in silence, wondering if the Davidsons were going to try and buy me and my wife out of our flat, so that they could return to the home they loved, above their friends of twelve years' standing. I felt a deep sadness for the demise of their dream.

Three months passed. By January we had found the stairs too much – I had to carry the carry-cot up and down them every day – and we put our flat on the market. I had cause to ring Selina about a key, and I asked her what Sheila had done when she was in the same situation.

"Oh I don't know," Selina said, "and it's difficult to ask at present. You see, there's a bit of trouble between Sheila and Gregory."

"Oh?"

"Yes, Sheila's not living with him now. She's living with another man. Actually, it's her boss from Harrods. It had been going on for some time. It began as a kind of game, but then affection crept in, and she had to choose."

I was reeling. "So Gregory didn't know when he went to Minorca?"

"Oh, no, he had no idea. He only found out when he was there. I feel very sorry for him. He's in complete despair, he has no interest in anything. He's over here now, living with his friend in Queen's Gate, and he has no interest in anything. Humphrey took him to a concert a week ago, and he couldn't come out of himself to listen to the music. He's in the depths of misery. He's finished with Minorca, he won't even go there to collect his clothes. Sheila's boss is only a year younger than he is."

Now I understood Sheila's reluctance to leave the flat. I also understood her tears when my removal men moved my furniture to the empty room, and I understood why she had come home every month. And pondering on Gregory's nightmare, I felt angry with Sheila for allowing him to sell the flat. If she was going to leave him, that surely was not necessary, even though it had been to my advantage. Now Gregory Davidson had nothing except a broken waiting for death.

LOST GLASSES AND CLANGING SEATS

The elderly RE teacher, Mr Cuthbert, took assembly that day. He was bald and boyishly enthusiastic, and he told amusing stories and then turned to his Authorised Version, which he quite rightly venerated, along with the Latin Mass, as a tradition that Christianity should be proud of rather than lose confidence in and change. He patted his pockets. "Oh dear," he said, "my glasses have done their usual trick of slipping down into the lining of my jacket pocket." And the hallful of girls giggled, and the Head stared stonily ahead, and I wondered why he had drawn attention to himself. It was as if he were trying to humiliate himself, it would have been so easy to pass the crisis off.

Being Head of English, I had to put in an appearance at the Dance Drama: the Head of English was in charge of the stage lights, and therefore ought to be present. Parents packed out the drama hall when I arrived that evening. I stood by the door so that the Head saw me – it *was* 7.30, definitely a time to be noticed – and then I settled down to watch the appalling turns. Dance Drama! How high-falutin' the words sound. Music and Movement was what it was called when I was at kindergarten. For a record was played, and a few girls mimed to it. After applause, another record was put on, and there was more miming – and thunderous applause.

When the interval came I stood up to slip away, and my seat clanged. "I was terribly embarrassed this afternoon by something like that," beamed Mr Cuthbert baldly behind me, as we walked outside. "I took the sixth form to a Magistrates Court, and I told them to be well-behaved and sit quietly. They were as good as gold, and when it was time to leave I gave them another warning, and they stole out on tiptoe – they were as quiet as angels. And then I stood up. I don't know what happened, but my seat fell against another, and it in turn fell against the next one, and they went along the line like a row of dominoes. Or should I say British colonies? Anyway, twenty-four seats fell, one after another. Clang, clang, clang, clang, clang, and so on. It completely stopped the Court's proceedings, and I had to apologise to the Magistrate. 'I am very sorry,' I said, and he said, 'Apology accepted.' It would have to happen to me, wouldn't it?"

And as I shook with laughter, he turned and like some Chaucerian monk was reciting the same tale eagerly and with great rotund gusto to another member of the staff. I wondered why he was so keen to humiliate himself in public – or was he merely going through a daily routine of humbling his pride?

SHOUT TO THE LORD

Sister Moore came and sat beside me in that girls' school staff room. She was Head of Science, and her Department had just moved rooms. "How's the move going?" I asked.

"Oh, not so bad," she said, pulling a face. She had a spiritually beautiful face. It was over forty, she had silver hair and deep eyes and very sophisticated smile, but I sensed she had not found true peace. "Did you watch the play on television last night?" she asked. "I seldom watch television," she went on, and as she told me about the play I looked at her. She wore a modern uniform for a nun; if it weren't for the ridged Catholic cross you would think she was in a blue sweater and skirt.

"Do you live in your order?" I asked.

"Oh yes, in the convent," she said, and seeing my questioning look: "Three years ago we had to decide how to set the balance between action and contemplation, and I was involved in the Nuffield Project, and now this."

"Contemplation. This can't leave you much time for contemplation."

"Oh, we rise early. I have got up at five-thirty all through my religious life. We pray in the morning and again in the evening. But it's no good in the evening, I find, when I'm tired. So I do my contemplation in the morning."

I thought of Teresa. I had often longed to ask the question that was on the tip of my tongue.

"Forgive me if I am asking something I shouldn't be," I said, "But is illumination featured in the convent? Illumination in the sense of light in the soul?" And I told her how Teresa had it, and how she had assumed everyone had it. I didn't tell her how she had introduced me to it. "I mean," I said, "this Light which you read of in the writings of the saints and mystics, from St. Augustine to today, is it a common experience in the Convent, or is it rare enough to make Teresa a woman with a difference, perhaps a spiritual leader?"

"Oh, she's a leader," Sister said without any hesitation. "Illumination is never mentioned in the Convent. We pray, and hope the Lord hears. If there's nothing, then we shout to the Lord." And I felt that all at the Convent were trying to achieve what Teresa had already found and taught me. I felt that for all her religious life, Sister too had yet to find what I knew.

I was due to have a staff meeting for the twenty-eight in my Department that afternoon after school, but it was cancelled for a show 3E were putting on. 3E were an horrendous class. The girls in it were only thirteen or fourteen, but they contained three or four who rivalled one coloured girl of extreme naughtiness who weighed twenty-five stone, or thereabouts, and who was three times the size of most of the women teachers. I sometimes encountered them queuing in the corridor to get into a classroom, and this procedure was frequently followed by the discovery of broken doorhandles, damage to the walls, and the consequences of furtive fights.

3E had, in short, been so appalling in every subject to every teacher that the Headmistress had decided they should give the staff tea and mincepies, and put on a display of work. After weeks of cajoling, their teachers had actually succeeded in extracting a few pieces of legible, if not entirely literate, work, and so we walked round the house-room making embarrassed approving noises. Then some thirty members of the staff sat down to watch a very short play, which was on a Victorian Christmas.

Emily was a great tank of a white girl with fat red cheeks and a voice like a police loud-hailer or the excessively loud school tannoy.

"I hate Christmas," she recited woodenly, wearing an absurdly floppy hat. "I– will– not– give– any– money– to– those– children. Who– are– they?"

"They are orphans."

Off stage, in the next house-room, a pop record was blaring a "love song".

"I don't care," shouted Emily. "Get – OUT!"

Off stage, sniggering girls in Victorian bonnets sang carols out of tune against the crooner.

Emily had forgotten her lines. There were whispers. The cast giggled.

"Oh yes," said Emily when prompted. "I– have– changed– my– mind. Let– them– come– in. I– will– adopt– them. They– will– live– in– our– family. I– will– give– thanks– to– the– LORD."

She shouted the word enormously loudly and put up her carol programme to snigger, and there she stood, in front of thirty teachers who were sipping tea and eating floury mincepies, shaking with unstoppable giggles, the menace of the thirds clad in her better self but exposed to the quick for all to see, and at that moment I looked at Sister. She turned and without meaning to I caught her eye. For no amount of shouting to the Lord would redeem Emily – or would it? God hunts us down, and where he eschews a nun, might he not storm the heart of this monstrous girl and flood it with Light? After all, where he had passed Sister by, he had shone on me.

A NICE DAY FOR THE MATCH AND A BOTTLE OF OPTREX

I nipped across the road near Gloucester Road Station, feeling a little overdressed in my striped shirt and tie and my flared suit.

There was one other customer waiting at the end counter, a woman in her forties or fifties. There was no assistant in sight, and as we waited she smiled at me. She looked slightly familiar. Did I know her? Was she the woman who cleaned our stairs? I have a photographic memory for faces I want to remember, but am quite hopeless at remembering faces I want to forget.

"Nice day for the match," she said, referring to the Cup Final.

"Yes," I said.

No, it couldn't be the cleaner. This woman was well spoken.

"Are you going?"

"No, I shall watch it on television."

I should have said I was the Fulham centre-forward, and that I was in a hurry as it was only an hour to kick-off.

"Who do you think's going to win?"

"Fulham."

Then the assistant came, and I gallantly waved my arm to indicate that she could be served first.

"I am being served," she said.

There was nothing for it. At the last moment I had an inspiration.

"I'll have a bottle of Optrex, please," I said. "Does it come with an eye salve?"

"Yes, the smaller one does."

"Oh good. And I'll have some of these."

Without waiting to be served, the woman turned on her heel and walked out of the chemists.

A few minutes later I recounted the events to my wife. "I don't know who it was," I said, "but I'm sure I've met her before somewhere. If it wasn't the woman who cleans the stairs perhaps I met her at Selina Montgomery's."

"Pixie," my wife laughed.

Then I realised.

"Oh, my God," I said, "yes, it was Pixie. I think."

The taboos that were still exist, and many who observe them prefer back-street shops.

CRYING EYES AND A NEARLY PERFECT ROSE (OR: OPTIC NERVE)

"Aren't you sending your daughter to this school?" Miss Saxena asked me as I sat down in the staff room, and for a moment I thought of all the Labour Ministers who had not sent their children to comprehensive schools. Miss Saxena was an imperious little Indian woman with grey hair and brown skin and magnifying spectacles that made her look like a beetle. Besides being anti-coloured she was a Housemistress of great ferocity. Woe betide anyone who had a class in her house-room – the slightest noise and she would be out of her door with the full sting of her tongue.

"No," I said, "I haven't been able to buy a tin hat."

"A tin hat? Why you need a tin hat?"

"Well," I said, "I've made enquiries and they have a fierce woman called Miss Saxena at that school, and my daughter'd be in danger without a tin helmet," and Mrs. Marsh laughed beside me.

"No," said Miss Saxena," she won'ter needer tin hat with me."

"Well," I bantered, "You look as though you've recovered from your illness."

"Recovered?" she screeched indignantly. Miss Saxena had been away for weeks with what we understood to be a nebulous headache complaint. We knew that no doctors had found anything wrong, and staff-room opinion attributed her absences to Miss Saxena's excessively worrying mind. "Recovered? I'm not recovered. I'm nearly going blind. I can't see properly." And she began to explain how she had had pains for two years and how her vision was going. "Oh," she said, "there's the Headmistress, I'd better not talk too loud."

"You saw her all right," I said.

"Yes, because I looked sideways. I can see if I look sideways. I can't see you if I look straight at you – it's like crying, I have something like tears in my eyes – but I can if I look sideways. I've been to hospitals galore and had dyes pumped into my brain and had X-rays, but they can't find anything. It's the flow of blood to the optic nerve, you see. I know that. When I am relaxed at home I don't have it. It's nerves, the flow of blood to the optic nerve is reduced. I tell you, it's this school. I was eight years at Holland Park and never had this. I was eighteen years at another school. I've been here three years and I have this. Yesterday I got dizzy and fell and hit my head on the door of my room. It's school that does it. That's why I don't come to school."

"The solution is to take it easy," I said, sympathetically now.

"The solution is for me to leave this school," she said quietly, rolling her eyes behind her magnifying spectacles. "I tell you, I am sixty, I could have retired last year. I can't afford it but the solution is to retire and do nothing."

There was a depressed silence. Then the pips went in the tannoy and I was up and thinking about the next class.

Mrs. Marsh caught me up as I walked to the upper block. "I think a lot of it's in her mind," she said. "It's her attitude of mind."

"Yes," I said. "She expects to have it, and so she does."

"Yes."

We chatted about Miss Saxena. Then I went to my room and she went to her class.

I did not see rotund Mrs. Marsh again until the end of the day. Then, as I was leaving school, she joined me and asked for a lift up the hill.

"Oh, look," I said as we walked towards the school gates, "there's Miss Saxena."

Miss Saxena was standing still with her back to the fish-pond. Her hands gripped the black railing, and she was looking at the roses.

"That's right, that's the solution," I said to Miss Saxena, "you should take up growing flowers instead of growing children. Then you'd have complete peace."

"I was looking at that rose," Miss Saxena said tamely, taking my ribbing in good part. "Look, it's nearly perfect."

I looked.

It was, indeed, a magnificent rose. It was a deep, satiny crimson, and except for one petal which had begun to curl and shrivel, it *was* perfect.

I looked at her. "Yes," I said.

"I like looking at that rose," Miss Saxena said. And then I realised. She had been looking at it perhaps for the last time. She thought she was losing her sight, and each time she looked at it, she was looking at a nearly perfect rose for perhaps the last time.

"Good night," I said helplessly, powerlessly, and I walked away, leaving her to her private dark.

A SITUATION LIKE NERVE GAS
(OR: A GAS MASK FOR A SOUL)

Senior Prize Day came round again, only this time it was called Speech Day. There was widespread relief that the Chairman of the Governors was in the USA, and would therefore not be able to invite the whole school to drink wine, as he had the previous year. His place was taken by the Vice-Chairman, a rugged old battleaxe.

The hall was full, the stage festooned with flowers, and we were all sitting in our houses when, at 7.30 the Senior Housemistress said "School stand," and the celebrities filed onto the platform: the Governors and ILEA authorities all full of their own self-importance, and a few inspectors worn out from teaching at William Tyndale School, which had been closed when the staff went on strike. They were given bouquets and reacted with suitably put-on surprise.

The Vice-Chairman stood and spoke through a microphone, saying that though she was not going to make a speech, she would introduce the Governors. Reading rather obtrusively from an enormous piece of paper, which she held out in front of her, she asked each to stand up. Once again, a Chairman at a function had no idea where they were all sitting, and once again there was the spectacle of heads popping over a wall, like the man in the advertisement who said "Wot no Watneys?" When she turned to the right a head popped up on the left. When she turned to the left a head popped up on the right. They were like marionettes. "Revealed as the puppets they are," I whispered to Miss Finnigan beside me, and she giggled.

The Vice-Chairman explained that there would be a breach with tradition. This year, there would be more participation. The girls would be involved in Speech Day more than last year, and so there was no outside speaker to distribute the prizes.

While she was speaking, Mrs. Parkinson left the orchestra, in which she played the violin, and squeaked noisily down the aisle to the empty chair between me and the aisle. It had a bag on it, and she rummaged in the bag. "Can't find my bloody glasses," she said in a loud whisper, and the girls around us giggled.

"That would have led to a few wrong notes," I whispered to Miss Finnigan after Mrs. Parkinson had found her glasses, and again Miss Finnigan giggled.

The introductions over, the orchestra played, and then Miss Chadwick, the Deputy Head, pulled the microphone towards her, unplugging it, and a fourth year girl stepped up and began to speak. The microphone did not work. The girl carried on, describing a school life that no one could hear, and during the applause at the end of her talk, the Medial Resources Officer, who was acting as technician, went and crouched under the main table and plugged the microphone back in.

The evening continued with the presentation of third year prizes. Names were announced in batches like roll-calls for executions. Then there was an awkward silence while their owners marched across the platform one by one to receive their books. At the end of each batch there was a round of applause. The ILEA men and women sat with their heads propped on their fists. They shifted their positions and listened with excessively attentive nods of the head and applauded with false loudness. The situation had imposed an unreality on them, and they had lost their human naturalness.

There was a recitation by a group of a passage from Dylan Thomas, Welsh accents and all. Then the fourth year "executions" took place. After that the sixth form folk group sang a jazzed-up version of "We plough the fields and scatter" – I looked for the disapproval on Sister Moore's face but it was enigmatically deadpan and suitably dead – and then we had the fifth and sixth year "executions". There was more orchestral music, a House Captain spoke, there were prizes for service to school and houses, and then an Art teacher gave an account of her first year at the school. It would have been easy for this to have sounded soppy, but she just avoided sounding soppy, though she was rather heavy-handed in dwelling on how maternal her tutor group made her feel.

At last it was the Headmistress's turn.

She was a little nervous. She was a buxom woman of middling build with perfectly coiffeured black hair and bifocal spectacles, and she read her speech from a prepared script, holding a large piece of paper in front of her without any attempt to disguise what she was doing. I knew her handwriting was tiny, and that she was myopic, and soon she was peering through her bifocals – and losing her place.

There was a long, long, long agonising silence.

"Sorry," she muttered.

Speak, say something, I thought.

Again she said, "Sorry." Then she found her place, and she picked her argument up while everyone looked at each other as if to say, 'She's fluffed it.'

Her argument – if her few disjointed remarks can be dignified by such a word, which implies a majestic sweep of thought – was that parents had changed, that no one should believe the adverse rumours about the school, that teachers were now professionals, and that it was not impossible for our girls to do great things. She talked about girls "only interested in fashion", and through the microphone it sounded like "girls only interested in passion". The ILEA guests sat with their heads on their fists.

The sixth form choir sang again, and after at least half a dozen votes of thanks from different girls, the Head of Music played a chord on the electric organ for the National Anthem. It sounded like the accompaniment to a high spot on some dreadful television show, like *Sale of the Century*, and it caught Miss Chadwick stealing unobtrusively over to the main table, so that it sounded as if the chord had been played for her.

After the Anthem the select few poured over to the house-rooms for the traditional wine. I soon found myself talking to Mrs. Leng, the Vice-Chairman of the ILEA. She was elderly and had trouble with her hip, but stood straight and talked at me without the slightest attempt to listen to anything I had to say in return. She just wanted to talk, and I wished I could have put a tailor's dummy in my place and escaped, for she would have been quite happy to go on talking at it. She said she was a solicitor and that her husband was a judge, she talked about her educational beliefs. She wanted all teachers to wear gowns, just as lawyers wore wigs, and she wanted larger schools.

"The Mrs. Thatchers of the future will have to come from these schools, and so we must make a route for them," I said.

"The Barbara Castles," she corrected me, and she went on talking. I half listened, and spoke to the Head Girl from the previous year, an Ibo who was doing Teacher Training, and her Deputy, who was now on the credit side of a large department store. Mrs. Leng talked on, unperturbed, and then I heard her say, "I am in charge of Staff Appeals for the ILEA."

"When staff are sacked, you mean?" I said.

"Yes."

"So if I get sacked, can I come to you?"

"Yes," she smiled.

"I hope you've got the Headmaster of William Tyndale school on you list," I said, and though he had not then been sacked, she practically fell through the window in horror at my having mentioned a case that was, after all, already virtually *sub judice*.

"I'm not discussing that case," she said, turning away with a slight glint in her eye, and at last I was able to escape from her under the pretext of finding another drink.

How feeble, I thought at a distance of ten yards. Even in this situation she was straitjacketed by her role. She was like all the other "celebrities", colourless, hollow, and pusillanimous when it came to being original. She was an ILEA stereotype. I thought back over the evening's format.

A situation had been imposed on everyone, compelling everyone to stand like automatons, compelling some to pop up like puppets, and deadening all with the paralysing numbness of a nerve gas. That was what a social occasion did. There were corporate disciplines to which the individual subordinated himself and submitted – whether he was in the Army or the Church or here in education – and once he had made this voluntary submission, he had a social role imposed on him that bore no relation to his true meaning in life, the state of his individual soul. That was how society worked, how individuals grouped themselves into a social organism.

It was false, this deadening of a human being. I did not want to submit to their nerve gas, I wanted to be *me*, not their idea of me in relation to my social rank. I was *not* a socialist, I loathed Barbara Castle and all social organisation. I wanted a gas mask to preserve my quickened soul.

THREE COWHERD ANGELS AND A CATTLE-BRANDING

The Christening Day was rather foggy at first. My wife drove down to Essex with our one year old son and her mother early that Sunday morning. I stayed and read the Sunday papers in our London flat until Jesperson and Teresa, two of the godparents, arrived. They both travelled up from the South Coast, and they arrived within ten minutes of each other around 11 o'clock.

Jesperson was the first. The distinguished novelist, fiftyish, a life-long bachelor, stoutly clumped up our stairs in a dark suit and matching overcoat, his long black hair swept back. He carried a hold-all which contained thirty thousand words of his latest endeavour, and watching him from above I looked for a slight reluctance in his footsteps that might match his slight unwillingness to be a "Polonius" and all the excuses he had thought of, such as "I haven't been confirmed". In fact, I knew that he was secretly pleased to be asked – he always went through his protesting rigmarole when he was invited to speak at a wedding – and he did not know that I was doing a bit of matchmaking.

He wandered restlessly round my books while I made him coffee, and then we discussed a book review about a scandal involving Henry James and Edith Wharton, and another one about a recent mock-heroic poem that was a blend of the *Dunciad* and *Private Eye*. Jesperson objected that the poet's subjects were already parodies, of themselves. "I was at the Soviet Embassy with Lord Longford two nights ago," he said, "and Longford said to the Soviet Ambassador, 'We don't like your social system', which was a complete conversation-stopper, a parody of tactlessness and what not to say. I sloped off." Then the buzzer went.

Teresa, the mystic artist, came up the stairs, weighed down with bags and a foxfur. When she unburdened herself of all these she sat down and prattled about her journey, paying no especial attention to Jesperson, whom she had so often belaboured obsessively in conversation, and whom she had never before met. Jesperson looked sharply at her, and probed her with jab-like questions and said "Ah" with cold detachment when she replied, and I tried to imagine the two of them living together, these two brilliant artists, the one emotionally dead, plagued with the bleakness of scepticism and solitude and full of negative remarks, a puritanical perfectionist about style with a horror of anything that sounded like mysticism; the other contemplating, at peace, brim-full of all the positive manifestations of religious love. What a combination!

The car journey proceeded smoothly enough. There was not much traffic. Jesperson sat in the front, Teresa at the back. The talk was about nuns at first, for Jesperson had described how he had driven three nuns round Ireland, and how they were only lecturers because they were nuns. "It's their Pelagian optimism that gets me," he said with a typically negative chuckle.

I told him about the card Sister Moore had sent. It was of a Russian icon, c1411 AD, called *The Trinity*, and it showed three angels, with haloes and wings, sitting round a chalice. With their thin sticks they looked slightly like cowherds. Sister Moore had presumably meant these to represent threesomes like my family and the godparents, though I thought she was also saying something about the left-wing activities of Mrs. Marzeki at our school: something like "the Communists may be strong today, but Russia has a Christian tradition, which will survive".

The talk was also about civilisation and the barbarian architecture of the Knightsbridge barracks and of other monstrosities we passed as we sped along the Embankment, past the Tower of London and along the Mile End Road. Later I raged against the barbarian driving of motorways through Forest land. We drove to the church in the Forest at High Beach, which is a little like Little Gidding in size and simplicity. The leaves on the surrounding silver birches were fantastic golds and greens and reds, the strong autumn tints having been caused by the dry summer, and I said, "I shall be buried in that churchyard," and Jesperson and Teresa were strangely, almost sadly silent. We drove past the pond of my youth to my mother's, where the lime leaves were a faded yellow.

We sat over sherry before lunch, or rather, they did, for I was teetotal. Teresa talked to all the ladies, my solicitor-brother – the other godparent – took his son off to play putting on the lawn so that the conversation would not be disturbed, and I sat beside Jesperson discussing Ronnie Knox, who boarded with a relative of his for a while and whom he did not like.

Lunch was taken in the Nursery, looking out at the pear-tree. After the melon I made sure that Jesperson's glass was kept filled with good French wine I had laid in, and somehow the conversation turned to experimental music. My mother said she was shocked to discover that it was taught at the school where she gave occasional violin lessons. She described it as rubbish.

I said, "That's how standards fall. The knowledge of one generation ceases to be transmitted to the next generation. It's happening right across our culture. The young in that school are having their heads filled with rubbish and they will have to learn the good things anew later on, by which time it may be too late, in which case it will be not at all."

"But is that true?" my brother burst out with unexpected vehemence. "*Are* standards falling? Surely there's a spectrum of pop *and* classical. My son will have the opportunity to appreciate all kinds of music, *I* never had pop."

"A good thing too," I said. "Taste has to be trained, our parents were right to teach us that a rose-bush is better than a rubbish dump. It's a question of ease and difficultness. L. C. Knights, the author of *Explorations* was saying on TV recently that the difference between a best-seller and art is that the best-seller appeals to our received responses, the easy emotions, whereas art opens us up and makes us experience new things afresh, in a territory of difficulty."

"I like rubbish," my brother said. "I come home tired and I switch on TV and I like rubbish."

When the hubbub died down Jesperson said with admirable restraint, "Surely, it's all a matter of choices, isn't it? Between ease and difficulty? And difficult is better than easy? So long as you can choose between pop and classical you are all right." Then he said, "Your brother does not like the society in which he lives very much, whereas I am fairly friendly towards it."

"Yes," I said, thinking of my equation of modern trends with the Seven Deadly Sins, "and there is a good case to be made out for the artist's being outside his society today, and opposing its standards and judging it." And after my brother looked at his wife, slightly bewildered by the turn of the conversation into an area that he knew little about, we talked about the easy values of society, its materialism and corruption as evidenced in the Stonehouse Affair and its possible ramifications, and the difficult values of artists and of churchmen like the new Archbishop of Canterbury, who had just launched a campaign against materialism. And Jesperson talked about the naive belief that English people had in the innocence of their public figures from Philby to Stonehouse.

Lunch ended with a line drawn. On one side were the friends of British society – or were they just cowards? On the other side were those who embodied something superior to its standards – the artists and churchmen. Teresa kept quiet. My brother was her solicitor, and I was her godchild's father.

After lunch I took Jesperson and Teresa for a drive in the Forest. The autumn tints were now lit by a pale sun. I showed them the madhouse run by Dr. Arnold where Clare spent some time; the barbarous site of what used to be the Owl, an old pub I nearly took Edmund Blunden to once, and which the brewers, in their wisdom, had pulled down; and the coach-house which was all that survived of Beech Hill Park, where Tennyson once stayed.

We came back past the semi-derelict Mansion, which I had contemplated buying, and we drove in, thinking it deserted. Jesperson and Teresa went into raptures about the view across the Forest from the field at the back, and the fantastic pine-trees, and then a young woman came out to meet us with the aggression of fear. She asked what we wanted. A guard dog barked from within and she said, in a very demotic accent, that the property had been sold and was going to be developed in accordance with the planning permission. "The barbarians," I said again as we drove back to my mother's. I disliked the organisers of the society in which I lived.

The christening was a double one. We parked outside the churchyard and walked through the graves by the pew and passed our guests who sat on the right of the aisle and entered the front pew, for in that church the font was at the front. The Vicar, a white-haired man with a deaf-aid, gave us all a chat to put us at our ease. He said it did not matter if the two babies cried, he could easily turn off his deaf-aid. Then he went off and robed himself in white and returned for the service. Reading from cards, we, the parents and godparents, renounced all evil ("I do"), and then the baptism of the two children took place, our son being first.

We, the parents and godparents, filed out and stood round the font, which contained a little water at the bottom. The Vicar took our son, asked my wife to name him, held him, wriggling, head down, scooped water in a pearl scallop, and poured it on our son's head. Then, raising his right arm, he brought a stubby thumb down quite fiercely on the little boy's temple, and marked him with the sign of the cross, rubbing it in as if he were holding a red-hot iron. Instantly our son was strangely still as if the Devil had suddenly gone out of him and his sins had been forgiven.

When the other baby had been baptised, the Vicar stood in front of us and gave us a long talk. It was all about the "perilous times" in which we live, and it referred to the bombers in Ireland and in London, and to violent fashions. "On that altar there is a cloth with all the cattle-brands of the Forest woven into it," he said. "The cattle were branded, then put out to grass for the summer until they were taken in again in the autumn. They could then be recognised by their brand mark. Baptism is like cattle-branding. These two boys have been branded with the seal of Christ."

This summed up perfectly why I wanted to have our son baptised. I had come to admire the tradition, two thousand years old, of creative men and mystics who had drawn strength and inspiration from the Church, and I had wanted my son to be marked with a sign that symbolised that tradition and its ideal of perfection in our increasingly pagan society. He had "Ideal of perfection" branded on his forehead – the ideal of the fourteenth century mystics – and he would wear that sign for the rest of his life, like a Roman slave, as I wore mine.

The Vicar talked on about persecutors of the Church being

converted and themselves being persecuted, "like St. Paul who persecuted the Church until he saw the Light". I glanced at Teresa. She was sitting serene. Beyond her Jesperson was looking down, and something was clearly going through his mind. I wondered what.

After the service the godparents signed a card for us, I slipped the Vicar my envelope containing my donation, and we greeted some of our guests. Then we drove Jesperson and Teresa back to my mother's, with a convoy of cars following behind.

"Vicars shouldn't bring politics and journalism into their addresses," Jesperson complained negatively. "Winklepickers!"

I objected that the Vicar knew he had a mixed audience of intellectuals and simple people, and that the "journalism" was all a part of his communication. "He was courageous," I said, "he stood up for what was right and truthful."

It struck me again: the Church and society were at loggerheads today. In the past the Church was central to society – witness the Cathedrals – but it was a measure of the disintegration of the West that the Church was now opposed to society's values, its violence and materialism. The Archbishop of Canterbury, now this Vicar had spoken out. Society was pagan, and my son would be like Wulfstan among the Danes. Like the artist who knew the Truth, the Church was a castigator of society's values, a protester against the Establishment, and Jesperson, being "fairly friendly" towards society, had been told a few home truths, and so he felt uncomfortable. Whereas I, disliking the sinful society in which I lived, was naturally on the Church's side. To condone society was the way of the coward.

The tea-party for over twenty found my wife sick. I poured tea, handed round sandwiches and sausage rolls, and directed our guests to the feast of flans and gateaux on the table with the Royal table-cloth, and later on I poured sherry or Scotch. I had little time to do more than observe the groupings. Jesperson sat opposite Teresa with Eric Ashby, whose scheme for bringing foreign Professors to English writers' houses had reached brochure stage. Fenwick, the famous journalist arrived – I put down one of my grandmother's 75 year old china teacups to let him in, my brother's daughter pushed the table over, and it smashed into pieces; my mother always thought he had a destructive influence on my life – and I was able to arrange for Ashby's scheme to be written up in the national press.

My younger brother came up and said, "Is Jesperson a bachelor? He's like ….," he went on, mentioning a teacher who taught us both Maths at school, "either you get on with him very well, or else you don't make contact at all."

In due course, Eric Ashby said, "It's time we went now. I'm giving Jesperson and Teresa a lift back to town." And I found their coats and Jesperson's bag of thirty thousand words and Teresa's foxfur, and went outside into the road where the car was parked.

There was a slight delay. "Your mother is very similar to how mine was," Jesperson remarked. "She has the same approach. The same family warmth." I had been going to take him up on two things he had said – "The C of E is class-based" and "*Does* the Church stand for the Truth?" to which the answer was "Yes, if *I* want it to, and it stands more for the Truth than any other institution in our society like the Social Security building or the House of Commons" – but he spoke so strangely that I did not say a word.

After our guests left, we had a drink with Fenwick and his wife in the local pub. We had not been there together since he incited me to make a disgraceful speech questioning the quality of the local religion towards midnight one drunken Christmas Eve, with the result that I had been thrown out. He said, "The Forest has obviously rubbed off on you more than it has on me. I don't like Forests, I prefer grasslands."

Later my wife and I drove back to London in our respective cars, and later still all agreed that the day had been a success. It had been an event, in the sense of an image to be remembered, an image that stood out of the flow of time like a building beside a stream. "E-venire" means "to come out of", and I ruminated much on the symbolic architecture that had erected itself round the branding.

The next evening Teresa rang from the South Coast and we talked for an hour or more. Jesperson had been subdued on the way back to Victoria, she said, after the initial laugh they had all had. She and Eric Ashby had talked about priests and nuns they had in common. Jesperson had listened. Once he had said, "I do like having a godson."

"You know," she said, "I felt something happen to him during the service. It was when the Vicar was speaking. It was something in himself that he had always rejected with negative remarks. He suddenly accepted it, I am sure. He felt, 'I am nothing'. He wasn't treated specially by your family – he was just one of the family – and I am sure he suddenly felt 'I am nothing, my reputation is nothing'. I was at peace. It was when the Vicar was talking about St. Paul and the Light, about the persecutors being persecuted in due time. Of course, he was guided in what he said. Jesperson looked down, it is a Catholic attitude. I know he's C of E, but you will be seeing a lot more of him now. He wants us all to visit him when you come down to the coast on Thursday.

"A lot of good came out of that service. You see, that was what all your divorce and suffering were for, so *you* could see the Light.... Yes, a lot of good came out of that service. But don't push him. I didn't push you four years ago, and you have grown something of your own. So give him time, give him time."

I sat for some time after I rang off. Could it be that I had been present at a miracle in that little church, and that the great sceptic who specialised in scoffing at – in persecuting – the Church had accepted something indirectly as a result of my invitation, as a result of me? I felt terribly humble, and suddenly I did not feel alone. I felt God beside me. I looked at the card of the three cowherd angels, and saw them now as Teresa, myself – and Jesperson. All three of us – Jesperson included – would wear haloes of Light in our souls as a result of the branding of this little boy who was crawling slowly up the stairs to see me, calling "Dadda" and now scampering for his favourite toy, my telephone, laughing with all the abandon of a child of Heaven.

THREE PURE CHRYSANTHEMUMS, OR FADED PETALS (OR: A WHISPER OF A QUARREL)

We nearly did not go to the South Coast that Thursday. I had a temperature the day before and Teresa said over the telephone, "This is given, don't force anything." We both wanted the sea air and so we did go – and found a room overlooking the Worthing shingle and a sailing boat. It was a white room with purple curtains, a purple carpet, purple wallpaper at one end, and purple eiderdowns and lampshades. They were all the same shade of purple.

Teresa's sister, Tamsin, was baby-sitting for us. When we arrived at her Shoreham house we fed our son and took him upstairs. I erected his folding hammock-like cot, and we put him to sleep. Then Teresa said she would like to show me her new picture. "Tamsin asked for it to go on her bedroom wall," she said. We went upstairs, and she took a smallish etching off the shadowy wall. "I bought it yesterday," she whispered, so as not to wake our sleeping son." It's only a line drawing with this one colour." She held it to the tablelamp. "You see, three white chrysanthemums."

I looked. Of the three chrysanthemums, two looked ragged and were sideways on. The third had leaves that curled down. Part of the background, and the wide frame was purple – the same shade of purple as the Worthing room.

"I think it's so beautiful," Teresa whispered. "You see, no more blobbing. You know, ugly blobs thrown at the paper." She was referring to Jackson Pollock and Action painting. "It's so living, so alive."

In fact, it all seemed rather dead to me, especially the curled leaves. They looked like chrysanthemums that had begun to go, that had reached the stage when they are thrown out of the vase; if they were ever allowed into the house in the first place, for the Italians do not allow them in the house as they are called "fiore del muerto", flowers of death.

Teresa saw the doubt in my eyes.

"No flower is perfect," she whispered. "You see, that's just how you see flowers in the field."

I certainly liked the work. It looked rather 1890ish, slightly decadent. "May I ask how much you paid for it?" I whispered.

"Just sixty pounds," she whispered. "There were others for three hundred, four hundred pounds, but this was just sixty. I looked at them all and then I said, 'That one.' He said to me afterwards, I'm so glad *you* had that one. I think he did this one for himself, I don't think this one was for sale."

The picture was obviously special to her, and the purchase was a special one. I wondered how she saw it.

"You know how I see it?" I whispered, leading her on. "I see it as slightly sad, as flowers past their best that have begun to fade, because of this purple soil perhaps, with its suggestion of death."

Such an articulation is natural for a literary man when asked about a book he has read. I should have known that Teresa lived by a complex canon of "don'ts", one of which was: "Don't say it, don't put it into words for you will destroy the feeling, but just keep it privately to yourself," a maxim that might apply to a painter but which certainly does not apply to a self-critical poet.

"No," she whispered, "don't see it in terms of anything like that, not life and death, not faded anything. You mustn't analyse it. It just is, you must accept it. It's there. Like Tamsin, 'I'd like that on my wall.' That's all. Don't pick it to bits and destroy it."

Amazed at the violence of her reaction, I whispered, "I am a literary mind, not a painting mind, remember, and as a literary mind I have every right to react to it in terms of myself, and as I am a symbolist, that means that I react to it as a symbol –"

"Rubbish –" Teresa whispered stridently.

"A symbol with layers of meaning, like the *Bible*, and if you disentangle one meaning only –"

"Rubbish, you mustn't look for meanings in art –"

"Of course you must," I whispered, diverted. "If you're a symbolist in literature as I am, you see in terms of symbols, and not realistically, as a realist does. If I want to take that as a symbol I have every right to, and that's completely valid. It's all part of the way literary art works. Eliot sees the Hollow Men 'whispering together' in the tube, perhaps, he makes his image, symbol, mask – the poem – and I can see those hollow men in the supermarket, perhaps, with my meaning. In the same way, this artist may have seen these flowers in a field, he has made his image, symbol, mask – this painting – and I can interpret them as a symbol if my symbolist mind, with all its symbolist training, chooses to. And no one can deny me the right to if I wish."

"Rubbish," she whispered. "Art doesn't work like that. You put your feelings into words too much –"

"And what do *you* mean by feelings, seeing that I am talking about a symbol," I whispered, amazed that she did not grasp the simplest idea in the symbolist canon, and wondering whether to refer her to Arthur Symons's book or Kermode's *Romantic Image* first.

"You over-verbalise," she whispered. "You write too much –"

"A writer *has* to write every day –"

"Rubbish. He's just the same as a painter, he should only write when he's forced to. You write too much, and you over-verbalise. You can't define feelings."

"Words are my medium, just as colour-tones are yours," I whispered. "Russet, rust, crimson, scarlet, red, pink are all different for you. Feelings, emotions, sensibility and a number of other words connected with symbolism are all different for me. If you say they aren't you're making an idea blunt that should be sharp. I am a literary man, and I have every right to insist on a proper definition of words, if you are making statements about my method."

"When you looked at my picture – *my* picture – you put your feelings into words."

"And since when was articulacy a crime? If articulacy is what you are against, find a four year old child who will give you 'um' and 'er'."

"It's better to be silent sometimes," Teresa whispered. "Look, if I'd known you were going to pick *my* picture to bits, I wouldn't have shown you –"

"And if I'd known you were going to deny my right to be a symbolist I wouldn't have come –"

"*I* bought this, *I* possess it, it's mine, and I share it with those who will appreciate it –"

"All art belongs to all mankind," I whispered. "Shakespeare and Michelangelo belong to mankind, not to one person who has paid money for it, and it's wrong of the Queen or anybody to hoard pictures, and then muzzle the honest reaction of people who look at them in terms of who they are."

"Rubbish," she whispered. "Good God, look, see how *pure* the petals are. The man is completely honest. This is about purity."

"To you," I whispered, "but there are layers of meaning. As with Kafka, a work of art can be given five or six interpretations at once if it merits them, like the universe. You can see it in five or six different ways. This could be about his family, these three flowers....It could be about –"

"Good God," she whispered. "You mustn't go on looking for meanings. An artist just has a blank canvas, and he does *that*, and suddenly *that* is there. It doesn't mean anything."

"It's perfectly valid for me to see that as a symbol if I want to," I whispered. "If that symbolises faded petals to me, and faded years, then I can take that meaning."

My wife had been silent. She had followed the whispered "discussion" with increasingly anguished looks, some in the direction of our sleeping son, some in the direction of me, in case I ended my plea with a blow, and some because she wanted to intervene and have her say.

"Even if the artist doesn't mean it?" she whispered.

"Yes, I can make those three chrysanthemums the title of a story if I wish."

"Grabbing," said Teresa. "'I want'. I wouldn't have shown it to you if I'd thought you'd grab it and use it –"

"There *is* a grabbing form of consciousness as well as the quiet, passive sort," I whispered. "It's called 'prehensile' consciousness, it's known to phenomenology and documented in Husserl. 'Grabbing' as you call prehensile consciousness is merely a reaching out at something significant, and remember that 'attention' comes from the Latin 'at-tendere', 'to reach out'. So what is wrong with grabbing consciousness?"

"It's my picture, after all –"

"It's mankind's," I whispered, on the offensive now. "I don't accept the rights of private owners of art as being legitimate. And who are you to tell me what I may or may not do with my consciousness?"

"Is it copying?" my wife whispered. "To refer to someone else's work like that?"

"No," I whispered. "Dostoevsky did it in *The Idiot* – with the Basel Christ – and *The Idiot* is not a copy. E. M. Forster took a movement from a Beethoven symphony –"

"That's different," my wife said.

"No it isn't: music and art –"

"It's copying to be influenced by someone else's work. It's better to create your own picture than to use that one."

"Of course it is," whispered Teresa. "Of course. You can't interpret that picture as you *want*, then use it in your work. You can't use that picture in a story. It's without, not within. You have to write what is within."

"But perhaps this situation will haunt me?" I whispered. "Perhaps I have caught it like a germ, perhaps it will lodge inside my soul and give me a temperature until I vomit it and it comes up in my daily spring, which is how I think of my daily writing flow –"

"Oh rubbish –"

"Perhaps the external experience of that picture will be made experience within. Perhaps by tomorrow morning it will be within."

"Oh rubbish –" Teresa whispered more urgently than before.

"No, it's not rubbish. Angus Wilson saw some external experience at a gate, a woman turning sadly away, and it passed within and became *The Middle Age of Mrs. Eliot*. Why shouldn't that picture haunt me so that it becomes *The Portrait of Dorian Gray*? And who are you to say it can't? It's damned cheek. Why it's impertinence. I am an artist, when I create I am like God, I alone decide what subject matter my work has. The symbolist aims at a fusion of thought and feeling, at a unified sensibility. Who are you to say I can't do that?"

That evening we dined at the Amsterdam. The "discussion" continued, a little more gently now that we did not have to whisper. Teresa, being religious and not "being a slave" to art, said that art was unimportant, that being an artist was no more important than being a roadsweeper. It did not matter whether an artist painted, she said, it was important for him to keep an open door to everyone and not mind being distracted. All are equal before God, she said, so there are no standards, and a work of art is not better than a well-swept road. She wanted people to say 'that's nice', and no more, about a painting, and approved of those who did, seeing it as a sign of depth, not realising that perhaps they did not have the words to say more. She had no time for education, and "No one will write a biography of *me* after I am dead," she said, an eventuality which I thought entirely likely, taking her views into account.

I disagreed with her "mind-suicide". Though all are equal before God, I said, all have talents which they have a duty to fulfil. I believed that Michelangelo was right to build St. Peter's and spend long hours each day painting the Sistine roof, and I was glad he had not become a roadsweeper and "left the idea for ten or fifty years because it doesn't matter, it's not important, I won't be a slave to it, it can wait for me", or kept an open door. In fact, I made a mental shopping-list of two large padlocks, and keys; three locks; four iron bars; and a hundredweight of heavy iron studs; with which I would barricade the oak I was going to sport on my study door from now.

I thought of Yeats's lines, "The intellect of man is forced to choose/Perfection of the life or of the work." They were ridiculous of course. Although some poets he knew lived and died badly, there could be a saint who produced good mystical work of great depth – of symbolistic depth – and I recalled Teresa herself saying once, "A tree labours for three hundred and sixty days of the year so that it can produce a crop lasting four," and there was no reason why there could not be a good life *and* good work. Nevertheless, I felt that Teresa was now extolling her life and denigrating her work.

We drove back to the Shoreham house and picked our son up, the atmosphere definitely strained, and then we drove back to our purple room. Our son soon went to sleep, and my wife and I whispered briefly, and looking at the purple curtains and the purple wallpaper and carpet, and the purple eiderdowns and lampshades, and thinking of the purple background to that picture, I felt angry. Something had been spoiled. Our whisperings in Tamsin's bedroom had drawn up a line between life and work, religion and art, realism and symbolism, that should not really be there. The sea washed outside our window. It would have been better if my temperature had not gone, perhaps?

'You can't use that picture in a story....' Oh can't I, I thought defiantly as I went to sleep.

Next day we called at Teresa's shop. She was alone and very welcoming.

"I must confess," she said to my wife. "Helen Jameson called in today to buy a blouse, and I asked her about writers. She said, 'They need to write every day.'"

"Yes," I said, slightly mollified only. "As I said, it's like a spring inside, a spring of words."

"That's what she said. We have nothing like that in painting. Good God, the painter has to discard all that. I was muddled yesterday. Writing and painting cannot be compared. In fact, Tamsin told me off. I told her the situation after you went last night, and she said, 'It's a bit much, seeing they were only down at the sea for one night, to go on like that.' She thought we had got lost upstairs, we were so long. Yes, I was in the wrong yesterday."

And again this elusive woman had surprised. It required magnanimity to accept the blame so simply and so humbly. And I was not without fault either....Even if she *had* not fully understood her picture of three "fiore del muerto", fading, within a deathly purple frame.

EARTH IN THE WAY
(OR: A POEM LIKE A MOON)

That evening I was taking a party of girls to see *The Taming of the Shrew*. I stayed at school until the meeting time at 5.45 – I had my sponge bag in a plastic bag and I shaved at one of the school basins – and I tried not to think of the poem I wanted to write. It was a bitterly cold November night and the moon was full. It was huge and round and coldly beautiful and out of reach like a haunting image that cried out to be preserved on paper. I cursed all earthly trivialities for coming between my inner inspiration and a beautiful work of art.

We met in the foyer of the hall. I called out details of who was travelling in which coach, and then we piled into the two luxury coaches and set off into the rush-hour traffic. Unfortunately the rush-hour traffic never materialised, and we reached the little Islington theatre three-quarters of an hour before curtain-up, and the doors were closed.

"Would you like to take them for a walk?" I asked my number two, a man more than twenty years older than me who had lost to me at the interview for my job, and, buried deep in a coat and a hat, he set off with a grand army of seventy-five fifth and sixth year girls while I went to the theatre Buttery and ate with the actors. There was soup and cheese and a hunk of bread and knob of butter and toasted cheese and nothing more, and all for a ridiculously cheap 29p. I sat next to Katharina and opposite Grumio and watched Petruchio strut round the tables, listened to his noisy talk about Hong Kong, reflected on the poverty of actors and their inadequate evening meals, and thought of all the mundane tittle-tattle that came between their deeper impulses and a perfectly presented play.

The play itself was all right, except for a strange, unnecessary blot at the beginning. The theatre was a bit of a cellar – it only seated a hundred and fifty or thereabouts – and the actors mingled with the audience and then went onto the stage and played the first scene (not the Induction, which was omitted) in the sweaters and jeans they were wearing. They changed into costumes in the course of the second scene, which made veracity a little difficult: that willing suspension of disbelief which is the ground of the theatrical illusion. Two things struck me about the performances. The first was Biondello's obsession with verbal precision, not just in the catalogue of horse-diseases but in the way he took every word spoken to him literally, at the cost of its real meaning. This was surely different from the usual logic-chopping of the low-life Shakespearian character, and anticipated twentieth century philosophy. The second thing was the ironical interpretation the play might have. Was Kate really tamed at the end, or was she making her last submissive speech in irony, just to keep Petruchio quiet?

The theatre told us the play would finish at 10.15. Instead it ended at 9.45, and the coaches sped back to the school gate by 10.30, and parents were not due to collect their daughters until 11. I had to stand with the party in the bitter cold and wait until each girl was collected. It seemed an eternity. The moon seemed obscured behind cloud, I could just see its outline.

Then I remembered what I had read in the paper that morning.

"Oh look," I said to the Head Girl's group, "there's an eclipse of the moon."

Suddenly all the girls stopped talking. They turned their heads up.

"Do you know about eclipses?" I asked. "Normally the sun shines on the moon, which reflects its light. Tonight the earth is in the way."

And I thought again of the poem I had wanted to write. It was in my mind like a sun – I could actually *see* it when I closed my eyes – and I wanted to project it out onto a paper-screen, so that it looked like a moon, but the earth was in the way: the every-day responsibilities that went with earning my bread and butter. Because I had to earn my money my art – not my creative power – was in permanent eclipse. I wished I was very rich.

APRIL FOOLS AND THE THIRTEENTH STREAM

That day was April Fools' Day. There was a letter on my desk addressed to Miss Earl. I gave it to her and said, "Watch out, it's probably an April Fool." She smiled and then laughed as she opened it. "My Darling Dearest Barbara," it said, "Please meet me outside the staff-room door at 1 p.m. I have something very private to discuss with you. Please do not tell my wife."

Later I took the Lower Sixth for Blake. There was a note on the door: "Please go to Room 39." I stayed put, and after ten minutes

A SMELL OF LEAVES AND SUMMER

the class arrived, saying "Didn't we have to go to Room thirty-nine?"

"Oh that was an April Fool," I said, and they were all subdued until I stopped teaching to give them a rest.

When I returned there was a lot of laughter, and one of the Asian girls hurriedly put down my copy of Blake. She had been looking unsuccessfully for my first name. An hour later I found a letter on my desk: "My darling dearest, I will meet you outside the staff-room door. We have very private matters to discuss. I won't tell your wife. I am enclosing this in an envelop (sic) so that everyone will think you have received a letter through the post."

At lunch I sat next to my number two, Mr Street. The CSE orals were on. The moderator had been to see Mr Street, once Mr Street had remembered that he was examining, which he did after I tannoyed for him.

"Your orals are finished now," I said.

"For 5S they haven't begun," he chuckled, "only three turned up. Forty-six out of two hundred and thirty haven't turned up in all. I said to the moderator, 'We're a thirteen stream entry, this is the thirteenth stream.' He said, 'They're not streaming in!' When they did turn up they didn't say anything. 'What are you going to do when you leave school?' 'Nothing.'"

He chuckled, and the Head of Geography and the Head of Commerce joined in. I laughed, and it did not matter that the moderator had complained that Mr Street had talked too much, and not given the girls a chance to speak.

I was on duty after lunch. The Head of Remedial, who had just canvassed for the Conservatives at the coming by-election, gave me some exercise books to assess. She thought their owners should be moved up. I looked through them while I was on duty, and later I returned them to her.

"In a word, no," I told her. "The top band have ideas and punctuate. The middle band have some ideas and tend not to write in sentences, like these girls. They're middle band." The Head of Remedial looked slightly rattled.

Later I was teaching the Upper Sixth and she interrupted my class and said to me in the corridor, "I've been thinking over what you said, and I've been thinking it's my fault. I don't punctuate. I put the punctuation in afterwards." She looked as if she were about to burst into tears.

I could have been severely truthful, but I was still laughing within at the April Fools' jokes and at Mr Street's account of his orals. "Look," I said, "look at the letter on that wall. It's got regular full stops. There's a subject and a verb in that sentence, and what is needed to complete the sense and then there must be a full stop. Otherwise there has to be a conjunction. You can't have a comma, you can't have a whole paragraph with commas, as the CSE girls sometimes write, especially the thirteenth stream. We're trying to teach them *not* to write in stream of consciousness."

And as I saw her shattered eyes, I saw a Conservative politician whose name was known to former Ministers, and I was sad that she had exposed her weakness to me. The Asian epistolist was nicely immature, Mr Street was nicely incompetent. But she was too much on my side to be an April Fool.

TATTERED WALLS AND A GORGON'S SCREAM (OR: CLASS ENEMY FOR A TROT)

We went to Versailles and walked through the Hall of Mirrors and the magnificently furnished King's bedroom, where Marie-Antoinette went out onto the balcony the night the mob were calling for her death. Then we walked back over the cobbles to where we had parked the car, and we drove to the Grand Trianon, where Louis XIV housed Madame de Pompadour. Then we walked to the Petit Trianon where Marie-Antoinette, fed up with her husband's passion for hunting – he killed 189,251 birds and 1,274 stags between May 1774 and the end of 1787 – played make-believe that she was not Empress.

On the wall by the entrance there was a shield with a face on it. The mouth was open in a horrified scream. It was strikingly out of place, and I turned to the French guide who stood nearby in uniform.

"C'est un Gorgon," he said, and he explained at unnecessary length how the Gorgon changed Louis's enemies to stone.

We walked round the four sumptuously decorated rooms of the Petit Trianon, two which were dining-rooms. Then I realised we had seen all that was on view. I asked the guide where the King's bedroom was: "Le chambre du Louis Seize?"

He said in French that Marie-Antoinette's bedroom was where we were standing; that Madame du Barry lived on the floor above, which we could not see; and that the King had a room above that, although to his knowledge the King had never slept there. "Un moment," he said, and dropping his voice, he said he would take us up to see.

We waited while a French family walked round and left, and then he quickly unhitched a rope and we climbed the stairs.

On the floor above, all the rooms were in poor decorative repair. Was this the truth? Were the apartments like this is 1789?

We went on up the stairs and the guide announced that we were in the King's room. There was no furniture, and a brown cloth type of wallpaper covered half the walls and hung in tattered shreds.

"L'originel," the guide said gravely.

On the floor, on its side, propped against a wall, stood a picture of Marie-Antoinette, this woman who, when Louis called, advanced the hands of her clock an hour so that he would go more quickly.

Looking at the derelict furnishings, and recalling the sumptuousness downstairs, and the propaganda of the French revolution, I felt I had seen deep into the end of the French Monarchy, I had caught them as they were. And the idea we had of them was an illusion that was not helped by the fine, modern hangings and the modern restorations below.

We returned and stood by the shield. Surely that was no Gorgon? Surely it was a post-1789 sculptor's reaction to the tragedy that befell this Royal couple?

We drove into Paris and were lost in the rush-hour traffic until we found L'Etoile. We drove along the congested Champs Elysées – the Elysian Fields – and past the Louvre, and we turned over a bridge to the Boulevard St-Germain-des-Prés. We found a hotel off the Boulevard St. Michel near the Rue Champollion where I had spent a week over twenty years before, when the Latin Quarter was full of Bohemian existentialists instead of cobblestone-throwing Trotskyites, and then we went out to eat. The woman at the reception desk had recommended us to a restaurant round the corner. "Madame will change your traveller's cheques," she said.

The restaurant was a large Baroque room. It was packed with French students from the University, and the two waitresses coped at the double, much to the amusement of some of the diners. We were gestured to a corner, where we ordered (and after a long wait were brought) potage and a half duck. The food was good value in this expensive city.

We were joined by two young French couples who read the menu noisily and giggled and whispered behind their hands, I was sure about us. They wore sweaters and jeans, like the other students, and the two young men had tousled hair and the slightly open lips of working class faces unused to thought. The young man next to me sprawled all over me; I was aware of his elbow digging into mine. He looked like Trotsky, and he jogged me as I forked duck, and once he bent over my plate with blatant rudeness to inspect what I was eating. He then leaned across the table and cupped his mouth into his mate's ear and whispered something which produced a loud laugh. They all put their heads together and continued reading the menu with exaggerated accents, especially English words, and there was much giggling.

Suddenly I understood that I was being referred to as an "English bourgeois". I wore a faded khaki jacket – KD, as the issue used to be called – and I suppose I had a slightly military air about my dress, but I resented being cartoonised in this way. He was projecting an image on me that was not me. We had finished our duck, and I raised my hand to catch the waitress's attention – and to my amazement, Trotsky turned round and did the same, a blatantly rude mimic that brought uncontrollable giggles from the group, who had been joined by another man who sat at the end of the table. Then I heard the words "class enemy".

So that was it. Trotsky saw me as a class enemy! Now I grasped the situation. There were fears (expressed by the US Secretary of State only the previous day) that France might go Communist, and the University was as much of a hotbed of that tyrannical creed as it was in 1968. These noisy, ill-mannered young people had rejected the traditional French politeness (if they had ever been brought up to know it) for the aggressive hostility of the revolutionary, and so they were tearing my accent to bits, and everything about me that coincided with their class enemies. I was like Marie-Antoinette, and Trotsky was the new Nicolas Jourdan, alias "Coupe-Tête", the hirsute savage who brandished an enormous axe at daybreak on 6th October 1789, and who beheaded the sentinel M Des Huttes.

Now I was, willy-nilly on the side of Marie-Antoinette. These Europeans would cut my head off without batting an eyelid, if given half a chance, and it was a matter of honour to fight back. Leaning forward I said to my wife, "I think they're Communists. This place is a left-wing restaurant, hence their rudeness." I analysed the background to the situation for several minutes, and hearing political slogan-words they recognised they fell silent. There was no giggling now as I ordered two crème caramels from the waitress and carried on my tirade against left-wing politicians, on how the old Bohemians had departed and been replaced by anti-intellectual political militants. "Why should I tolerate a few Trots?" I said. "They'd kill me if they were given half a chance."

Before I could say, "Long live Marie-Antoinette", Madame called us to the cash desk so that she could change one of my wife's traveller's cheques. Immediately we were mobbed by half a dozen more left-wingers who apparently felt I was trying to cheat Madame by swinging low-value sterling across her. One very aggressive girl had the £5 traveller's cheque, and was very reluctant to release it as I took it from her hand, fearing she might bolt for the door with it.

I explained the rate, magnanimously said I would accept a low rate in the interests of fairness, and fought off a suggestion, moved by our waitress, that we should not pay with traveller's cheques after all. I may have been a capitalist in an army uniform, but Madame passed judgement in my favour and gave me change in francs to settle the bill ("l'addition"), and the direct action students ended satisfied, wishing me "Au revoir".

We went for a walk in the backstreets off the Boulevard St. Michel. Droves of students wandered near the restaurants and bread-shops and bought hot dogs or stood in late-night shops that sold the works of Chairman Mao in plastic-looking red covers. We walked across the bridge to L'Isle de France, and passed droves of gendarmes in riot vans near Notre Dame, where groups of thirty students were clapping and chanting. Not realising that they were massing for the next day's 15th April riot, when tens of thousands of students fought police with armed bars and bottles in the Boulevard St.-Germain-des-Prés, and were tear-gassed, for the right to work without having their educational system reformed so that specialisation led to more jobs in big business; not grasping the significance of the slogans painted on all the walls, "L'Oeuvre Francais"; not appreciating that I had dined with Trotskyite student activists on the eve of their big demo when they were obviously going to be suspicious of their neighbours in case they were agents of the French government, and when high spirits and cartoonising were obviously going to be at their height; I said, caricaturing with a clarity of judgement I stand by: "The hell with their new regicides' new man and his hostile rudeness and caricaturing eye. I view their coming regime with the horrified eyes on Marie-Antoinette's shield: with a Gorgon's scream."

A WAG IN LYONESSE

That summer we went on a Sunday charter excursion to the Scilly Isles. We took a coach from St. Austell at 7.30 and were driven to Penzance, where we caught the Scillonian. It passed the Wolf Rock lighthouse. By 12 we were passing St. Mary's, and the loudspeaker on the back deck drew our attention to some gannets, a Dutch submarine and a Russian "trawler" (or spy-ship) which pulled aggressively across our bows. "When Sir Harold Wilson was PM," the loudspeaker told us, "there used to be a Russian boat here. It intercepted all telephone calls between the Scilly Isles and the mainland, i.e. Downing Street, and it bristled with electronic equipment. Now you can see the strange rock formation on the right." We stood, packed on the rear deck, and looked, and I felt that this must be what it was like to enter Hell. A voice over a loudspeaker would explain the sites of Hell to help us settle in.

We disembarked at low tide, having to climb up the gangway to the harbour wall, and we walked up to the main square of Hugh Town, where we found a bus waiting to tour the island. We sat in it with some elderly folk, one of whom said, "Look, there's Harold Wilson," and the red face and silky hair and blue suit of Sir Harold appeared across the square with three detectives behind him. He was hunched like an old man and he shuffled, and while everyone slowly identified the frizzy-haired woman beside him as Lady Wilson, I thought how ill he looked, how demanding the cares of office had been, and I wondered if there was more to his resignation than we knew. I watched the Wilsons encounter a group of tourists, all of whom had their eyes fixed on our bus. They bumped into the ex-Prime Minister without realising it, some fifteen of them, and they were so unobservant that they did not look round, but kept their eyes fixed on our bus and our watching faces.

The guide boarded the bus now that it was full. "Harold

Wilson's meeting the Duke of Gloucester, who's in that landrover," he said, and everyone craned at the figure in the landrover. The guide was a young, reddish-faced man with a curly quiff to his hair, and he seemed a bit waggish. "We're going when *I'm* ready, ladies, but if you want to go to the loo, don't let me stop you. But if you're going for a drink, then I'll go without you," he said, and after we had pulled out of the town and admired The Lady among Rocks and made our first stop at a beach: "It's cold bathing here, but safe. No currents – and the raisins aren't much good either."

I groaned and prepared for a pathetic show, but his next effort was better: "We are so mild down here. We have no snow. In 1963 we had four inches and didn't know what it was. Some of our wives came up and scooped it up for mashed potato." There was a laugh all round.

Then an American woman with spectacles asked, "Are those Christmas trees?"

"Windbreaks, madam," the guide said. "We've tried Rennies and they don't shift them." There were tee-hees from all and sundry.

"He's a one, he ought to be on *New Faces*," said a voice at the back. And the two girls in dark glasses and headscarves looked at each other in convulsed giggles.

Soon we could see Tresco. "It costs eighty p landing charge," the guide said, "and you have to walk a mile and a quarter to the gardens, and a mile and a quarter back. There are more dead bodies of day-trippers on Tresco than any other island in the United Kingdom. You can tell when it's been a good tourist day by the vultures, you can see them flying round from any part of St. Mary's." Again there were hoots.

We came to a coastguard station. "What's on that flag?" the American woman asked.

"It's got a crown, a rope, and 'GG' on it," the guide said. "Does that sound plausible? Because I made it up." Now everyone fell around, and there were tears streaming down faces.

We stopped at a point where there had been wrecks. The Torrey Canyon had just missed this rock. "We have a wreck every four years," the guide said. "Guinness have just chartered a new tanker, and we're hoping that'll be the next wreck." Again there was general laughter.

We came to the bulbs and he took the American know-all to task.

She said, "They're tulips?"

"No, daffodils," said the guide. "We have a virus down here, it makes the tulips go streaky. If we're to sell tulips, we must have perfect flowers."

"These are for market?"

"No, stock. We have to rest the field after bulbs. We put potatoes with kale or corn then, but not bulbs."

Later on he explained why a beach was not sandy: "The sea from the ocean crashes in and doesn't give the sand a chance to settle."

"Yes," said the know-all, "I understand that very well," and the whole bus muttered in irritation with her.

We stopped at another beach where Sir Cloudesley Shovel was shipwrecked and drowned in 1707. "He was the Admiral of the Fleet," said the guide, "and he lost a third of his fleet." (He was, in fact, Little Bo Peep who lost her sheep or ships.) "His treasure was found a few years ago in The Association. His body is rumoured to have been found by two local women who robbed it of its rings. And the Torrey Canyon went down here."

We came to the Old Town and saw the Union Jack above the white beach. "She has days," the guide announced of the owner of the flagpole. "When the Queen and the Duke of Edinburgh came, it wasn't the UN's day and she flew the Tricolour."

We returned via Harold Wilson's bungalow. It was hideous. It looked like a church hall. Paddy, Wilson's labrador, was sleeping on the lawn and there was an empty deck-chair near the window. These were the trappings of power; this unattractive bungalow in this quiet, peaceful place.

"What about the rabies laws?" asked someone. "Oh, this is like the UK, we're clean here," said the guide, serious for once, and it was now time to disembark. "Forty p for the bus, ten p for me," he said. "No, forty p a ticket." But everyone gave him 10p extra. With six trips a day he would be making £18.20 on the side in tips. And as I saw the queue for the next trip, I realised that his patter was rehearsed and learned, like an act. He churned out the same jokes several times each day.

Later we took a speedboat round the islands, and saw Cromwell's castle and various lighthouses. The swarthy, ruddy seaman (John Nicholls) showed me where Lord Hamilton's wreck, the Colossus, had been found; men were diving for treasure while we watched. He showed me the ocean-bed through the clear water and said he believed in Lyonesse: "From the air you can see a causeway between St. Mary's and St. Martin's over there. This was clearly all one land mass. I haven't seen any houses or church spires, though."

His straightforward approach was strangely effective. Now I liked the Scillies. The magic showed through. It had not been destroyed by the "witty comments" of the jaunty guide. I gazed at the bottom of the sea and it did not even occur to me that it was unfair that Prince Charles should own such beauty in place of the British people; I was blissfully content that there was no wag in my Lyonesse.

DEATHLY WHITE BOY AND A PACT
(OR: MORTGAGED TO GOD)

Simon fell downstairs on a November Friday and bumped his head. That Saturday morning he was flushed. He slept from 10.30 to 2.45. I went to the library off Kensington High Street to research into the Holy Grail, and he went into convulsions. He twitched and bubbled at the mouth, and had a fit. Pippa, who was pregnant again, seized him and put the side of her hand in his mouth so that he would not bite his tongue, and as he frothed he stopped breathing.

At the library I had a sudden intuition that I had to get home. I left the Reading Room, bringing my books with me. I drove into our road as an ambulance screamed round the corner. I saw two uniformed ambulancemen throw our front door open and run in. I rushed upstairs hoping that it was for someone in one of the other flats, but no, it was our door that was wide open. I arrived to see them holding a limp Simon, who was in a coma. He was deathly white, and life had gone out of him. As I took this in Pippa said, "It's Simon, he stopped breathing." I felt a trembling nausea in the pit of my stomach.

The ambulancemen took him down the stairs to the ambulance. One carried him with a blanket round him. Simon's eyes were closed, his mouth open. We raced to St. Stephen's Hospital. One of the men bent over Simon the whole time, and I expected him to stop breathing again and prayed silently, "Please God, I'll do anything, but please let him come through."

The ambulancemen took him to a cubicle just inside the hospital doors, a young doctor fell on him, and I said it again to myself: "Please God, I'll do anything, but please let him come through."

This time I felt a shiver up my spine, and within a minute there was a surge of life in Simon, the colour came back into his cheeks, and he came round. I felt absolutely drained as if life had gone out of me, I felt sick and was so weak in the legs that I had to sit down. I felt as if a tremendous current had leapt out of me, though of course it had not come from me, but had merely passed through me. I felt as I felt when I touched a faulty light switch when a boy at school, and received a substantial electric shock that left me shaking all over.

Soon they took X-rays of Simon's head, which showed there had been no fracture or bleeding, and eliminated the fall as a cause of the convulsions. They diagnosed acute tonsillitis, the high temperature having caused the fit. Simon was put in a ward with a wet sheet round his cot and a fan played on it to bring his temperature down. He lay in an unco-ordinated heap, his eyes bleary and unfocused, naked except for his plastic pants, and after being given red anti-convulsant medicine and an injection, he slept.

He had another three fits early next morning, the workings of the trigger mechanism whereby fits breed fits. He had a lumbar puncture, which showed there had been no haemorrhage in the brain, and he had to lie flat on his back or on his side for 24 hours. There was a yellow stain on his back, and his eyes showed a glazed discomfort. His movements were jerky and his co-ordination had gone.

But he slowly improved, and despite doctors' fears that he might have an abnormal EEG, he was back to normal within a week. He suffered no ill-effects. His co-ordination was good again, he remained intelligent to the point of brightness. He did not seem to have changed at all.

But something had changed in me. I had made a pact with God, to which I was now mortgaged. I had felt a power come through me and heal him, and I now had to keep my side of the bargain. I could sense that Eternity would play a more important part in my life from now on. I felt sombre.

PART TWO

THE CLEAR, SHINING SUNLIGHT OF ETERNITY

STORIES OF SPIRITUAL LOVE

THE CLEAR, SHINING SUNLIGHT OF ETERNITY
(OR: A FEW YEARS IN THE SUNLIGHT)

In the car I changed into my black tie and drove to the Catholic Chapel of Rest, the Holy Ghost, in Nightingale Square. Girls waited in the porch, there was scaffolding in the main part of the church. I lingered until I saw the mourners sitting quietly in the Lady Chapel. Among them sat my old Head, black-haired and upright in a dark overcoat, and aloof from the rest against a wall.

The coffin stood to the front of the aisle. It was on a stand, of yellow wood with gold handles, and six candles stood round it. There was a mauve cusp on top. I found a pew and sat next to a handsome, dark-haired, Bohemian young man with hair over his collar, and thought of how the train had hit James and blasted him to bits at Clapham Junction the previous Friday afternoon and closed the lines for three hours, and how my own son's breathing had stopped twenty-four hours later. Simon had been given back, but James had been taken. There was a silent wait while the Lady Chapel filled. Soon it was packed; many of the local people had read about the tragedy in the local papers, and had come to give quiet support. A bell rang, and the bereaved came in, Italian Mrs. Burns wearing black, her black hair hidden beneath a black head veil. She was supported by a group of relatives and friends and clutching white roses, and I thought how nearly it was me that was led in.

The local junior school trooped in. This was the choir, and it was led by a bald man with insincere eyes. Mass commenced, and for the next three-quarters of an hour I kneeled, sat, stood, sat and kneeled through a threnody of singing and praying. The priest wore a surplice with a Y-shaped cross on the front. He spoke of James as "having been baptised in this chapel". At one stage he spoke of James as "joining the saints" and the Bohemian man next to me pulled a face. I thought of the pinched, black-haired boy I brandished my cane at – he had bent down at the back of the class, inviting me to swish him – and of all the terrible things he had done after he ran away from home and before the remand home, and I avoided my old Head's eye. James was out of harmony with the universe, he was in opposition to it rather than in harmony with it, there was self-assertion, he hit policemen in the face – and I thought of a line from the *Tao Te Ching*, "He who is against Tao perishes young."

The Eucharist was served in a white goblet that glowed in the light like the Holy Grail. At the end of the Mass the priest walked round the coffin, shaking incense over it in a way that would have made James bristle with indignation. Then, standing by the coffin, he gave a short address. He said: "James died at the age of sixteen. This is young to die, but in the clear, shining sunlight of eternity a few years do not matter very much. Children die at one or two, and we will all die one day, and in fifty years' time a few years will not matter very much." I thought of the truant James as a Shining One, standing before the Clear Light of the *Tibetan Book of the Dead*.

At last it was time for the coffin to be carried out. The pall-bearers came down the aisle, dressed in black. They all looked over sixty, and one had a patch on his shoulder. They hoisted the coffin up and turned it round, and as they advanced down the aisle Mrs. Burns leaned out and touched it, and the two women next to her did the same.

Then suddenly the aisle was full of jostling women in black. Mrs. Burns passed me, her cheeks soaked with tears beneath her black veil, and then out they all went, blubbing and sobbing, and I found myself walking beside my old hunched Head, his well-parted black hair greased flat.

"Didn't expect to see you here," he said.

I explained about the letter Mrs. Burns had sent me through a girl-friend of James's who went to my school. I said I had often seen him up and down the road, and that apparently, he had always liked me. "A miserable business," I said.

"I suspended him," my old Head said, "and now I'm attending his funeral." He added: "A myth is already growing up about him."

"The murder story," I said, "The suggestion that he was chased onto the railway line by a gang of coloured thieves."

"Yes. He was playing on the lines. He was in trouble as recently as last week."

I stood with the Head and watched the coffin in the flowered hearse. Mrs. Burns sat in the Austin Princess behind. She looked distraught. I gathered that she did not believe her son was dead. They would not let her see the remains as there was nothing to see, only a few bits of flesh, and she still hoped against hope that it was not James who had been killed, even though pieces of his clothes had been retrieved. She had a lot of suffering ahead of her. Once again I thought of James travelling unknowing towards this. He had been taken, my own son had been given back after the screaming ambulance-drive to hospital. There, but for the grace of God....

"Cigarette?" the Head asked, offering me a packet as he fumbled, and I said, "I don't," and we walked up the road towards our cars to return to our respective schools and normal living. Life went on. Those who died were losers, and besides, in the clear, shining sunlight of eternity – in the sunlight – what did a few years matter?

BONHOMIE LIKE AN OXBRIDGE SMILE
(OR: AN EARL'S DAUGHTER AND A TRAITOR'S SON)

Jesperson gave a dinner for the son of a famous British traitor who had defected to the Soviet Union after handing over our atom secrets. That morning my wife was admitted to hospital with high blood pressure – our second child was due in six weeks' time – so I arrived alone at the crumbling street off Liverpool Road, in whose faded Jamesian charm Jesperson lived.

He had borrowed his Foreign Office cousin's flat, and her sister's illegitimate son greeted me at the door, a naked child of three. Jesperson led me into a room of leather armchairs and fin de siècle elegance. Jesperson told me that the lad's father, a card-holding member of the Communist party and Director of Studies at a Cambridge college, and his mother, an Earl's daughter, had between them brought great embarrassment on the head of his Foreign Office cousin. Former prep school masters asked her, "Why are you living in the same house as a Communist?" to which she had replied, "My sister's love life is her own affair." The presence of the Communist had much to do with her absence that night – and with her loan of her flat to Jesperson.

The traitor's son was a *nice* young man. In his early thirties, with a shock of hair, he sat foppishly in a sports jacket, legs crossed, looking straight ahead, avoiding everyone's eyes, and smiling. He joked in a very dated Oxbridge English which he had acquired from his father, and his infectious laugh put everyone in good humour. He said very little about his Russian background, except to say that he had spent twenty years in Moscow from the time he was nine, and that some of these years had been spent in Philby's house; and his wife, a black-haired Russian, looked quietly on, saying very little.

The Cambridge Communist and the Earl's daughter came in noisily. The Cambridge Fellow dominated the conversation by telling his wife, in a working-class accent, that they needed fluorescent lighting upstairs. He described her as "silly" and "wet", and the Earl's daughter fought back. She was a redhead with slightly parted lips and a hunched posture, and he had a sweater over an open-necked shirt. He talked rapidly, interrupting himself to nod and giggle with his listeners.

We were all restrained. The forbidden subject was spying. We succeeded in keeping off it until dinner ended. We talked about translators. The traitor's son was a Russian translator, and he said that *Room at the Top* had been translated into Russian as *The Attic*, a splendidly Soviet view of the squalid goings-on at the top of British society. The Cambridge Fellow (whose undergraduate career coincided with the 1968 Student Revolution) wanted more girls from comprehensives to go to Cambridge, and he suggested I should send him some. We talked about my former tutor, who was now a Cambridge Professor, whom he detested to the point of wearing a sweat-shirt with a slogan against him. We talked about the élitism of Cambridge, or rather the Earl's daughter did, and there was the obligatory talk of subjects that were once taboo. Circumcision took ten minutes of the Greek meal – at this topic the Russian girl suddenly came to life – and there was consideration of a pornographic movie in which a "member" had been thrust through a Japanese paper screen. The Earl's daughter described who "f—d" whom and what with great relish. She had seen the film when alone in Paris. There was talk of Cambridge humour.

Over brandies we got onto politics at last. I said that the traditional distinctions between right and left wing were breaking down: Mrs. Thatcher was in China allying against the Soviet Union. The Cambridge Fellow said, "China's always been right wing," and Jesperson scoffed. I said what if Europe expanded at the expense of the Soviet Union and Carter's Human Rights put Eastern Europe into turmoil? Would the Soviet Union split and part join Europe? The traitor's son, beaming, said, "No, it'll all change, or all stay the same," and his wife, who, as a waitress, was surely in the KGB, nodded in agreement.

I then passed on to Admiral Gorshkov's strategy of sea-power and asked his opinion. "Are you critical of Podgorny's visit to

Africa?" I asked. "Or do you support it?"

He said, "If the Soviet Union is defending the status quo, then Podgorny should not be in Africa."

"Does it mean you are against the policy of the Soviet leadership?" I asked.

"He shouldn't be there, as their policy has gone wrong."

"Will you go back to Moscow?"

"For visits."

"And take part in Russian politics?"

"No, I've excluded politics."

There was a silence.

The Earl's daughter said, "The trouble with the Soviet Union is they never intervene when they should. Chile was the worst case. The Soviet Union did nothing in Chile." She was opposing her parents who were in favour of the regime in Chile.

And that was how I saw them. The traitor's son was essentially against the ideas of his father, just as the Earl's daughter was against the ideas of hers. Neither could be held accountable for what their fathers had done.

The conversation passed on to bugging, and whether this room was bugged. "The difference between dissidents here and dissidents in other countries is that dissidents here can say things like 'This room is bugged' and not receive a visit later," I joked, and the traitor's son collapsed with laughter.

It was amazing. Here we were: a Communist at Cambridge; the near-Communist daughter of an Earl; the son of a Russian spy; a presumed KGB agent; and Jesperson and I, who had been to Oxbridge and China, and I with a rightish outlook. And there was no acrimony at all. Like an Oxbridge smile, the bonhomie was stronger than our views. It was not a social constraint, it was the *niceness* of these people that triumphed, despite the way that two of them quarrelled with each other.

I saw deep into the Philby years. Why had Philby remained undetected so long? Because of this bonhomie, surely. It was a consequence of the upper class code of talking about other things than about oneself and others present, which in turn was an aspect of upper class concern for a high style at the expense of warmth of feeling. So long as spies talked about other things and observed the high style and were nice, you left them alone and did not pry into their ideas or their political inclinations.

ETERNITY BESIDE THE TRAFFIC JAM
(OR: ELDER DICK AND ELDER DUNCAN)

My wife was in hospital with high blood pressure in late pregnancy. I pushed my son's pram towards the Tooting chemist. Two clean, bright, well-dressed young men were wandering towards me. They looked woefully lost and lonely.

"Excuse me," one of them said in an American accent, oblivious of the enormous traffic jam beside him and the chugging of a hundred exhausts that clouded the air. "I can see you're going somewhere but you've got a family and we're doing a survey on families, and we'd like to ask you some questions." He raised a black file he carried, but he did not actually open it. "Do you believe that family life is the best experience there is?"

I thought. I could have given him a half-hour's lecture on good experiences, but I did not want to disappoint him. He looked terribly earnest. "One of them," I said, slightly amused.

"And do you think that there's an After-Life, and that you'll meet your family in heaven and know them for Eternity?"

I thought of my ex-wife as he developed the idea. "It's a nice thought," I said non-committally.

"Because we belong to the Church of Jesus and Latter Day Saints," the spokesman of the two continued in his American drawl. "Our Church teaches that, and no other church does, and we'd like to share our teaching with you. Why don't you come along some time and see us? We'd like to call on you one evening. Then we can share our belief that family life continues in the After-Life. We do this voluntarily."

"We don't accept donations," the quiet one chipped in. He had a round scrubbed face and freckles.

"Perhaps I can have your address," I said, brushing them off like two wasps, indignant that the survey had somehow turned into an attempt at conversion, resentful at the con-text of the black file. There was a debate as to what address they should give. They decided on the Church as "we'll be moving from our lodging in Trinity Crescent within a few days".

"Have you been here long?" I asked, wresting the initiative with a question.

"About eight months in London. We're here for two years altogether. We've given up our jobs in the United States to do this."

He seemed to be looking for praise.

He wrote the address of the Church on a pad. It was in Nightingale Lane. "I'm Elder Dick," he said. And the quiet one chipped in, "I'm Elder Duncan." They held out their hands and I swatted them away with a handshake.

I escaped to the chemist and bought razor-blades. When I came out, wheeling the pram down the two steps, Elder Dick and Elder Duncan were standing among the petrol fumes of other families further down the pavement. They had an Asian boy between them, and they looked as if they held an arm each. As I watched, they turned and headed towards the traffic-lights, and I thought they had actually found someone to visit, with whom they could share their lonely belief that family life would last through Eternity.

A BAFFLEMENT LIKE A NETTED FISH
(OR: SISTER KIM AND THE MYSTERY OF LIFE)

My son, being premature, was put straight into the prem unit, where he was discovered to have air round his left lung. He was wired up in an incubator, like a prize fish under glass, only there were sundry alarms on top. He had tubes for the internal monitor and the oxygen, and he was fed intravenally through a drip into a vein in his head until they threaded a tube with lead on the end down through his stomach to his upper bowel. By then he had had jaundice, which was disseminated by a bright light. His breathing was rapid because of the immaturity of his lungs. I rang every morning and visited every evening, and was baffled by this thing which had come from nowhere and whose chest fluttered and gasped like a netted fish. I marvelled at the mystery of life.

Paul was so ill, in fact, that I did not introduce Simon to him. Then one Sunday when I visited as usual, my wife was all smiles as she would be coming home on the Tuesday. "Sister Kim says let Simon go and see him," she said.

I took Simon to the prem unit and put on a back-to-front gown and tied the white strings in front. I carried him in for a look. Simon, two and a half and blond, peered into the aquarium and said, "Baby." I pointed out the pink little toes and the slightly opened eyes under the oxygen box, and then I noticed that the Pakistani baby in the next incubator was missing. It had had hot-water bottles packed round it. "She died," the staff midwife said. I was shocked. It was so much better developed than the frail little Indian thing which had been delivered after twenty-eight weeks, and which lay fetally and pot-bellied and still.

Outside I took off my white gown, and joined my wife. I remarked on the death. "Yes," she said, "the mother is in the room by herself, number ten."

Later the bell went for the end of visiting. I passed Room 10. The door was open. A dozen Moslem Pakistanis stood tearfully round the one bed, and four children – the dead baby's brothers and sisters – came out and ran up the corridor. I followed them and waited while my wife took Simon to the loo, and Sister Kim came up, a youthful Singapore Chinese in violet uniform. She accosted the Pakistani woman who was collecting the four children.

"Will you please control your children," she said. "They are very noisy. And will you try not to bring them next time. They are too small. Older ones, yes, but not so young."

She spoke haughtily, like a racial superior to a racial inferior. Then she turned and saw me looking. She smiled as she turned away.

As I left the hospital, I thought of the two babies in the next-door incubators – my Christian son, who had survived, and the Moslem Pakistani's girl, who had died – and again I felt the sense of bafflement at the mystery of life which it was my purpose to record before I returned to the great ocean. And I thought of Sister Kim. She was not baffled. She had guided Simon to meet my newborn, and she had banned the Pakistani's children from the hospital, even though they had been bereaved (though they probably did not fully realise it). She presided Providentially over birth and death, she accepted the process like the keeper of a shop full of fish-tanks. She saw their lungs grow like gills and their skin pale like dry scales, and she did not stop to speculate. And in that blind process and in her blind, unquestioning acceptance of it, perhaps, lay the answer to my questioning bafflement.

A MOUSE UNDER THE COUNTER

I went "under the counter" (as I referred to the House of Commons following the deal between the Liberals and the Labour Party, a deal about which it was much said there was "nothing under the counter"). I waited a quarter of an hour for the MP who had invited me to the House. As I watched, several MPs in succession tottered into the Central Lobby and theatrically threw up their arms, sticking out their bellies as if they were exposing themselves, and communicated pleasure at seeing their petitioning constituents. I waited among the statues under the fine vaulting, and eventually the deputy Shadow Minister came. He threw up his arms – I thought in horror, at first – and pumped my hand, and I thought how yellow and bloodshot his eyes were under his balding head.

"Oh, and I've had to keep you waiting," he said regretfully, theatrically reviewing the last quarter of an hour and stating the facts. "And I've got to be back there by six so we've only got a few minutes. I've been reading your papers, they're very good." Then, like a small boy proposing that we should get down on our hands and knees and sit under the counter, he said conspiratorially: "Let's go out on the terrace."

I stressed how kind it was of him to see me as we hurried down a passage. I wanted to use his name. We stood on the terrace. Boats plied down a choppy brown river.

Eventually the Deputy Minister nodded. "Good," he said, and we turned and went back into the electronic echoes of the passage which led back to the Central Lobby. He escorted me to the exit, talking, and shook my hand. "Do please use my name," he said. I thanked him. For a moment he stood, looking yellow-eyed and curiously soft, yet very much like the photographs of himself, and then he turned and hurried away into the darkest recesses of the Central Lobby, like a mouse scurrying for an under-the-counter hole.

A BODY FOOLED INTO MILK
(OR: LIKE FLOWERS IN A FALSE SPRING)

I bumped into the Italian Mrs. Burns. She was crossing the road outside my school wearing a coat and holding a shopping-bag. She looked sallow and lined under her straight black hair. "How are you?" I asked, meaning 'How is your grief?'

"I don't mind telling you because James liked you so much, worshipped you even," she said. "I had an operation ten days ago, it's all right now. I was pregnant during the funeral, not by my 'husband'. They used that magic paste and brought it on. My 'husband' came and visited me in the hospital, he was horrible to me. He didn't know, he thought it was my change. I had a dream as I came out of the anaesthetic. James, you know, my dead son, was standing by my bed, and when I woke up I thought he was really there. Then I realised he was dead, and I'd lost this one too. I felt terrible. But it wouldn't have been fair to let it live. Not after what happened to James. He was never the same after I told him my 'husband' wasn't his real father. No, I couldn't go through that again. And my actor-lover didn't want it. Besides, children are all right until they're three, while they're cuddly little babies, but after that they grow away from you. I don't want any more children.

"The trouble is, though, that magic paste makes it like giving birth. It's a kind of mini-birth, so much so that it fooled my body. The other morning I woke up and my breasts were squirting milk all over the sheet. Luckily, he was asleep, he never saw. It's like flowers coming out in a false spring, being cheated. The mini-birth fooled my body, and for several days I was full of milk."

I stared at her. She was a body, and she had been a fool. And she had talked too freely out of her lonely grief, which had lost all sense of social propriety. How wonderful that her irresponsibility should have swollen to milky bloom.

A ZOO OF BUFFERS

The Jubilee Garden Party of the European Movement, Kensington and Chelsea Branch, was held below the Brompton Oratory, in the gardens, and as I walked along the alleyway that led to them, an old buffer with a bald head turned from his wife, who was in a long dress, and peered at my long hair.

I was not sure what to expect. In the event I went into a hall and was greeted by a man with smarmy hair. I took a fruit juice and stood and surveyed a generation of buffers. It seemed as though the whole European Movement was aged sixty. Perhaps this was the generation that had suffered most in the war, the generation to which European unity meant the most. Then I realised that everyone was from the upper classes. Everyone I met was Lord this or Lady that or the Duchess of the other. One of the organisers told me: "There was trouble over Lord Swainham's tickets. I founded this branch, it was my idea. I now want it to turn from being a social thing to a more intellectual movement."

There was a band in the gardens. I talked to a few members of the ruling class and then the Chairman tried to speak through a defective microphone. He read a letter from Princess Alexandra, who was sorry to refuse her invitation. The Mayor spoke, and Sir Con O'Neill, the former British Ambassador to Brussels and leader of the "Keep Britain in Europe" campaign, also spoke, a bald, wizened man. While their words were lobbed out into the air among the higher intelligences, buffers turned and peered indignantly at me, and their elderly wives looked at me with smiling eyes.

Neither of the two local MPs had turned up. There were no European MPs present. After the speeches I wandered round and saw the bearded founder of the Branch with a white-haired woman on his arm. She pushed his arm and left, laughing, and the founder said to me, "The Chairman's wife has just been rude to her. That's the Countess Natalie Szekely. She keeps us all sensible."

I stood and looked at them all. It *was* a social gathering. It was like a reception abroad. No one was talking about Europe. That was just an excuse, everyone was socialising. "There are fifty members and a hundred and thirty here," the founder had said. "There must be a lot of hangers-on."

As I looked at them, they turned into animals. There were bulls and bisons of the especially thick-necked variety, and there were thin, slender ostriches and giraffes. I who should have kept an appointment with the angels had somehow lost my way into a zoo. I surveyed each occupant of each cage and left their world of the senses for more real things.

A SHERMOZZLE AND A FREUDIAN SLIP

I went to the Conservatives' Queen's Gate Branch drinks party in the New Town Hall, Kensington. I climbed the plush stairs and paid at the door and entered a wooden-panelled suite. Drinks were being served in the doorway and I was caught up in ageing, clutchy women. An elderly Tory, the leader of the GLC, said, "If we're not careful there's going to be a shermozzle." Someone introduced me to my constituency chairman, an elderly soft-looking man with furtive eyes and grey hair. He limply gripped my hand and said sadly, "We'll put you on the committee," which I did not think a good idea. He introduced me to a young man who had an egg head, who was starting a London European society. He was all manner, and he broke off our conversation to listen to a large plump woman who talked derogatorarily about socialist speakers for Europe.

Later, I found myself talking to the sister of an MP. Her husband was the new Branch Treasurer, and he said, "I am seriously worried about funds. We are two thousand in the red. They had to repair the roof and the membership is ageing, as you can see. The old die and only foreigners are coming in to take their place. Look, you're the youngest here." A clutchy woman came up and talked, brushing her hand against mine. "We are all oldies," she said sadly. "No one here is young."

Everyone was a Lady or a Lord. I walked round. My clutchy woman came with me and introduced me to a peer as "a young man who taught in Libya".

"Good God," the peer said.

This was a generation I had nothing in common with. Suddenly, someone was clapping for silence, and a woman was thanking the organiser, for whom there was perfunctory applause. Then it was announced that "Lady R— will make the draw". This was the local MP's wife. The large plump woman was standing in front of me, a little sozzled.

"My husband was hoping to be here," she said, "and he had a pairing arrangement, but he must have been double-crossed. There's something happening in the House until three a.m., and he hasn't been able to get away. I am sure that he would want me to give *your apologies to him*."

There was a stunned silence. She had meant to say "to give his apologies to you", but her Freudian slip had revealed what she really thought of the party and of her husband's constituency duties. The "shermozzle" had happened.

Lady R—, unaware of what she had said, was making a great thing of identifying the colour of the tickets she drew. Exaggeration was the game, and there was applause as the "unlucky" peer won a bottle of whisky. Lady R— was the famous MP's wife, she was the centre of attention, and she wore her mask effortlessly. But I knew what the MP had thought of this junket.

Later I was taken round the New Town Hall by a Councillor and when I saw the extravagant large hall I joked, "I hope it's not my rates that are paying for the carpet." But I could not forget the MP's wife's blunder. Somewhere in the House of Commons he was voting or moving amendments, unaware that his public pose looked very naked.

AN ORGY IN THE CHURCHYARD

"Virginia came round yesterday," the school-cleaner Mrs. Jenks giggled. "She makes me laugh, she's so crude. 'You ought to have it all out like me,' she told me. 'Since I had it all out, I can't get enough of it. I had my man round last night' – she's having an affair with her husband's best friend, her husband works nights and the best friend comes in when he goes out, and the husband doesn't know – 'and he's not as good as my husband,' she said 'but it makes a change. Anyway he had a go, and then when he woke up he wanted some more, and then my husband came home at seven and he wanted some, and gor, am I tired. Makes me think of that orgy I went on in that churchyard.' She went on some orgy without her husband knowing, and everyone made love to her. I told her, 'Virginia, it's not the quantity of the sex, it's the quality.' 'Yes, you're right,' she said, 'you know my man came round last week, and we got into bed, and he couldn't do anything at all. Was I disappointed!'

"She keeps wanting to take me to the Spiritualist church at Tooting Bec. You know, she's very spiritual. She said to me about you, 'I'm sure he's one of us.' Anyway, she took me along – I went just to get away from my old man – and she thinks I went into a trance, but the truth is, I was so tired and bored by all the weirdos there that I went to sleep. Really, I went right off. When I woke up they were calling out to the dead, and I got up and I left. Virginia was in a trance when I went, she really believes in it."

Mrs. Jenks chuckled to herself, and I contemplated Virginia, the parent I had met at Parents' Meetings at school, and thinking of her infidelities and her spiritual zeal, I wondered who she would smuggle in at nights when she put off her fleshly clothing and became one of the Shining Ones in the other world, I wondered what orgy she would join in her final churchyard.

TWO SMILING BUDDHAS AND HE WHO SPEAKS (OR: SHINING ONES AND A STOPPED WATCH)

I went to a New Age conference on Ancient Egypt and the Essenes, the sect in which Christ may have been a Master and which produced the Dead Sea Scrolls. It was scheduled in a London church from 11.15 a.m. to 9.45 p.m. one July Saturday, the day before I was due to join my wife on holiday in Cornwall, and when I arrived some four or five hundred people thronged the church interior, which had Renaissance pillars. The altar was curtained off to make a stage, on which there was a microphone, and while I took stock of the elderly age-group and bought the recently translated Gospel of the Essenes (billed as the pure, uncorrupted words of Christ), I observed the seventy year old, grey-haired organiser theatrically mingle with his audience and bestow exaggerated embraces and hug each group in turn until he came to me.

"Have we met?" he asked, thin and pale, a baronet with long grey hair over his shoulders. I gave my name, unflustered and calm in my illumined serenity, and he bent deafly and listened. I looked deep into his eyes and felt he was an actor, perhaps even a charlatan. The feeling was confirmed when, soon afterwards, he called for silence from the front and announced in a slightly Scottish accent, "I have just broken my spectacles. Can anyone lend me a pair of fairly long-sighted ones?"

The chairs were bagged with coats in the front half of the hall, and I sat in the back half as Sir Thomas Roper began: "The question is, why have five hundred people come to an all-day conference on the Egyptians and the Essenes?" He spoke slowly, without notes, in a slightly Scottish lilt, introducing the ideas of the ancient Egyptians and the Essenes – they had the Light in common, which was my reason for being there – and talking to the inner mind, planting ideas like seeds, making statements, not arguing. He made it clear that there are spirits, and that we have had numerous incarnations, two heresies I found attractive. He often referred to "the Shining Ones", as enlightened souls were known in ancient Egypt.

He was succeeded by a balding composer who had communed with Sir Thomas Beecham for a number of years, and he presented his Temple-Dancers. They were dressed as the ancient Egyptians dressed, and they danced soulfully, moving their arms very slowly into the gestures you see in Egyptian temple frescoes and in the illustrations to *The Book of the Dead*. I took extensive notes.

Lunch was down in the crypt. This was surely how Heaven would be, a congregation of angels like this, jostling shoulders. I collected my box of sandwiches, a pie and an apple, and took them to a table. The young man and two women who had sat next to me upstairs approached and said, "May we join you?"

The younger of the two women said, "We're faith-healers. We've come up for the day from Cardiff. We're spiritualists. We heal through spirits, or rather, spirits heal through us."

"Oh yes?" I said, immediately interested. "You all heal?"

"Yes," said the old lady. "An eighteenth century spirit heals through me. We believe that God does not come down to our level, but intervenes through intermediary angels and spirits."

"When I heal someone," the younger woman said (she had a craggy face), "it's different each time. I can feel the peculiar character and individuality of the angel or spirit that is doing the healing each time."

The elderly woman was tiny, and she had the white-yellow skin of a spirit. "You'll get plenty of kicks in the back from bad spirits," she said, and she put her finger on the top of my spine, and I felt a burning sensation that left me quite weak.

I recovered to question them all at length about their healing, and I established that the young man was a Minister. He had been asked to leave the Congregationalist church as a heretic, and had just been accepted as a Unitarian Minister. I also established that God used them as channels. They prayed quietly to God and God did the healing. They merely applied their fingers to the part of the body which they felt was weak. Absent healing worked as well as immediate healing, for prayer was a living, healing thing. Every condition was alleviated.

"You'd better ask a spirit to heal my wife's headaches," I said, and I told them how she had had headaches after her difficult pregnancy.

They said that if I put my hand on the back of her head at 9 p.m. the following evening, they would ask God to heal her.

The afternoon session comprised readings from the *Egyptian Book of the Dead* (or "Book of the Great Awakening" as it is better translated) and from the *Gospel of the Essenes*, and the extracts about "the Shining Ones" were accompanied by exegesis and more dancing from the Temple-Dancers. I was able to speak to Sir Thomas Roper again just before tea. I asked him what evidence he had for saying in the hand-out that Christ was initiated in the Temple of Isis at On (Heliopolis). "It's not in Josephus, for example," I said, "and I'd like chapter and verse."

He looked at me as though I had hit him across the face. "Oh, er, it's an esoteric, occultist tradition, a Gnostic-Essene one," he said. "It hasn't been written down, but I can assure you that He was there."

I also asked him about the New Age. "Oh, there are hundreds of groups," he said vaguely. "It's the sort of thing my lectures are about. You can buy them at the back."

"Yes," I said, "I know New Thought, the movement which began in the nineteenth century, and which is reflected in works like Trine's *In Tune With the Infinite*. Is the New Age an extension of this?"

"It's the upsurge, the bursting up of new energy in our time," he said in words that themselves had an occult, esoteric meaning; bursting up from where?

I saw it in waves. After New Thought, New Age. Because each generation was a new wave, the tide was coming in.

I drank tea standing in the crypt with the three faith-healers. A small youngish dark woman with brown eyes came in on the conversation. "I couldn't help hearing what you said," she said in a Birmingham accent. "I've always thought disease was caused by a disorder in the mind. You confirm that, do you?" We stood in a circle talking about healing, and when the faith-healers withdrew to return upstairs I asked her about herself. She was a Yoga-teacher from Birmingham, she said. She had come down for the day with two friends.

On the way up she asked my interest in the Egyptians and the Essenes. At first I lied. "Oh, I'm interested in ancient Egypt and *The Book of the Dead*."

"And the content of the *Essene Gospel*?" she asked.

She had drawn me out. "And illumination," I said neutrally.

She seized on this. "You've had it?" she asked. Surprised, I nodded. "So have I," she said excitedly. "I got it through Yoga, and so did my friend and our other friend. But I haven't met anyone else who has. You're the fourth person. Tell me, how did you do it?"

Astounded, I said, "Oh, I went to Oxford. Most of my generation became left-wing journalists, but some were interested in the East. They introduced me to the no-soul and other Eastern concepts. I went to Japan and sat in Zen temples, and it came like that, the first time was in the bathroom. It only finally happened when I returned to the West."

She said: "It often happens in the bath, they say. If I hadn't seen it, I'd be envious."

I said: "You have to rebel against the materialistic Western tradition and culture to have it. I did it through Zen, you did it through Hinduism."

"Yes," she said excitedly, "if we hadn't done it through Yoga, we'd be just housewives."

"The Light," I said, checking that she really *had* seen it, "you actually saw the Light?"

"Yes," she said, "you know what I mean. But don't you have to suffer for it? There's no easy path, is there? All these people here think it's easy, but it isn't, even though you're guided Providentially. And when you've had it, it's like that Zen story of the Master who was asked 'How do I achieve enlightenment?' and who replied, 'Have you had your tea? Then go and wash your cup.' It's that easy, isn't it? Provided you have the tea, which these people here haven't had. Fancy you having seen it. And we've got nothing to say to each other now, have we? They say that when two Buddhas meet they have nothing to say to each other, and just smile."

Amazed that someone else had experienced the Light, I said, "You're right. I was not going to tell you, I was going to lie."

"'He who knows does not speak, he who speaks does not know'," she said quoting the *Tao Te Ching*. "I know, I drew it out of you. I knew you'd had it, I felt it somehow. But did you *cry* a lot on the way, really cry, tears I mean? Or is that just something that women do?"

"Men do, but not in public," I said, remembering a decade's pain with some unwillingness. "First everything's futile, aimless, meaningless, hollow, unreal, purposeless, and you're depressed. That's the suffering, and you MUST suffer, there's no other way, you have to go through it. Then you see the Light and you're calm and still and purposeful and have an aim."

She nodded. "And before, you seek out people who are in a mess," she said.

"Whereas afterwards, you avoid them and seek out those who have an aim," I said.

"And you pity them," she said. "We have a friend who's gone into a mental hospital because his wife left him. That's about the level of the suffering here."

THE CLEAR, SHINING SUNLIGHT OF ETERNITY   169

"He should realise," I said, "that it's a good opportunity to grow. His wife was taken away from him, perhaps she was wrong for him. He is now unimpeded by what was not right and can now grow."

We were standing in the aisle waiting for the conference to restart, and I looked at my watch. It had stopped at 4.45. I calculated that it was the moment when she told me she had seen the Light. I left her to return to her friends, and sat down next to the Unitarian Minister. I shook my watch and wound it, without success. The Unitarian Minister suddenly said, "Oh, my watch has stopped." His also said 4.45. I wondered what Uri Geller type of power was around in the atmosphere.

The early evening session was devoted to the Temple-Dancers as "Shining Ones", and I met Dot (the Birmingham housewife) down in the crypt for supper. "Would you like to join our table?" she asked as I looked for a place, my hands laden, and I sat in a circle of her friends including the one who had seen the Light, a quiet shy mother whose daughter of fourteen sat beside me, and I discussed the Light with Dot.

"I'm free, unattached inside," she said. "I'm a free individual and I'm detached from all sects."

"We're all climbing Mount Fuji," I said, "but some take the Western path and others take the Eastern path."

"Yes," she said, "our friend doesn't need to come to a conference like this, she knows. She's stayed at home to put on a party for some children." I thought of Teresa, who would have done the same. "I feel that this is all intellectual clap-trap," Dot said. "Once you've seen the Light, you don't need all this. We went for a walk by the river during the last session. Did we miss anything? And the river was very beautiful."

I agreed with her attitude, but said it was useful to have one's experience confirmed by the tradition. I told her about Sister Moore at work who had never seen the Light, despite a lifetime of getting up at 5.30 for it in her convent.

"No, that's useless," Dot said, interrupting. "She's wasting her time if she hasn't seen the Light."

I talked about the energy illumination gives, and she said: "I have the energy too, but I don't know what to do with it, what group to channel it into, that's my trouble. I shall give up teaching Yoga but I don't know what is to replace it. We've tried several groups. This one is the latest."

I told her to organise a group; St. Teresa founded the Carmelite Order after her illumination, and involved St. John of the Cross, and we should do the same, but in a European context. We should address ourselves to Europe and work for one world government and one world religion.

She said, "They'll all recognise what you say because it's the Truth. That's brilliant. I've never met anyone like you. You're a once-off."

I left the crypt and returned to the faith-healers in the conference. Sir Thomas Roper was summing up. He spoke for an hour about the Light of the Egyptians and the Light of the Essenes, about the way the Christos was the Amon-Re and is a living idea for today. He said that the Renaissance pillars of the church protected the souls of the worshippers, and were living things. At the end he made us stand for a prayer to the angels and spirits.

My faith-healers had had to leave to catch their train to Cardiff. I looked for Dot, who, I knew would be catching a train to Birmingham with her friends. Not seeing her, I went to Sir Thomas Roper, who was embracing a party of Dutch grannies on the "stage", and, feeling the power come in and fill me like a tide in an empty harbour, I said, "Why don't you organise a day like this on *The Experience of the Light*? Not Light in the Essene times, but Light today."

He looked at me as if I had slapped him. "*The Experience of the Light*," he said in raptures. "I can just see it. An excellent title. Thank you for the idea." He turned away and resumed his exaggerated farewell kisses on the Dutch ladies. And then I saw Dot, who had listened in to our conversation without my knowing it.

"Do you think he's *experienced* it?" I asked.

"I don't know," she said. "You'd think he'd have to to talk about it for an hour, but 'he who knows does not speak, he who speaks does not know'."

"I'll ask him," I said, and she smirked to herself all the while I waited for the Dutch ladies to finish.

"Further to what I said about 'The Experience of the Light'," I said, "my friend here and I are both illuminated, having achieved enlightenment through Hinduism and Zen Buddhism. We'd like to know about your experiences of illumination."

Sir Thomas Roper looked as if I had hit him. "Oh, er, I'm not a sensitive. I'm an interpreter," he said evasively. "I haven't had

THE CLEAR, SHINING SUNLIGHT OF ETERNITY   171

experiences." Then, evidently realising the enormity of what he had said, he recovered his composure. "On the other hand, perhaps I am a sensitive. Perhaps to feel the life of pillars is to see the Light."

I interrupted indignantly, objecting that the Light can *actually* be seen.

"You mustn't press me on this," Sir Thomas Roper said. "Talking about an experience disperses it and....No, I'm not saying any more."

Dot and I did not dare look at each other until we had left the church. We picked our way through a circle of long-haired people in jeans who sat in ostentatious harmony, their hands on each other's shoulders. Outside we both said together, "He *hasn't* seen it!"

"He talked about it for an hour," I said, "but he hasn't seen it."

"It's what I said," Dot said, "I knew he hadn't, I felt he hadn't. 'He who knows does not speak....' You see what I mean, we've been trying various groups and now *he's* no good. It's all very depressing. Has no one seen it besides us?"

"Don't despair," I said, *"we'll* form a group."

I drove home, waving to Dot and her friends as I passed them on the Embankment.

Reviewing the day in my mind, I thought of Sir Thomas Roper and his theatrical behaviour, and his sheer panic when I had confronted him with the question that had found him out. And I thought of Dot, the enlightened housewife who knew more than he did, more even that did the faith-healers of Cardiff in her own way.

Involuntarily, I looked at my watch. It had irrevocably stopped at 4.45 in true and final memory of a timeless moment: the power – so much greater than time – of the meeting between two "Shining Ones".

SPIRITS UP THE SPINE AND A BUCKETFUL OF STONES

The faith-healers I met at the conference were mobilising their group in Cardiff to heal my wife of her headaches. The heretic Unitarian Minister had explained to me at great length what to do. At 9 p.m. the following evening I had to surrender my ego and ask God to use me as a channel, I had to picture my wife healthy while I compassionately touched the back of her head. I had to concentrate on her being well, and his wife and the old lady would be doing the same in Cardiff. Thoughts were living things, and God would do the healing through spirits for God did not come down to the level of human beings but healed through intermediaries – provided I opened myself to the Infinite. Spirits would come into me and God's power would flow through me and make me burn, provided I allowed my body to channel it like a pipe that is not blocked by an ego. Each spirit that entered me would make me feel slightly different. All disease was the result of disharmony, the heretic said, and was healed through God's peace.

On the train down to Cornwall I sat opposite a freckled lad who precociously drank beer, which he slopped over my *Book of the Dead* on the small window-ledge, and travelled with a set of adult golf-clubs. My wife and first son met me on the platform – "I've found my Daddy," my son said, "he was on a train" – and as soon as we reached the Cornish bungalow I began to put the theories into practice. By 9 I sat with my wife. I said silently, "God, please use me as a channel, send power through me to heal my wife here of her headaches so that she will be well." I pictured her laughing, very headache-less.

I was relaxed and breathing deeply, and after about a minute I felt a surge of power that left me cold. It hit my back around the base of my spine, and ran through up my cheeks and into my arms and out into my wife. It was a cross between a rush and a shudder. I was not afraid. I tried again a few minutes later and felt power sweep through me again, only this time it was faster and slightly different, as the Minister's wife had said. My wife felt an accumulated warmth in my fingers, and she felt a lurking headache in the middle of her head rather than at the back.

Later we drove down to Charlestown harbour. The sun was a deep red through mist, and the harbour was silent. A bat flitted by, and the air was full of spirits wheeling and ducking and weaving.

The next night, a Monday, I tried again. I touched her hand and silently asking God to make me a channel for healing power. After about a minute my prayer was answered. Four times in quick succession I felt little rushes enter my back and sweep along my arms out into my wife's head, like clouds across the face of the sun on a windy day, or like sudden shivers in the night. Each rush was slightly different in character from the others.

Then there was a massive surge which lasted twice as long as the rest. I had to ride it, and then it was over and out of me after a little puffing and blowing on my part, and my wife felt a shiver and her headache lurked at the front of her head instead of the middle.

At 9.15 p.m. we drove to Par beach and looked at the full moon over the headland and the white china clay chimneys.

The next afternoon I got through to the Unitarian Minister on the phone. I described what had happened and said I thought I was pushing the headache from back to front, and he said, "That's most interesting. Cold is very often something people talk of, and burning. I'd think the four 'rushes' were different spirits that entered you. Incidentally, my wife complained of a headache at the back of her head last night about five past nine. She picked it up. It's clearly working. We'll keep it up. The whole group will be doing it at nine p.m. tonight. Keep doing it until you get a hunch that 'the other side' wants you to stop. And make sure your wife's relaxed."

We relaxed in good time, at 8.50 p.m. There were a lot of distractions, one way and another – I heard clattering pans – and I found it much harder to surrender my ego and be a self, a channel. Then the surge came at the base of my spine and went up my back. It was hot and cold at the same time, and very restless; it made me wriggle and fidget. This lasted about thirty seconds, and then four more rushes came, one after another. At the third one – I counted each aloud and actually murmured "number three" while it passed through me – my wife burned. But I did not feel the power as deeply as I had the previous night. At the end my hands were cold and my temperature was low. I was shivering and trembling and shaking as if I had the heebie-jeebies, and my fingers shone electrically in the electric light. I had a slight headache in my forehead, over my sinuses, and my wife said she felt very "light" and "free".

We drove down to Charlestown harbour. There was no sun or moon, and we walked along the dark and deserted harbour wall and then I rang the Unitarian Minister from a call-box. The group was there, and he said: "What you've got is nothing to worry about. It's unlikely that you've picked up a negative influence or that you've taken something from your wife to disperse." He spoke to the group over his shoulder and then said, "We were concentrating on both of you and perhaps you picked up what was designed for your wife as well."

"Like a plus *and* minus charge of electricity," I said.

"Yes" he said, "that's a very good way of putting it. Don't worry. It'll go. It's obviously working, that's the main thing."

My wife was cured of her headaches. For the first time for weeks, since the toxemia, she was normal again. They never returned, though I went on with the healing for a while.

The following day my wife and I took Simon to Charlestown beach, and we caught shrimps and crabs in the rock pools, thrusting a net among bladderwrack and limpets and green and red seaweed. Simon filled his bucket full of large stones and carried them back to the car. Walking beside him with the net, and watching him waddle and labour with his stones, I thought of the world of the senses, which people carried round with them like a bucketful of heavy stones.

A HANGED MAN'S GIFT AND A MONGOL'S EYES (OR: WHEELS ON A HOBBY-HORSE)

We went on a coach around Dartmoor. We stopped for lunch at Badger's Holt, Dartmeet, where a brown stream bubbled through Cyclopean boulders towards a bridge under lowering wooded heights. Our youngest son had been ill – the change of water had upset his tummy – and my wife rang her mother from the call-box by the little shop. She was a long time, and she came out and said: "Paul's all right but Mr Shipman's killed himself. It happened this morning in his garage, some time between seven-thirty and ten. He definitely did himself in. The nurse came down to my mother's with Mrs. Shipman and she couldn't say anything in front of Mrs. Shipman, but when Mrs. Shipman wasn't looking she put her fingers to her throat, like this, and later she said, 'He hanged himself.' It's terrible, I feel quite funny. I only saw him on Sunday – he came round and put the wheels on Simon's hobby-horse – and my mother saw him last night. He was sitting on his sofa when she went round and he had his arms over the back of the sofa and he turned and waved very hard through the window. Apparently he and his wife had had a row about the house."

I frowned, for I recalled the balding, freckled, silver-haired Mr Shipman with his ruddy weather-beaten face and I knew that Mrs. Shipman had moved house and now wanted to move again. She had wandered into the kitchen only the day before to see my wife's mother, a dark-haired woman in her fifties in a sweater and slacks. I had taken Simon out to buy the papers at eight that morning.

We walked down to the stream and sat by the clear water that looked brown, as if the bed were rusty. "You know," my wife said, "Mrs. Shipman used to live next to my mother. Then she wanted to move elsewhere on the estate, so they moved where they are now, just up the road. But she wasn't happy, and she wanted to move again. They were going to sell and buy a house near us. They had some people over the house last night and Mrs. Shipman changed her mind again – she's a dreadful ditherer – and she refused to allow the prospective buyers to see her bedroom. They were going on holiday in October. He was such a quiet, cheerful little man, he wouldn't say boo to a goose. He worked at a joiners' down the road, he was a Do-it-yourself man, just the person to fix wheels on a hobby-horse. Now he's dead."

I sighed. "Assuming he *did* kill himself," I said, "he obviously wanted to be dead rather than go on living. I don't know what drove him to it: his job, the fact that he was working and his wife was never contented and he had no family and felt isolated and everything lost its point. But if it was the house that did it, then Mrs. Shipman is learning a terrible truth, that the art of living is to be content with what you have, and not to seek to change it all the time, because suddenly what you have been discontented with is taken away, and you realise too late that you were happy."

We ate our sandwiches by the brown stream, and then my wife telephoned again. When she returned to me, trailing her long dress in the dust, she had a different story to tell.

"Mrs. Shipman's been down," she said, "they didn't only quarrel over selling the house. It began with some 'literature' she found in his haversack, which he brought back from work at lunchtime. Normally she never looks in his haversack, but she did, and what she found was 'disgusting'. She didn't think he was like that. She challenged him about it, and he said he was given it at work. I don't know whether it was a joke, or whether he had been lent it, or what. Then came the house incident – he showed these people round – and after they went she shouted at him and said, 'I'd be better off without you.' She went off and slept in a separate room.

"He was up some of the night. He doesn't drink, but the whisky bottle and the sherry bottle had been left out. He was supposed to give two cousins a lift at seven-twenty and she said, 'Drive them and then come back and we'll discuss it.' He said, 'I can't miss work.' The quarrel seemed to be over. He left the toaster out for her, and her paper. He drove the red mini out of the garage as usual, and left it with the window open, to close the garage door. She didn't see him after that, she went up to bed because she hadn't slept. She slept until ten.

"When she came downstairs she found his haversack in the kitchen. The 'literature' had gone. She thought it was strange. Then she saw the red mini outside the garage. The fold-up door was down. She pushed the door up, and then she saw him. He was on his knees, his knees were grazed. The garage is low and he'd kept his feet on the ground and bent downwards over a tea-chest using a very fine cord. It wasn't even an eighth of an inch thick. He was in the Navy during the war – he had an anchor tattooed on one arm – and he must have learned about knots then. He'd never gone to work."

I sighed again. "It's all very unfortunate: the 'literature', the house," I said. "It could be that he was thoroughly confused. He possibly believed her when she said 'I'd be better off without you' and thought his marriage was over. Mrs. Shipman will want to believe that the quarrel was finished because it will exonerate her. He probably hadn't slept all night, and the alcohol confused him, if he wasn't used to it, and he couldn't face discussing a divorce. He probably sat in his garage, and then realised he was late for work. What should he do? Ring and say he would be late, and be told off? Ring and say he was ill, and have to face the talk with his wife, about the dismantling of his home, everything he had worked for? Everything got on top of him, and at the end – you can imagine it – the words 'I'd be better off without you' rang through his ears and he gave her her wish. Words are like boomerangs, and her words boomeranged straight back. The question is," I said, "did the 'literature' warrant criticism, or should it have been tolerated in a permissive society? Should she not have let him be?"

We returned to the coach. A Mongol of about twenty sat in the front seat with his mother. He had dozy slit eyes and an open mouth, and he stammered in a loud voice, "It's qu-quite n-nice, qu-quite n-nice here," to the coach-driver, who said in embarrassed Cornish, "It is, isn't it." This Mongol had more reason than Mr Shipman to hang himself in a garage, yet there he was, eagerly drinking in the peace of the gorge with greedy, slit, Buddha-like eyes. In "this strange disease of modern life", the norm was to be sick, the rarity was to be healthy – health being calm serenity.

I thought of Mrs. Shipman. She had the quarrel on her conscience. It was axiomatic in life that you should only say what you mean, or else you are responsible for any misunderstandings that take place; also that you should never sleep on a quarrel. Having had everything, she now suddenly had nothing: no companionship, no income. She would look back and see how good the time was that she had never been contented with, she would grasp that she was one of those women who kill their husbands, who ride a hobby-horse over them, and make them put wheels on it for good measure. I thought of how I had taken Simon to buy the papers at eight. While he sat in his push-chair, white-haired, and I wheeled him, pointing out the clover and the dandelions, a man had been hanging himself in a garage I could see as I walked. There was no knowing who was doing what in their garages as the coach trundled along the road. Life changed so suddenly, and human beings were taken from the heights and suddenly, within a morning, plunged to the depths.

After a while we passed Warren House Inn, where a guest woke up at night to discover a man's body in the chest of drawers. In the morning he was told, "It's only fay-ther." Opposite where the ponies grazed there was a fire that had not died for a hundred and thirty years. There was no death, I knew, and even Mr Shipman would one day become one of the "Shining Ones". His body was dead, and the post-mortem (which would be delayed because of all the drownings off the Cornish coast) would perish, but the important part of him – the soul and spirit that had fixed wheels on my son's hobby-horse – would survive. It was a pity that Mr Shipman could not have read about the Angels of the Essenes when I read them to my wife the night before, for then he might have learned sufficient about the art of living to know there was no escape into extinction, and to stay his cowardly hand. But then that was *my* hobby-horse – on which Mr Shipman fitted perfect wheels.

The inquest established that the balance of Mr Shipman's mind was disturbed, and he was buried in a little church where he attended Sunday school as a boy. The Minister spoke of the Valley of the Shadow, and said that we did not know that Mr Shipman had not seen the light at the end of it. Mr Shipman's cousin expressed the opinion that his wife had "driven him to it".

A COBWEB CHRIST AND A FEATHER DUSTER
(OR: A PILGRIM'S SCALLOP IN AN ANGELIC LIGHT)

We stopped at Buckfast for two hours. We walked up to the Abbey which Canute founded, and which had been rebuilt in the twentieth century. From 1539 to 1882 the Abbey was a ruin, and not even the foundations were visible when some French Benedictines settled there. They found the foundations and the monks did the rebuilding from 1907 to 1938. The grey square stone tower looked clean, and inside the brickwork was new. The mosaics and the corona were imitations of German Romanesque work.

We wandered down to the Chapel of the Blessed Sacrament at the back, which the guide-book said was added in the 1960s so that the monks could have a place of stillness apart from the tourists. We recoiled. Through the glass, in a garish blue light, was a huge Byzantine Christ in stained glass; five times life size and verging on the abstract. There was an abstract mural nearby. I stared at the forehead. It looked at if it had cobwebs across it. Of course, it was magnificent that twentieth century monks could make all this by themselves, but why had they fallen back, archaistically, on the past? Why was there so much imitation? This was a cobweb Christ.

We walked up to the Post Office and had a cream tea. We ordered it in the Post Office itself and carried it out into the small garden and ate it among roses. A chaffinch perched on the next table. When we had finished our scones and jam and cream and drunk several cups of tea in the sun, we wandered along to the House of Shells and went round the exhibition. There were shell flowers (flowers made entirely from shells) dating back two hundred years, and there was a sea-devil rising from a melon shell. There was a giant clam – the longest shell in the world – and there was an underwater display under mauve fluorescent lighting which threw a glow on both of us and made us appear like luminous Angels.

There was a scallop shell there – mounted, for it was an old badge for pilgrims – and it was inscribed with Sir Walter Raleigh's poem, "Give me my Scallop shell of quiet", the poem he wrote while awaiting beheading in the Tower. Looking at it, I knew I preferred being a pilgrim in the world, for all its movement, to the life of stillness of the monks in the archaic and abstract surroundings of their new chapel.

When we came out, I went to the Abbey bookshop and looked at a book of Herbert's poems, and my wife went to another little shop and bought a feather duster for her mother. And walking with her later, I saw her as an angel with a feather duster, with whom, by my spiritual endeavours in the world – the moments of stillness I stole from the movement of the crowds – I would sweep away the cobwebs in the country's soul and reveal the third eye of its illumined, peaceful vision.

AN EAGLE AND A BASKING SHARK

Mrs. Shipman's cousin Jean, a wizened, crabbed woman, had been in the house as Mrs. Shipman was away for a couple of days and she did not want to be alone. She had apparently pointed out that I had scratched the table with my typewriter (despite the padded cover), and that I drank too much coffee and therefore used the electric kettle too much.

To escape, I took my wife to the local cinema to see *The Eagle has Landed*, a film about a German attempt to kidnap Churchill. Alderney, the Channel island, had been recreated in the local Cornish harbour, Charlestown, and the IRA man came flying through the Pier House Hotel window, Michael Caine wandered on the Charlestown quay, and the too trusting German with an eye patch faced his firing-squad against the breakwater below the Harbour-master's house, with a final adjustment to his coat and tie, at low tide.

Next morning (a Saturday) my wife set off for Par beach to make the final arrangements for our beach hut. I typed until 11.30 and when I went through to the kitchen for coffee, Jean was sitting there. "Haven't you got the good manners to come through and see your wife's aunt and cousin? They've all gone to Par."

I was amazed. "Are they here?" I asked.

"They dropped in," she frothed negatively, her mouth a forbidding slit. "Driven all the way up from the other end of Cornwall, and you couldn't come through and see them."

"What a pleasant surprise," I said. "But why didn't someone come and tell me?"

"They were out in the garden near your window," she complained.

"But when I concentrate I concentrate," I said. "I'm not aware of people in the room or what they say, let alone what's going on in the garden. Why didn't someone come and tell me?"

I was civil, but firm. I was amazed at the violence of her emotions. I watched her with eagle eyes from my great height, and circled over her, self-defensively, to make sure that she was out of my range. I wheeled over her and watched her turn beneath.

My wife returned from Par with her mother, Aunt June and

Henry, and I was there to greet them enthusiastically outside the gate. In the kitchen I caught up with their news. Porthleven had been sold; what did they think of the buyer? Was Henry still fishing with "the Reverend"? What about his sailing yacht? We all sat around and talked, and ate a lunch of rolls and pork.

That afternoon my wife and I took Simon to Par beach to see the beach-hut, which was a brown wooden box, and Simon jumped in a deep hole in the sand. When we returned, Jean was still there. She was better, as if she was basking in the terror she had caused.

That evening my wife and I went down to Charlestown Harbour to look at the places that had been filmed for *The Eagle has Landed*. It was late dusk when we looked in at the little shell-shop, and I heard the owner say in a Cornish accent, "There's been a shark round all day. It's a six-foot basking shark, and it's got a wounded tail."

We hurried down to the 1790s harbour wall and peered into the gloomy sea towards the bright yellow lights across the bay, and there was a triangular dorsal fin just off the end of the short stone "pier" where some thirty locals and holidaymakers were standing excitedly and pointing. As we joined them and craned over their shoulders, the shadow of the shark was visible in the clear water. It nosed slowly in and crossed the harbour bar, and as the thirty people scrambled down the steps and walked back along the harbour wall to keep pace with it, it swam slowly round the harbour before turning and heading back towards the open sea. Its sinister shadow was right beneath me, as fifteen foot up, I followed it like a hovering eagle. Just once it surfaced its dorsal fin.

"It's gummy, it's got no teeth," an old fisherman said. "It's only a plankton shark." I watched its black shadow nose lazily out in the clear, twilit water. There did not seem to be a wound in its tail. It might have had no teeth, but I was glad I was not down in the water with it.

When we returned home, Jean was basking in her front room chair. She nosed into the kitchen. I went to the bathroom and saw a set of false teeth in a glass. I did not worry about her negative comments. They were "gummy" comments. She had no teeth. Also, she dwelt in different surroundings from mine. She lived in the little life with its unharmonious pettinesses, she was confined to the low restricting waters of materialism like the basking shark, whereas my domain was the upper reaches of the air, I could soar through my typing like an eagle. She had nosily intruded into my haven just once, trying to terrify with her dorsal fin which looked as sharp as a thorn, and she would continue to live at conflict in her world, instead of feeling a lofty peace and serenity, in tune with the universe, in the upper atmosphere, like me. I felt sad that she was condemned to her world, and I was glad to have the free heights of mine.

A SANDCASTLE AND A SUN-KITE

We spent all that day on Par sands. I sat on my sun-couch in my swimming-trunks and gave my body to the sun and the air and the wind. In the morning the tide was out half a mile, and it came in quickly after lunch. A girl with a good body in a bikini the colour of the sun flew a kite. It took a long while to get it up, and she stood in front of me, seemingly oblivious of the people on the beach, and played it gently until it rode the wind. Then she tied the string to a lump of wood and left it to soar, a yellow sun over the sand dunes by the beach-huts. It was good that the kite displayed a sun.

Later I went down to the sea with Simon. I shovelled some wet sand into his yellow bucket and upended it when the waves went out, and we watched the sea wash round the castle's base, dissolving and shrinking it, until the top crumbled like a Carolingian tower on a deserted Scilly island coast. I made a dozen castles, and the sea swooshed them all down, and after three gentle waves there was no trace left.

"Sea won't knock *that* one down," Simon said, pointing to the one farthest inland – but it did, and he looked disappointed, as if he were not familiar with the ravages of time.

"You stood in a castle the other day," I reminded him to console him, and he said, "I did," and I could tell that he remembered standing in the crumbling ruin of St. Catherine's Fort, which dated back to Henry VIII, the sea below him.

I left the flattened rampart and returned to my sun-couch and watched the kite which soared safely above the waves, high up on the wind.

That night my mother-in-law went to see Mrs. Shipman. When she returned she and my wife spoke at length in the kitchen. When I went in she reiterated, "I was just saying, she feels she has no purpose in life now that she's a widow and alone, she can't see the point of carrying on. She told me, 'I've got nothing, it's all been knocked down. I haven't got any children. You've got your daughter and your nephew, but I haven't got anybody. I can't see the point at all.'"

I said, immediately running up my kite, "I know it's terrible, but I've got ten books by my bed that would help her. They were all written in the 1890s. Her purpose will not lie in social relationships with non-existent daughters or nephews, it will come from making a journey through herself until she locates the 'peace that passeth understanding'. If she searches through all the teachings in the Middle and Far East as I did, she will find that the answer is within herself, in her mind, or rather in her soul. But for that answer to be born, for the deepening to take place, suffering is essential. I had to suffer for it, and so must everybody, so will she. I know it sounds hard, but this suffering she must do is a gift, if she will only see it in the right way. Traditionally, the Church would help her find peace, but the Church is in decline, along with our society and our civilisation, and the Church probably won't be of much help. I had to go to the Far East for it. The saints of the past went out into the desert for it. The best thing that she can do is to shut her door to other people like you, who only act as aspirins, or morphine, and get on with her grief – which is terrible, I know. But until she has done her emotional prison sentence, there cannot be a release. The trouble with our society today is that there is no one, except for some writers and a few good parsons, who embodies the Truth, and so when a woman is bereaved late in life, she is taken unprepared. She questions the values she has had, the clothes and the houses she has wanted suddenly seem the illusions that they are, and she discovers too late that it is the real things that matter. The smart ones latch onto the real things when they are young, and they hold on to them, and are not deflected by criticisms from those who are living in Maya, the world of illusion."

And as my mother-in-law turned away, unable to control this dipping, dancing kite that mocked her concern, I realised that Mrs. Shipman had built a sandcastle against the sea, and, like little Simon who was not yet three, she was shocked that it had crumbled. It would have been better if she could have flown a kite instead, for she could have put that up at will and taken it down again. A sandcastle was doomed from the beginning, but a kite would have done her until the day she died.

THE WATERS OF THE OCEAN, THE UPPER REACHES OF THE AIR (OR: THE SUN AND TWO WORLDS)

We looked at alternative places in Cornwall with space for small children. We drove to the Duporth Holiday Chalets, a holiday camp on the nearby cliffs. It was like a housing estate, and there were hundreds of cars in the car-park, the notice of which said "Please park prettily". We walked in the evergreen gardens, where the sound of running water never left us, and passed the huge dance hall and a sing-song. It was all a bit vulgar, it reeked of the material world, and I didn't like it. So we went and looked at the caravans near Par Beach, which were more simple. They looked like the homes of gipsies by a road, complete with washing on the line, and I found the air of squalor faintly depressing.

We returned to our beach-hut and sat in deck-chairs, and while Simon played in the sand I said to my wife, "You know, thinking of Jean, I conclude that there are two worlds. Hers is human, mine is divine. Hers is the world of the waters of the ocean, and mine is the world of the upper reaches of the air. She is a shark, and I am a sea-eagle. I fly up to the sun. It is absurd for the eagle to say, 'It is ridiculous to live in water like a sea-mammal', and it is absurd for a shark to say, 'It is ridiculous to live in the air and soar', and to try and splash the eagle's wings to keep it earthbound. The fact remains, the eagle points the way to the sun."

"I agree," my wife said, "but whereas the spiritual world needs the material world to do the shopping, the material world doesn't need the spiritual world."

"It *thinks* it doesn't," I said, "but that is its blindness, as Christ pointed out in his story of Mary and Martha. It skulks away from the sun in the depths of the ocean, and does not know true peace, and so it will be reborn to more suffering. If the sea-creature could see truly, it would emerge onto land, like a seal or crocodile, and try to grow wings to fly so that it could be above the clouds and near the sun." My wife was silent.

"Anyway," I continued, "the eagle will lie down with the shark in Paradise. Until then, there is enmity between the eagle and all sea-fish. The eagle eats the fish, as I do when we attend a social occasion. I devour the sea-people in my art, all true artists do. It's also impossible for the eagle to *represent* sea-fish, so I can forget about being a politician, either in Britain or in Europe. I would have to be a full-time land creature, I wouldn't have time to soar on a St. John of the Cross-like flight, and I'd have to sympathise with the material worries of crabs who scuttle under their self-blinding shells and who belong to the sort of people Pope spoke of: 'Most souls, 'tis true, peep out but once an age.' It's bad enough being a teacher, for at school I have to pretend I am a land-creature instead of an eagle."

Simon had put on his Tiger-mask, and he jumped out from behind the beach-hut door, roaring terribly, and shouted, 'Frighten Mummy.'" Mummy said, "Very frightening." And I was suddenly reminded of two lines in Eliot: "Why should the aged eagle spread its wings?" "In the juvesence of the year/Came Christ the tiger." If I had to come down to land sometimes, then the tiger would be my ally. The tiger would make the land an unsafe place and make the divine air, the world of the higher mind, of religion and poetry, more appealing. And I saw souls flitting and dancing where the bees buzzed in the sea-holly.

CARAVAN PEOPLE AND A FUN-HAT

Having had the idea of renting a caravan on Par Beach next year, I did some unenthusiastic homework by picking a good caravan and calling on the owner, who lived next door but one to my wife's uncle. She was elderly, and with an impeccable London accent she invited me in and we sat down while her bald Cornish yokel of a husband stood and grinned in the doorway. In a very upper-class manner she told me she had lived in Stanhope Gardens and at other fashionable Kensington addresses, and she mentioned Bailey's Hotel as a place where her boy-friends had taken her for a drink. Her yokel of a husband nodded and grinned. She said she had sold the particular caravan I wanted (F25), and that she was selling her other two caravans for £450 and £350.

My wife had said she wouldn't mind buying a couple of caravans secondhand and renting them, so I showed interest. "But you have to be on the Council waiting-list," the old lady said. "There is a list for those resident in the borough of Restormel – that will take two years to clear – and there is another for non-residents, which is already eight years' long. There is a third list for those who already have a site and who are waiting for a second one. The whole thing can be wangled, though. If you get a relative, your mother-in-law for example, to put her name on the list, in six months' time you can ask the Council if you can buy from me, and even though you're not at the top of the list, they will say Yes. For many of the names on the list are duds. Go and see Mrs. Underwood at the Council. She's very attractive. As to the profit you make, you have to pay a hundred and twenty pounds a year in site dues and rates, and you net about two hundred and fifty to three hundred per caravan, for it's only a twelve-week season at Par, and outside that you get the rag, tag and bobtail who are on social security and make a mess."

It was no good. We did not want to burden my mother-in-law with financial arrangements. We went to see Mrs. Underwood at the Polkeith Recreation Centre, a striking woman in her late forties who was probably attractive once, and she confirmed that we had no chance of obtaining a site now that the Council was tightening up, unless it was all done through a local resident.

I called in on a private caravan company to see if we could obtain a private site, and found myself speaking to the boss of the whole chain. He was fat and sixtyish, fierce-looking and softly spoken and all beaten up. "I'm closing at Newquay on October 1st," he said wearily. I gathered he had financial worries. For a private site you had to pay about £800 entry, which lasted eight years, and be residential, he said. Letting was not allowed, and you had to have a new caravan, which could cost around £2,500. I returned to Par Beach in some frustration, having walked through three people's lives.

The woman in the ice cream booth wore a black hat which said "Kiss Me Quick, Squeeze Me Slowly". She was fortyish, but attractive. She was knitting, and as I passed she smiled cheerfully and we fell into conversation. "Have you got a caravan here?" I asked.

"No," she said, "I cycled in from up the road, St. Blazey. My two children are here somewhere. I'm so bored...." We chatted about Par, and then she said, "My husband walked out and left me two months ago. He took all the money and I had to get a job. He's in the Navy and they didn't want to know, they didn't help me at all. I do school-lunches usually, and I took this as it was holiday time. This is my last day though, I can't stand the boredom any longer."

She chattered on. "Does anybody take you at your word," I asked, "and kiss you quick?"

"Oh no," she said, the mood changing. "Anyone who asks gets told that I'm old enough to be their mother. No it's just a bit of fun to make me feel better." And she took her hat off and tossed her head slightly to straighten the pony tail which I now saw was beneath it.

"I've got to think out what to do," she said. "If I had my way, I wouldn't see him again, but there's the children to think of. The younger one's clingy, you know, more clingy than usual. Anyway, caravans. Have you got a caravan here?"

"No," I said, "I was thinking of buying one, but I'm not going to now."

"There's no one to guard them in the winter," she said, "they get overturned by the gales and vandalised and I don't know what. You'd be better off at Pentewan, they have people looking after them there."

At that point two young girls approached the booth and asked for hats like hers, and then they ordered ice creams, and as I left her, I thought of her spending the winter up the road with her husband away, possibly for good, putting out subconscious signals like the wording on her hat. I thought of all the caravan people she might become a watering-place for, like the old yellow caravanserai I stopped at on my way to Babylon, out in the sands of the Iraqi desert.

A BUZZING BLUEBOTTLE AND A FROZEN FISH

I went to the Charlestown estate office to enquire about holiday flats. The girl smiled and said, "Go to the last house on the right, the one on the edge of the cliff overlooking the sea. She has holiday flats." I walked down in the rain and climbed the steep path with a lawn on either side to a modernised stone cottage. I knocked on the front door and a holiday-maker who had been playing cards in the window opened up and tapped on an inside door, and I found myself in a room with a stunning view of the harbour and the cliffs below, talking to a white-haired woman.

She was an active seventy, with glasses, and she wore red trousers and red lipstick. She described the flats and said she was not booking until January as she had to give her regulars a fair chance. She gave me a leaflet from a desk in the huge picture window, and, looking at the view and thinking I had found my eyrie – here the sea-eagle could perch over a typewriter and look for fish while business went on next door and upstairs – I said, "It is lovely here, isn't it. Don't sell without letting me know, will you. This is just what I've been looking for."

She said, not contradicting me, "Oh, it might be pricey, for it's a business as well, remember." And soon after I left and squelched back through the rain to my wife and Simon who were in the car.

That night, after a lengthy discussion, my wife and I returned after dinner. Mrs. Vine was trying to catch a bluebottle in a duster. She abandoned the attempt and sat us in comfortable chairs, and I asked her, looking down at the harbour, what she meant by 'pricey' as I would be interested in buying. She looked at me and said, "Are you psychic? You read my mind. I *am* thinking of selling as I haven't been well. I'm seventy now, and I've been here twenty-three years. My husband had six years to live and he lived twenty because the air's so good. I've done holiday flats for nine years, and I'm ready to retire, it's getting a bit much for me now. I've been very happy here. I first saw the place during the war. I was in the Admiralty, and we had to make a survey of the harbour, and I sat on the beach down there when it was full of barbed wire and thought how lovely this cliff was. My mother was with me, actually. She died before I bought this place, she never knew I came here. Anyway, I'd like to go to Jersey to live with my nephew and his wife. We're very close, it's more like a mother-son relationship. Now I don't know how much you have to have to get into Jersey, but I understand I will need fifty pounds a week for a flat there."

She prattled on, buzzing like the bluebottle I could hear as it made low passes, zooming from end to end in the room, and it took me three-quarters of an hour to wring a price out of her: "Thirty-five thousand at least. After all, it's freehold. We had a devil of a job getting the freehold from the estate, we had to take counsel's opinion, and it's only one of two freehold houses in the village, and it's possible to build in that front garden and the back garden. There's a lot of back garden, you know." And she took us through her kitchen and showed us an enormous lawn with two outhouses and a greenhouse. "It may be Providence, you know," she said. "It's very strange that you came up in the rain like that and read my mind, it hasn't happened before. It may be Providence that brought you. But," she said, suddenly changing her mind, "I don't have to sell, I can stay here, don't get me wrong," and the bluebottle zoomed on the window, and as if it were a thought that had escaped the normally careful controls of her conscious mind, she caught it tenderly in her duster, and drew back the double glazing, and flapped it out into the gathering dusk.

The next day I returned to the estate office and spoke again to the girl. I asked about properties in the area, and casually asked how much, just for sake of example, the property with the holiday flats was worth. "It's larger than the ones next to it," she said without hesitation, "and it's got more land, and it's a business. I'd say between eighteen and twenty thousand."

I took this item of information back to Mrs. Vine at lunch-time. There was no bluebottle around now. She was hunting in her freezer, and I explained what the estate office had said. When I mentioned the figure she dropped a frozen fish on the floor. It slipped awkwardly down the side of the freezer, and it took her some while to retrieve it. Then she reacted. "What cheek. Twenty thousand? I wouldn't dream of selling for that, I'd rather stay here, I don't have to move. The girl hasn't been there very long. She was being bitchy because I got the freehold through counsel's opinion. What cheek! Why, you see that property across the harbour, that *barn*. He advertised that in the *Times* two weeks ago for thirty-five thousand. In fact, he annoyed us. He had a ninety-nine year lease, and for ages he said 'I don't want the freehold.' We went ahead and broke the estate office with lawyers, whereupon he stepped in, on our back as it were, and bought the freehold for himself. No, I wouldn't dream of letting it go for less than thirty-five thousand."

I emphasised that I did not necessarily agree with the estate office's opinion, but the atmosphere was frozen now, and she showed me out holding her icy frozen fish. As I walked down the garden path another dream seemed out of reach.

TOY PLANES AND DOGGIES, AND A MERRY-GO-ROUND

We drove to Fowey to see the Carnival air display, and right on time, at 6 p.m., as we left the car-park, Simon sitting in his push-chair, the Red Arrows screamed by, nine red Gnats with yellow lights in their noses. We sat on a wall, and I pointed them out to

Simon in language a two and a half year old would understand.

They roared up into the sky, trailing red, white and blue smoke, and after disappearing behind large, scudding clouds re-emerged against blue in first diamond, then arrowhead formation. Then they dived down, wing to wing, and scattered in different directions, and one skimmed the water below us, and roared up into the sky, while another screamed above the trees in front of us at 760 mph and flashed over the roof of the house behind us, seemingly little more than twenty feet overhead, and hurtled up to the topmost depths of the sky. I held Simon's hand and squeezed it tight and shouted, "They're saying, 'Look how well we can fly.'"

He said bravely, "Yes, can we go now?" and just after I reassured him the plane came back, thundering overhead and roaring away, leaving a hundred reverberating echoes. For fifteen minutes they made low passes and shot high up into the sky, and Simon was quite at ease now he was used to them. I recalled the time I nearly had my head taken off by a low-diving Israeli Phantom in Luxor, and when I saw American jets going in against the Viet Cong just outside Saigon, and I thought what it must be like to be strafed by these terrifying machines, and I don't know why it was – whether it was the moving clouds or whether the noise had slightly disorientated me – but I felt myself giddily clutching the garden railings, just to cling on to earth and not fall deep out into outer space, and I held on to Simon more out of support than to support. Simon squinted unmoved up at the sky and said, "Planes too little to talk to me," and I knew he saw them as toys without men inside.

When the aerobatics were finally over, with one last spectacular fountain-like dive and fall-out of planes which raced away in different directions and did not reappear, we pushed Simon along to a field high up under the scudding white clouds. It had a view over Fowey sea, and we joined the several hundred spectators who stood behind a rope and watched the tug o' war between teams representing local pubs.

Then there was a police-dog display. There were three dogs, each of which looked like the Wolf in Simon's *Little Red Riding Hood*, and with varying degrees of discipline they walked to heel, lay, sat and stood while their handlers walked on. They jumped hurdles and a nine-foot wall and ascended steps to a high plank before rejoining their handlers. Then a plainclothes "villain" with an enormously padded right arm that was full of teeth marks "stole" a handbag and ran across the field to be brought down by his sleeve. Another "villain" fired shots from a long gun at one of the dogs which, after whining and straining at its leash, chased him and brought him down. "He was a burglar," the loudspeaker announced as I recalled the gunfire of the Libyan Revolution and the shooting round Saigon.

"There," I explained to Simon, "man went bang bang but the dog helped the police."

"Yes," Simon said delightedly, "man went bang and doggie caught him," and he was completely at home with these images of danger, too. Fast planes and savage dogs were part of the safe universe he had inherited, they were toys and doggies. They were there, like the crescent moon with its eyes and nose, they were an aspect of good that contained evil, as I contained his occasional naughtiness.

On the way home we stopped at a fair, and Simon had a proper adventure. He went on a small roundabout. First he had a ride in a steam-roller, which he thought was a train, and then he had a ride on a boat, which he drove. The boat went round and round in a fast, dangerous, exciting blur of which he was a part, in which he was involved. He was not a spectator, and the safe world out there had ceased to be for the giddy whirl of this slowly trundling merry-go-round.

THE LITTLE LIFE AND A MIRRORING HIGH SELF

I had seen Mrs. Cumberland when I was watching a thousand house martins and swifts soaring up on a thermal current one warm evening. She tottered down to her greenhouse, a noble eighty-four, her arm in a sling: she was suffering from incurable cancer, as her white face showed. Her son was on leave from the RAF, and he had told me that the nine boats in the bay were naval minesweepers.

"Jean took Simon in to see Mrs. Cumberland, "my wife said as we headed off for Padstow. "Mrs. Cumberland loves children and she watched every move Simon made and said, 'I love to see them developing.' Jean said, 'Oh, I've no patience with them half the time,' and Mrs. Cumberland said, 'You must learn, you must work on yourself.'"

I had just been criticised by Jean for not helping to pack the car, or so my wife told me: "She said, 'You'd think he was Lord of the Manor the way he sails out and leaves you to do everything, it's a good job you're young and can do it all.'" I had been typing up my researches into Huna, the Polynesian Mysteries which believe that the low self must give *mana* or vital force to the High Self, which can then reflect the Light of God in its mirror and beam Light back, and I immediately said: "And Mrs. Cumberland is very wise. Jean *does* have to learn patience. If she had patience and worked on herself, she might break the seal round her heart which prevents the golden flower of her High Self from emerging, she might develop from the bud of her low self to the full bloom of her High Self."

"But she thinks you're unfeeling and intolerant," my wife said.

"I'm no more unfeeling or intolerant than a teacher who says to a girl who will not do her homework, 'You *must* work.' You're a teacher, should you be unfeeling towards, and tolerate, and explain that she *must* work? It's the teacher who does nothing who is tolerant, who is unfeeling. Jean is a low-self person who has to discover her middle self, let alone her High Self. She has done no homework, so she will have to repeat her life in a new incarnation. Fair enough, that's her choice, but the trouble is, she therefore stunts the growth of all about her with her low pettiness. It's the little life." And in the ensuing silence we passed Roche Chapel (Tregeagle's Dilemma), on the top of which a saint perched like St. Simeon Stylites a hundred feet above the central Cornish plain.

We had our sandwiches near Padstow, overlooking yellow sands and the sea, and my wife drew me a map and I said, reading her mind, "You are about to ask me why it's low tide on the north and south coasts of Cornwall at the same time, is that right?" It was: I received hidden powers from above. We went to the Tropical Bird and Butterfly Gardens, which are near the Elizabethan Place House and opposite a pump dated 1592. We walked round the Gardens and observed, through netting mostly, Chilean flamingoes, a crowned crane, lorikeets, love-birds, hoopoes, a minah, a macaw, and a host of other species and butterflies. I kept thinking of Blake's line, "Robin Redbreast in a cage/Puts all Heaven in a rage." Then we drove along the coast to Newquay and past golden, rocky beaches to St. Agnes, where we visited the model village.

It was gardens again, with models of Cornish buildings that were smaller than Simon: Trerice Manor House, Restormel Castle, tin-mines, Polmear cottages, Penzance heliport, Norway Inn,

Culdrose air station and the like, including the hideous Truro County Hall. It was the little life to scale, measured accurately (and not inflatedly) in terms of Simon, its Lord of the Manor; the world of the low self in all its smallness. We went through an arch, and were dwarfed by a gigantic Mad Hatter and a huge Alice, and now we were in Fairyland, and here, in all its correct proportions, was the magnified world of the imagination, of the High Self of religion and poetry and art. We walked through more gardens and at each turn encountered scenes from children's tales and nursery rhymes – Simon saw Little Red Riding Hood and a moving Wolf, and Snow White and seven moving Dwarves – and in one scene there was a tree with eyes, a nose and hands.

Later we went down to St. Agnes bay and ate a cream tea in a café, and later still, standing under cliffs thick with bracken and purple heather, I did my Huna breathing exercise. I breathed in through my nose and blew the air out through my pursed lips so that the colours were mirrored more vividly in my purified eyes, and I knew that, despite the little life in Cornwall, I belonged here, for the sun and air and wind would nourish my High Self, if only I could buy a Roche-like eyrie high up on some cliff where, eagle-like, I could contemplate the rough sea breaking gloriously on the rocks of some bay.

LAD'S LOVE

We went to hear a band play at a pub near Par Beach. It was next to the Polmear almshouses, which had fallen into neglect. I stood and looked at the ruined slate roofs and overgrown windows and open "church" doors and long chimneys where, since the 1850s, the local poor had lived, and I felt sad among the young people in the pub garden. The Lostwithiel Youth Band played *All through the Night* under fairy lights while dozens of lads jostled for beer and sat in the twilight. There were a lot of young children there, probably from the caravan site, and the mood was the sort that might never have heard of the almshouses no one would support.

On the way home I stopped off at the house of the old lady who had the yokel of a husband, to tell her we would not be buying her caravans. They were feeding the dog with beetroot which stank, and Jim sat bald and beetle-browed and grinning under the bright main light while his wife sat opposite him and disturbed a silence that was as deep as the almshouses' neglect.

"Don't go into caravans," she said, "I'm sick to death of them. You have to put a bucket underneath for the oil, and you get filthy dirty, and there are thirty-six blankets to be washed, and the gas cylinder needs changing. Don't do it if you're not down here. They're putting the site rent up again next year, and the cost of caravan parts goes up each year, and it's so expensive to move the things, it can be twenty-five pounds a time if they ask you to change your site, and then all the crockery has to be packed away. They're squeezing the profits, and there's a limit to what people will pay. I mean, they won't pay fifty-five pounds a week, will they. They're pricing themselves out of a market. We've had the best years. Then there are the people who are on social security, the winter lets. That's why there's a list, there was never a list three years ago when it was summer lets only. The good families, the Hodinots, the Hancocks, the Griggs and the Williams" (she stated her own name with pride) "won't touch them."

And Jim interrupted to say in his rich Cornish, "We're old, no, we are, we're old, and it takes us longer to do things. But if we was your age, I'd still do something on the letting side."

We talked about holiday flats as an alternative. The old lady said, "One of the white cottages down the road went for four thousand. We think it was bought by the woman who used to live over the road. She's on her own and she bought two cottages for eight hundred pounds each a few years ago, and did them up, and she sold one for two thousand and the other for three thousand, having lived in it to avoid some capital gains tax. Then she moved down to Mevagissey with her profits and did the same."

I expressed interest and brought my wife in from the car: I had dropped in for a minute and had got involved. "Oh," the old lady said, "I knew your grandmother and your great-grandmother. You look so like your grandmother. She often came to the shop two doors down." She had obviously lived in this house since she was a small child. "When I was first married, in 1921," she went on, "we bought a property...."

Her latest husband, Jim, grinned and took the story up and told a long, rambling, interesting tale about a cottage he bought for £90, which went through half the neighbourhood, and which would soon be on the market for £4,000 because its present owner was ill and hadn't long.

"There's another white cottage going soon," the old lady said, "this side of the one that's been sold. Don't go the other side, that's the Tilleys' and he's dying too. You could write to the Treffry Estate. It'll be about four thousand and you can let it for fifty pounds a week in the summer and twelve to fourteen pounds in the winter."

The elderly couple came to the gate to see us off and the old lady pointed out the white cottages through the arch of the railway bridge. Jim picked a handful of spikes from a feathery plant, sniffed them, rubbed them between his hands and pressed them into my palm like an elderly uncle giving a small lad a sixpence. "Lad's love," he said.

"It smells of sandalwood," the old lady added.

As we left he looked in the opposite direction and waved in a sort of salute, and looking down at my bare feet and sandals, I guessed how much he envied our youth, how much they both did. I smelt my lad's love, and thought of the profiteering eye we had in common, and the roving eye the old lady had evidently once had, and I was full of good feeling for a splendid old couple.

A GRANDFATHER AMONG RAS TAFARIAN HATS

I had to take Simon with me to the Housing Agency. We had to wait on the landing outside the door to the tiny office, while the housing agent finished with a visitor, and then he greeted us warmly, "Ah, the man from Cornwall, and with....How are you, darling?" He smiled at Simon behind his rimless glasses, all parchment yellow and thin and lined behind his beard.

He chattered while I handed over my rent and discussed the new agreement. "Where's your wife? At the dentist? Abscess? Terrible. I hate the dentist. I have a low pain threshold. My wife and my son and my daughter, they have the drill and don't think about it, no injections, nothing. But me...." He shook his head. "My dentist said, 'Your teeth are softer and thinner, you feel pain more readily.'" Simon sat on a chair, his bare legs just reaching over the edge of the seat. "Would you like a biscuit?" Mr Parker asked.

At that moment, as if she had been listening, the ravishingly dark Mrs. Parker, his Italian wife, put her head round the door and said to Simon, "Come in and have a biscuit."

"I haven't had a holiday for two years," Mr Parker said,

watching Simon's brown legs disappear round the door. "My wife has, but I haven't. She goes on her own. My Cornwall's Cumberland. I go up there for a weekend and hear the birds croak. They sing down here, but they croak up there, it's the mist. No, you can't have a holiday if you run this sort of business. You see, landlords' money is due at different times, and they ring, and if they don't get hold of you for a week or more, they think you've gone, and they come round here to see." (I had been ringing him for a week, and he was either permanently engaged or else there was no answer.) "And tenants complain about the plumbing." He shook his head. "The black ones are the worst. They come in here and loll on the wallpaper, chewing gum. 'Wanna bedsitter.' They say, 'It's because we're black you don't want us.' and I say, 'You *know* the reason.'

"And the Asian and West Indian landlords, they don't want them. They come here, rubbing their hands together and doing a Peter Sellers and they say" (he imitated an Indian accent) "'I want a gooda tenant.' I say, 'Here's the card of the Race Relations Board, you go and tell them what you're going to say next.' They look at me and they say, 'Europeans only.' I say, 'I told you, go and say that to the Race Relations Board.' They get angry. 'How did you know I was going to say that?' I've had slammed doors. You see, you can come in here and I can say 'No flat because you've small children' and that's that. If you go to the Race Relations Board, they're not interested. But if you were black, they'd say, 'What's the name of this agent?' And they'd ring me up, and I have to speak to them, the bastards. The law's all tilted on their side, not ours. Only the British could be stupid enough to let it happen, elsewhere they chuck them out. No, I've seen Tooting go down over the last five years. These blacks, they leave school and no one wants to employ them. They walk up and down the road in their Ras Tafarian hats and they go to the Amusement Arcade, and then the Notting Hill Carnival happens and they all pour in there and there's a riot. And many of them are young Mohammed Alis. They grow up so quickly."

He looked at Simon, who had returned with two biscuits and who was patting his beard with wondering curiosity. "They're like dogs," he said, picking Simon up and sitting him on his knee, "they know when someone likes them. I remember when my son was this age, nearly three, and now he's got more hair on his chest than I have on my head. My daughter went to Paris the other day. She's twelve but she looks sixteen, she had her first period when she was ten and her bust....She told her mother, 'A man tried to kiss me and I told him off – in French!'" He chuckled.

"No," he said, "the children grow up so quickly, and I'll soon be a grandfather." He said sadly, "Time goes by so fast, and it's the grandparents who have the time for their children, the fathers are all too busy making a living in goddamn places like this."

LIKE BRICKS ON SAND

After walking by a green sea at Worthing, we drove to Shoreham. Teresa was sitting alone in the back garden of her gallery in the early September sunshine. She was strategically placed so that she could see anyone who opened the door. She came through and greeted us, and we carried the pram out onto the sand and sat in the sun while she caught up on her godson.

I asked her how the paintings were selling, and she laughed and said, "I'm thinking big. I've decided, if I'm going to fall, I'll fall big and not small. I've just been to Vienna. It was terribly expensive, I spent eight hundred pounds on taxis and food in three weeks, and I had no hotel bills, but I've fixed up a business there, exporting paintings to the Continent. It'll have to be another company, it must be kept separate from all this. If you have more than one company, one will offset the loss of the other, it's what they all do. It's the same with boutiques. You see, the commission you get on those large paintings in there, which the artists bring and leave and take away if I don't sell them, is so little, and people don't buy much round here. It's got to be the Continent.

"You know, it all happened because of an exhibition sponsored by the British Council. The British Ambassador was there. It was for five British artists, and it was *rubbish*. Bridget Riley was one of them. Look, I've got the expensive brochure here, you see how much it cost to advertise their trash when good artists are unshown? Look, stripes. Wallpaper stripes. And one of the artists showed a huge tray of sand and just two bricks. See? All right, he was trying to say something about foundations of sand and foundations of brick, but it's rubbish. You see bricks on sand in a rubbish dump. And it took space that could have been given to a good British artist. An Austrian I know went, and he said to me, 'What's the matter with them in Britain? Have they lost their values?' I told him that the good artists are producing good works, but that the commercial establishment prefers bricks on sand. He said, 'Find the good works and export them to me.' So now I have a new business. That's how it happens." From her combination of frankness and her boast of expansion, I sadly realised that business was not going at all well. Her gallery was founded on sand.

After a while my wife took Simon to buy some striped Wellington boots she had seen, and, rocking the pram and putting Paul's dummy in his mouth when he cried, I brought Teresa up to date with my mystical progress, as I always did: sharing the experiences I had had and listening to her expert observations on them as a neophyte listens to a spiritual initiator. I told her about the faith-healing and she said, "Such people are good. There is no distinction between prayer and healing." I told her about the conference on the Essenes and the *Egyptian Book of the Dead*, and she said, "I always said to you there is strength in silence. Recently someone said to me, 'No, silence is weakness,' but it is not, silence is strength. If there were more silence, and fewer lectures, there would be more Light. People are looking for the wrong kind of Light. They see it as out there, like a candle or an electric light."

I told her about Dot, and Teresa said, "Those who find the Light do not have to trail round the country looking for the right group. They can find it at home, in the Church. She is sitting at lectures, but she should sit in the silence of a church. No "group" will work because everyone is at a different level of spiritual development. You at your level cannot tell others what to do because they are at their level, it may be that they are below your level. You can tell them the truth, in which case you are guided, but there is no need for a group, and the 'I–I–I' of the leader. Yoga, what is yoga? Prayer and helping people is how to live, and should we say 'I cannot help you through prayer because I am doing Yoga?' Everyone has a guardian angel who tells us things. She will learn that, through silence.

"I have just been reminded of it myself. I had a Green sculpture. In fact Green died recently. He was cleaning his car with a vacuum cleaner, and he stepped into a puddle and electrocuted himself, at sixty-two, leaving his work unfinished." I frowned and shook my head. "I did not know this," Teresa went on, "but all of a sudden I wanted to get rid of his sculpture. It was no longer living for me, it looked dead. A voice in me said 'Out, at any price.' So I rang the Tate, and they recommended two buyers. Then the Royal Academy came in, Casson. I am still waiting to hear the result. It will sell for a lot of money."

And I realised that Teresa was subsidising her gallery out of her own private collection which, I knew, she had formed when she was married to her multi-millionaire. She had shrewdly picked up a painting here for £50 and a sculpture there for £100, and now, through her foresight, they were worth hundreds and thousands, and she was selling them off one by one for a good price. These investments in her private collection were her bricks.

My wife returned, and Teresa showed us round her gallery. I recognised several of the pictures from my last visit, the previous February. They were still unsold, in particular the Guy Worsdells.

I saw three peeping Virgins on a shelf (see *A Vision in Winsor and Newton*) and when I pointed them out she said indignantly, "Do you know, a man came here several times, and he kept looking at them, and in the end he said, 'Can I take this one away and fire it for you?' My black Madonna. You understand, if I had wanted to I could have asked the woman down the road to fire it. I was minding my own business, I did not want him to take it away. Stupidly I said, 'Yes.' he kept it a long time, and when he next came back, I immediately knew it wasn't mine. You see, it's a cast, a mould *he* made. I said, 'What went wrong?' He said, 'I'm afraid it broke.' But look, it's just the same as mine, though the little hand round the angle is missing, and how could he have made a cast if it broke? My black Madonna was made of stone, and stone doesn't break easily. You have to try very hard to break stone. I have not seen him since – he's been up north, and I am waiting for him to come back – but I am sure he has made hundreds of cast Madonnas from my original and is selling them by the dozen in eight different colours for thousands of pounds. You see, it was my idea, not his, and there is only one like this in the whole world, and I chose not to make casts from it, and now I am sure he is making money out of it. I am going to ask him for my one back."

I thought of the gift shop at Buckfast Abbey where there were rows and rows of cheap Madonnas for sale, and I squirmed at the idea that a con-man should make peeping round angles a subject fit for mass production and misunderstanding.

My wife had picked up a pendant made from driftwood. The wood had been chiselled and burned and an Old Master Madonna had been stuck on it and varnished. It was £2.95, and I bought it for her. "Two-fifty for you," Teresa said quietly.

I imagined the driftwood lying on sea-sand. It had been thrown up by the tide, given to the artist by a great, rolling force of giving, the sea. Then I knew that the sand on which this gallery was built and the driftwood Madonna were worth more than dead sculptures and fake casts: in this case the sand was a surer foundation than the bricks. Teresa had made her peeping Madonna out of stone, which was as enduring as the pebbles on the beach down the road, and so long as her values were right, what did it matter about the business side, which was suddenly as ugly as builder's bricks on the wonderfully natural, sparkling sand.

SODA WATER AND A SCALLOP SHELL

The day of Paul's christening, a September Sunday, was wet. The family gathered for lunch at my younger brother's, and then we drove up to the little church in Epping Forest. The vicar, a silky white-haired, deaf man, greeted me with, "I looked out a candle for you but I forgot it." He poured water in the font from a bottle that was labelled "SODA WATER", and he giggled and said, "It's not what it says, and it's not Scotch either," inviting me to ally with him against the idea of Holiness.

Simon ran round the font and his cousin clambered up it and peeped over the stone rim, and my other brother gathered them both up and restrained them in a pew, holding them in improvised stocks (crossed legs over ankles), while the Vicar began his opening address in a suddenly serious tone: "It may shock you if I say that I think Baptism is immoral. We are making promises today that a child may not be able to keep. There are so many influences, at school and in society, which can prevent a child from keeping the promises of his parents and godparents, and in my view it is better for a child to make the promises himself, on his own behalf, when he is old enough to do so. I am not criticising the parents." I sat and thought of the appalling loss of confidence in the Church's spiritual power that accompanied a vicar's inappropriate anxiety to be naughtily with-it.

The godparents were only two instead of the expected five: my younger brother and a journalist friend. Of the other three, one had been taken to hospital and two were in remote parts of the country and could not travel down. So my wife and I acted as proxies and made the responses, reading from the cards we had all been given. We went forward with the two godparents for the Baptism. There was a scuffling behind us, and sounds of a struggle, and with a last defiant gasp Simon broke free and ran round behind the font for a better view as the Vicar scooped water in his scallop shell and splashed it on Paul's forehead, and marked him out for eternal life.

There was a moment of confusion when the Vicar, having finished reading from the card, asked us to form a procession and follow him. No one was sure whether we had to go up to the altar. We did. Then there was a closing address, in the course of which the Vicar spoke of the traditional nature of Baptism and said, "I cannot condemn anyone for clinging to traditional things. I do so myself. I am glad I am about to retire. I leave the future to a new generation of priests."

The congregation came back to my mother's for tea, and again the Vicar was full of jokes. He told me a long story about a man from Leeds University. He ended with a roar of laughter and said naughtily, "I've had three cups of tea, and there are no facilities in the church, and I've an evening service to get through." I looked at my journalist friend, who specialised in scoops of another sort, and I thought of the Church's dwindling influence and this man's reluctance to use the scallop shell. I was for quiet – I spent my life stating non-sense experience in sensual terms – and watching Simon fill a blue watering-can with wet earth out of the window, and muddy his trousers and boots, I felt that I embodied the true reflective values, while the Church was like the bubbly soda water on the drinks table.

PEOPLE LIKE US AND A SASH-CORD

I went to my SW7 flat to return my tenant's £200 deposit. Mohammed was a Kuwaiti diplomat who had spent time in Morocco, and he greeted me at the top of the stairs, all sallow-skinned and greying and stout in a Western suit, while his round, dark, heavily made-up wife beamed from ear to ear and his three mouse-like daughters scurried away in the background.

"Everything is here, nothing has gone," he said in a thin voice that ill-befitted his weight, "believe me," as I walked round with my inventory.

His wife said, "It is hard in England."

It appeared that Mohammed only worked from 8 to 1 in Kuwait. "We didn't use the washing-machine," he said, and I realised, looking at the beds, that they had spent three months sleeping *on* the sheets without changing them; they had covered themselves with blankets which had therefore been three months next to their skins. "The hoover was no good, so we used the brush," Mohammed said. I surveyed the filthy carpets and immediately checked the hoover, sensing that I could keep £50 of the deposit for damage they had done; but it was simply jammed with a hairpin, which I removed to sighs of enlightenment.

"Very good flat," Mohammed said as we resumed our tour, "except for the stairs. I have heart condition, I do not like the stairs. Believe me, you are lucky to have people like us. You want to have Americans and people like us. Don't have any Arabs. These people from Qatar, for instance, they have many small children who damage the walls and spoil the bathroom."

Mohammed told me he did a little business. "Last time I was here in England," he said, "I sent cloth*ers* back to Kuwait. I take a profit." His wife kindly provided baclava and pistachio, and I learned that his daughters would be staying on in London at the lycée. He and his wife would be going to his brother's and thence back to Kuwait. "Yes," he said, after I had washed my sticky fingers and counted out twenty £10 notes, "you very lucky to have people like us."

Next day they all left in a taxi. I arrived in time to see them off and carried an enormous leather suitcase down the stairs, and nearly ricked my back in the process. As we shook hands I noticed that a sash cord had snapped. "Three days ago," said Mrs. Mohammed, following my eyes, "it was no good." It clearly did not count as damage as it was my fault for having "no good" sash cords. It cost me £8 to renew the sash cord for these good people.

AN ARCHANGEL AND PERSONAL RESPONSIBILITY

I went to a conference entitled *Rediscovering the Angels*. It was at the Christian Community's Temple Lodge in Hammersmith on an

October Saturday. The hall was in fact the former studio of Sir Frank Brangwyn, the artist who died in 1956 and sometime friend of William Morris. His observation platform took up half the hall. A line of elderly ladies sat behind the white fence above the rest of us, and Sir Thomas Roper stood before pink curtains and a pink-draped altar with seven candles and a picture of an angel and spoke on *Angelic Impulses within the Unconscious Mind*. He was a presenter. As much as a media man like the presenter of *Nationwide* or *Tonight*, he took alien material and absorbed it and made it personal and understandable. From time to time he pointed to a blackboard on which was charted the angelic hierarchies according to Rudolf Steiner.

We lunched from picnic boxes in the studio, and after I had been for a cold walk to the river, Sir Thomas Roper and his sister and Elizabeth Sharp, followers of Steiner's, answered questions. Elizabeth Sharp was grey-haired and sallow-skinned and spiritual-looking, with grey eyes, and she said that the present epoch began in 1879, when Michael took over from the archangel Gabriel.

Afterwards I talked to my neighbour, a middle-aged woman whose husband had died an alcoholic, and who had found that God helped her in numerous small practical ways. "I say 'It's your problem, God,'" she told me, "and when it turns out well people say 'You are lucky', and I say 'It's all because of up there'." We discussed the chakras, the psychic centres which are the gateways for the angelic energies, and as Elizabeth Sharp was standing nearby, we approached her and asked for her view on the workings of the chakras, to which she replied by quoting Steiner.

I said that Steiner had little to say about mystic illumination.

She said, "Oh, illumination's a relic of the old age. Mystics belong to the old Christianity, when men were obscured from the angelic intelligences and so they experienced Light as a compensation. Today man is not obscured as a result of the change in our epoch, and he can speak with angels, and so he does not need illumination. Also he has personal responsibility, which means an ego, and so he cannot see the Light."

I frowned. "But surely, man is a being of Light and becomes *more* of a being of Light," I objected.

"No," she said, the representative of a sect that had to regard Christianity as out of date so that it could be "born again" (in the wording of her leaflet), "no mystics can have illumination now, not since 1879."

Who fixed the date 1879 as a turning-point?" I asked.

"Steiner did," she said.

I did not believe a word of it. Illumination was eternal, it had not suddenly stopped happening because the epoch had changed. To believe as much meant carrying the hierarchies to absurd proportions.

The middle-aged woman wore a scarf round her head. She was asking about clairaudience: "I've heard a babble in my ears, in the middle of a supermarket, and I felt I was leaving my body."

Elizabeth Sharp said, "Oh, that's to be discouraged. You should have personal responsibility, and any form of illumination or sound that comes in diminishes your personal responsibility, that's what Steiner would say."

And as the woman with the headscarf turned away, disappointed and shaken and confused, I turned away to console her. We would ally against this archangel Steiner, who died in 1925 and who had taken away Elizabeth Sharp's personal responsibility for her ideas, and made her a mouthpiece for his own dubious system.

A CLOWN AND A VOLCANIC ERUPTION

At the end of October we went to Worthing and walked on the wet front, and I showed Simon a primitive chalk drawing a child had done on the pavement. It was of a clown, and he had a pointed hat and buttons and round cheeks and a sad, sad mouth, and Simon said, "He's got no arms," but they were folded across his front. Simon stood and looked at the clown for a long while, and I remembered how he had come home from the circus earlier in the week, holding a gas balloon that clung to the ceiling, and waving a clown's mask.

We drove to Shoreham and I carried Paul's carry-cot into Teresa's gallery and put it round the corner at the end while Teresa greeted my wife and Simon. She had large round rouge marks on her cheeks and a white mask of a face, and before she had taken in the new baby she erupted over me: "You know, I was just thinking, I'm going to the West Indies to live with my ex-husband" – she called him by his surname – "for he's retired there, and he's got all my paintings in a house, and I'll be with them again and away from all this dirty business. There's been a robbery. I loaned a thousand pounds worth of paintings and sculptures to the Hotel Metropole, including Connie's limited edition which is irreplaceable, and they put them in a showcase and the lot were stolen. No one wants to know anything or pay compensation, nothing, and they're all hiding from me." She had clearly been smouldering and full of tremors all day, and she had erupted volcanically over me. "It's the head man of the Hotel himself, he's involved," she stuttered, agitated, "I know. He's a crook. It's dirty, corrupt, it was arranged. I'm getting your brother to sue him. I told his man, he's not making a clown out of me, he will be hearing from my lawyers."

I thought of *Brighton Rock*. Who was the leader of the gang that was based in the Metropole? Colleoni, that was it. Teresa showed me three paintings she had done of flowers. "I wanted to paint beautiful, clean things," she complained, "and then this mess, this ugliness." She sat down on a chair, slumped back looking baffled and bitter and angry, and at that moment one of her supplying artists came in with his wife, and she leapt to her feet, far less calmly than she normally would, and strode to the front of her shop and engaged them in a long, worked-up conversation about a paperweight they were offering her. She talked about how easy it would be to sell their work, putting on an act, making out that business was all right, trying to convince herself that she could ride the loss of £1,000. She waved her arms to strengthen her points, her two cheeks heavily rouged, her face a white mask, and while we waited Simon, kneeling on the floor at the back of the shop amid layers of stacked paintings, drew a face and two round eyes and a nose and a sad, sad downturned mouth and two round cheeks and said, "Look, a clown." From the front of the shop Teresa gave a laugh and went on talking rapidly, performing for all she was worth.

CHAIRMAN'S ACTION AND A RED-EYED COMEDY

The interviews for the vacant Scale 2 post were conducted by Chairman's Action. In other words, there was no quorum of Governors – in fact, of the Governors only the Chairman attended – and the Chairman had the casting vote as to which of the two external and three internal candidates would be successful. I took one of the two external candidates round the school. She was rather drippy. The other one, I knew, had been in Tripoli and was a

THE CLEAR, SHINING SUNLIGHT OF ETERNITY

woman of the world.

Outside the Head's door again, I joked with the internal candidates, who were in my Department: "Perhaps one of you has dumped Mrs. Balmoral in the fish-pond out there, to eliminate the competition." They laughed, and the atmosphere had the hilarity of a farce, their nerves were relaxed, as I had hoped they would be. Young Miss True, who was in her second year of teaching and whose heroine was Ursula in Lawrence's *Rainbow*, had only been at our school seven weeks, and she laughed with leaky eyes. Older Mrs. Simons, who had been in my Department for four years, smiled nervously.

The interviews took a quarter of an hour each and were in reverse alphabetical order: two internals, an external, an internal and then the last external. The Head had changed the rules for Scale posts. She wanted them to be awarded for contributions to the school and for work on the curriculum, rather than for odd jobs, and so as Head of Department, I asked each candidate where she wanted to contribute towards Language Development.

Young, long, dark-haired and beautiful, Miss True interviewed well: in her seven weeks with us, she had started a dance club and a house folk club, and she had reformed the Departmental filing system and built a material bank. She wanted to contribute Language Development in years 1 to 5. Unattractive, warty, bespectacled Mrs. Simons came in with a strange, unco-ordinated walk and appeared thin in content by comparison. In her four years she had contributed little, and she wanted to contribute Language Development of the West Indians; she was married to a West Indian and had a half-caste son who made her late most mornings. The other three girls were not really in it. One had trained in Drama, and was not qualified to develop language; one was vague; and the woman of the world was good but inexperienced in Britain. She could have a Scale 1, if she would accept it. It poured with rain outside and became very dark, and the Head did not put on the lights because there was a power-workers' go-slow that was causing electricity cuts. Towards 5, we discussed which candidate should be given promotion.

The Head was reluctant to appoint as Miss True had been with us only seven weeks, and Mrs. Simons had not contributed enough: length of service was not the criterion. I protested that I needed the help in the Department. "There will be criticism," I said, "but we must meet it head on." The Chairman backed me up, and in the end the Head agreed a compromise. She was trying to save points because of our falling roll – the Inspectors were taking Scale points from us – but she agreed to award a Scale 2 to Miss True from the coming 1st January, on condition that another Scale vacancy would be held back until the following June. This should be for West Indians, and would probably go to Mrs. Simons. Miss True was called in and told of her success.

The Head went out to see the two internal candidates who had not been successful, and when I found them outside the Head's door, they were both looking very pale. Mrs. Simons was blubbering with red, swollen eyes, "It's so unfair. After all I've done…." I took her downstairs, wondering why she was so attached to the idea of the job. Had she, like me, got a bank manager on her back? I dived into the first door, the Deputy Heads' room, and began to explain that she had in fact taken a step forward in her campaign to be promoted, for she was nearer a Scale post. Outside the window there was a flash, and I interrupted myself to say, "Lightning," and it occurred to me that a similar lightning had flashed from Mrs. Simons' brain to annihilate me.

I came out and ran into the female Deputy Head. "It's like a French farce," she said to me, when Mrs. Simons had gone, tripping sloppily in her loose, unco-ordinated walk, "doors opening and closing, people avoiding each other, I've never known anything like it." But the truth was, it was comedy, not farce: it was about man – or rather, woman – as a social being rather than as a private person, and it had had a corrective purpose. For Mrs. Simons would have to face the blindness in herself, and the folly, that had led her to believe that she would get the job, when Miss True's personality, looks and dynamic outlook were so obviously more suitable. Mrs. Simons' red eyes signified the wound where she had gouged out an illusion.

A SPOON-FEEDING BULLY AND A PACIFIST

I went up to a local school to make a complaint to the Head of English. Our girls were not being taught properly under the new consortium arrangements. I parked and wandered past fountains to the receptionist who directed me upstairs to A2, where the Head of English, an elderly, white-haired, balding man was seeing a boy about career options in a large room. He smiled and waved me into a chair, and we chatted about the syllabus. He searched without success for past exam papers, and I detected chaos. He told me he was leaving at the end of the year because he was disillusioned with the comprehensive system. "We've had a hundred remedial boys a year for the last six years," he said, "and I've seen this school change character. I am a bully and a spoon-feeder now. I joined the profession to teach, not to bully or spoon-feed. I'm retiring early. I could stay five more years."

He passed me on to Mr Harris, the girls' teacher. He was eggshell bald with a small fringe round his ears, and he had a wide waist that gave him an awkward, top-heavy look that would have been easy to mimic. He gave very precise, correct replies, and he consulted his register unnecessarily in a fussy desire to be exact about our girls. There was an impression of killing thoroughness.

He was teaching the poets of the First World War, and to make conversation I said, "You may have some memories of the Second World War."

"Yes," he said, "I spent it in prison. I was a conscientious objector."

Startled into embarrassment, I said, "Good," though I believe in defending national values against Nazi-like aggression. "There weren't many who had ideals in those days," he said with pedantic attention to the articulation of each word, "but the young of today seem to have more ideals. It is very encouraging."

I came away. There were a lot of coloured boys in the long corridor, and there was a lot of noise in the playground. I thought of the two men. Both had ideals. One loathed the present and looked back to the past. The other, his subordinate, loathed the past and found encouragement in the present. One loathed his job, the other liked it. One loathed his society, the other liked it. One stood for standards, the other for humanitarian values. It was a measure of the change that our society had seen, that one was a has-been, the other's pacifist time had come.

A DOTTY BARD AND A COTTON-WOOL EAR

I went to Jesperson's and drank tonic, sitting in his leather chair, while he changed. I leafed through some books on the First World War, on which he was writing for an American publisher. "It's on a theme," he said when he returned, "I'm taking the money and running." I felt a little sad; he was a novelist, he should have been writing a novel. We drove to a nearby bookshop for the reading the ancient bard David Marchant was to give. Jesperson had been invited by the bard's wife, and having identified her, Jesperson shook hands. I found myself shaking the limp hand of a tall, distinguished-looking grey-haired man who was a cross between Yeats and Lord Shackleton. Then we plunged down the tiny staircase to a tiny brick cellar and sat in the back of the four short rows where Jesperson said, "The entire Hampstead of the forties is here." Jesperson let the side down dreadfully. He said, as a lull fell, referring to the bard's manic-depressive nature, "He's quite dotty, he's been in bins."

Maud Rand introduced the ex-surrealist who sat in a high-backed armchair, a whisky bottle within reach. She said, "I was in Paris last week, and they were asking about you, and this turn-out proves that people haven't forgotten you here either. It's an eternal occasion." Marchant read in a thin, prayerful voice rather like a Nonconformist preacher's. His poems were in received diction and contained many abstract words. It was as if he had cotton wool in his ears: he wrote in monotonous iambic rhythms, a dead language from a dead mind. There was little direct personal experience. It was not until half an hour had passed that there was a poem (about a field) where the 'I' was directly and freshly involved: he had failed to exteriorise his interior, and the evening confirmed that Marchant was a very bad poet.

The interval came after an hour, and the chairs emptied. Most went to the pub. Jesperson and I hung around and talked to Mrs. Marchant and to Maud Rand, and I heard Marchant say to a German poet, "I'm in great sympathy with the Baader-Meinhoff group. You aren't? Oh, I see." He was an alienating figure, and I went upstairs and found a copy of his verse.

The second half began with readings from George Herbert, in whose tradition Marchant clearly saw himself. He was right up to a point; neither were mystics. He seemed set for a good two hours – he obviously liked the sound of his own voice – and as Jesperson and I were hungry, we stood up and left, tiptoeing up the stairs and fighting with the shop door, which had shut us in.

Jesperson gave me an Arab meal. I dipped Arab bread into ratatouille and ate kebab on skewers, and rice and a garlicky salad.

THE CLEAR, SHINING SUNLIGHT OF ETERNITY

We discussed poetry.

I said, "A poet has to discover something in himself, and then the technical side carries it."

Jesperson said reflectively, with more than a touch of autobiography, I thought: "I wonder if he couldn't face himself because he was afraid to find out that he wasn't a poet."

And I thought of the cotton wool the depressive had put in his ears and round the inside of himself, to shut out the inner voice that also tormented the flawed genius who sat beside me.

AN IMPERIOUS NEO-PLATONIST, AND A GENIUS'S VOLUME OF VERSE

The ticket Dr. Rand promised duly arrived, and I attended the première of a film which had been sponsored by the Arts Council. It was near St. Paul's. I bounded up the stairs of a plush, modern building into a comfortable, full hall and sat through an hour about how Nature's patterns are reflected in ancient stone buildings. There was quite a lot on Chartres, and the sound-track was by Kevin Freeling.

As the lights came up there was perfunctory applause, and the audience drifted towards the Exit and down the stairs. A small woman got under my feet, and I found myself towering over the tiny but imperious Dr. Rand, who, with her cottage loaf hair and straight back and piercing gaze, looked just like Madame Blavatsky. She was with a tall, white-bearded gentleman who had been at the Marchant reading, and his lady friend. I thanked her for sending me the ticket. "Oh, did you enjoy it?" she asked. At the foot of the stairs there was a reception, and she drew away with her friends. I took an orange juice and surveyed the two hundred drinking, talking people, and to blend in, latched on to the first man who passed. He turned out to be Musical Director of the Arts Council, and he had a cautious attitude towards esotericism.

Later I found myself near Dr. Rand, who was sipping wine. "What did you think of the film?" she asked. I said in the course of my reply that some images evoked the Findhorn community, and she exploded: "I can't stand that set-up. I think it's phoney, commercial, and imprecise. I'm sorry, but this is my third glass of white wine. What I like about Kevin Freeling is that he's precise. There are no geniuses around in poetry or painting. He's the only genius in London today. I mean it, he's a genius."

I could not allow that to pass, so I objected that there are two traditions; one logical and mathematical and Pythagorean and Euclidian, and the other emotional and intuitive and mystical. I said that Freeling belonged to the first, whereas the Findhorn view of mystic unity belonged to the second, as did St. John of the Cross, and I said I preferred the second kind of genius to the first. I told her about Teresa in Shoreham, and said she was an example of a mystic genius.

The white-bearded man nodded and took my side. "It can be argued that the eternal world has nothing to do with logical geometry," he said. At the end of our exchange, Dr. Rand brought up Marchant and said: "He's an example of a mystic genius, isn't he?"

Again, I could not allow that to pass, so I said: "No, he isn't. It's one thing to have mystic experience from the inside, as Freeling hasn't, and to express it in good poetry, and it's quite another thing to stand in front of a painting in the National Gallery and reflect on the agonies and wounds of Christ. Marchant tends to do the second, and he's no more of a mystic than Herbert is."

Dr. Rand was very cross at this. She turned and introduced me to someone as "he doesn't like David Marchant", and then she stood apart, peering imperiously for Freeling who was supposed to be joining us at the end of the second showing of the film. (We had attended the first showing.)

Dr. Rand waited some ten minutes, craning her neck for Freeling, and then she uttered a cry and put her head down and charged for the swing-doors, having sighted Freeling's mop of bright grey hair. The white-bearded man and I set off in pursuit, and I saw Dr. Rand fighting her way through the crowd round Freeling, trying to reach the great man, who was holding a volume of verse by – none other than Maud Rand.

Freeling was a weird-looking man with a disconcerting squint, and he mimed a shady sideways shuffle and a furtive showing of the title to Maud Rand, who looked pleased.

I was appalled at the mutual self-congratulation. Had she called him a genius because he was a fan? I went off and bought the booklet on Chartres that was on sale at the cinema door, and as I left the two admirers were beaming at each other in a crowd of disciples.

In the tube I looked at the booklet. I immediately gathered that Kevin Freeling had applied geometric principles to ancient monuments to prove that they symbolised a Neo-Platonist journey from the One to the Many. His most recent effort had been on Chartres Cathedral, the maze in the floor of which he saw as a 13-pointed star. More interestingly, he had proved that the maze was based on a diagram in Macrobius' Commentary on Cicero's *Dream of Scipio*, a Neo-Platonist work.

Now I understood. Both Maud Rand and Kevin Freeling were Neo-Platonists, and when Maud Rand called Freeling a genius, she was in effect saying 'Freeling agrees with me.' So do even the most apparently objective judgements have a subjective base.

LAUGHTER IN THE DARK

"My tenant has had a breakdown," my mother said. "There were signs. Every day there was something abnormal about him. You know he was at Winchester and Balliol? He told me he spent four years on his course at Oxford, and then he never took his degree because he had hitch-hiked to London and he could not get a lift back. He missed the first exam. I thought when he told me: 'That wasn't very responsible.'

"He came to me because he was teaching at the School for the Partially Deaf nearby, and I immediately noticed he had no sense of time. He'd be lying in bed at eight-fifteen, and I'd say, 'You've got to be at work at nine,' and he'd say 'Oh,' and then get up very slowly. His room was in a terrible mess. He put wet sprout ends and potato peelings in the waste-paper basket instead of in the bin-liner I provided, and the chest of drawers was covered with a half-eaten loaf, butter in its paper, open, old socks and wet soap all together, and he'd put a cup of tea among it all so it tipped. One day he upset a bottle of milk so it was all awash. He'd prowl around at night. He'd go downstairs – I knew it was for the time – and then no matter how late it was he'd BANG his bedroom door, and then I'd hear him laughing in his room. He had no radio on, he just laughed to himself. He'd go off at weekends with an enormous rucksack, one so enormous that he might be climbing Mount Everest, and he never said where he was going. When he returned he'd try and let himself in through the front door with the wrong key. I used to think: 'Balliol, Oxford, and he can't even find the right key to the front door.'

"He was like it at work. I was going to ring the Principal of the School for the Partially Deaf when she called one Saturday afternoon. As I let her in I heard his door upstairs, and she had the good sense to go into the kitchen, where he couldn't see her. He came down the stairs with his rucksack. I called to him, 'Where are you going?' I wouldn't ask normally, but he'd been very odd. He said, 'Oh, to see my married sister in Manchester. She was married this afternoon.' He was going to disturb the honeymoon, in other words. I said, 'It's a long way to Manchester.' He said, 'Oh, I may go south, then.' His parents live in Bognor. I said, 'Will you be back tomorrow night?' He said, 'I don't know.' I said, 'But you've got to go to school on Monday.' He said, 'Oh, I'll be back for that, even if I'm not back tomorrow night.' The Principal heard this and shook her head. It was just how he was acting at school. The breakdown had been coming on. She left me and contacted his parents in Bognor and said, 'He's not to come back to school. He needs help.'

"His parents told him. He was so angry that he wanted to return and confront the Principal. But he didn't. He saw a doctor and was given some drugs. He was not admitted to any hospital. He left his parents, and he hasn't been heard of since. His father doesn't know where he is. He has just disappeared. I rang his father last night and asked him, 'What are you going to do?' He said, 'I don't know, I just don't know. We've tried everything.' I think he may commit suicide."

My mother sat in silence. I brooded. It was terrible to be that rootless: from Oxford to an alien room and teaching the partially deaf, and then off to nowhere fast at the weekends, with a rucksack. What had caused him to go like that? What had made him lose grasp of the "real" world, lose his grip over keys and watches, over the top of his chest of drawers and his waste-paper basket? And more frighteningly, what perception had made him laugh madly at night?

A STUMBLE AND A SLAMMED PHONE
(OR: A VICTORIAN POLLY AND THE MOON)

I had received two offers for my flat, and we were looking for a large property. An advertisement in *The Sunday Times* caught my eye – an "Enormous House" with four storeys, the top two of which needed improving – and the following Tuesday I rang the number from my Housemistress's room while an Old Folk's party next door made a background hubbub. I found myself talking to Stuart Williams, a self-employed-property-developer-cum-self-employed-estate-agent who had several companies. He said he worked from a place near home. He said the "enormous house" had been sold two weeks back, but later he rang me to say that the sale had fallen through because the buyer's wife had had an accident and was in a plaster cast and could not cope with the stairs. That December evening I drove my wife to see the mansion.

It stood in a waste land of Council flats Dulwich way, a former millionaire's row now fallen into decay. It was fortress of a place, a narrow towering Victorian folly set back from the road behind a wall with a drive up to the front steps and the massive front door between two columns, and there was a low wide garage beside it. It was dark save for a light in the lower ground floor.

We rang the bell and an elderly small man came to the door with a hooked nose and a Jewish cap on the back of his head. He extended a hand and welcomed us in, saying Stuart Williams had not arrived. He wanted to give us a drink, but we preferred to look round, and found our way up to the top of the folly and peered into derelict rooms with peeling wallpaper and bare floorboards, and gazed with dismay at the lights of the local comprehensive which adjoined the back wall.

Then there was a tread up the uncarpeted stairs and a well-spoken, carefully groomed, youthfully middle-aged, slim man with crushed ears came up. He wore a suit. I greeted him, and in holding out his hand he lost his footing on the top stairs and stooped into an undignified, grovelling position. He seemed a little put out at this mishap, and immediately launched into technical surveyor's English about joists and water-courses, pausing to ask if we understood his meaning.

Stuart Williams showed us round from top to bottom. He went into all the technical details, having seen a surveyor's report which the previous buyer had commissioned, and he presented himself as someone who had every contact one could wish for. He would provide unlimited tenants, he would obtain baths, basins and lavatories at special rates, he would advise on carpeting, he would introduce cheap decorators. He said, "If you do as I direct, you can sell this for a good profit if property values go up in the coming year." From the magnificent tapestry walls on the upper ground floor I could believe it. "Everyone's buying property now," Stuart Williams said. "I bought eighty-eight flats last week, and I bought another house yesterday. I live down the road in a house the same size as this. I shan't buy this one because I don't touch anything unless it brings me a thirty per cent profit, and with capital gains tax it would net me twelve to fifteen per cent. It would be different for someone like you."

The plan, I told him, was to let seven of the rooms on the upper two floors, and sell the property at a profit after a year. Outside in the cold garden, which was clods of earth surrounded by a brick wall, we discussed the financing of the plan. The problem was, I would be dependent on tenants to meet my monthly total outgoings. I was doubtful, but Stuart Williams insisted I could do it. He said, "I will say that your wife is employed in one of my companies as a secretary for a salary. I can get you the mortgage you'll need." He clearly knew how to raise money and pass it between his companies, and I could imagine his ending up in prison one day; he was a bit of a Stonehouse. He pressed me like a salesman, and I was coolly defensive.

We went inside and talked to the old Jew and his wife, who was sixty. The Jew taught Modern Languages in a grammar school in central London. He was retiring in two days' time after forty-five years' service, and they wanted to buy a house in Bournemouth. He told me he was a cousin of a well-known elderly Professor and literary critic. He said he had lived in the folly for twenty-seven years. Stuart Williams left, promising to obtain a quotation for me from a building society.

I rang Stuart Williams with some questions the next day, and was impressed by the way he had an answer to each problem I raised. He had the quotation. The mortgage was guaranteed. All I had to do was to add my capital and a mere £5,250 which I would borrow from a bank. He would guarantee seven tenants within two weeks of my taking possession. He would sell the house to a stockbroker when I had done it up. He would tell the stockbroker that it would cost him much more to buy such a house in a "good" area. I could always sell off the basement for £12,000 if the market turned against me. He wanted me to drive over and sign the mortgage application form the next day. I said I would have to see over the property again, and so that night my wife and I drove round the waste land of glass and concrete and entered the dark drive and knocked up the old Jew, who, with some incoherence occasioned by a bottle of whisky, stomped round ahead of us, turning on all the lights.

The next day I left a message on Stuart Williams's answerphone, saying that nothing could proceed until I had had a chat with my solicitor-brother; which I could not have until the following Tuesday night, when I had been invited to dinner.

The night before, on the Monday, Stuart Williams came round with the mortgage application forms. He was unexpected, and he stayed from 9 until 11, and kept asking if I saw any problems. "It takes imagination and courage to make a profit like the one you're going to make," he said. He was very cunning, he knew how indirectly to flatter. He was engaged in a form of brainwashing, and I did not like it. By introducing an element of coercion he had stumbled up the stairs of his argument.

To deflect him, I proposed that he should look at a plot of land I knew, which might make us both a profit, and when he flattered me by saying "what a sharp sense of the property market" I had, I proposed that I should help him with the estate agent's side of his business. He said, "You might be able to help me on Sundays. I advertise in *The Times* and you could take people round, the keen ones who want to be first over, for one per cent of the commission. On a thirty thousand pound flat that would amount to three hundred pounds. What you have to do is to find out their problems and solve them. I always have a nine out of ten success ratio." I grasped that this was the technique he was using against me. When he left my wife remarked that he never seemed to see his wife: he had talked of being at the office until 10 p.m. on the next day, and had tried to make an arrangement for Boxing Day.

I drove down to see my brother. We talked from 7.30 until 11.15 and covered the objections to the project: it would be difficult to evict tenants promptly in such a large house, for a judge might allow them to stay six months as I did not need the room, and so I might not be able to sell quickly; tenants might apply for a "fair rent" and involve the planning authorities, who might inspect for fire doors and outside fire-escapes and bathroom and parking facilities, and then close me; banks were not allowed to lend for property speculation following the collapse of the secondary banks, and so I would have a seven-year loan and would have to repay capital each month as well as pay interest, which would bring my monthly mortgage and bank interest to much more than Williams had said; only the first £25,000 I borrowed would receive tax relief. There were a dozen other objections. I drove home through thick fog, and when I came out of it I saw very clearly, and the moon was a brilliant frosty yellow.

I rang Stuart Williams the next day and left a message on his answerphone, saying that I had decided against the enormous house, and, briefly, why.

I rang him an hour later. He would not accept my 'No'. "All your points can be answered," he said. "You can gain possession from the tenants if you serve them breakfast. The planning authorities won't be involved, only aggressive landlords have problems like that, tenants are nice if you treat them right. You should tell your bank that your mother will pay off your loan out of the sale of one of her properties."

I objected that my wife did not want to serve breakfast, that I did not want to involve my mother, and Stuart Williams started to become nasty. He raised his voice and said, "Your brother sounds very inexperienced, he sounds muddled and ignorant. I deal with you, not your brother. I haven't time to deal with stupid solicitors who don't know what they're talking about."

I pointed out the risk that had to be considered.

"Of course there's a risk," he snapped, "but there's a risk in crossing the road."

I said: "I've got my family's home to think of. I'm not just taking a chance for myself, but for my wife and children as well. I stand to lose *their* home, not just my own." The pips went for the fourth time, and he slammed down the receiver like a spoilt child who had not had his way.

I walked slowly back home. Stuart Williams had revealed the self-interest in his motive. I thought he needed the commission to fund some of his flat- and house-buying. He wanted me to have the property because it suited him, not because it suited me, and he would stop at nothing to make me have it. He had violated my freedom of choice, he had stumbled again.

That afternoon I heard that the first (and larger) offer for my flat had collapsed. The enormous house would anyway have been out of my reach.

A FLASH IN THE CHEMISTRY LAB
(OR: AN ELBOW JOGGED BY PROVIDENCE)

The fire-alarm went at midday while I was on the telephone. I rang off and joined the hordes of girls pouring outside into the snowy playground. There was a fog and the air nipped the cheeks, the school building was a faint outline in a ghostly mist.

The Senior Housemistress bustled up and said, "This is it, this is the big one. The chemistry lab's on fire, and girls have been badly burned." I shivered, hands in pockets, over to where our house had lined up by the tiled gate. Three fire-engines screamed down the road and turned into the main gates, blue lights flashing – they were the red ones, not green goddesses, for the fireman's strike was just over – and then three ambulances whined up, and a couple of patrol cars disgorged squads of uniformed policemen.

The Deputy Head strode by, bald and flushed and tall, and said, "Mr Hosnani's experiment went wrong, and there's been a fire. Some girls had their hair and clothes on fire." Then I saw one of my English second year class, a notorious thief, being escorted by a member of the staff. The girl had her head bowed, and she was sobbing, and her hair was singed and burned brown.

"You're not hurt," I said, almost too sick to look, but saying the first reassuring thing that came into my head, whether it was true or not.

On the whole, that class was appalling, except for half a dozen little angels who sneaked on the misbehavers, six I called "the moppets". The class contained two brilliant thieves, who, within six weeks of their arrival at the school in their first year, had perpetrated no less than fifty thefts from other members of the class, who had been terrorised into keeping silent about their losses. The ringleader was Lisa Belfast. I had spent two hours in the Head's room with two uniformed policemen trying to crack all her expert lies about just one of the fifty thefts.

"You can be sure of one thing," I said, turning and hiding the welling lump in my throat beneath a veneer of caustic cynicism, "if *that* class has been blown up in Science, then Lisa Belfast is at the bottom of it."

I headed for the Medical Room. The warm air hit me as the swing-door shut out the cold – and I was sickened by the stench of burnt flesh. Then I heard the screams, the groans. It looked as if a bomb had gone off. Some sixteen girls lay, sat and stood in twisted postures of pain in the small room, many shivering and trembling from shock. All were being sponged by ambulancemen and comforted by stooping, crouching teachers, and some were being supported by one or two harrowed parents, who had arrived amazingly quickly.

Some of the girls had appalling burns, great rings of

skinlessness on their swollen faces, arms and legs, and many had limbs in cold water. Everywhere there were bandages, and one girl – one of my moppets – shrieked of her arm, "Ooooh, ooooh, it stings, it hurts, ooooh, ooooh." She was in the grip of an uncontrollable force, and Sister Moore, the flushed Head of Science, gripped her shoulders and said, "You're being very brave but it doesn't help to make a noise, think of the younger ones." One of the worst burned was sitting huddled under a sheet, her black cheeks white rings where the fire had burned her away. "Don't touch my hands," she screamed to an ambulanceman who squeezed water over her arms. Another who was very severely burned, lay in an improvised stretcher, shivering in several inches of water, whimpering feebly, too ill to moan. Several teachers had tears in their eyes.

I was stricken. I knew them all as human beings, I knew the strengths and weaknesses, the foibles and mannerisms and character of each. They were not limbs on an operating table. I was in a relationship with them all, it was horrible to see people I knew suffer so dreadfully, and I knew a little of what it was like to witness a disaster like Aberfan, when a whole community was struck down. I wandered from girl to girl, showing them the secure front they saw me as, just being there, saying what consoling things I could muster when the lump in my throat went away, and feeling very bleak.

The girls were moved to the fleet of ambulances which lined the main entrance, and soon afterwards the press arrived. The men gathered round the main gate, asking for a statement, and the Head, unsure of the facts and uncertain whether she should speak without consulting County Hall, shooed them away. Some of the pressmen went up to the local hospital, and one reporter for a national evening paper attempted to photograph the disfiguring burns on a girl's face. Other pressmen lay in wait for girls and took down as eye-witness accounts the rumours that spread on such occasions: there has been an explosion (as opposed to a flash), the worst injured were going to East Grinstead for plastic surgery, and one teacher, the pregnant Mrs. Runcey, had been pushed down some stairs in the hysterical panic and trampled to death by escaping girls.

The facts emerged during the afternoon. The Asian teacher had conducted an approved experiment which illustrated how a mixture of water and alcohol can burn in a controlled way inside a beaker. It should have been like brandy burning on a Christmas pudding, and he had invited the girls to gather round the beaker to look –

which was wrong. The appalling girls had been closest to the beaker, and, as he had confessed to another member of staff at the hospital, where he was treated for severe burns on his arms, he was jogged while adding more alcohol to the mixture. Girls – Lisa Belfast was the main suspect – had crowded him and jogged him, spilling alcohol on the naked flame, which went up with a WHOOSH! His own jacket was on fire, girls' hair and pullovers were on fire, and part of the lab caught alight. Several girls ran on fire into the corridor, and Mrs. Youldon, the enormous Housemistress, happened to be passing. She shouted, "Get back into the classroom at once." So the defined procedures of the school's administration were observed, regardless of the inconvenient flames.

The hierarchy had revealed great confusion and inability to cope, and in her disarray the Head had inadvertently switched on the tannoy in her room, and had unfortunately broadcast a number of confused and despairing mutterings: "Why aren't the firemen here? Where are the bloody ambulancemen?" One member of the hierarchy had flapped in and out of the Medical Room at the height of the crisis, giving meaningless instructions in an urgent tone.

To cap it all, the fire chief had said that the building was so badly designed that it would have been gutted in twenty minutes if the fire had burnt through the ceiling into the air-flues.

But all this was nothing beside the grand climax to the day. For *BBC News* devoted a whole minute to the incident in its 5.40 news, and the culmination of the story showed the return to school of two of the less badly hurt girls. And there, stepping out of a taxi, relatively unscathed because she had been behind Mr Hosnani's elbow, smirking at her greatest disruptive triumph and giggling scruffily at the sight of the camera, presenting herself before fifty million people in the very way that she presented herself to her class and to me, stood none other than Lisa Belfast. I had always known that when our school's moment came and we appeared before the nation, it would be by Lisa Belfast that we would be judged.

It was the next day that the damage to the school's reputation became apparent. A primary school cancelled its visit without explanation, thus adding to our falling roll. Distorted reports appeared in the newspapers, some very sensational. (These were deplored at the lunch-time Staff Association meeting, the "weekly hate meeting" I called it, for if they had flashed the Head's face on a screen for two minutes and hissed "Hate, hate, hate", they would have achieved the same flush round the heart that these protracted half-hour vendettas achieved.) In the local supermarket I overheard two ladies talking: "You'd think children would be safe in school, wouldn't you. You wouldn't think they'd blow them up there." There were mutterings that Asian teachers were poorly qualified and badly trained, and the staff decided not to send a card to poor Mr Hosnani.

Two days later three girls were still in intensive care, and the Head and Sister Moore were both exhausted. The Head kept forgetting what she was going to say, and her sense of time had gone; she could not associate days with events that week. Both she and the Chairman of the Governors had visited the parents of all the burned, but it was clear that one flash in the class of a weak disciplinarian had undone what she had spent four years striving to build up. Or, to put it differently, Lisa Belfast, who should have been expelled following the thefts, had survived to destroy all her hopes.

And yet, I cannot be that pessimistic. In my experience, some Providential good comes of every disaster or misfortune. "Why?" we ask, seeking to make sense of what we have surrendered or lost, and only later do we give thanks that it was taken away from us, for it was not right for us, and we did not realise that we were being protected from something. So I see the incident as a timely warning. The disfigurements, mercifully, were not permanent, and can we be sure that there was not a terrible weakness in the elbow that allowed itself to be jogged, a weakness that might, had it not been checked by Lisa Belfast, have resulted in an even worse disaster than that flash – a disaster of Aberfan proportions, in which a whole class, or, if the fire spread rapidly along the air-flues, *several* classes might have been burned to cinders? Perhaps the scruffy Lisa Belfast was in fact an angelic messenger from the divine who had intervened to *save* the school; in which case she richly deserved her place of honour on the *BBC News*.

IRISH FISHING AND A HURRIED GRAVE
(OR: A LITTLE PLACE AGAINST
CREEPING TIME AND DEATH)

Mr O'Leary lived near Tooting Common, in a seven-bedroomed house that had three storeys. I rang the bell by appointment, and he showed me round, a creased and crumpled Irishman with a melancholy, battered face and a thick brogue. His wife was a good forty-five, but she had retained some beauty; she was dark. She sat with their daughter by the back fire. I was set to buy, and Mr O'Leary and I discussed our plans in the main room.

"I'm just lookin' for a little pla-ace," he said in his Irish lilt. "My idea is to get a little place, somewhere nice in Norbury, for about sixteen thousand, and put nine thousand in the bank against a rainy day. That's what I want to do."

His wife came through and asked where I worked. "Oh, do you know Miss Scott?" she asked. "She was here for lunch yesterday afternoon, she's often here. You might have come when she was here." Miss Scott was a raven-haired, brown-eyed Inspector, a former displaced Headmistress who laughed with leaky eyes, and I thought what a small world it was.

The arrangement was that I should ring Mr O'Leary every week while I sold my flat. I warned my wife, "He's Irish, you are never sure where you are with the Irish." But I rang three times, and each time he said, "No news, I haven't found anywhere." The last time he shocked me by adding, "It's hopeless, there's nothing. I'm taking the house off the market. I may put it back on in the summer, when it'll be more expensive to find somewhere else, I don't know. But I'm taking it off now." It all sounded very Irish.

I saw Miss Scott a few days later. She came to my school one January day to see some of my young teachers. We sat in my room and talked teaching, and then she said, "But I'm off the subject. You've met some friends of mine," and for the next half hour we discussed the O'Learys. She said, "I met Vivien when she was a nurse. She was looking after my mother who was dying, and she was so good to her that we kept up afterwards. You know, they were left that house by another patient of hers. They were very close. The O'Learys were tenants of his and she nursed him and.... It couldn't have happened to a nicer couple. I think they're reluctant to move for sentimental reasons. Certainly, I saw a house with them last September. It was in Norbury and it would have suited them excellently. But he dragged his heels. He doesn't want to leave. I've said to them, 'As my name's been brought into it, if you're not moving, for Heaven's sake say so, so that they're not misled into waiting for you to move.'" I said I would go round and clear up the O'Learys future intentions.

I called unannounced two or three times on my way back from school, hoping to catch Mrs. O'Leary, but she was always "out shopping" and would not be back for two hours according to her daughter. Eventually I rang her and she asked me to call at 8.30 p.m. when her husband was there; and so I found myself sitting by an electric fire on a bitterly cold night while the creased and rumpled Irishman sat in a depressed melancholy. His daughter Edna was doing her homework on the floor, a project on Egypt.

"You've taken this house off the market," I said.

"That I have," he said, "that I have." I said I wanted to know his future intentions. "I can't say with certainty that I'll move out on the first of May or the first of June," he said. "My hands are tied, that's the trouble. My hands are tied."

It sounded very mysterious and not a little Irish, so I asked, "What is uppermost in your mind?"

He said, "I'm thinking of staying here three years till Edna leaves school. She's thirteen now. Then we may go to Ireland. You can get a little place in Ireland – the South – for sixteen thousand and I could have a nest-egg in the bank and get a little job and have some leisure, have time to go fishing. For you feel it when you go down to the south coast from here, you breathe that fresh air and you feel hungry. But up here.... Up here we're all hurrying towards the grave and we're eighty before we're fifty, aren't we. We're all going to a hurried grave."

He sat on in a melancholy silence, his skin loose like fine clothes gone to rags, and while I grasped that he had been fishing for a dream all along, first in Norbury and then in Ireland, I realised how important the nest-egg was to him. He did not want a "little place" so much as the security of something he could hold on to against creeping time and death.

ANARCHIC LAUGHTER IN THE SYSTEM
(OR: A CROSSBOW AND PAINTED ARROWS)

Mrs. Marsh came in and said, "I was with the Head just now, Mr Rawley, and you figured strongly. She looked at her diary and said, 'Not Friday period two, I'm with Mr Rawley.'"

"That's news to me," I said.

"'And not Friday three, I'm with Mr Rawley and....' She paused and it was on the tip of my tongue to say 'The rest of the gang of six', and then she said 'The policy group'."

I said, "You'd have called her a Madame Mao."

"And then," Mrs. Marsh continued, "she asked me about a girl, and I was just about to say 'She's a dreadful Jew' when I bit back the word and said 'miser'."

I smirked. The Head was Jewish. "Mrs. Marsh has been using her crossbow again," I said. "She's been suggesting that the hierarchy are 'out of their tiny Chinese minds', and she's been striking anti-semitic, Thatcherite racist attitudes. We'll have to 'haul her before the sheriff for breaking curfew.'" In two sentences I had included topical references to the Chancellor of the Exchequer and to the Leader of the Opposition, and the Liberal Mrs. Marsh threw back her head and went out laughing.

At break there was a staff meeting to discuss fire procedures. All girls should follow their teachers – "If they follow this one," I whispered to my neighbour, "they'll be going down the nearest drainpipe" – and the women worried. There were complicated schemes for arrows to indicate the exits along the corridors.

I left with Stan Hauler, the international shot-putter who was on the staff. "I've got it," he said, "we'll all go round with arrows on our foreheads."

I laughed at his irony. He had a good sense of the ridiculous. For a moment I saw him as a robot chuntering down the passages of our system, a great feathered arrow above his much-televised eyes. But no, those of us who were capable of anarchic laughter were human. The robots were those who took the system seriously, who thought of policy groups and fire procedures rather than of gangs of six and arrowed submen; they were slaves to the system. One anarchic laugh was worth a hundred appointments in desk diaries, and thousand cyclostyled books of rules. It was a paean to all that was individual.

AN EXILE IN NOYNA ROAD

"We're retiring today," said the wizened, silver-haired Asian newsagent who had put aside my newspapers for a year or more. "We've been here twenty-three years. We're handing over to a young couple."

I expressed sorrowful surprise – "Really?" – and asked if they were "leaving the district".

"Yes, we are living in the district," he said while his Indian-looking wife nodded. "Two roads down. I have my property there.

We have a daughter who is doing 'O' level at Ensham. We will continue to live in the district. This is our country now, we will stay here."

It was the height of the public row about immigration – Mrs. Thatcher had said she would reduce immigration, and Enoch Powell had said that meant repatriation, as the Sunday headlines screamed from the crowded counter in front of me – and I asked where they had come from.

"From Tanganyika," the wizened man said. "In the fifties, I worked for the East African Railway. I was Chief of the Expenditure Section. I knew the British Governor, Sir Richard Turnbull, very well. I knew a number of the present Ministers. We left in 1964. We had British passports. I was active in a number of social causes – Red Cross and Labour organisations – and I knew people like Oscar Kambona."

"He's a London exile now," I said.

"Yes," the wizened Asian said, "in a way, so am I. We won't go back. Politics....Things can change so quickly over there, and once you have been in politics...." He shook his head. "No, we will stay here. This is our country now. I have my property just two roads down, behind Liptons: number 32 Noyna Road. You can come in for coffee next week, all my customers are invited. This is our life now, and what is past is past. I knew every district in Tanganyika and spoke at a lot of public meetings, but now I have my property in Noyna Road, and with my daughter taking 'O' level, that's the main thing."

He fell silent behind the counter where he had stood for twenty-three years, a British passport-holder who had known the Crown Governor, and the headlines screamed repatriation.

YES PLEASE TO A PEELING HOUSE
(OR: "ARE YOU GOVERNMENT OFFICIAL?")

The house was near Streatham Station. As we parked in the dark road my wife said, "The man's nervous, he doesn't want anybody and everybody seeing round, so the estate agent's written something on the leaflet." There was a strong smell of curry in the front garden. I sniffed and wrinkled my nose.

The door was opened by a dapper Indian in a suit, a man who looked like King Hussein. "Come in, sir," he said after examining my credentials on the leaflet, the ex-colonial greeting a descendant of the British Raj. He waved us into a peeling interior and sat us in the front room with two other Indians while he found an enormous bunch of keys. Then he took us round his squalid house, unlocking and relocking doors, wheezing asthmatically. In the back room half a dozen swarthy children were clambering into one huge double bed, and in the adjoining kitchen (whence seeped the aroma of curry) a woman pulled her sari close round her face and stooped over the stove. Upstairs, another woman in a sari stood hunched in a bedsit while snores came from under the lumpy bedcovers. Mr Khan wheezed his way to the top of the house, and when I asked him how much I might get for letting, he looked furtively to left and right, bent slightly forward, dropped his voice and said in a whisper, "One room can be twelve-fifty a week, and for two people, fourteen pound." I gathered from his secretiveness that he was not merely considering the feelings of his tenants, on whose sleep he had so indifferently intruded. I gathered that there was something illegal about his letting.

Mr Khan wheezed out into the garden and said, "I am a sick man, so I am not gardening. It is a mess. I am being in hospital four times this last year."

"The climate doesn't suit you," I said.

"Yes please," he said, "climate suit me." But a moment later he said, "My doctor tell me I must go to warm country. We leave, go back."

"Where?" I asked. He was reluctant to answer as if he had something to hide, so I pressed him. "Where are you going back to? Where did you come from?"

"India," he said evasively, at length.

"Ah, I've been there," I said. "Calcutta, New Delhi, I'd like to go back. What part of India?"

"Are you government official?" he asked suspiciously. "Did you go India as government official?"

"No," I said, "I was in education, I was living abroad at the time."

"Ah," he said, "Bombay. We go back Bombay. I sell this house, we go back Bombay." And with an intuitive flash I knew that he was less worried about the taxman than about Immigration, for he was an illegal immigrant. I knew he was harbouring illegal immigrants. They were his tenants. No wonder he did not want anybody and everybody seeing round.

Mr Khan's relief showed in his smile, and I was sad to have to say an Indian "Yes please" to his peeling house.

A CHILE BADGE AND A LANCED BOIL

Lisa Spells was a plain girl with a widow's peak, a spotty face, and the most appalling spelling. She came on supply to the English Department, having worked on an ice-cream van, and she obtained a permanent post before her spelling showed up on reports. She wore a Chile badge until a controversy involving the National Front required all badges to be banned from school. She questioned the school system. As Mrs. Marsh remarked, "Lisa Spells is one of the first to have come through of the generation that was taught to question everything. Nothing is free from her questioning."

Mrs. Buss, the Head of Drama, saw it differently. "I can't work with Lisa Spells," she told me for the umpteenth time. "She's incapable of accepting any system without changing it. It's because of her political outlook. She can't accept Western capitalism without changing it – witness her Chile badge – and she can't accept a syllabus without changing it. The idea of accepting anything makes her feel swollen up inside. It's the left wing temperament; I know, I was in the Young Communists a long time ago."

It was the job definition which brought me into conflict with Lisa Spells. She had been in for a Scale post – the one which had gone to Miss True – and she criticised, or rather "questioned", the distribution of work within the Department, which (as she saw it) required Scale 1s like herself to do work that should be done by the Scale 2s like Miss True. She went round the probationers (the teachers who were in their first year of teaching) and persuaded them that they were doing too much, and then it came to my attention, through a whisper from Miss True, that she had been to her union to complain that my job definition was illegal. She made me out to be a Watergate figure, a cartoon of corruption which I both rejected and resented as totally untrue. I was not going to accept the mask she wanted to hang over my reasonable face. The atmosphere of the Department was being poisoned.

The atmosphere was like a boil that needed lancing to let the puss out, and, wearing the mask of a surgeon in an operating theatre, I lanced it. I called a mini-meeting of Scale 1s and 2s, and I outlined the difficult situation we were in, and called for help. I outmanoeuvred Lisa Spells, and the puss came out, and after half-term, which followed two days later, the muttering was over, the wound had healed. The next meeting Lisa Spells chipped in a couple of times and confessed to feeling paranoiac, but after that she settled down and improved, for her questioning was outlawed.

But a spotty face is not free from boils for long, and the puss began to form again deep within her soul. The collective soul of the Department was immune from it now, her jealous witchery had no magnetic field in which to spread in our school, and so she left to find a more suppurative atmosphere.

WHITE CARS, BLACK HANDS

I renewed my car through *Exchange and Mart*. I advertised my old car, a battered white Triumph, and one Saturday night a couple of louts rang the bell, glanced at the car in the dark, sat in the back while I took them for a drive, and then – without so much as looking underneath for rust – announced they would buy it. One of them had black hands, and he produced a roll of notes and peeled off the price in £20 and £10 notes, thumbprinting each with grease, pocketed the log book and MoT certificate, and drove the car away, just like that.

I immediately set out to find a replacement. My wife and I toured all the local garages from Balham High Road down to Mitcham, and the most attractive cheap car was the Marina Coupé. I found an *Exchange and Mart* that was two weeks old and hunted through the Morris columns and identified the cheapest Coupé de Luxe and rang the telephone number. The car had not been sold yet. It was having a scratch removed, and it was not being advertised at present, the man said in a demotic accent. I arranged to see it on Saturday.

I took my neighbour. An Italian, he had been a fitter in East London for twelve years, and had had to give the job up because of ill health. He was now a schoolkeeper, and he did service and repair work on cars in his spare time. He was always tuning the engines of different cars in the road, and there was never any space to park because of his waiting fleet. Sometimes his two sons helped him – they had a garage in Carshalton – and that Saturday afternoon I found him holding a hand against the vaporous exhaust of a Volkswagen, wearing blue dungarees.

He got into the back of my wife's car, his hair smarmed back over his bald pate, all unshaven round his glasses, his hands black from the exhaust, and as we drove to Sidcup he remarked on things out of the window and commented on them in his thick Italian pidgin English. He was chained to the outer world.

The Marina was a white one with two doors. It was four years old, and the owner, who worked for a company, was a tousled-headed youngish man with red cheeks and blue eyes. He took us for a drive. The car was spacious and smooth, and conversation centred on the throbbing gearstick. I wondered whether the clutch was wearing out, and the owner said it needed adjusting. Pasquali sat in disapproving silence. "Why you no buy a car from a garage and have a warranty?" he had asked me. I pointed out that I would be paying £200-£300 more, and he had shrugged.

The owner said in his demotic accent, "The clutch is very near to the floor, and it's very positive." He let me try on his runway, and the car shot forward and nearly smashed into the garage doors.

We all went into the luxurious front room, and the owner's wife joined us. My wife and I sat down. Pasquali stood in his filthy dungarees and waved his black hands and muttered in thick Italian, "Clutch last twenty-five thousand miles. You ask RAC or anybody. Clutch plates gone. Car needs a new exhaust." Waving his black hands about, he looked strangely impressive, and the owner stopped him and asked if, price aside, I liked the car; for if I did I was to make an offer.

"In view of what has been said," I began, "I think £875 too high. Will you accept £800?" I expected the owner to explode, but to my surprise he said calmly, "I would think that's a little low, a little low. Would you like to try another offer." We settled for £820. I whispered to Pasquali, when there was a discreet moment, "You said just the right things, thank you very much."

I drove Pasquali home in the Marina. At the end of the journey I asked, "How much do I owe you?"

After a pause he replied, "Nothing."

But I insisted that he had earned something, and gave him a fiver. When I got in, I was glad the renewal of my car was over for another two or three years. Seeing the lout thumb banknotes with greasy hands, and Pasquali standing in that plush room, waving his black hands to denigrate the price of the car, I could not help feeling that car-selling is a dirty business, and that anyone who barters over those clean, white pieces of machinery has unclean hands.

A BOAST AND A PROVOKED FATE
(OR: A STOP-OUT AND A CORONARY)

Mr Street showed me a discoloration on his ankle one day. It turned out to be phlebitis. I told him he should rest, but he came back to work the next day with some pills and said he needed more exercise. He used to be an international athlete before the war, and he had given up running after some cartilage trouble, and subconsciously he had stopped all forms of exercise ever since.

"I'm going to go for a walk in the lunch-hour," he told me, and he asked me for my book of Canadian Air Force 5BX exercises. A couple of days later, on a Thursday, he confided to several members of the Department, "I'm so happy now. I'm enjoying my teaching, I leave all the hassle to Mr Rawley, and I can stay out late. You know, sometimes I don't get home until five a.m., and I'm on the gate at eight-thirty. I can overdo it and get away with it, I'm on top of the world."

It is very unwise to provoke Fate. Providence heard the boast and Providence, as the ancient Greeks knew, sees a boast as a challenge. Hubris was dangerously close to arté, and Providence measured up Mr Street and turned the Wheel of Fortune, which struck him down from behind, cast him down. He gave me a lift to the bank that Thursday afternoon. He was as jaunty as ever – I can still see him walking briskly to the car-park as the pips went and getting into his Avenger – and then on the Friday morning I was told he was seriously ill. Mr Simpson, the School Secretary, had taken the call from his wife.

I rang him for details. There was an awfully long delay as the switchboard tried to put me through to the Secretary's room, and I said to the other teachers in our Departmental room, in exasperation, "Ringing the Administrative Building is like getting through to Moscow. Perhaps they've got the lines in such a muddle that they can't put me through." I painted a cartoon picture of the telephonists getting the school lines hopelessly crossed – the cartoon picture was a way of communicating with the other teachers – and there were chuckles all round, concerned faces split into broad grins. In the end I gave up.

Then the telephone rang. We shared a party line with the library, and the librarian banged on the wall with her umbrella, the signal that the call was for me. Mr Simpson said, "Mr Street's very seriously ill indeed. He had a coronary at one this morning. He's in intensive care at Lewisham Hospital."

I told the Department at break as we sat together over coffee. Twenty teachers were very crestfallen. Earlier I had been making one of the youngsters laugh with my cartoon pictures – she had slipped a disc and was going to an osteopath, and I have given an exaggerated account of how I had slipped a disc and of my osteopathic treatment, and I had warned her, "Don't let me see you on crutches on Monday," and she now looked harrowed.

I gave Mr Street's wife time to have a good sleep and then phoned her mother's house, where I knew she was, and her mother said: "The hospital's very concerned, dear. He's in an oxygen tent, and he's got a drip up, and a plug in an arm and a plug in his chest. He's been screaming and groaning with the pain, the pains have been all along his chest. The next few hours will see which way it's going to go."

I rang the next morning, the Saturday, and he was off the danger list, and out of the oxygen tent. The pains had gone. The old lady was overjoyed, and she kept thanking me for phoning. "He's going to be all right," she said.

But he was an invalid. He would have to retire. Unbeknown to him, that walk down the path to his Avenger had been his walk away from his working life. At one blow, Fate had struck him down. The ancient Greeks were very wise to beware of boasting. Or was that another of my cartoon pictures, to communicate?

A BLEARY-EYED LOOK AND A BELLY-LAUGH
(OR: THE ONLY PAIN IS IN MY HEART)

I visited Mr Street in Ward C1 of Lewisham Hospital. He was lying in a ward bed, and he sat up and waved his arms and shouted "It's Philip," and pumped my hand and said, "Oh, it's my favourite," as I handed over a primula plant. For a moment he was so lively that I could not guess that he had had a coronary. His wife stood and extended a hand, and then he subsided, and I saw how grey he looked, and ill, and with his hair in straggly, uncombed wisps that stood on end, he had aged. Then I noticed his bleary eyes.

Pathetically he groped for a key. "You can find my record book in my cupboard," he said in a thin voice, "and my work forecasts. And here are some reports. I can be light-hearted, but I just can't concentrate on serious matters." He was obviously under sedation.

I told him not to think about work – I had come to see *him* – and I said he was a lucky fellow.

"I am," he said, "the specialist told me, if I'd arrived five minutes later at this hospital, I'd have been dead. I had these pains in my chest. I thought I had cramp, and I was perspiring. The sweat was pouring off me. They put me in intense care" (he stumbled on the word "intense") "and I was like a fish on a slab. They spent two hours working on me, like artists. They're perfectionists there."

"Fishmongers," I said with a glint in my eye.

"Yes," he laughed. "They fillet us. I've been on morphine. I'm on these pills now. I have to take four. I've had ten wires in me until today. This is the first day I haven't. Last night I had pains from eleven a.m. until two. See?" He showed me a bulletin. "A nurse came and said 'Are you all right?' and I said 'Yes,' for she couldn't do anything. She sat and watched me have these pains until I sucked a pill – you keep it under your tongue – until the pains went away. You can get some sleep between the pains." He looked grey, and I felt how sad it was that he should be at death's door alone in the dark night.

"It's angina," he went on. "The blood can't get through to the heart muscle. The muscle has to become strong. That's why they get me up to have a shave. It makes demands on the heart. They get me up, but they won't let me – or anyone on this ward – cross legs in bed. You mustn't cross your legs, it's bone on bone. Bad. No one here's got his legs crossed. I can honestly say that the only pain I've felt is in my heart. Nothing else they've done to me has hurt me. They come and powder my bum and inject me in my chest, but that doesn't hurt. Ah," he cried as a dark-haired, rather pretty nurse came up, dressed in white. "This one's my favourite."

The nurse said, "You'll make me blush."

His wife said, "I know he's a rogue, but he's a pleasant one." She was approaching fifty, I thought.

"You know," Mr Street went on, "this is the first time I've been in hospital since 1938 – for forty years – and then there was a chap in the next bed who had been blown up in a ship. He had no skin on him, except on his bum. The two most famous plastic surgeons of the day removed the skin from his bum and put it on his face, on his cheek and nose. He used to say, 'I'm all bum'" (he laughed) "and, 'They don't give me a handkerchief, they give me toilet paper.' The humour!" And he threw back his head and gave a healthy belly laugh, and his bleary-eyed look disappeared, and with it his matter-of-fact self-pitying self-absorption, and he was back to his old self again, as I remarked.

"It's your visit," his wife nodded, saying the polite thing to her husband's boss. "It's the stimulation."

"You'll be better now," I said. "You've got your mental faculties back, it's mind over matter. You'll control your body now, like keeping a class firmly under your thumb."

They both laughed, and I shook hands with both of them and prepared to leave. He was a different man, he was back to his old self, he looked as good as he had ever looked, and the bleary-eyed look had been transformed by a current of laughter, a current that was somehow in my aura, but which had not come from me but from somewhere outside myself. He gazed on me with envy as I went to the door, and I knew there was another pain in his sixty year old heart.

A BIRD'S SONG AND A SPREADING YEW

We came home through Hayes. "We can visit Miss Nightingale," my wife said, and so I swung off the main road through Hayes Common and drove to a Georgian house in woods and rang the bell by the grand white door. "They like you to ring and make an appointment," my wife said while an auxiliary nurse took my request up to sister, but she returned and showed us into a long room with a colour television where, hunched, white-haired and nearly blind, Miss Nightingale sat in far-away silence among half a dozen silent old ladies.

"Who is it?" she asked as the auxiliary bent over the walking frame that stood in front of her. "Is it Quentin? Oh, Philip and Pippa." She extended a scraggy hand and rose, hunched, to her feet. "How nice of you to come."

"Will you see them in your room?" the auxiliary asked.

"Yes, of course I will. If I'd known you were coming we could have gone upstairs for tea. You'll excuse my not being dressed, won't you," she said, and she led the way on her walking-frame

THE CLEAR, SHINING SUNLIGHT OF ETERNITY 233

into a room that looked out on grounds, and an enormous yew.

"It's supposed to be four hundred years old," she said, hunched, white-haired and nearly blind in her chair, gesturing at the yew. We listened to birds singing. "I listen to the birds in the morning," she told me. "It seems to attract them. I lie in bed and listen. It's one of my comforts, to listen to the birds. I can't see any longer, I can only just see the outline of the tree. I can see shapes. I can just see you. You're looking well, Philip. I can see that Pippa is wearing a fawn top and red bottom. It's like the newspapers. I can read the headlines only. I've had a good life, I've just got to put up with it. But I haven't been too well lately. I've had some falls. They won't allow me up on a stick any longer, I have to use this frame."

She reminisced about the past. "To think, I knew you as a small boy," she said. "Do you remember going to hear Billy Graham at Haringey? I should think that was in the early fifties. I was there the same night with your aunt. Billy Graham was staying with a friend of mine, the Earl of Lonsdale, who was *not* an evangelist (though his wife was), and Billy Graham did *not* succeed in making him teetotal. Oh yes, I've a good memory. It's the one thing I've got left. I remember you visiting your grandmother. I was when your aunt had a party in a hotel somewhere off Regent Street. She came into some money, and that was her way of spending it. One of your uncles brought me back to this home. I was a sister here for a few weeks twenty-three years ago, you know."

I reacted with incredulity – "*Really*?" – for I had not known.

"Oh yes," she said. "We worked harder than they do today. There are two sisters now, and two auxiliaries, and they have their tea-breaks and lunch-breaks, and they all seem to have most of their weekends off. I should think this place will close soon. There are only twelve of us – all ex-nurses – and it's run by the State. It's dead you know. There was more life in those days. We don't talk to each other. There's only one here who's nice: Miss Partridge, who was at the London Hospital. She's over ninety. Oh and there's Miss Hawkes, whose lectures I remember attending from 8 p.m. to 9 p.m. after a day's work, and we used to fall asleep." She smiled and nodded her head forward, eyes closed. "She's ninety-five. Your aunt says she was an awful dragon. We don't talk to the rest. We are...." She put her finger to her nose. "I share this room with another woman, but I don't like her very much. I think it's because she's not a Londoner. She boasted to me, 'I was in the...Something Hospital for twenty-three years.' I said, 'I was at the London for thirty-three years.'"

Miss Nightingale sat hunched and white-haired and nearly blind against the spreading old yew, and having heard her song, I thought she belonged in its aged, evergreen branches somehow. I felt sad for the world of the old, in which what you *were* is important in determining status, and I thought how like the yew this home was; it had seen generations of transient people to their graves, and there was something durable, permanent and eternal about the way it survived. Miss Nightingale was as transitory as the singing birds that flitted in the yew's spreading fingers.

A POKER FORK AND A BURSTING BUBBLE

I hiked the price of my flat before I sold it. My buyer was a doctor, and before he made an offer I received a telephone call: I had been offered an extra £3,450 by a solicitor. This took my flat back to the original price plus £500 for fixtures and fittings, and the estate agent was Harrods. Teresa had advised me to use Harrods, and in some strange way I felt Providence was behind them.

The solicitor rang me. She sounded young and scatty, and wildly excitable. She seemed to know very little about the Law, and had little idea of how to set about obtaining a mortgage. She was under the impression that I would want the entire purchase price immediately. When I told my solicitor-brother he said, "I know her. I met her last week. We're on the same case." He advised me to proceed with her to investigate her offer, and I met her at my flat early one morning. She had blonde hair and she giggled.

After a couple of weeks we had to tell the doctor. I elected to follow the moral procedure and give him a chance to match the offer. I rang the estate agents (Donaldsons), but my girl had flu. I delayed until after the weekend – and the doctor had gone to Thailand for a holiday. The doctor had weakened his position. He would not be in London to look for other houses. Selling property is like playing chess, and I had him in a fork. I could take him whatever he did. I told Donaldsons of the situation, my girl sent a cable to the doctor, who rang his solicitor and raised the price by £3,450.

My brother invited me down to his office and we discussed the situation. The Government were forcing Building Societies to clamp down on lending and extend the mortgage queue, and the crunch was coming on Friday. "This recent rise in prices," I said, "is a bubble, like the South Sea Bubble. It's getting bigger and bigger, but it's going to burst."

"*I* think it's going to burst," my brother said.

"We agreed that we would exchange contracts on the Friday morning, but that meanwhile we'd blow up the bubble still more."

The doctor refused to pay any more, and the solicitor found she could not obtain a mortgage, and with Friday's prospect ahead, she withdrew. She would have to wait three months before she could be granted another mortgage. Now I knew it had been a game of poker all the time, with bluff and counter-bluff as the determining skill, and I exchanged contracts with the doctor's solicitors on that Friday morning.

I felt I was very lucky. The solicitor Harrods found had been a gift from Providence to raise my price £3,450, and as in a nightmare, I had been playing the wrong game by different rules, and had somehow won. The solid-looking counter which I had used as stake-money now looked as insubstantial as a gigantic soap-bubble.

ONE OF GOD'S CHOSEN
(OR: A BRANDED FOREHEAD
AND SCREAMING NIGHTMARES)

"Hello," I said on the Head's stairs to beautiful Mrs. Sharman, "Jane seems to be coming on well."

Mrs. Sharman frowned.

"I mean," I said, "she seems to be perfectly all right in class now, she's working hard, she isn't self-conscious at all."

Mrs. Sharman pulled a face. "It comes out in dreams," she said. "She has nightmares. We have them once every two weeks now. She's scarred, you know – she combs her hair forward, but underneath she's scarred – and she wakes up screaming. In one nightmare, she had a shotgun fired in her face, and she looked in a mirror at herself. In another, she fell through a window and cut her face and was scarred. It's never fire and burns, but the idea's there. She puts a bold front on in class. She's naughty, you know, you musn't let her get away with it, some of the things she tells me she's said to teachers....But underneath she's very sad. It was the same at hospital. She was super, smiling, laughing....But as soon as we got home, she cried and cried and cried. No, I'm afraid the accident has marked her for life."

There was a depressed silence. I thought of all the suffering and pain she would go through, growing up with a scarred face, and I thought of the improvement in her work for me. Already she was growing in creativity, she was deepening herself: her ordeal would unite her with God sooner or later.

She was one of God's chosen, and she wore the badge of her office, like a K for Kalends branded on the forehead of a Roman slave, under her combed-forward hair.

FRENCH HOWLERS AND SPILT WINE

Mr Sykes came in towards the end of the sixth form Parents' Evening. "Hello," I said, "I heard you on the radio the other day. I was in the bath, and I heard this mellifluous voice talking about prisons, and then they said it was you."

Mr Sykes was Secretary of the Howard League for Penal Reform. He was a sandy-haired man with a small goatee beard and eyes that twinkled behind his spectacles in the Cambridge manner. It was only when he spoke that you knew he was a radical. "Oh, on *PM*," he said, after we had shaken hands. "It helped pay the gas bill."

We sat down and we talked about his daughter, who had been accepted for Cambridge. I had offered to help and had arranged for her to meet the Cambridge Fellow I'd met at Jesperson's, but she had turned him down, preferring to enter through Modern Languages rather than English. Sophie needed an A and two Bs, and he said she gave the appearance of working hard – I wondered it if was just an appearance – but that in Modern Languages she had made some "dreadful howlers". Modern Languages had not got anyone through 'A' level last year, let alone anyone near an A grade, whereas we had had an A and a B, and I thought that her howlers were the working of some cosmic boomerang, which was punishing her for her hubris in turning down my Cambridge don.

The next day the Heads of Department had a lunch-time gathering. I arrived late and helped myself to some red wine which the Head of Maths had distilled. It was very rough wine. The Head of Home Economics took the bottle from me and did the rounds, and in refilling the Head of Maths' glass she spilt wine all down his front and trousers; he was reclining in the Roman manner on one elbow on the floor. There was considerable banter. There were ribald suggestions, and there was talk of the "gang of six", the policy group which ran the school, of which I was a member. I said it was an "Upper Chamber", like the House of Lords. There was much talk about "Giovanni", the Heads of Departments' nickname for the Deputy Head, who was renowned to behave like a member of the Mafia in his capacity as the Head's hatchet man.

In the middle of all this bibulous mirth, the telephone rang, and the Head of Art jumped and jogged the Head of Home Economics who slopped her own glass of wine down her front, and everyone hooted with laughter.

"It's the karmic boomerang," I said, and I thought of Sophie Sykes. She had spilt wine on me, and had had wine spilt on her by being penalised for howlers, and no amount of penal reform by her father would remove the stains from her 'A' level chances.

THE ORDINARY IN PEARLY KING CLOTHES
(OR: A MIRROR IN BATTERSEA PARK)

My wife had been talking about the Easter Parade in Battersea Park for some days. She wanted us all to "go out" to it, which meant that I would be taken away from my desk. I was tired and ill – the holidays had only just begun, and I had a sore throat and a stiff neck – and I wanted to withdraw energy from all trivia so there could be a superabundance for important things.

It was with some reluctance that I mustered the energy to set off after an Easter Sunday lunch of turkey. This was part of the Western way of life: earning cars we did not want, to go to functions we did not want to attend. I affected not to know the way, and I groaned at the lack of parking-spaces; Battersea was like Wembley on Cup Final day. We entered the Park to the sound of bands.

Pippa ran ahead with Simon. I followed at a deliberate, leisurely pace with Paul, who was in the push-chair. Suddenly, they had gone. I found a place at the back of the crush of people and watched bands blare past, floats trundle by. Elephants loped up, and there were several beauty queens, all goosepimpled from the keen March wind, and there were Edwardian figures on penny farthings. By and large, they were received in silence, and the participants looked cool and faintly embarrassed, especially the trick cyclist with a daffodil in his bowler hat. There were several Pearly Kings, one of whom shouted, "Come on, let's 'ear yer," and then there were clowns and some men on enormously long stilts. One with red and white striped trousers doffed his wig to reveal a head as bald as an egg, and there were cackles from the ageing women, and one or two cat-calls. I watched crossly, fed up at being there rather than at my desk.

I looked around for my wife, but she and Simon were nowhere to be seen. Then they came up, and I lifted Simon onto my shoulders so that he could watch the huge polar bear float, and the giant King Kong gorilla, and the daffodil sun from Jersey, under which sat the smiling but freezing Jersey beauty queen. I looked at the crowd, alienated and disgruntled and resentful. The women's eyes had a slight shining glow, the men looked withdrawn and resigned. This was society, and the Easter Parade, for all its glitter, mirrored it. The crowd, looking at the tawdry, tinselly procession saw a mirror-image of itself. There was no Easter procession to any Golgotha, no Resurrection from any tomb; just a long, winding show of modern affluence and nihilism. The crowd saw itself in the pearls of the Pearly Kings' caps.

Slowly I grew more tolerant. It was good to see the women with naked waists and the two huge papier-maché boxers who wobbled round the tiny ref, I did not mind being invaded by the West Indian steel band and the sleek shire horses. Soon my mind was as empty as the next man's, and I was looking for the next distraction, as though I came from a pre-TV age of self-amusement and self-entertainment, which needed its Parades and Carnivals.

"Oh, it's Mister Rawley," called a West Indian I must have taught some time during the previous eight years. That was the trouble with teaching south of the river, strangers called your name. I waved and then ignored him and went on allowing myself to be distracted, I surrendered to the Carnival atmosphere and allowed some energy to flow towards it, and I came away as tired and blank and mindless as anyone in the crowd, and I had completely forgotten about my destiny.

I had allowed the world outside to intrude on my monastic quiet, I had sacrificed some of my inner flow – poured its spring water like a libation to the ground – to placate a restless ghost who did not acknowledge the disciplines of greatness and who had a love of the dressed-up ordinary: of those ordinary Cockneys in their shining Pearly King clothes.

A PIGGY-EYED BROKER AND A CONNIVING SMILE
(OR: A WIZARD LIKE THE WOOLWICH FERRY)

I met Mr De Souza through an advertisement in the ILEA *Contact*, a weekly for teachers: "100% mortgages for ILEA teachers. Top-ups, remortgages. Ring."

I rang, wanting a top-up on my mortgage at a time of mortgage famine, and after doing some figures over the phone he said in his demotic Ilford accent, "A top-up will cost you more than if I get the full amount for you, because of the loaded insurance premium. It will be easier if I get you the full amount. It's better for you to have only one charge on your property. We can definitely help you. Can you write me a letter."

I wrote him a letter and the next day he told me over the phone that he had received an offer, at 12%, which was confirmed in principle, from a North American Bank. I pressed him and he said it was the Philadelphia National Trust: "The form's in the post. Can you come in after the Easter weekend and complete it?"

I rang to confirm that the form had arrived – the bank was in fact Citibank – and on Easter Tuesday we all drove off to Ilford. We crossed the river by the Woolwich Ferry. After a short queue behind Continental lorries with huge containers, we drove down the ramp of the South Pontoon and onto the boat, and Simon was convinced we were still on dry land.

We arrived in Ilford around 1 p.m., and I climbed the stairs to the tiny, plush, two-roomed office of a small mortgage brokers'. An attractive girl sat at a desk. The demotic Mr De Souza, bald and piggy-eyed and chubby-cheeked, sat at one of the two desks at the far end and spoke to a loutish long-haired young man. There was nowhere for me to sit so I had to stand and wait.

Mr De Souza's partner came in, and immediately I saw him I recognised him; but could not place him. He was slow, and he spoke in an Essex working-class accent that was at once open and furtive: there were secretive silences round the chirpy remarks he made as he hunted for a file. He accidentally bumped bottoms with the attractive secretary, who was making me some black coffee ("there's no milk or sugar"), and he said, "Ooh, I enjoyed that." He was very slow, and the figures he gave Mr De Souza were wrong. He gave me an apologetic, conniving smile and disappeared into the next room, leaving me wondering where I had seen him. He looked like Val Doonigan. Was he a cricketer in the 1940s or 1950s, perhaps, or had I run across him in a former life?

Mr De Souza gave me the Citibank form and asked me to leave "Capital repayment or endowment" blank until he had explained what was involved. He returned when I had finished filling it in and sat down to explain. He drew graphs. My salary would rise over the years. The tax I paid would fall if I opted for capital repayment, and so would my tax relief. If I opted for an endowment policy, the tax I paid would be a straight line, and so would my tax relief. I would have more tax relief in ten years' time. It may seem that an endowment policy was more expensive at first, but if I considered the net position, and the return on maturity.... If I chose endowment, he would charge no fee but would take £45 expenses, a fixed rate calculated at half a per cent of what it cost to run the office per annum. If I chose capital repayment, he would charge me £250 plus £45 expenses. "The form says that Citibank agents are not allowed to charge a fee," he told me, indicating the huge slogan across the top. "I can't declare it openly, so it'll have to be unofficial, on the side."

I was appalled and rang my solicitor-brother, who said, "It's blackmail. Don't sign anything that makes you liable to pay any fee at all."

Mr De Souza was a wizard at doubtful argument. He was an accountant as well as a mortgage broker, he told me, but most of the figures which his partner provided, and which he checked on a brand new calculator, and on which he based his championing of the endowment method of repayment, were wrong. The gross interest, I objected after some simple mental arithmetic, should have been £250, not £229.25.

"I said the list was one per cent out, do you remember?" he countered quickly. I remembered nothing of the kind.

The premium of £70.75 was uncompetitive; my solicitor-brother quoted £58.90 for a Norwich Union policy. "I just quoted the first one I could find," Mr De Souza said quickly, not to be caught in the act of raising his commission at my expense. "We don't like to involve the companies in work at this stage, we just take the first quote we can get." Which happened to be the most expensive quotation in the business.

The capital repayment figure his partner provided was too high, and so was the mortgage protection policy. Mr De Souza had clearly tried to make me choose endowment and not capital repayment by rigging the figures, he was trying to make me choose what was to his advantage rather than to mine, and he was prepared to charge me exorbitantly for doing so.

He was very cunning. He was deferential to the point of obsequiousness towards my brother because it suited his interests: "I agree with you, I completely agree with you," he kept saying. And during the last half hour of his "explanation" he kept the next clients, a couple, standing without so much as looking at them, and ignored several phone calls, to suggest to me that I was the subject of his attention, and that (by implication) he was earning his high fees. He was very subtle.

I drove the form to Harrow and handed it over to the Citibank man. I pointed out that though I had written "endowment" on the form, I would prefer capital repayment, if there were no question of any fees being charged. Mixing with tough businessmen had taught me some of their ruthlessness, and Mr De Souza was a piggy blackmailer, as my brother had said. I had to defend myself against his greed. I told the Citibank man that I would be pressed for around £300 in fees, contrary to what was written on the form, but emphasised that this was between the two of us, and was not to go further.

The Citibank man was young and English and in his twenties; he had just been in the computer room. "I don't know why he has to do that," he said, "most mortgage brokers live off their commission from policies, they don't need to do that. I suggest we cut him out of the deal. Tell him you've got a top-up privately, and that you've withdrawn your application."

It turned out that Citibank could top up my existing mortgage for a monthly sum which, contrary to what Mr De Souza had told me, would be considerably cheaper for me than to borrow the full amount from Citibank. From the outset Mr De Souza had championed the scheme that would give him the maximum fees.

And so I meted out summary justice upon Mr De Souza's greed – he had been a pig – and my ruthlessness slightly shocked me. I was glad I did not dwell permanently in this cut-and-thrust city world, and I could understand why my brother needed to go to church every Sunday, just to flush all this dirty dealing out of his system.

As I drove home, the Citibank man's words "They don't need to do that" went on ringing in my ears. Mr De Souza had told me it cost £9,000 a year to run his office. The tiny room, the lack of chairs for his clients, and his underhand methods all, perhaps, hinted that he was a mortgage "broker" in two senses of the word. I thought that his company was going broke. He was like the Woolwich Ferry in Simon's eyes: he seemed to be on *terra firma*, but he was really up the creek.

I saw Mr De Souza as a desperate man who needed money to stave off a horrible crash, knowledge of which his Val Doonigan partner had somehow shared with me: hence the complicity of his apologetically conniving smile. I suddenly felt very sorry for Mr De Souza, and very sad that in this Maya of indefinite possibilities I had just contributed to the realisation of his worst fears.

ALISON BUSH, EIGHTEEN, WANTS PROOF
(OR: ICE DRIPPING FROM STEEPLED HANDS,
AND SAINT THERESA'S EYES)

The sea was green with galloping white sea-horses. The foam hissed on the shingle, the spray threw a mist over the coastline under scudding clouds. There were lashes of rain. All being was in the cosmic dance of Siva as we scampered out of the wet into Teresa's gallery. The halo in the window – her red earthenware circle – had been arranged in pieces, as if it had been blasted into fragments, and I knew instantly that Teresa's mystic peace had suffered the intrusions of the world.

Teresa rose from her bed in the back part of the gallery. She lived like an anchorite in primitive conditions. Her one-roomed hermit's cell had one old basin and no wardrobe or chest of drawers, and a few simple clothes hung from a peg on the wall; the back of the gallery was very old and had a preservation order on it. She lived out the rôle of a spiritual nun among her paintings with great simplicity.

"It's been a terrible day," she said, dabbing at her headscarf over her lined face, "one of the worst in the year in every sense. I've got a touch of flu, but it's not catching. It's good to see you."

Pippa released Simon and Paul onto the floor, and while they occupied themselves Teresa listened to our news.

"I'm so glad you've sold your flat at last," she said. "Actually, this gallery's on the market. But I must clear up the mess first, the theft at the Metropole. You see, there's a Court case to compensate my artists, and they've withdrawn all their works until I compensate them. It's been six months, and nothing's been done, and I can't get hold of your brother, who's handling it for me. He

THE CLEAR, SHINING SUNLIGHT OF ETERNITY

was supposed to serve a summons, but whether he has or not I don't know. I've spent pounds ringing him to find out, but he's never there. I know he's lost his secretary, and has to depend on temps, and I know he's had big cases in London, but I must get hold of him. I can't sell this place until the mess is cleared up." I frowned and promised to speak to my solicitor-brother.

"I've been painting again," she went on, "and selling my paintings too, more than I sold of all those who withdrew their work. Look, I'm having an exhibition here." She showed me a poster. "There's a lot that's coming out, but I feel impeded, as you did by your flat. I know how you felt now. I want to be in London, and free of this. I've got to get this gallery sold, then I can be free."

We talked about a conference I was going to attend while Paul lay on the floor and kicked a canvas out of its frame with thuggish effectiveness. The conference was about how modern physicists were coming to the conclusion that the mystic view of the universe was right all along.

"Do you know, that accords with what I was trying to say the other day," Teresa said. "My niece Alison is eighteen. She's going through an independent phase, as they all do. I'd just been to a church service where everybody lighted a candle and held it, so the whole congregation was composed of lights round the Easter candle, and she said to me, 'How do you know religion is true, are *you* God?' and 'I want proof'. Those were her words, 'I *want* proof.' Alison Bush, eighteen, wants proof. I mean...." Teresa shook her head. "I said, 'Alison, pray for guidance.' I will go on praying that she does not leave the Church. There's hope. We've a new young priest. He's like Father Felix, he's beautiful and intelligent and up-to-date. Alison hadn't been to 'communion' (as you say) for two months, but she dressed up and was first up for him on Sunday." On the wall was a painting of Teresa's: Alison knelt, her hands were steepled before her in prayer.

Then I saw, hidden at the back of dozens of propped up canvases, a stunning nun. She wore a blue head-dress, and had the shiny glow of innocence and youth on her forehead, and she had the most haunted eyes, and I immediately thought of Eliot's lines, "Will the veiled sister pray/For children at the gate/Who will not go away and cannot pray." It was the contemplative ideal incarnate, and I said excitedly, "Who did *that*?"

"I did," Teresa said calmly, "a week or two ago. It's Little

Theresa, you know: Theresa of Lisieux, the most recent saint. The world thought she....But never mind. Father Felix in Cornwall told me something about her, and I've come to know her recently, I've just seen her."

"In visions?" I asked, awed.

"Yes, she just came to me, looking like that, and I put it down. Someone said it's just like her. Someone else said her eyes watch you. It's not for sale."

I was very excited. There, I said, was the refutation of Alison Bush's *desire* for proof. St. Theresa did not need proof, she accepted and looked with pity on Alison Bush. I said she had defined the mystical-contemplative tradition – "you see," Teresa interrupted, "one day it will hang in the Royal Academy" – and I told her about my researches into the chakras or force centres of the etheric body.

"The seven senses in the head, according to Catholic teaching," Teresa said, "Father Felix mentioned something to me about them once, and I have seen them in my visions."

I told her how modern physicists had proved the existence of the aura. "We represent the mystical-contemplative tradition," I said, "of man defined in terms of the currents or rays that flow into the spleen chakra and light up the head and then pass out into the aura, so that all of us have fields round us that pick up forces from the Deity, are receptive to prayer."

"Don't put it into words," Teresa interrupted, "don't inquire what the Light is, don't analyse it; just feel it."

"But the scientists *are* putting it into words, it's their way of stating the mystic truth," I said.

Teresa said she had found a sketch she did of me eight years back, and I found myself looking at a long-haired Nureyev-like image of other-worldly beauty, a dreamy mystic-contemplative face – with penetrating eyes which (I guessed) were meant to be excessively analytical.

Teresa suggested we went out and had coffee in the community centre. She would shut up shop. We would walk through the churchyard, it had stopped raining. I looked round her gallery while she and Pippa dressed the children. "Would you like to spend a penny?" Teresa asked Simon, who held out his hand and said, "Yes."

I came across a stunning sculpture, which was priced at £300. A small black iron spine was entombed in a dripping block of ice. I saw it as a definition of man. The backbone was buried deep within the flesh which was ephemeral, for it would melt like ice. Only the bone was real. So were real values frozen within the watery values of the flesh.

I thought of the worldliness that iced round our hearts, I thought of Alison's proof which had frozen round the knowledge of the nun's eyes, and I knew that the cold ignorance of the materialistic and intellectual minds would soon melt away from the mystical-contemplative ideal that held all real things together, like discs in a spine.

A ROLLS ROYCE DAY-DREAM AND A NAIAD'S CHIPPED NOSE (OR: A CHURCHILL FIREPLACE AND A BRUISE)

Near the bank I ran into Mrs. Burns who told me she was now employed as a temporary nanny in a house that had just been sold to American film people. The vendor was a famous photographer who had spent thousands on it. "It's full of things to do with films," she said, holding her shopping-bag. "It's only round the corner. Come in and have a quick look; the baby's asleep there."

We went down some steps to a basement, where a green spiral staircase led up from the kitchen area through where the ceiling should have been to the front room, which contained one of Liberace's pianos.

"This is going to be in *Charlie's Angels*," Mrs. Burns said. "It's so dirty here, she isn't a clean woman at all. She doesn't wash the baby's nappies till they're white, she uses detergent instead of soap. And the place smells of cats. I won't have them in the house."

She spoke as if the house were hers, and the owner were her servant. She showed me the fireplace which had come from one of Churchill's houses – two breasty naiads (water-nymphs) leaned out on either side, one nipple exposed in each case, and one had a chipped nose – and I thought how thin and pale Mrs. Burns looked.

"I've lost two stone," she said. "I've got a lump on my breast, I ought to be in hospital, my doctor wanted me admitted. I told him, 'You know it's cancer, I'm not going in any hospital, they're dirty.' It's just as well, I'm not complaining. I'll be joining James. Oh, I think of him so much. You can see the railway line from the upstairs window, and the children playing on the green, and I miss him so much. The council house creaks a lot, I'm sure he visits me each night, I hear him moaning 'Let me come in.' I want to believe he does because I dream about him so much, but I know it's all rubbish really, and that death is the end. And yet I don't really believe that, I know I'll be joining him. I'm more with him now than I am with the world. I'm dying, I'll be dead soon, but I don't care. It's a good thing really.

"The trouble is, I'm short of cash. I've thrown the old man out, I literally kicked him out of the door and he stayed out two nights and rang today to know if he can come back home. You see, he got jealous. They sent me home from here in the Rolls Royce – it's nothing, it's just the company car – and his jaw dropped, and he started complaining at me for being up here so much, and I lost my temper and got angry and kicked him out. The thought of him touching my body makes me physically ill. He's not my husband, he was bankrupt when I took him in, I'm only his common-law wife, and being in the furniture business, he's terrified I'll tell the truth. Anyway, I'm paying my own rent now with money sent from Italy.

"All I have to do is look after this little boy" – she had fetched a curly-haired brown-eyed baby of eight months – "and they're rolling in money. They pick me up in a Rolls and pay me fifty pounds a week, and the nanny gets thirty pounds for four hours – she came from Princess Anne, and she has her own cup and saucer – and the cleaner's on the shiny floor advert on TV, and *he* has a phone in his car and he rings me from his car in New York. It's easy money, but they take advantage of me. I'm up here at six in the morning, which means I have to get up at four, and I don't go home until after midnight. I'm more or less living here, and I see nothing of my daughter, who's admittedly working in her shop. They take advantage of me. Never again." I stood and looked at a photograph of the exploiter, the wife of the photographer, and, driven by loneliness and her compulsive need to talk, Mrs. Burns produced a photograph of the wife with Lawrence Harvey, who was once the wife's lover.

"You know, Tom, my actor-lover," she went on, talking too freely, "comes up here sometimes. He's not at all well-known, not like Lawrence Harvey, but he's very *sympatico*. I push the cot round the corner and draw the curtains in case the gardener's next door – he's the 'What your right arm's for' man on the TV advert – and....It's my change, but I'm terribly greedy for him. I don't know if it's James or having the baby around, but I want a child by him.

Is that very wrong? Anyway, there's not much chance, he's really mean. He makes sure I don't get pregnant. He makes me so angry."

We went back to the Churchill fireplace, and Mrs. Burns put the baby in the pram and prepared to strap him in. I stared at the naiad with the chipped nose, which reminded me strangely of Mrs. Burns, and she stopped what she was doing and prattled on about how warm the fire was when the photographer and his wife had dinner parties and how the Churchill marble was valued at £8,000.

Suddenly there was a thud on the concrete floor, and the baby was screaming. There was a bruise on his forehead and dirt on his flat nose. Mrs. Burns fell on him and nursed him and rocked him backwards and forwards while I made reassuring noises and left. The strap lay neglected on the floor.

Mrs. Burns' day-dream had been broken into by reality, which had proved her negligent and left her image as chipped as the marble naiad's and as bruised as the wauling baby's nose.

SUBTLE BODIES
(OR: A DOUBTING FLAMINGO
AND A SEA-EAGLE'S FOOT)

At a conference I met Sally James, a gangling bird-like woman in bifocals who seemed to stand on one leg. She picked her way across the hall and sat next to me and asked, "Are you a scientist? Oh, I thought you might be, judging from a conversation I overheard between you and Dr. —" she named a subatomic physicist. "I'm a Radionics Practitioner."

"Oh?" I said. "What exactly do you do?"

She said: "There are only forty of us full-time, actually, and we all work in England. I have an office, and people send me a hair or a blood sample, and I put my fingers over it and...receive an impression. I may find illness or stress – the person may be living in the wrong place or have a child at the wrong school – and if it's a medical problem, I take measurements and plot a graph and give treatment from special machines. People consult me for all kinds of problems, like predicting the future, but I won't do money, stocks and shares, for that comes back on you. I am really curing the subtle or etheric body. I sometimes send written answers, but sometimes I send out messages across the unconscious web."

"Telepathy," I said.

"Precisely," she said.

"Oh," I said, "scientists speak of their theories as being nothing more than 'models', and do you regard the subtle body as a model that works, and so you see no reason to doubt it, or as a Reality you clairvoyantly know?"

"I'm not clairvoyant," she said, "and so it's the first. I go on what people have told me. I have doubts, but I go on doing it, and it seems to work. I can see people's auras."

"Do you actually see them, like Bagnall, or do you see them with your inner eye?" I asked.

"On my inner eye, I suppose," she said. "It's difficult to talk about these things, we need a picture-language."

And once again I was in that no-man's-land across the frontier of language, where one encountered Reality like an enemy in the dark, and attempted to interpret the confused alarums of metaphysical experience. During the lecture, which began soon afterwards, she stood up and picked her way over to a woman friend, who would not leave with her; and I last saw Sally James wading doubtfully through rows of chairs to the exit, alone, like a ruffled pink flamingo.

At the end of the conference a thin, brown-haired woman crossed over to where I sat in the cafeteria, drinking tea and eating bread and butter and clear honey. "May I join you and ask if you're a scientist?" she asked in a slight North American accent, her hooked nose like the bill of a fluffy-headed sea-eagle. "Because I heard you talking, and I thought you must be a scientist." Later she told me, "I'm married to a Foot Therapist. He discovered that the foot corresponds to the stages of pregnancy. The top of the toe here" – she showed me a stockinged foot – "is the pineal gland, when the intention of life becomes formed. Further up the toe is the pituitary where life begins to form. They join with the sole, here, is the moment of conception, and the heel is the moment of birth. He massages between the toe and the heel, going by feel, and soothes away the tensions of pregnancy. It works. Of course, he's massaging the subtle body. It's like acupuncture, but he does it with all his fingers. He discovered all this on this very foot. I was married to my first husband when I met him, but even though he was spotty I knew I had to marry him, and I did."

I asked her where her husband was.

"In Germany," she said. "I'm looking after the children."

She wanted to know where the guru was. I said he was in his room, "and you might surprise him in disattire if you go in."

"Oh," she giggled, a hot, pleased glance in her eyes, "I'm not like that." And I looked at the feathered body she was reserving for her spotty husband.

I walked down under the fir-trees to my car. Both the Radionics Practitioner and the Foot Therapist's wife had thought I was a scientist, and both owed their livings to the subtle body. I felt I had been approached by two very subtle bodies.

THE MYSTERY OF THE GREAT PYRAMID (OR: MIND-AND-FESTIVAL-OF-BODY-ING KHUFU)

I visited Caxton Hall to hear a lecture entitled *The Mystery of the Great Pyramid*. It was given by Albert Chamberlain, the son of the distinguished Pyramidologist whose four volumes were on sale at the back of the room, price £27.

Albert Chamberlain was a precise man with brown hair, strangely evasive eyes, and a formal, blue suit. He fussed over his slide projector, raising the beam with books. When the room was full, he stood at the front and, lit only by the fading summer light from the dome above us, apologised for having left an important part of the slide projector in his Hertfordshire home in his haste. He spoke briskly about the antiquity of the Great Pyramid – in relation to which Alexander the Great was only half way from us – and then gave us a slide show, from which the mystery and the solution were to evolve.

We looked at numerous stills of the interior of the Pyramid. The main point was that in seventy-nine of the eighty Egyptian pyramids, the burial chamber was below the ground, while the Great Pyramid was the only one to have two burial chambers *above* the ground, and two seemingly unnecessary air channels which would not be needed for the "ka" (soul) since the Egyptians provided for the "ka" with pictures. There were no pictures of doors for the "ka" on the walls of these burial chambers, and if the new concept of building above-ground chambers evolved in the time of Khufu by accident, as the Egyptologists maintained, why did not Khufu's son, Chephren, continue the concept instead of reverting to the traditional design?

The slides began to repeat themselves, the disc had turned full circle, and Albert Chamberlain apologised for not having filled it correctly in his haste. There was some confusion as he returned to the front and proceeded to the solution to the mystery.

He pointed to a chart of the Great Pyramid and showed how the passage down to the underground chamber represented death. In that case, the passage up to the two upper chambers represented...? He looked around like a teacher and pointed to a raised hand.

"Life," said a woman.

"Absolutely right, top of the class," said Albert Chamberlain. "Now," he went on, "there is a text in *Isaiah* which in the Hebrew contains thirty words. The text is *Isaiah* 19, 19-20. Now in those days they used letters of the alphabet as numbers, and if you add the letters up, you get, five thousand four hundred and forty-nine, which is the exact height of the Pyramid in Pyramid inches. Now each Pyramid inch is a five hundred millionth part of the earth's polar diameter, which suggests a knowledge that the earth is round when everyone believed it was flat. No one had that knowledge. The Egyptians had the knowledge to *build* the Pyramid, but not to *design* it like that. And so who could have designed it? God is the only person who had the know-how. God is the architect of the Great Pyramid, which, being built under divine inspiration, is a symbol for all the divine secrets and contains prophecies about the future.

"Now the most important part of the Pyramid is this intersection of passages here. This represents the Resurrection of Christ. It all works out because the inches of the passages represent years of future history."

I was giddy at all the leaps in his interpretation. I was staggered at his Christ-centred view. He was imposing his Western ideas on the ancient Egyptians, and seeing the time of Khufu in terms of his own Christian belief. It was all so daft that I thought of Swift's Academy in Book 3 of *Gulliver's Travels*. The Academy contained rationalism gone mad, with Professors looking for sunbeams inside cucumbers. Here was a crank looking for the laws of God inside a Pyramid, basing his belief on one weird rational theory or speculation or supposition that was totally divorced from experience.

Now Albert Chamberlain proceeded to prophecy. According to the slope of the down passage, and counting inches, 1914 was the beginning of a new time of troubles which would not end until 2274, while the millennium of Christ's reign on earth would start in

1978/9 with economic crisis and war involving the Soviet Union, which did not need a navy, being landlocked, and was arming for expansion. His lecture was a warning.

On this apocalyptic note he stopped for questions, and a filthily dressed, balding man, who, judging from the askance looks round the room, ought not to have been there, asked, muddling his words in his nervousness, "I went to the Mind and Festival of Body last week and they told me that next year is the beginning of the Aquarian Age, and you're saying it'll be a great disaster; what am I supposed to believe?"

Albert Chamberlain said thinly that the two ideas were not mutually exclusive, and he passed on to other questions.

I was speechless, marvelling that people could believe such rubbish, and at last I could contain myself no longer.

"Is it not likely," I asked, "that Khufu built the Great Pyramid as a place of initiation, so that neophytes could be initiated into an ancient Mystery religion, like the worship of Isis? If so then the initiate underwent a ritual death and was ceremonially reborn to Light in the upper chambers; and perhaps the air channels let in a little light? They would anyway allow the initiates to breathe."

There was a ripple of approval around the room. "But our solution answers points which that solution cannot answer," said Albert Chamberlain, and he passed on to another question before I could object that his answers were crazy.

I thought of his muddled slide show – he was like the revolving disc on his slide machine, he went round and round – and I thought of his confused logic: he was "mind-and-Festival-of-body"-ing Khufu's Great Pyramid; and I was indignant at the way he had rationalised History away with such indifference to the intuitive, mystic veracity of Khufu's time, some of which he could have gleaned from the *Book of the Great Awakening*, the correct translation for the mistitled *Egyptian Book of the Dead*. Or had his language been imprecise; was the Pyramid a symbol from the collective unconscious that really did foretell the millennium?

ACROSS THE FRONTIER
(OR: DEATH IN A BACKWOODS CABIN)

I drove down to Norwich to be hypnotised. I had met Henry Coleridge at the Reincarnation conference, and had opted for him.

Pippa was against my going, but my search had reached a point where it had to go beyond one lifetime, and although I knew the dangers, I now had to cross the frontier of death. I told her it would be like going to the dentist: I can still remember coming round after having gas, spinning until the room slowed and stilled. And so I arrived at a tiny modern bungalow in a clean modern road that would have graced a surgery, and was admitted by the elderly, balding hypnotist himself.

He barely greeted me for I was late. He lay me straight down on his wide sofa, assembled microphones, for I would be his hundred and eighty-first "tape", and started the process: "Relax, re-lax, re-lax. I will count to five. With each number your relaxation will go deeper.... Now imagine you are at the top of a staircase. We are going down ten stairs together and you will go deeper into relaxation with each step. One – two – three...." Soon I was breathing very deeply. "Now raise your left arm. Hold it up at an angle of ninety degrees," he went on. "You will feel no sensation in it. Now let your right arm rise. It wants to rise slowly, let it float up of its own accord. Let it float up, don't try to prevent it." My left arm was in the air, my right arm rose of its own accord. "Now let your right arm fall slowly back."

Soon he was satisfied, and I was completely aware of what was happening. He took me back to the age of sixteen and asked me a few questions about my life then. "Now we are going back – fifteen, fourteen, thirteen, twelve, eleven – ten, you are ten years old." I answered some more questions. "Now you are nine, eight, seven, six, five – you are five years old now." I saw myself being taken to school by my mother and being left in a lobby and not knowing where to go. "Now we're going back – four, three, two, one, now the great moment has arrived, and you're about to be born. You are being born now." I saw a great blackness but felt cold at my extremities, especially at my toes.

The preliminaries were over, and Henry Coleridge said, "Now you're going to have a very interesting experience. You are going to go back in time to your previous life. Your subconscious contains the record of all your past lives, and I want you to answer my questions just as your subconscious provides, don't filter anything with your intellect. You will answer my questions and suffer no ill effects. I want you to go back now, go back, go back to your former life. Now where are you? Where do you find yourself?

THE CLEAR, SHINING SUNLIGHT OF ETERNITY

What do you see?"

I was completely conscious and could understand all he said, but talking was difficult for my breathing was very slow. Slowly an image formed in my mind of someone wearing a white shirt and high trousers with braces and sideboards. I was looking at him in a clearing of pine-trees somewhere in the backwoods, and on my feet were boots.

"Where is this settlement?" Henry Coleridge asked when I had told him.

"Canada," I said, "it's called Sirioux."

"What are you called?"

"Abbé."

"Now tell me about where you live."

I saw a log cabin – "the cabin" we called it – made of reddish pine trunks stripped of their bark and bound together, and there were steps up to it and a woman sat in the doorway with her grey hair in a bun. She had a wizened yellow face and she wore a white smock that had black and grey in it. "She looks after us," I said.

And there was another woman in a white bonnet with a bell-shaped dress, who was rolling pastry and she was called Emé or Esmé. I could not see her face.

"How old are you?" Henry Coleridge asked.

"Twenty-six," I replied.

"I want you to look at a newspaper and tell me what year it is," he said.

"Eighteen twenty-nine," I said, for I saw the date on the top of a faded yellow newspaper that looked like *The Times*, which had advertisements on the front.

"Now go forward ten years," Henry Coleridge said. I could not see anything – all was black – and I somehow could not speak. There was a long silence, I just could not speak a word.

"Go forward to the year of your death," said Henry Coleridge.

I said, "Eighteen thirty-six." I was in a pitted single bed in the corner of the cabin. There was a lamp. Esmé was around in the shadows. I was thirsty, so thirsty. My mouth was dry, my lips were cracked, but there was no water because of the contamination that had caused my illness. It was bad water that had brought me to my end.

"You are reliving your death," said Henry Coleridge, and my breathing came and went, my feet and legs went numb, my hands were numb, my breathing became more laboured, my mouth was parched, and then I knew I had taken my last breath. I felt a tremendous relief, a great peace. Then I was floating up to the top of the cabin, feeling light, weightless, looking down at Esmé, who pottered in the shadows, and then I was outside, high up over the settlement. I could see there had been a camp-fire in the mud, and there was a river near by.

And then I saw my tombstone: "John Barfield d 1836." The letters were carved on a curved rough round stone. Abbé John Barfield – I was a Jesuit who had lived in the camp, I had been unmarried because I was a priest. Hence my obsession with Esmé....Leaning on a long-handled axe, the blade of which I could not see for it was out of the daguerreotype, was the man with the sideboards and braces. He was looking at my gravestone, and I could not contact him. Then I was in a mist of light, and I went on and on in the mist of light....

"Now it's time to wake up," Henry Coleridge said. "You have had a very interesting experience, and it will not affect you badly in any way. We are returning up the steps: ten, nine, eight, seven, six, five, four, three, two, one...."

Soon I was awake, and the feeling returned to my left arm, which had been up at a right angle for over an hour, and I had total recall, and I was discussing my life as a priest among simple woodcutters. They called me the Abbé, Abbot. Now I had no fear of death. "There's nothing to death," I said, "dying's simple."

But underneath there was a question. I had seen images like the pictures I saw when I had a dream. Were these images far memories? Or were they a waking dream of the imagination, a fantasy, albeit without much wish-fulfilment? Were they inherited or forgotten memories: cryptamnesia? I thought of Paul Solomon's Source which had also been evoked by hypnotism. The answer to my question meant an answer as to whether I believed in his Source, and in the whole phenomenon of the collective unconscious which accounted for such New Age "certainties" as telepathy and mediumship.

"It was all historically convincing," Henry Coleridge said as he fiddled with his equipment, but I was thoughtful as I drove home. The universe looked entirely different. I felt a growing conviction that I had lived and died a hundred times before, that the human condition was *not* confined to one lifetime. I felt a great sadness for

THE CLEAR, SHINING SUNLIGHT OF ETERNITY

Esmé, a woman I had genuinely felt affection, perhaps love for, Esmé, my Emé, who was hidden behind her bonnet, cut off from me by time, irreversibly back in 1836.

Two weeks later I found a book in a junk shop called *From Log Cabin to White House*, a study of President James Garfield. In it I found descriptions of log cabins in Ohio in 1830 and a picture of a long-handled axe, and of high trousers. All the details tallied with what I saw, and I now accept them as memories like the fir-tree in the back garden of the house I lived in during the war, which had frogs in the cellar. I saw, and can remember, my dead father going to work as I stood in the window, an infant; he walked to the left and waved his stick over the privet hedge.

Emé in her bonnet, and my dead father over that hedge, both were a part of my life at different times before the present. How many more did I love and lose, how many more are locked up in the records of my darkest memory?

A CAUSEWAY OF LIGHT

Over Wiltshire a parachutist hung still in the air. He landed in a field, and his tiny limbs only moved when he hauled down his billowing red and blue chute, and from a distance he looked like someone stretching after a long meditation. Pippa drove us on, and I read a review of David Gascoyne's *Journal* in the Sunday papers. It called Gascoyne "brilliant" and quoted a judgment by Durrell, "one of the finest and purest metaphysical poets of the age". It quoted Gascoyne's aim as a young poet "to make coherence of oneself; to see...a finally convincing image of the significance of one's life, an assurance of destiny."

Over Somerset a glider went round and round on thermal currents, sinking lower and lower each circle, and looking up, I felt that gravity might suddenly snap and plunge me from land into the sky, like a parachutist on a film run backwards. I felt as if I were on the verge of a high flight.

As soon as we arrived at my mother-in-law's in Cornwall, I left Pippa to put the children to bed and drove down to Charlestown. It was sunny, and there was a blue, calm sea. The rocky headlands were covered in bright green turf, there were sunwashed cliffs, and I walked along to the old 1790s harbour wall and watched boys swim beneath me and fish. One boy held a wriggling silver fish.

When I got back we told my mother-in-law about our decorating, and she said, "Now you're here, I wasn't going to tell you, because I didn't want to spoil things for you in London, but Pippa's grandma died last week in the nursing home. The funeral was on Thursday."

I expressed shock and sorrow and watched Pippa, who was close to her grandma.

"My sister-in-law wrote and told me," her mother went on, "the letter arrived on the morning of the funeral and look, it only had a seven p stamp on it. I wonder whether it was deliberate. Pippa's grandma was well off, and she always said Pippa would benefit."

Suddenly a way seemed to have opened. Of course, one expected nothing, but for the next hour we were caught in the toils of worldly considerations, and I was unaware of my true nature.

After dinner we both drove back to Charlestown. It was dark, and there were few lights round the small harbour. There was an enormous deep yellow moon on the horizon and a causeway of yellow light across the calm water. The moon reflected the sun as my mind reflected the spiritual sun, and standing by a rusty capstan I saw that causeway of light as a straight and narrow road to my destiny which spanned the waters and rose where it reached the cliffs of Polkerris.

I crossed the bridge to the Harbour-master's house so that I could have a better view, and the night was full of brilliant stars, and again I felt I might fall out into space and live as a consciousness and being of air. Suddenly, like a finger, a shooting star gleamed and was gone; and slowly a cloud obscured the moon and the causeway faded, leaving my vision of my destiny the merest glimmer on the quiet dark waves.

I turned and walked back from eternity towards the lights of the road, I crossed back over the bridge to the world. A middle-aged man stopped me and asked, "Do china clay boats come through here? They're mainly from Fowey aren't they?" he said, wrongly. "Why's this called Charlestown? Because Charles fled from the battle of Worcester down here and went to the Scillies, I expect."

"No," I said, "it's after Charles Rashleigh."

"Oh," he said, "Charles Rashleigh. Where do you come from?"

I turned the question and he said, "Worcester." Hence his knowledge of the battle of Worcester.

I was completely back in the world now, and my realisation of the spiritual nature that gave me coherence was gone, the "gathering together of the dispersed powers of one's personality...(that) might, nevertheless, permanently alter the level of one's life" which was Gascoyne's coherence. My glimpse of my destiny had passed away, and the moon was hidden in a thick black cloud, but I had brought back with me a renewed conviction that I was a messenger from the unknown, a parachutist who was entrusted with a dark truth about the most secret Light.

PINNED BUTTERFLIES AND AFRICAN CARVINGS

They were sitting at the bar of their front room in shirt sleeves as we walked up the path. Pippa and I were greeted by Berry, whom I had not met. She extended a hand and we stood rather formally. Then she took us in and I sat beside the curate and drank cold apple juice and prattled about houses and listened to his move while I weighed the others up: the curate's wife who liked sleeping late and who looked sulky under her long hair; a quiet, bearded accountant and his rather intense, small wife, who spoke as if she had a plum in her mouth; a Unilever man with a thin, ferrety face and horn-rims and receding hair, and his spiky, bespectacled wife who had been a Head of Department at a comprehensive school; and lastly, our host and hostess, a bearded anaesthetist from the local hospital and a seasoned, still attractive physiologist whom he had met out in Zambia.

Dinner was in the front room. The curtains were undrawn and we were on display for the street to see. The space was cramped. I had met none of these people before, save to say "Hello" – the women were all friends of my wife's through children or housewives – and the conversation was a little laboured. I was down the window end of the table with the Unilever couple – the anaesthetist couple sat together near the door so they could transport the numerous curries – and I had a weird conversation about how propagandist the media were becoming, how *1984* had arrived.

The Unilever man had some ideas, but they went round and round like prejudices, and he remarked rather sadly, "I can see from your face that you don't agree with me, and that you find it boring." He lamented the meetings he attended. The Unilever people all conversed in the currency of cliché, and their brains were not involved. I said, "I don't know how anyone can measure himself in terms of an organisation."

"Yes," he said, "that expresses what I feel exactly," and he sat in silence, a sad organisation man who lived in terms of a "U" and would never be a director, and who cared about the size and brand of his car.

On my right the small, intense accountant's wife kept trying to come in. She was a history graduate, but found difficulty in expressing her ideas succinctly or holding attention because of the plum in her mouth, and her observations degenerated into reminiscences. Though I was touched when she described her reaction to being burgled. "Ronald and the children are so much more important than my things, I was just glad they hadn't been hurt," she said, and her quiet, bearded husband beamed.

It was all a bit painful, and I squirmed inwardly, though outside I was poised. I missed the stimulation of someone like Jesperson, who always said in the course of an evening at least ten things that came back next morning. I was sober, they were all anaesthetised with wine and average, that was the trouble.

After dinner we ascended to the sitting-room, and some of us sat on the floor. There were butterflies on the wall, beautiful, exotic butterflies pinned under glass. That was how the women were: pinned and exotic and under glass, and a little dead.

There were five carved African figurines on the otherwise empty mantelpiece, and when I commented on them the anaesthetist reached over and handed me one. It was a figurine from Katanga, he said. It was of a black man kneeling with his eyes closed, and looking at him I asked, as if I were looking at myself in a mirror, "Is he praying or is he miserable? See, he looks ill. Look at his belly. Has he got beriberi?" and Berry looked up, thinking I was talking about her.

The name of the carver, Loti, appeared on the bottom. I put it back on the mantelpiece and looked at the four other men who were sipping brandy. We were like the five black carvings kneeling in a semi-circle with their eyes closed, while our wives were apart, separate, together, like exotic butterflies under glass that could not be touched.

DOORHANDLE FOR A SLAMMED DOOR
(OR: GLISTENING EYES AND DROPPED KEYS)

The builder's wife rang and asked, "Is Robin there? We're trying to get hold of him. His father's died. Can you ask him to ring when he arrives?" It was a bad line, and my wife could not obtain any details.

Soon there were two rings on the bell and Robin walked jauntily in. "Your doorhandle," he said.

"Robin," I said, "I don't know what the news is, but your wife rang about your father. She wants you to ring her immediately."

He stared at me for a moment, tousled-haired and dark in the hall, while the news sunk in, and then said, "Father's died, I expect," in a casual tone.

"It may have been that," I agreed, preparing him as sensitively as I could, and before I could guide him into the sitting-room he was in the kitchen and dialling from the wall extension.

I closed the hatch and shut the door so he could be alone, and then I heard squeals. My eldest son had been in the garden and was swinging on Robin's arm as he always did when he greeted Robin, his three year old mind not understanding this crisis of grief. He resisted when I tried to move him, and he kicked and wriggled as I removed him to the playroom, where his friend was playing, and where Pippa sat with the friend's mother amidst sounds of inappropriate merriment. I heard Robin say, "OK, love."

He came out. "Go straight home," I said quietly.

He avoided my gaze and shook his head. "I'll fit your doorhandle," he gulped, and he bounded miserably upstairs, his eyes glistening. There was a long silence, and I called up, "I'm bringing some tea up."

"No," he called down.

Eventually he came downstairs, under control, to hoots of mirth from the playroom, and said, "You've got a doorhandle now."

I said, "Get straight off home."

"I'll just take the glass from outside," he said.

As he eased it into his van I said gently, "Was it expected?"

"He hasn't been well," Robin said, "and they were very concerned about him two days ago."

There was a silence in which I pondered his choice of tense. "I think I'll take his business over," he went on. "He's got six men. More problems."

I sympathised, and said how I felt when my father died. "He'd be pleased it's going to his son," I said of the business.

"I dunno," Robin said. "We fell out and I slammed the door on him and we haven't spoken for four years."

"He'd still be pleased," I said.

He thought. "Maybe," he said. "I'll go home now and sort things out, look after my mother and work out what's going to happen. I'll ring you."

He stood indecisively and then he dropped his keys. Suddenly he seemed at a loss as to what to do about retrieving them, and I bent and picked them up. He took them limply and got into his van. He nodded and drove miserably away.

I was sad for the obscure pride that had divided the two men. The surge of feeling into his eyes had taught him that he had loved his father all along. He had fitted a doorhandle to that door he had slammed, but now he was ready to open it, there was nobody the other side.

A DESTINY IN HEBREW LETTERS
(OR: A BRIDGE OF SIGHS)

I took five girls to Cambridge to "show them the way", and to support Jackie, who was being interviewed for a place that day. We were going to have lunch with Dr. Molloy, a friend of mine. We met at the local tube station in London and took the train from Liverpool Street.

We arrived at Cambridge about 11 and took a bus into town, and I entered King's with three Asians, one Moslem, and one West Indian. It was a glorious summer's day, and I immediately felt relaxed. The wide open spaces were immensely uplifting, and we walked through to the gardens at the back and ambled across the green lawn to the river. Then we gazed at the water from the stone bridge.

Eventually we returned to the Chapel. I had a book on the mysteries of the Chapel, and I marvelled at what the Freemasons had built in the second half of the 15th century, and identified the fan-vaulting as papyrus, the Egyptian plant.

The Chapel had been built in accordance with the principles of numerology, as a microcosm of creation, and it reflected the Kabbalah. I knew that the Hebrew for JHVH was on the west face – the letters counted 26 and represented the secret name of God – and we looked at it, first on the inside and then on the outside.

"Look," I said, "it's there in the sun."

Between two angels on the door there was a sun, and the

THE CLEAR, SHINING SUNLIGHT OF ETERNITY

Hebrew letters were across it, and I knew immediately that the secret name of God was written across the Divine Light.

We met my tousled-haired friend, who wore jeans and an old sweater. Jackie joined us, looking studious in her spectacles. She was pleased with her interviews. She said she was all tensed up for the second interview, and the don walked in in jeans and said, "Hi." We went to the Fellows' dining room near the Hall and served ourselves at the canteen and carried a tray of greasy food to the table where three dons had to move up to accommodate six comprehensive girls.

Dr. Molloy answered questions about the courses the girls wanted to choose, and then he took us to an ante-room with old paintings of the College, and I sat in a leather chair and drank my coffee and chatted until the Senior Tutor came in. She was youngish and wore casual slacks and a jerkin, and she laughed a lot and flirted with my eyes. I sparkled. I felt at home. I revelled in the play of witty conversation, while the six girls sat in silence. This was where I belonged, in this sort of environment.

Later we looked at a student's room, and I saw where E.M. Forster died. We revisited the Chapel, and I tried to show Jackie the manuscript of Rupert Brooke's *Soldiers* which I had seen that morning, but the room was closed for hoovering.

Once again I stood before the Chapel's west end and looked at the secret name of God in the sun. The Light shone out into me.

Later we walked to Trinity, where Marvell was, and to St. John's, where we saw Wordsworth's room and the fireplace he sat before. Then we walked to the Bridge of Sighs and soaked in the red ivy and yellow flowers the other side.

Men punted lazily, and I stood on the nearby bridge and sighed. For it occurred to me that I had thought I was showing the girls the way, whereas perhaps they were showing me the way without my really realising it. Soon I would be returning to the greyness of London and my glassy comprehensive, but mentally my direction had changed. I wondered if I would work in Cambridge, somehow. In some strange way I had been guided there, I had been shown Cambridge because it held something for my future.

I sighed again on the bridge, and thought of the lettering in the sun. The Light had shone on me in Cambridge, and my destiny was written in Hebrew letters whose details were obscure, although the whole meaning was plain.

SHAHITES IN OUR ROAD

"I came from Persia originally," said Semira, the girl from down the road as the train sped home from Cambridge. "My great grandmother was married to the Shah of Persia, and the present Shah's father took over and persecuted the former royal family, and she fled to India. It was the time when the British set up the Pahlavi Dynasty. We are Shiite Moslems, we follow Ali and the Shah's opponent, the Ayatollah, who is in Paris, and we stayed there until the Indo-Pakistani war in the 1960s. Then we fled to Pakistan. I went back to India last year, for much of our family is still there near New Delhi, and I caught malaria. I was away all the Michaelmas term, but I still passed my English Literature 'O' level. My uncle lives further up our road, in the Hotel."

"Not Mr Bhavani?" I said in astonishment. "I've met him."

"I know," she said. "He has a son, Sammy, who needs to learn English."

"My wife was going to teach him," I said. "He told me he was from Persia. He has a house full of tenants a few doors nearer us from the Hotel." I did not say, 'And he charges exorbitant rents.' "He has a house on the Common," I went on. This was bought out of his high rents and overcrowding, he had told me.

"That's right," she said. "It is very dangerous for him. That part of our road is very bad. There are muggings and murders. The house next to him was burgled only two nights ago. There was a kidnapping up our road last week. Did you read about it? A girl was kidnapped and raped all night, and she threw herself out of a window and broke her legs. She is critically ill. They caught the two men. We were near Clapham South before. We moved because there were two murders behind us. Our end of the road is all right.

"My father is a printer," she went on. "He works for the *Daily Mirror*. He leaves for work at half past six at night. He is an expert on ancient religions. He knows many things. He says that Shakespeare was an Iraqi Arab, Sheikh Beer, whose father came from Spain to Italy. He arrived in England and Anglicised his name. My father has over two hundred books on ancient religions, including the Persian religions. But we are not Parsees, we are Shiites. He is glad that I want to become a doctor. I have always wanted to go to Cambridge, and I shall never forget today, September the twenty-second. Thank you very much for taking me. I shall never forget it."

THE SWEET SMELL OF DECAY
(OR: A COLLEGE OF FLOWERS,
TWENTY YEARS AS A DAY)

I went back to Oxford for a gaudy. It was to be paid for by my College, I merely had to hire a dinner-jacket from Alkits. I drove up from London and arrived around 5.30 p.m. on a cold, bright, autumnal day. I collected lists of my contemporaries who had accepted, found my room in the eighteenth century Terrace and then climbed the winding stairs to the library, revisited the scene of whole nights of labour and recalled the twitter of the birds in the dawn gardens as I crept to my bed.

I went for a walk in the gardens. I went through the tunnel, and was hit by the smell of decaying flowers. There was a riot of rank sunflowers, dahlias, roses and overgrown hollyhocks, and one or two pansies, all of which looked storm-beaten and neglected, and I identified the smell as carbon dioxide, the smell that rises when dead flowers and stagnant water are tipped out of a vase.

I did not know what my contemporaries would be like, and I was a bit appalled that I had come back, twenty years after matriculating, to the deep silence which had once been a loneliness disturbed only by the swishing trees. I returned to my room and changed into my DJ while draughts creaked in the bare boards of the staircase outside, and at 7 I went into the sumptuously decorated Burges (1866) Chapel. I sat among still men in DJs and listened to the choir sing High Church music, and then a tousled-haired man in spectacles came and thumbed his way through the gold Bible until he found his place and read a lesson. It was how "a thousand years are as a day in Thy sight", and I thought 'Twenty years as a day'. For really, it seemed only yesterday that I had sat beside the familiar, ageless expressions of my contemporaries.

Afterwards we went out into the Buttery and immediately I was mobbed by familiar faces and there were excited cries of recognition and pumped hands and raised silver tankards. "I feel just as young as I was twenty years ago," one of my contemporaries told me. After a word with the Deputy Provost I went into Hall in high spirits, and took my place at the ancient long table for a sumptuous five-course meal. There were three wines, and the sconce pot was ceremoniously out, and I admired the decor of Thomas Wyatt (1784), for the walls had been restored to the original. The few survivors from twenty years ahead of my time sat white-haired on top table, and I joked, "In twenty years' time we'll be on top table," and the company around me laughed as if Time were a containable evil.

At the end came the speeches. The tousled-haired man turned out to be the new Provost, and he raised laughs. We thumped our approval on the table. Then the Deputy Provost called on the ageing Law tutor, shortly to be a laurel-leaved Emeritus, to make a short speech, and my first tutor rose, pale and bald and eighty and Churchillian in his frailness, and croaked, "Gentlemen, this is not going to be a short speech, this is going to be a speech."

There was a roar of approval, and we thumped the tables, and the Emeritus told a long story (told to him by the late Provost) about a preacher who asked his Presbyterian congregation, "Do you know what I'm going to say?" When they called out "No," he replied, "Neither to I," and sat down. This was deemed a promising beginning, and two weeks later he was invited again, and again he asked, "Do you know what I'm going to say?" "Some of us do, and some of us don't," they called back. "Then," he said, "let those who do tell those who don't," and again he sat down. There was laughter and deafening applause, and everyone was slightly drunk. My neighbour said to me, "I find all this poignant. It'll seem like a dream tomorrow. It's a trip back into the past. I feel so young."

There was a boring speech by one of the white-haired oldies, and with the Hall reeking with cigar smoke, we adjourned to the Buttery and drank beer until three in the morning.

I talked to some thirty of my contemporaries and near-contemporaries. They were all in education, journalism or the Law but we were all back as we were twenty years previously. "Charles Nones," one said (a BBC economics correspondent), "now there was a name to conjure with – and he ended up in a university in Alaska." Names were exchanged, and I heard apocryphal stories about myself: how I climbed over the wall onto the garden roller, which they named after me, and how I broke a toe in Greece, though I have never broken any toe. One said, "Most of us here are the same, but you've changed." Another said, "You were very daring: while we were all in cavalry twill you were in black jeans. You were ahead of your time."

I felt I had changed. I was a part of the college now; I was no longer an outsider, I was more in charge of the evening than they were. I sparkled. I had a long talk with the Provost who said, "You are a member of a college for life, not just for three years, and I would like old members like yourself to come here and teach for a year, and let in some life from the outside world. Because it gets very enclosed here." I said I would like to be seconded for a year and he said, "We will talk about it. I will talk privately with you about it."

At 3 a.m. I went to bed and slept under a quilt, and I just arrived at breakfast as the doors closed at 9.30 a.m., with the timing I perfected in the old days. I sat again in the Hall and talked with a Headmaster of a public school who said, "I have a permanent smile on my face. I practise what I used to condemn in others. Whatever I do, I'm thinking 'Who's watching me?' Because if I'm gloomy, people may think the school has problems and take their children away." I was the last to leave the Hall. Like the Old English Wanderer, I felt I belonged to a Hall.

I went for a last walk in the gardens. A chill wind swooshed through the trees, and blew brittle yellow leaves on the grass. Birds sang. Chinese geese honked. Once again the smell of decay rose from the flower-bed. Far away a group of my contemporaries stood in a ring on the grass. There were ten of them, and they were as still as flowers till the wind came, and then they swayed slightly.

Twenty years were as a day in their sight. They all felt as young as spring flowers, but they had all begun to go, and the sweet smell of decay was on them. Rooted in our college, we were all like that bed of decaying flowers. We were a college of flowers, struck by time, leaning storm-beaten and neglected together, supporting each other as we withered sweetly away.

RÔLES LIKE FANCY DRESS
(OR: A FLURRIED HEAD, AN ICY INSPECTOR,
OR: DETACHMENT AND INVOLVEMENT)

The school was being subjected to a Full Inspection, and the loos and lunch queues were cluttered with seedy-looking men with spectacles and baggy, disillusioned eyes. There were some fifty of them. They stood at the corners of the corridors during afternoon tutor time, and the Deputy Head told me, "I've got Raymundo of the Mafia himself coming into my General Studies class now, I've just written my record book for the year."

Then the Head clucked into the staff room, looking flurried, and shouted, "*Will* you all go to your tutor groups," and, taken aback at being addressed peremptorily, the staff indignantly stampeded out into the lower block corridor, pushing a throng of senior girls before them who, in turn, pouring through a bottleneck caused by a loitering Inspector, pressed on a group of first year girls, one of whom fell and was trampled on. Her cries under the scrimmage immediately told that she had broken an ankle.

Mrs. Gandhi, an RE teacher, fought her way through the mêlée and lifted the injured girl, broke the medical rules to get her out of the way. As she backed out, holding the girl, she saw the Inspector who had caused the bottleneck. He stood icily against the wall, like a lamp-post, at the very spot where the accident had happened. He was scribbling in his notebook.

"Can you call an ambulance?" Mrs. Gandhi called. Perhaps he did not hear, but he made no effort to intervene. He went on scribbling in his notebook, and it was left to girls to raise the alarm.

After the ambulance had taken the injured girl to hospital, where a cracked shoulder was diagnosed, and paralysis of one leg, the Head's voice came thin and strained over the tannoy, a tone higher than usual. It identified girls who had been recognised as having stampeded, and said, "All these girls are to come to my room *immediately*."

Rumour had it that the Inspector was still there on the corridor with his notebook. After all, are not Inspectors the public's eyes and ears? Was he not there to inspect the operation of the system? Could he have observed the incident if he had involved himself in that schoolgirl's raucous pain?

For days afterwards I could not get the image out of my mind of a flurried Head who caused the stampede, and of an icy Inspector who recorded a girl's pain in his notebook while she screamed for help. How much better it would have been if they had both taken off the rôles they wore round their hearts. How much better it would have been if the Head had hung her frown on the peg behind her door, and been detached at the start of tutor time, and if the Inspector had stopped being a sodium street-light and become involved in the corridor. How much better it would have been if they had not hidden their hearts under their social fancy dress.

PROVIDENCE LIKE A RETRIBUTION
(OR: RUNNING EYES AND AN EOKA GUNMAN)

A parent came up to school to see me, as Head of English, about his daughter, who had wept for two days since being told that she would not be taking 'O' level. He was a thickset, pugnacious Greek Cypriot with spivvy black, greased hair; he could have been a forty-five year old Teddy Boy.

As soon as we had found an interview room, he sat with his legs apart and weighed into Mary's English teacher, a young girl who was with me; wagging his finger: "I know you, you have caused trouble for Mary, you make her unhappy and so you make us unhappy, why? Mary was good at English last year, and her teacher said 'She is fine', and now you give her poor marks. Mary is a very hard worker, she should have good marks. Another girl copies from Mary and you give her better marks than Mary, and she does not drop. No, I no tell you any names. You must find out. I have lost today's money to tell you this. Mary does not know I am here. I work at a garage, but I do not care for the money I have lost. In fact, the wife, she wanted to come too. But I say, 'No, I will go.' I am a fighter, and when I fight I hit back. I tell Mary, 'I do not mind if you drop, you going into hairdressing, you not going to be a bank clerk or go to university. But I want you to be happy and not have running eyes.'"

The words came out as a stream of feeling, and all the while I kept thinking how his spivvy Teddy Boy haircut made him look like Nicos Sampson, the ex-EOKA gunman who was President of Cyprus for a week by accident after the coup that overthrew Makarios. I could not help liking his forthright approach, and I stilled the teacher's protests and said: "We accept that Mary is industrious, but the only thing that matters is what *is* her standard? An 'O' level C would be hard for Mary to get, because at 'O' level all mistakes are marked. Her English is inaccurate, I know, and no dictionary or course work is allowed at 'O' level. She might obtain a CSE grade one because only the first two hundred words are marked at CSE, and thirty pieces of course work make up thirty per cent of the total marks of the examination. She needs a certificate to obtain a job – she might change her mind after a year of hairdressing – and a grade two at CSE means something whereas an 'O' level D does not. Mary herself should choose and then she would be happy. We have made our recommendation, but we are not preventing anyone from taking an examination they want to take, and if Mary wants to do 'O' level and fail we will accept that." I knew Mary would choose CSE if her choice were sufficiently informed, and her teacher understood my tack and nodded her agreement, and he nodded.

He looked so much like Nicos Sampson, I had to ask him about EOKA. "Mary is from Cyprus," I said. "She does very well to write English as she does. But she speaks a lot of Greek, and that is why her English is inaccurate."

"She has been here a long time," the Greek Cypriot said. "I was in Cyprus, but we have been here, and I work in a garage."

"When were you in Cyprus?" I asked as we left the interview room.

"Back in the 1950s," he said.

"Did you see anything of the troubles?"

He looked startled. "Oh, no," he said, "not in our village. We saw nothing. We heard about them though."

"I once met Colonel Grivas," I said, and he looked hunted and said quickly, "I never met him."

I chattered on about my encounter with Grivas, but he repeated, "I never met him," looking sideways, and I was sure he was lying. Then he said "Well...." He shook my hand, and nodded to his daughter's teacher, who said quietly so that only I could hear, "Seethe, seethe", and then he was off, scuttling across the playground as if I had just said I would be asking the Home Office to investigate his background during the Cypriot troubles, and I was sure he would never come near the school again.

I was sure I had spoken to one of the EOKA gunmen, and I wondered who I was avenging, what British soldier had fallen in a Nicosia street at his fighting hands, leaving Providence to cast me as disturber of his peace, a voice from a past he had tried to forget, who brought a divine retribution upon his daughter.

MIXED METAPHORS AND A DIAMOND LIGHT
(OR: CLEARING THE BOWELS OF THE MIND)

Black-haired Mrs. Gandhi, an ageing Jewess who had married a Hindu, showed me an "essay" she had written. We were sitting in the staff room, and half-term had just begun, and glancing through it and recognising an expanded rehash of some ideas I had expressed, I suffered an acute bout of mental constipation. It began: "Meditating with other Zen Buddhists in search of Enlightenment, even though we were unsure what this was, the Master would walk up and down behind our backs." Later on it contained the sentence: "What we did begin to understand was that there is a ladder of self-transcendence, a gate of illumination."

I pushed her "attempt" tiredly aside. Apart from the dreadful words, all the "wills" and "begin tos" were in the past tense for me, and it was all so utterly turgid and boring.

"What do you think of it?" she asked.

I was sharp from an afternoon with my 'A' level class, and the way she fawned for praise cried out for some Practical Criticism. "It's all a question of language," I said, nauseated at the fustian. "You have put down what I have told you, but an idea is sharp if the language is sharp, and blunt if the language is blunt. Look at the wrongly attached participle in the first line. Who was meditating? Only the Master? Look at the metaphors in paragraph two. You can't have a *gate* above a *ladder*. You can have a gate above steps, or a loft panel above a ladder, but you can't mix the two ideas. And further on, look at 'luminous channel'. A light is luminous, a channel can't be, it is a conduit. And in the same passage, a channel becomes a knot and a key. This is the trouble with the language of Mysticism. It can be too imprecise. It is like the Staff Association Meeting the other day. 'We want to extend the car-park' means 'we want to bulldoze the bank of flowers next to it'. 'We want to extend car-parking facilities' is horrible jargon." I put her "essay" down.

"Yes," she said, crushed, "but what do you think of the contents?"

"More and more I come round to the view that only the poets can catch the Light in writing," I said. "Only sharp language can wrest meaning from the unsayable, and only poets purify the language. Poetry today has fallen into terrible disrepute, but traditionally poetry sharpens language, its imagery is consistent and united, and it is founded on experience, and not theory. Mysticism has fallen into disrepute because of its imprecise language, and is knocked by Ayer. Only a purified language can restore it. And so more and more I am going back to the Metaphysical poets. I should go to Oxford and write a series of lectures on the mystic line in

English poetry. Mysticism is like gazing at the sun, like the contemplative gazing at the sunrise. Channels, knots and keys get in the way of the gazing-on-the-sun, they get between me and the sun, they do not add to the description of the sunrise, they interfere. A Metaphysical poet describes the sun shining, and sun-basking, better than an 'essayist' who uses clichéd jargon. It's a personal point of view, but I see with a Metaphysical poet's eye now."

She looked slightly hurt. "I agree with you," she said, looking up to the height from which I was speaking. "I have to go now, my husband is waiting for me."

I watched her put her coat on and go. I sat on in the corner of the staff room. I breathed slowly and heavily, and closing my eyes, for the third time that week I gazed on a clear blue diamond of Light, which sparkled and glittered and flashed with a sharp cutting edge. I could not gaze on it for long, for members of my Department sat across the room, and one wanted to speak to me; but I felt wonderfully close to the truth about myself and the world, I felt beautifully serene. It was as if I had taken a laxative and fizzed and cleared the bowels of my mind, and flushed away something indigestible that had given me a pain.

LIKE THE SMELL OF FRESH BEANS
(OR: WOODWORM IN THE SOUL)

I wanted four trees lopped that autumn: the two acacias in the front, the pear and birch at the back, all of which overhung the road. My mother had had four of her fruit trees pruned down in Essex for £8 (no cartage), and knowing no more about the going rate than that I rang the Council and confirmed that they would only lop rent-payers' trees. Ratepayers had to lop their own.

I then rang two numbers in the local paper – "free estimates given" – and made arrangements, and soon I was rung back by the second man, who began abusively: "I understand you've asked someone else to come and look at your trees. It's not good enough. Is it worth my while or isn't it?"

I was taken aback by his assumption that an invitation to estimate was as good as a commission, and in the end he slammed the phone down.

When the first man arrived, a long-eared giant with a turned-up nose and a wrinkled brow, he said, "Did you ask someone else to look at these trees? Because a total stranger rang me up and asked me if I was coming up to you, and he was very abusive." The giant had two men and a van, and he seemed very anxious to be given the work. He made "expert" comments, and then said, "I'll give you a price for the whole job, and then you tell me what you think, and we can negotiate. My price is: a hundred and thirty pounds."

I nearly fainted.

He must have seen my look, for he immediately made me a second offer. "We won't do as much as we were going to, and it will be eighty pounds. And we'll burn the wood here."

Again I can't have looked very enthusiastic, for he said, "I'll tell you what I'll do. I'll do it for sixty, and you can pay me the other twenty when you have it, perhaps three months later." I deflected him and promised to give him an answer the following morning. "Can you ring by 10.30?" he said. "I want to be there to take the call myself."

Meanwhile I found a man who would cut the trees for £40. When I rang the giant the next morning and told him, he did not seem unduly surprised. He immediately said, "One of our lads is on holiday, and he'll come along. Can I send him up?"

"It'll have to be for significantly less than forty," I said, and so curly-headed Jim, a hulk of a bloke with slow, stupid eyes, rang our bell and could hardly get out who he was. He agreed to do the job for £25, including carting everything away on a lorry. "I'm getting married," he said very slowly, "and I need all ve extra money I can get."

He returned that afternoon with a lad and gave the trees a haircut. He climbed the pear-tree and, wielding a hack-saw to good effect, soon had the overgrown foliage looking like a groomed fruit-tree. "This'll let some light in," he kept saying. He then turned to the birch, and the garden was filled with lopped boughs, dead bits, and brittle autumn leaves.

The lad and I loaded the lorry and then Jim sawed off all the acacia boughs, leaving (or unleaving) the trunk and ear-like stubs. "This'll let some light in," he kept saying, and, "Smells of fresh beans, don't it?" I smelt the round sappy end of an acacia bough and I marvelled at the sudden accuracy of this stupid-eyed fellow's sense-impressions: it did smell exactly of fresh beans that have not been sliced. Then I saw that the branch it had come from was riddled with woodworm holes, and I pointed it out to him.

As he sawed out the rotten knot of wood the phone rang. I answered it. It was another man I had rung for a free estimate. He too was abusive. "I happened to be passing, and I noticed you've had the trees done. What do you mean by ringing and asking for an estimate if you're having them done by someone else? I've a good mind to send you a bill." I told him plainly that while estimates varied from £130 to £25, I reserved the right to shop around, and I rang off.

Back in the garden, I thought how desperate some of the loppers must be. They were all on the verge of bankruptcy, I decided, and so they abused each other, and conned and bullied their clients, and were generally sour; unless there was a tender, in which case, like Jim up the tree, they were pleased. I thought how lucky I was that I had not professional woodworm in my soul. I held a sprig of acacia to my nose and exuded a serenity that smelt of fresh beans.

LOYALTY LIKE A COMPANY LABEL
(OR: DRAIN MEN ON THE FIDDLE)

The builders had destroyed everything. In removing old slates and gutters they had broken the conservatory glass. In removing the boards over the French windows they broke four panes of glass. They had made a fire in the middle of the lawn. And now – I was convinced of it – they had blocked the seven foot deep drain that ran to the sewer in the middle of the road. Something had clearly blocked it: fetid greeny brown water lapped six inches from the garden as, taking it in turns, they thrust long supple rods downwards, felt for the overflow, and plunged them backwards and forwards without effect. In the end they resorted to baling out. They turned the two dustbins upside down and gently scattered the contents so that wrapped tins and decaying chicken bones lay on the concrete, and then, destructive to the last, filled the two dustbins with the foul water, one whiff of which reminded me of stepping out of the aircraft at Hong Kong airport. "At least our tenants should feel at home," I remarked to my wife.

The men prodded and poked all morning and half the afternoon (a Friday), and finally asked me to ring Drain-Rods. They emptied the contents of the two dustbins among the rose bushes, so that a brown pool of slurry and sludge vied with their late scents, and they stood and watched as Drain-Rods came, at £10.40 an hour, wearing smart green boiler suits with their company's name on the back, and lifted down a machine that looked like a rotary mower. The two Drain-Rods men revved it and played cable down through a pipe and into the water. A curly-haired young man with dreamy eyes was in unenthusiastic charge of the operation, and after three-quarters of an hour of revving and lulls, the machine shuddered and screamed, and there was a terrible jar.

"The cable's snapped," the dreamy young man said in a very unbothered tone. "I'll have to ring my depot. Do you mind?" He made a phone call to his superior, calling him "mate" and saying "Right?" at the end of each sentence: "Look mate, we got fifty feet under the road, right? But the storm-flap hasn't opened, right?" Then he turned to me and said, "My governor says I must repeat the operation to recover our cable. This will be at your expense. But quite frankly, there's no more guarantee of success than last time. I'd advise you to have the high-pressure water-machine at forty pounds fifty for two hours, plus VAT. I'll have to get it from the depot. It may only take two minutes to blast the drain clear with water and break up what's there, but it'll still cost you forty pounds fifty. Are you prepared to pay?"

My builders, gleeful that their lack of success was not being shown up, pointed out that the alternative was to spend £3,000 digging up the road, so after unsuccessfully telephoning the council to see if they would open the storm-flap I reluctantly agreed, and Drain-Rods returned to their van.

"How can I keep the cost down?" I asked the builders.

"Bribe 'em," Robin replied.

"Sling them some money?" I echoed.

"Bung, not sling," Robin said. "Look, give me some notes. A couple of nicker. Bung 'em a couple like this. Oi."

His shout prevented the Drain men from driving off. I watched as he approached their van and tossed the two notes through the window. I saw hands grasp.

Robin returned without saying a word, so I advanced. "Can you keep the cost down?" I asked.

"I'll do my best," the dreamy young man called through the window, brightening up for the first time since his arrival. "But I can't promise anything."

He was gone a couple of hours. He returned after dark with a water-trailer on two wheels at the back of the van, and with three other fellows. They ran and lifted the sewer manhole in the middle of the road, and we bent and craned our necks and peered as they shone a torch at the stream of muck that trickled below us. "We can't possibly crawl down there and open the storm-flap," said the dreamy young man. "The opening's so small we'd have to crawl, and we'd be overcome by fumes. We haven't got masks."

So they replaced the manhole lid and returned to their water trailer. They unwound hoses and connected one to a mains tap in the house, and put a hose down a bent pipe into the drain, and soon the top of the trailer was bubbling like a loo tank. There was a revving, a needle moved round a dial, I peered down the drain, and the fetid water ran away. They blasted the sides of the drain with a jet of water, and there at the bottom lay their cable, and slates from the roof.

"Your builder hasn't been roofing the drain has he?" one of the Drain men asked as he lowered himself into the hole and scooped out handfuls of slate and rubble. "I could kiss you, girl," the dreamy young man said as his colleague hauled in yards of expensive broken cable.

Following some advice Robin had given me, I said, "If I give you some more money, can you lower the price? Can you fix it?"

"I'll see," he said, and he had a word with his "guvnor", a tall young man in a T shirt and jeans, with long matted hair.

Sitting in his van the "guvnor" said, "It's twenty-one pounds for the two hours they were here, plus VAT. That's already been written down. If I make your bill twenty-five pounds, I get a drink, right?"

"Right," I said, "a fiver?"

"Look," he said, "your bill should come to sixty or seventy pounds. You're thirty-five in the clear, that's not very generous."

"A tenner," I said.

"All right. I'll write twenty-one sixty-eight, VAT included. It had cleared itself when we arrived and we didn't need the trailer."

"Right," I said. "Payment would be what it would have been had they opened the storm-flap the first time."

He wrote out my receipt while I paid him twenty-one sixty-eight and two fivers, and the three others stood around, grinning.

Nearly £35 in all was down the drain, so to speak; but it was a drop in the ocean – or rather, sewer – compared with what the house was worth, and what I had paid to the destructive builders. I was sure they had lifted the drain-top and swept down all the sweepings-up after their work on the roof.

It was an unnecessary expense, but I could not help smirking when the Drain men had gone. It was the blatancy of the operation that amused me. Poulson, T. Dan Smith and other professional men and politicians had done the same with contracts, except that thousands had changed hands rather than fivers. They had been veiled and subtle. Moral considerations aside, I would not dare to take a bribe in front of three of my colleagues for fear that one of them might tell my "guvnor".

Yet here were four men who were in a conspiracy to defraud their firm, and not only were they not veiled and subtle, but they did not even have to be sounded out. Robin had taken it for granted that they were on the fiddle. It went without saying. To such a pass had things come in England.

We had become like an Arab country. There was a general assumption that everyone was on a fiddle. May be it had something to do with union attitudes towards management and the pay freeze, but personal gain had become as blatant as the unenthusiastic manner in which these Drain men wore their company label on their backs.

WHITE GLOBES AND A BLOOD-RED SUN
(OR: A PAINTED NUN AND A SMASHED HALO)

We drove down to Worthing that late October afternoon. The sea was a long way out, and there was a whiff of low tide in the air. It was misty, but the sun was trying to break through. I drank in the sea air and planned the next twenty years, pondered on life and art. We walked to the end of the pier and looked at the small fish that wriggled near the barnacled stays, and then we walked on the pebbles and combed for shells. There were several severed fishes' heads near where the fishermen drew their boats in, and a pair of pink claws from a crab. I reflected them in a line of poetry. I felt a resigned peace, as though I had succumbed and revisited a lost love.

We drove to Teresa's shop. It was closed. Every other day was closing day now, for she was painting again. In the window stood the finished nun, St. Theresa with a blue top and a white wimple under her throat, her masterpiece, her Mona Lisa, framed in gold and surrounded by water colours of flowers; the religious life in one pair of haunting, divine eyes.

Below it the red baked halo lay in three separate pieces, as if blown apart in some awful explosion. It was utterly smashed, I knew she was in turmoil. She left the secret signs of her spiritual life on public display in her shop-window, for all who knew to read.

We called in at her sister's, and Teresa came and talked through the window of the car. "I can't wait to sell that gallery," she said. "I'm mentally in London now, but I'm tied by what's happening – or not happening – down here. And then there's the Continent. I am in three pieces at present, but I am painting."

We drove back to Worthing. It was twilight, and the setting sun was a round blood-red ball in thickening mist. All along the front were round white lamps. They were strangely incandescent. I looked at the blood-red sun and the white copies of it, and suddenly I grasped something very elusive about the meaning of art. The white globes were all down the promenade, but I fixed my eyes on the blood-red sun and vowed that even if it took me twenty years, I would keep faith with the disc of blood in my life; and the globes would take care of themselves.

STAGNANT EYES AND A VEIN

I saw the Holy Trinity as I came out of Assembly. They were standing grimly together, the three ILEA English Inspectors: Ireland with moustache and glasses, Oldfield tall and gangling and uncannily resembling George Orwell, and Martin dapper in a dark suit and coat, the *Guardian* tucked under his arm. As I approached, Ireland said to Martin, "Are you allowed?" and Martin replied, "No, I'm a quiet."

I pumped their hands and greetings trickled muddily from their dry lips. I gave them up-to-date class lists and timetables, and Oldfield and Martin disappeared to classrooms. I took Ireland up to the Departmental Room.

"Why are you out this afternoon?" he asked suspiciously. I showed him my green hospital appointment card and told him how the valves had gone in my right ankle, leaving stagnant blood that varicosed the veins, causing me to wear an anklet, and I said I was going to have my blood rerouted. "Oh, Alan Oldfield has just the same," Ireland said, "you must talk with him."

I did not see Oldfield until lunch-time. Then, as he scraped his plate clean on the trolley he called across to me, "You're having your ankle injected, I hear." I repeated what had happened to my valves and said non-committally, "I have an appointment with a consultant, but I don't know whether he'll recommend me to have it done."

"I had it done in Cheshire," he said, the stagnant blood in his jaded eyes. "It didn't work. My valves went, I had eczema because of the stagnant blood, and they injected me at a hospital. There was no local anaesthetic, it didn't hurt. It thrombosed up. They made me walk three miles a day for six weeks, my wife used to pick me up in the car. Then the eczema began again. A complete waste of time. Go and try it, but I warn you, it may not work."

He had a slightly hooked nose, and he gave me a bleak, severe look that somehow summed up the disillusion I expected from an Inspector.

Thus encouraged, I drove to the Hospital, congratulating myself on avoiding Ireland's censorious gaze in my fifth year class that afternoon, checked in at Out-patients, presented my urine sample in a plastic bag, was weighed, and then waited my turn over the *Times*. After half an hour I was called to an empty room where a nurse appeared, briefly, to ask me to remove my trousers and socks and sit on a high, short bed with a sloping end where the pillow should have been.

Mr Gilligan came in. He was a smiling, bald man. He examined my right ankle and then asked me to stand on a raised platform with rails. Immediately the blood filled my varicose vein. "I can do this," he said, "I can thrombose it up and make this side vein disappear. The front one is shown in classical Greek sculptures, so normal is it, so I'll leave that one alone. I'll do it now if you like."

"Will I have to walk three miles a day for six weeks?" I asked and to delay the stab I told him about Oldfield.

"Oh no, I don't go in for any of that," Mr Gilligan said. "You'll only walk your usual."

He already held a syringe and, still standing, I bit into the side of one hand and screwed up my face and felt a searing pain that lasted a good twenty seconds.

"Sorry, that was bad," said Mr Gilligan, "I'll have to do it again."

I bit into my hand a second time, and shut my eyes so that I could not see the pain, and as the agony swelled I felt a little giddy, I was hot within but cold to the touch.

"It's natural," Mr Gilligan said, "it's because you've been standing. Lie down a minute. Then you'll be all right."

It took me twenty minutes to hobble back to my car, and I hurt all the way home. I limped for the rest of that evening, and when I took the small plaster off my varicose vein, it had gone, and there was a red thrombotic patch under the skin above my ankle. The next day I walked carefully, but all was well. I told Oldfield about my ordeal.

"Obviously a new technique," he said, "trust Cheshire to have an old technique."

"I think it's worked," I said.

He looked thinly at me and said, "It's too early to say that, you may find it doesn't work. I'm on the waiting-list for having mine stripped out, and I'm having a hernia done at the same time, so I won't try your Mr Gilligan. No, you may find it doesn't work." And he sauntered off across the playground, leaving me wondering why he wanted to believe so positively that it wouldn't work.

Was it because he could not bear to think of the hundred and twenty-six miles he had walked in vain after his injection, or was he just as stagnantly disillusioned and uncharitable towards another human being's convalescence as he was towards human teaching methods?

A SMILE AND VIOLENT STREETS
(OR: A PRIZEWINNING HEART)

We went into the Old Town Hall, Chelsea, and entered the reception where Butcher waved and greeted us. We took a glass of wine each and met Lady Ash of the Chelsea Committee for Overseas Students, and the Lady Mayoress, who, in the Mayor's absence abroad, was in fact the Mayor's god-daughter, and the Deputy Mayoress. Then we wandered round the room, where Commonwealth mixed with non-Commonwealth. There were numerous Africans, Asians and Latin Americans, their countries on the badges on their lapels, and American girls spoke together near a Russian girl from Moscow. There were representatives from every nation.

Then the Irish Peace Movement people arrived: one of the Nobel Peace Prizewinners, a glamorous dark small woman and one of her blonde assistants, along with the widow of the British Ambassador to Ireland who was blown up and killed by the IRA. They were introduced by Lady Sims, and the Peace Prizewinner smiled a simple, unaffected smile at no one in particular, as if she were slightly diffident.

There was a contrast between the frail beauty of her simplicity and the appalling violence that had killed her two nephews, and I went over to her.

"I felt we should have said something when we were introduced, but I didn't know what to say," she said with a disarmingly shy smile in her Irish lilt, and I was quite captivated. I asked a banal question about what she was doing in London, and she said, "We're here to canvass against the Emergency Powers Act. You know, it came in after internment. We want it ended, and we're pressing the British Government, lobbying MPs. It's a measure of how much better things have become that we can do this. We just articulate what people feel. I think that's the power of our movement. It's not us, it's what people feel."

"Do you ever feel a target?" I asked.

"Sometimes," she said with a nervous smile. "There were death-threats a month ago, our offices were supposed to be blown up, but they weren't."

"Do you have a bodyguard when you walk the streets?"

"Oh no," she said. "We reckon that if the IRA blew us up or shot us it would be counter-productive to their cause, so we never have any form of protection, and we never look over our shoulders. We don't think about death-threats. If they're going to do it, they're going to do it."

We were having too real a conversation for such a false occasion, and the Head of a local College was on hand to divert and trivialise the talk. I turned aside and found myself talking to the widow of the former British Ambassador to Ireland, who was being remembered in some lectures which were to be published, she said. I suggested that Sean McBride, a former head of the IRA and a UN Commissioner, the son of Maud Gonne, Yeats's mistress, by the McBride we executed in 1916, should be approached, and later I found myself talking to an author who was writing a book about Isadora Duncan, "that nymphomaniac". But I still thought of my

Peace Prizewinner.

I thought it was clever of her to turn her protest from the IRA and the Provos to the British Government – neutrality would help her survive – and I watched her smiling happily and apparently not thinking at all about the violent streets that awaited her, if not outside the Old Town Hall, Chelsea, then certainly when she returned to Belfast. She had a prizewinning heart.

A COLONEL IN CIVVY STREET

A fat man with a moustache and a pinstriped suit lurched past me at the reception, took another drink, turned, and said something incoherent to a couple of black Rhodesians, who laughed and exchanged glances, finding him a figure of fun. On his way back he stopped and asked me "Are you a Friend of Chelsea?"

I beamed the question back to him, and he said, "Oh, I'm a nobody. Colonel Bond, formerly Commandant of Sandhurst. I retired eighteen months ago. Do you know Butcher?"

It was Butcher who had invited me, and I said I did.

"I used to know him in Berlin," the Colonel said. "I don't know why, but I *liked* him, and I think he liked me. I still don't understand it. I was Military Attaché in those days, and he was in the British Council. Then I saw him a few months ago out of a bus, walking near South Ken station. I said 'Butcher'. My wife was sitting beside me, and I said, 'Butcher'. And so we met up. I invited him to something and he couldn't come, and then he invited me to this.

"You used to be connected with the British Council didn't you say? Then why the Hell aren't you abroad? The taxation's killing me, taxation's what sends people abroad. Take me, for example." He ogled my wife. "I retired eighteen months ago – all right, I have a job in the Ministry of Defence, but I retired from Sandhurst – and I have a house in Chelsea, but I *hate* it in Civvy Street. I hate it. All I do is drink too much and wish I was abroad. Like the old days in Berlin, with Butcher."

He swigged the last dregs of his wine, then turned and lurched disdainfully over to the table for another glass, and the last glimpse I had of the ex-Commandant of Sandhurst was of a big man surrounded by more black Rhodesians who laughed and exchanged glances.

CHRISTMAS-TREE PATTERNS ON THE LUNATIC FRINGE (OR: LIGHT IN THE FINGERS)

That morning I had an hour and a half with two Inspectors. Then I had lunch and played truant. I drove across the river, parked at a meter and meditated in my car until it was time to descend the steps to a basement. I found myself in a kitchen full of munching, white-haired male healers and sipping grey-haired female healers. I found the Major and reported in.

"Grab some wine and some food and a girl or whatever takes your fancy," he said airily, looking straight ahead and sticking out his enormous paunch. He pointed out everyone in the room and then introduced me to all in a loud voice: "About to join the lunatic fringe. They're all phoney," he added quietly, and there was such sincerity in these last words that I wondered why he had devoted his life to healing after discovering his gift on the Dunkirk beaches.

I poured myself an orange juice.

"No, that's my collaborator," he said, pointing out a famous man with a moustache, who had invented the machines that lay round the sitting-room behind him. "His wife will put you on the machine. We'll have you first on." This item of information was communicated as an afterthought, as though it had only just occurred to him, and I gathered that the organisation was very far from being military. "The machine will show up how relaxed you are," the Major said, and then he went through to greet a mother who lay a hand on the shoulder of a boy with spectacles.

One of the white-haired healers said: "That's one of our most interesting patients, Geoffrey. He's been coming for two years. His mother drives him up from Devon, he's got a damaged brain."

I wandered through and sat in a chair with rounded arms and had a constricting hairnet placed round my temples. Electrodes were smeared with paste and stuffed under the headband, and then I was plugged in to the mind mirror. Lights jumped and ran both ways from the centre into symmetrical patterns, each side of the machine representing a side of the brain.

The boy sat in front of me. He had his back to me, and he looked docilely at his machine, and with his headband and feather of hair he looked like a 'redskin' who had opened his stocking and was now gazing at the fairy lights on a Christmas tree. His mother sat and watched.

I closed my eyes and asked God to send His power through me, and use me as a channel. I opened up the back of my spine, and, waiting for the power to flow in, I concentrated on a picture of a Geoffrey healthy and well, and gave thanks to God because the normalising of his brain was already completed. I scanned Geoffrey's head with my hands and picked up little tingles in the little finger of my right hand, and I concentrated on these areas, moving my hands slowly above his head and down his spine, and slowly I sank deeper and deeper, and I loved him with the deep, detached love of God.

"Lovely relaxed rhythms," I heard someone say, but I kept my eyes closed and sank deeper and deeper into my timeless state, and I was hardly aware of the flickering red torch-strobe that the Major's collaborator put on, and after a long nothing the four surges came, one after another, and I heard a gasp, "They're the best brain rhythms he's had in two years."

I knew there wouldn't be any more surges once the fourth was through, and so I slowly allowed myself to float up to the surface. I saw the shapes on the machine.

"Lovely Christmas-tree patterns," the collaborator's blonde wife said, "they're the best Geoffrey's had in two years. That's the healing pattern. You've got him over to your side, you've given him your pattern."

I asked them when they were aware of the Christmas-tree patterns, and the moment coincided with the first of my four surges. I sat on, letting the power flow quietly through until Geoffrey began to fidget. Then I sat back. I felt tired.

The blonde wife came and put a band round my fingers and measured my skin resistance on a dial. "Yes, you're two hundred," she said. "Healers are generally around that mark. You're very relaxed, and you can channel and communicate the power. You're definitely a healer. You can be very successful, I would say. I'd like you to come again in December, and I'll give you longer on the machine, and you can use it to direct your healing." I showed her my shiny fingers.

"Oh I say," she said, "look, we haven't seen this before. That's the power in your fingers, it's a kind of Light in the fingers. That's how you know it's coming through."

Geoffrey sat fidgeting on his chair. It was time for him to go.

"Thank you so much," his mother said to me, as if I did this sort of thing all day long.

"My pleasure," I said. I got ready for the next patient – a young man who had a blood clot in his neck – and came across the list of forthcoming patients. They included Lord H—, a famous elderly politician, at 5 p.m.

I would leave before then, for being a healer was an amateur pastime, not a social rôle. I looked at the mentally defective, brain-damaged boy who was being helped into his coat. I hoped he would not be long on the lunatic fringe.

TWO BURPS AND THREE CHEERS
(OR: ONE JOLLY GOOD FELLOW WENT TO MOW)

I took a party of a hundred girls to see *Julius Caesar* at a small theatre in Canonbury. We filled the front half of the auditorium, and the girls paid attention for the first few minutes. The actors took the play very fast, and Cassius tended to shout at Brutus instead of being cunning and devious, and Brutus was a posturing ninny who resembled John Cleese.

Antony wore a very short tunic and was bare-legged to his loins, and there were titters. He did look like a Welsh rugger-player. After his arrival there was a perpetual whisper and there was a rustle of sweet-papers – it was as if the girls were behaving in the theatre as they behaved in class or at the cinema – and then, scandalously, there was a very loud burp, at which half the theatre giggled. A few minutes later there was another, answering burp, and again there were general giggles, and I thought Casca showed great restraint in not gesturing towards our seats when he spoke of "a hundred ghastly women".

In the interval the manager told me that a hundred boys had been present the previous night. They popped beer cans and competed with the actors and barracked, and he had thrown six out, even while the play went on. I understood that the actors had been sufficiently unnerved to gallop through the text, and I felt sorry for them: they were amateurs, they had had to learn their lines, they deserved better than to be ridiculed by unappreciative school-children in a civilisation whose public standards were breaking down. Throughout the second half of the play, during which I saw Cassius as the would-be ruler of Rome, the would-be deposer of Brutus once he had served his purpose, an Elizabethan,

Machiavellian view of the text, I hated the monstrous regiment of women I had brought.

On the way home our coach was filled with song. "One man went to mow, went to mow a meadow" was one of the favourites, and there were numerous attempts at more salacious songs, which were accompanied by hoots of raucous laughter.

But as the coach turned into the dark road that led to the school, the girls broke into "For he's a jolly good fellow", and as I turned and beamed, there were a spontaneous three cheers for me, the coach rang with hurrahs, and it would have been a very hard-hearted, uncharitable fellow who dwelt on their burps and ghastly disruption then.

A LIGHT ON DEAD ANEMONES
(OR: MOMENTS IN AN URN)

Pippa's old college friend, Julie, came to stay that Friday evening. She was plump and bubbly-haired and wore a tight-fitting black dress. She looked like a barmaid, and she had a voice that could look after itself. She brought a large bottle of white wine, which I opened. She told me her decree nisi was just through. I knew from Pippa that she had wanted to get married at college because she feared being on the shelf, and that her boy-friend had gone into Guinness and led a comfortable life, and that she had rebounded into a Manchester rugger crowd, where she had met her husband.

"He had another woman on the go," she told me. "I actually caught them at it on the sitting-room floor. I went to my sister's, and then I rang home and if there was no answer it meant they'd gone, so I could return home. He was so childish. When I finally moved out he cut off all the plugs on the electrical equipment – lights, fires, hair-dryers and the rest – just to inconvenience me. The parents where I teach are a rough lot, but they've been a great help. 'Just tap on the wall if you want me to sock him one,' one of them – my neighbour – said."

I left them to reminisce, and two hours later the bottle of wine stood empty beside the glass vase of faded anemones on the marble mantelpiece, and their faces were lit up. They were talking about the boy-friend who went into Guinness. "It became his life," Julie said. "We couldn't go into a pub without him buying Guinness and telling the landlord how he shouldn't keep his pipes like that, and the rest."

I said that my generation knew very early that serving a company – whether it was Unilever, Shell or Guinness – was a waste of a life. "Imagine spending all your life promoting the sales of a product – a soap powder, an oil, a beer – you secretly care nothing for, imagine selling your soul to a company," I said with a shudder. "All right, in return they give you a house, a large car, private school fees, but you've sold your life away. You've sold out to the system. We knew we'd be better off in education or journalism, where at least we'd have some leisure and harmonious living, where at least we'd be free to think for ourselves. I'm against these companies that take our lives away."

And I realised I was anti-capitalist, as I was anti-Communist. I liked the dwindling freedom in our society which the companies created from the wealth they made through trade, but I loathed the cheapening of values they were responsible for, the waste of millions of lifetimes. There had to be a revolution in our attitude towards living.

I went to bed surprised at my own reaction – dinner parties enable us to discover our own opinions – and they reminisced on about their days in college, the days of long ago. They were preserving moments that no longer had any life, but whose dead forms occupied space in their minds, and next morning, when I went down to that room, I found the light still on, and the faded anemones bent their dead heads down onto the marble mantelpiece like dead moments round a transparent urn.

STONE LIONS AND MARBLE VEINS
(OR: A ROSY SKI-LOOK AND MELTING EYES)

We went through a gate into a garden that had two stone lions in it, small versions of the lions in Trafalgar Square. The front door had coloured glass that included a snow-scene in mountains, and the Unilever man let us in, the horn-rimmed man whose life was ruled by a U. We went up carpetless stairs to a small room with a grand piano and many paintings, and there were Georgian bookshelves on either side of the white marble fireplace. The walls and radiator were brown, and here sat the spiky Elspeth in a low cut dress, having just got over her second miscarriage; the Deputy Librarian of the local borough; and a neatly groomed blonde who also had a leonine fringe. She looked as if she had just been skiing she had such rosy cheeks and frozen eyes.

We sat and sipped sherry and talked about the cold snap and the closure of a daily newspaper. This led to the U man saying that academic achievement was overvalued in relation to manual achievement, and soon we were discussing whether Western civilisation was disintegrating. From time to time the blonde mentioned a shop, and I gathered that both she and the librarian were single.

Dinner was served in an adjoining room. We ate avocado pear, beef stroganoff and rice, and Elspeth praised the drama of ideas.

I said that drama should be about real people, that you cannot feel pity or terror for a walking idea, and I talked about the whole man. Intellect, feelings and sensations all ought to be developed, I said.

Elspeth talked about her philosophy class, where she had been introduced to Sartre. She said there are no absolute values.

I said there are, and one has to have the confidence and experience to know them. I said that philosophers who stress linguistic absurdity or egotistical freedom have lost sight of the eternal values.

"Imagine a Club of six hundred great men, from Homer to Tennyson," I said, "and ask each member 'Is life sacred, or can you put twenty million Chinese in football stadia and shoot them as reactionaries, and justify the act as a "culture pattern"?' You will receive the same answer from at least ninety-five per cent of the six hundred. The eternal values were traditionally guarded by the Church – they *were* the Church, especially in the days when the Cathedrals were being built, they were in the stained glass of the Church – and they are now looked after by the public libraries. Because of our lack of leisure, and our specialisation, few are able to read the works of the six hundred and achieve a holistic view. All people can make the journey from egotistical relative values to selfless eternal values, undergo a mystical development, but in the twentieth century the intellects of analytical philosophers have exceeded their inner developments, and so men like Ayer are not whole men, they lack warmth and feelings."

The ice cream arrived, "melting" – "like relative values melting into eternal values," I said, and everyone laughed – and the blonde looked at me with melting bedroom eyes.

"Today," I went on, "there's too much living at second hand through television and the media. The ideal life is the one the six hundred lived: being rooted in the community, travelling little, and being ignorant of much of what is happening in other countries and places, but experiencing everything directly, including the sun, the stars, the trees, the earth. One should watch TV as little as possible, and have as much leisure as possible, and not be ruled by a U for Unreal, but by an R for Real." And when mildly challenged: "Change is good and one should be a dissident, but ultimately change merely compounds the process of disintegration. The more you change the status quo, the more you help to break a civilisation down."

There was a silence when I had finished, and sipping red wine from my silver goblet I thought they were all fundamentally uninvolved in ideas which were living to me. "Let us hear" they seemed to say; they were hearers rather than passionate talkers, and so they had frozen eyes.

Afterwards we had coffee in the piano room, where music, art and literature embodied a profound detachment. Elspeth said of the blonde, "She's very self-effacing, she runs a large shop for cosmetics near Harrods. It's her concern, and all the top people in films and television go to her for make-up."

The blonde flushed underneath the fake ski-look of her rosy make-up and spoke loudly and quickly. She had obtained a university degree and had taught chemistry before going to Unilevers and then Yardleys, and she had set out alone in the middle of the three-day week, when firms were going bankrupt. The risk had paid off.

"I had a very famous actress wife in the other day," she said. "She's very nervous, she twitched, and her face was white with the strain of her acting. She told me, 'It's squeezing out the emotions that drains me.' Her face was as white as that marble."

"And it had the same blue veins in it," said the U man, for the marble was veined blue, and everyone laughed.

The blonde spoke of a pop star who came in. "He was so relaxed he was obviously very successful," she said, and relaxation, it struck me, was an aspect of her lack of involvement in what she was saying.

Elspeth spoke disapprovingly of her latest live-in help, a teacher training student, a boy from a broken home who criticised her and her husband for being bourgeois, and who had joined the Hari Krishna sect, where it was a paternal lights-out at ten every night. Nervous tension and transcendental meditation were frowned on, and on the way down the bare stairs I passed the ideal: the portrait of a young Victorian, the U man's great-grandfather, I passed the snow-scene in coloured glass, and out in the garden I pondered the two stone lions.

And thinking of Elspeth and the blonde, I could not help feeling that there was a stony coldness about the pair of them. It was somehow connected with the made-up rosy enthusiasm that concealed the lack of passion in their ideas, and their marble veins.

THE COLD HEAT OF ALPHA
(OR: A MAJOR IN NEED OF DELTA)

That morning I was wired up to the machine in a bedroom of Victorian prints, and I started with Max's wife who sagged at the knees and muttered, "Can you bring me a chair?"

Later she said, "It's like liquid nitrogen going in. It's cold, and it's pressing down into me, and my body needs to swallow it up."

I said, "It's the psychic heat," and we spoke of the waves up the spine and Kundalini. It was time to stop and I sat alone for a while and Max said, "Your rhythms are a bit peculiar, but they may be affected by Kundalini. We're doing a study of Kundalini at present, and we think that Kundalini replaces alpha rhythms. You have few alpha rhythms at present when your eyes are closed, and you have quite a bit of beta, awareness of the outside world."

I tried an old man next, a Prussian Jew who shifted about and fidgeted and made sceptical remarks until in the end he said, "I am not relaxed, it's not working, the telephone broke my concentration."

Max asked the Prussian Jew's wife to lie down on the table that had an oval hole for the head, and I kept my eyes slightly open, like a meditating Buddha, and immediately I was full of alpha and I went straight into the healing pattern. "There was a flow of power going down through my shoulders and my arms," the Prussian Jew's wife said later, and Max said, "You were in the healing state. There's a lot of theta and delta: imagery and intuitive, unconscious rhythms."

When I had finished the Major came and sat on the table. He

talked to Max about his insomnia while Max's blonde wife swung a dowsing pendulum behind his back and mentally asked it questions: clockwise meant 'Yes', anti-clockwise 'No', and a straight swing backwards and forwards meant 'No answer' or 'A bad question'.

"I feel so enervated," he said. "Perhaps I have a hole in the throat of my astral body. Should I give up healing? I haven't had any sleep for so long, it's feeling responsible for all my healers."

"Lie down," I said, and the Major was wired up and lay on his back, his head in the oval hole, and I put my fingers on his forehead and went into trance.

Later he said, "There was a pressure, it was almost painful, and then an energy going into me which I saw as flashes of light, and which my body wanted to soak up."

"Your pattern was bloated at the beginning, but slowly you entered the healing state. You were soaking it in," Max told him. "And there was a lot of delta."

"Delta is the sleep wave," I said. "I was putting in the sleep wave because he needed it."

"That was very interesting," the Major said, and he gave orders and lunch was brought up to the three of us: the Major, Max and me.

We sat wired up, sipping red wine and eating bread and paste and talked about how enlightenment would appear on the machine.

"A blue light is the throat chakra," Max said, "and a blinding white sun the eyebrow chakra. The crown chakra is mauvish to me, with petals that expand, and in my experience it is experienced with great relief: 'I've made it, I've got there.'" I told him how I did Zen in Japan and he said, "Zen holds back the chakras and Kundalini until they're ready. You were very lucky, it delayed them until they opened naturally."

After lunch I said I was feeling tired: I *had* healed for four hours.

The Major said, "We'll restore you. Healers up here." He lay me down on my front and my face was through the oval hole looking at the carpet, and he dowsed me and manipulated the knobs on either side of my spine and my neck – the intersection between mind and body, the centre of the psychosomatic – and, though I only realised it later, intensified my sexual flow. Meanwhile the grey-haired woman worked my toes and my feet and told me things about my prostate and pituitary glands. Then other healers came and lay hands on my shoulders and the small of my back – I saw their shoes under the table – and I nearly drowsed off to sleep until I came to with a start, recharged.

"Your pattern remained the same," Max said as I thanked them all, put on my socks and shoes, and left.

On the way home I reflected on what I had learned. I could heal with my eyes slightly open, when there were no waves up my spine, and that was the healing state. But when I closed my eyes and approached the Kundalini waves, I got a different pattern, one akin to deep meditation, one connected with Kundalini, without alpha rhythms. I had made a gain, I had progressed: I had separated the healing pattern from the Kundalini pattern, I had distinguished the healing experience from the experience of Kundalini.

MULLED EMPIRE AND A HYMN-SINGING FLAG-PLANTER

We went to a Catholic seminary in Chelsea. It was within the grounds of the old Beaufort House where Thomas More lived, and belonged to the old Douai order, and there was a library and a mulberry tree that went back to the time of More. We took glasses of a very spiced mulled wine and mincepies in a long room of old Masters and balloons, and took stock of the ex-colonial black and brown and yellow faces, and Lady Sims, one of the few white faces there, came up and sang in her upper-class dying fall, "How nice to see you."

We had a chat, and I thought how stunned and confused she looked, as if she had never come to terms with the loss of the British Empire in the post-war years. Then a black man sidled up and said to her, "How ya doin'?" and she said, "Oh not so bad," and, smirking, I turned aside and refilled my glass with mulled wine and found myself talking with Eric Ashby, the organiser who had spent a lifetime promoting British values among the nations with the British Council.

He mentioned Jesperson's latest book and said, "He's writing the same little thing over and over again," and I said, "He's found a tiny garden in the great territory of literary England, and he has fenced it in, and he walks in it every day and won't allow anyone else within a stone's throw of his mulberry tree, and that's *his* voice," and Eric Ashby smirked and turned aside to his mistress, a grey-haired woman who handled gardening for a publishers.

A black Rhodesian accosted me. "You've come from a hot place," I said, for the illegal oil dump had just been blown up and Salisbury was under smoke, and there was an uneasy moment as he sized me up and went through his "horror" at the latest guerrilla strike, and later, talking to a swarthy Mauritian about Russian intentions in the Indian Ocean, I saw myself as a latter-day empire-man. Our respective cultures had been mixed together and mulled, and I spoke to the ex-colonials as an equal, just as they drank the wine that I drank.

Later, one of the fifty trainee priests handed out printed sheets and gathered everyone round the grand piano for traditional English carols. A trainee priest played the piano, and the leader, a clean-shaven young man in glasses, conducted us through *O Come all ye Faithful*, *Silent Night* and *Jubilate Deo* (in Latin). Then he handed out Douai hymn-books, and *While Shepherds watched*, *Good King Wenceslas* and *Hark the Herald Angels* followed in rapid succession.

The leader conducted more and more vigorously and sang more and more loudly, and the blacks and men of brown skin all bellowed obediently, and as they went on to *O Little town of Bethlehem* (the governments of most in the room being anti-Israeli) I suddenly realised that the empire was built by such zealous young men as this clean-cut priest. He had been born seventy years too late, and I saw him striding confidently out into uncharted Africa with Cecil Rhodes, lining a crowd of blacks up, and, by the sheer force of his arm and voice, welding them together into a choir of conductor-respecting hymn-singers.

Lady Sims sang with a distant, faraway, stunned and confused look on her face, but we were full of certainties as, with a final flourish of his arm, he appeared to plant a flag in this clearing in the bush.

A CHAUFFEUR FOR AN INSPECTOR
(OR: A HOUSE-HUNTING HEADMISTRESS)

After the Inspectors' report, which praised her "strong and courageous" leadership, the Headmistress invited the Inspectors and Heads of Department to her room for wine. The two Deputies were not there. They took a dim view of some of the criticisms the Heads of Department had made, and one of them put up a notice saying, "O judgement! thou art fled to brutish beasts (*Julius Caesar*)."

The general opinion about the report was that it was far too vague for the £100,000 it had cost to involve sixty-six Inspectors, and more than one member of the staff told me that I was in the wrong job: I should be visiting one school a term and saying nothing about it at the end.

I told the Chief Inspector that he seemed to have missed the main point about the school – that there was too great an emphasis on the pastoral side at the expense of the academic – and while he was defending the general nature of his conclusions there was a knock on the door behind me and a schoolkeeper asked me, "Have you ordered a car?"

"Probably," I said flippantly, and then, "Oh no, it'll be for one of the Inspectors, his name is like mine."

I went over to the Inspector and plucked his sleeve, and he said "Oh yes, where's the chauffeur?" As I pointed to the door the schoolkeeper ducked out and someone else stepped forward, and before I could stop him the Inspector advanced and said, "Are you the chauffeur?"

"No," the Sixth Form Tutor said, "he's the Head of Geography," and while the bearded worthy blushed and grinned through his spectacles, and the Headmistress looked horrified, I said, to save the situation, "He makes a good chauffeur, I've used him myself in the past, you want to try him."

The Inspector retired in confusion, having demonstrated that at the end of four weeks' Inspection he did not know who the Head of Geography was.

Later the Headmistress talked about her house-hunting. "We visited a house in Cheam," she said. "Three bedrooms, one long through-room downstairs, forty-four thousand." Her circle of listeners winced theatrically and whistled sycophantically. I did not say, 'I've just bought a double-fronted six-bedroom Vicarage nearer to London than Cheam.'

The next day a young lady teacher in my Department said, "I'm so frightened of the Head," and I told her about the house-hunting episode. "Why?" I asked. "She's a house-hunter – one they saw coming – not a tyrant. 'Si le dieu n'existe pas, il faut s'inventer.' You need a figure of terror, and you have invented it and pinned it on the Head and unfortunately she sometimes obliges you by acting in the rôle you have cast her for."

And then I thought of the poor Inspector. Perhaps he, too, was a house-hunter – he certainly was not a car-driver – and perhaps I had a need to see Inspectors as incompetent bunglers just as junior teachers needed to be terrified of their Heads, and perhaps I had invented a persona for him and had unconsciously contrived a situation in which he acted in rôle.

FIRST MATE IN THE COLISEUM

My Department came to afternoon tea and drinks. There were some twenty women sitting round the front room, many squatting on the wine carpet in front of the marble mantelpiece where an old colour picture of an Edwardian fairground cinema proclaimed "Electric Hagger's Coliseum". They drank tea and sherry and ate savoury puffs and quiche Lorraine, which our ancillary helper served. She had made it the previous evening and it was full of garlic; she catered for four hundred at functions held by the Rangers at Hampton Court, where her sons went riding.

The new number 2 sat next to her retired predecessor, Mr Street. They had been out a couple of times while Mr Street's wife rehearsed for concerts, and their complicity showed in the way their elbows touched. I sat and looked at the good ship I skippered. As in an old fairground film show, I stood at the wheel and steered the Department through the Scylla of the Inspectors and the Charybdis of the Head and the deceiving siren's song of progressive education, and the crew manned (or wo-manned) the rigging, and there, straight-haired and puppet-like, sat the first mate, and looking at our ancillary helper, I thought how much better a number 2 she would make from the personality point of view.

Most of the Department had to leave early because there was a Dress Rehearsal for the school pantomime: *Snow White and the Seven John Travoltas* was the title of that fairground film show. Mr Street and the ancillary helper and another teacher sat on and drank and talked. I felt vital, alive – electric – and though I often wanted to scupper her and return to a cliff in Cornwall, I did not then mind skippering the good ship in this fairground Coliseum.

A SPEAKER LIKE A HURRICANE
(OR: THE CALM BREATH OF A WARM SPRING DAY)

"Mr Davies-Brown," said the Clerk to the Governors on a bitterly cold evening when one candidate had already been snowed up, and in walked a ginger-haired young man with a woolly gollywog hairstyle and a moustache and flared blue suit. He placed a file on the desk, said, "Good evening" all round, and sat down.

I thought how like a car salesman he looked. I had met him briefly before the interviews – he had arrived at 4 p.m. from Wiltshire – and I had had difficulty in getting away. I had left him selling the contents of his file to anyone in the staff room who would listen, and one of my staff said, "What an ebullient young man."

The Chairman of the Governors started the questioning, and it soon became apparent that his problem was to get a word in edgeways, so full and long were Mr Davies-Brown's answers in a slightly working-class accent. The Head took over, looking spikily through her bifocals, and Mr Davies-Brown answered her first question by rising and walking over to her and placing an agenda before her as if he were handing out a worksheet to a girl.

Eventually the questioning passed to me. I asked how he would bring a language policy to the school, and soon he was telling me how he would develop the language of our first year girls. "The method of teaching is very important," he said. "For example, recently I have debated bloodsports." He held up a stack of papers from his file. "My classroom is arranged like the House of Commons."

"And you're the Speaker," I said, and the Governors fell about laughing.

When I could next get a word in, I said, "I have no doubts at all about your abilities as a salesman" (though I was not sure that I would buy a second-hand car from him) "but can you be a member of a team and modify your strong opinions to blend in with other personalities?" There was a silence. I had evidently touched a sore spot.

"I admit there have been clashes of personality where I am," said Mr Davies-Brown, who had only been teaching three years, and the Governors exchanged glances. "But that's in a small Department. In a large Department this need not happen."

He went on and on, and when I could next speak I said, "I see from your application form that you have written a paper on *The Politics of the Comprehensive School*, and on page three, that you want to make our girls more aware of 'the political realities' of a comprehensive. What do you mean by the words 'politics' and 'political'?"

I expected a reply about the balance of power within a school, but Mr Davies-Brown jumped straight in: "I was brought up in Argentina. I'm not exactly a Marxist, but I saw the gulf between the rich and the poor, and I believe that all schoolchildren should know more about socialism and subjects like secondary picketing. These subjects could be taught in English classes."

The Governors looked aghast. It was evident that Mr Davies-Brown had blown aside his candidature for this particular job, but he did not stop there. "For instance," he went on, overselling himself again, and nothing could stop the tide of disastrous words that surged from his mouth until in the end the Chairman of the Governors intervened and there were two perfunctory questions from other Governors. The first was a question, "Tell me, Mr Davies-Brown, in your classes girls do manage to ask a question now and again, do they?" The second question established that his father had been an Anglican priest, which was how he had come to be in Argentina.

And then Mr Davies-Brown was prevailed upon to take his leave. He stood up and after bowing all round, left the room. But even then he would not disappear. He hung around near the door, and the Deputy Head went out to investigate and found he wanted the Head to sign his form for his travelling expenses from Wiltshire. The Head said the normal procedure did not require any such signature, and then Mr Davies-Brown was apparently asking if he could visit the Head the next morning, and there was a chorus from the Governors, "No, tell him to go."

The Clerk to the Governors read out the confidential report. It was the worst I have ever heard, and it contained the words, "Mr Davies-Brown is his own worst enemy. He has excellent ideas but he pursues them so intensely that he clashes with all around him, and threatens teachers who like to lead a calmer life." The Head who wrote them had obviously had enough of Mr Davies-Brown, and I wondered at his honesty, which would mean that he would be stuck with him for a few years to come.

The Governors then considered the application of Mr Davies-Brown, whose interview was the last of the evening. "The question is, can you control him?" asked Mr Herring, a balding man with an enormously bulbous nose.

I said, "It might be a bit like trying to control a surge tide up the River Thames."

The Head said strangely, "If he were on the staff, no one's job would be safe, he's a natural leader of a pressure group."

Mr Herring said, "If he were on the staff I think that within a month he'd be doing secondary picketing outside the school gates, and the staff would walk out, and the school would be closed." Everyone laughed.

It had already been agreed that no appointment would be made that night because of the appalling weather conditions which had prevented one candidate from appearing, but everyone agreed that Mr Davies-Brown was not the current favourite, and we broke up and went out into the cold. The roads were like glass, and most of the Governors abandoned their cars and set off on foot.

I drove slipping and sliding home in second gear, and all the way I was haunted by the ginger-haired, moustached, woolly, tactless golly who had so vividly oversold himself, whereas a quieter approach would have walked him the job. Whether it was because he was young and naive, or whether his excess of energy had left him slightly emotionally disturbed I did not know, but he had made the mistake of wanting something too strongly, and of letting it be known that he wanted it, instead of making us do the wanting.

A hurricane had blown through the room carrying before it a flood tide of words, and it made the two previous candidates seem like gentle breezes, and I knew, as I slithered sideways down a hill into a blizzard, that I wanted my Department to work through the calm breath of a warm spring day, and not anything so unseasonal as the buffeting winds of Mr Davies-Brown's unfulfilled ambition.

AN IMPERIAL EGOIST AND A CAR WALLAH
(OR: MW MW-ED, OR: THE REVERSAL OF THE RAJ)

Mrs. Mahawal, our Indian tenant upstairs, had six academic degrees, including a diploma in Russian, and she ran the government newspaper in Delhi. She was in Britain for three months on a Central Office of Information course, and it was soon apparent that though she hoped to become an Indian Ambassadress, she lacked all sense of diplomacy.

"I am not a true Hindu," she told me on her first evening with us putting her long black hair behind her head, "I am an admirer of Ayn Rand, I am an egoist, I believe in egoism."

And she wasted no time in putting her belief into practice. She left the girl she shared a room with (a beautiful young Bhutanese with the clear skin of the Himalayas who read *The Tibetan Book of the Dead* and worked for the government newspaper) and came downstairs and opened our door and announced, "I want to watch your television, our course director said we must watch the news on both channels every night so I will come down before nine and stay till half past ten or eleven every night, unless you have a visitor."

We were so taken aback that we could not think of the words to object, and we allowed her to park herself in front of the television for the next three hours, during which she talked non-stop and asked numerous questions about British life with barely a glance at the screen. At half past eleven she ordered my wife to teach her English "because I need to know about British etiquette and intonation", and she was put out at being deflected.

"I am used to having servants in India," she declared, "normally I do not have to cook or clean or empty bins." It was soon clear she had found servants in Britain. She ordered us to make available a pressure-cooker "so I can cook rice", to arrange for the milkman to deliver two pints every morning "as I do not want to go to the shop on my way back from the course", to empty her bin, to put 10p in her electricity meter, to change her sheets, to hot up her radiator (which on principle she never turned off), and to pass on our newspapers.

Mrs. Mahawal lived out her egoism. She chattered non-stop late at night, opened the door to let out the smell of her curries "because it's a bit stuffy in here", and woke the children who complained of the stink. She never wrapped her rubbish, and besides ventilating her room, I was forever scraping wet onion peel from the side of her bin. Her baths mysteriously lasted three hours, during which the hot water in the house ran cold and no one could get into the bathroom to clean their teeth, and when she emerged with a bowl of wet washing she said disarmingly, "I was doing my exercises, you know, my Yoga exercises. They should be done in quiet, and I cannot do them sharing with Nima." She got herself into the bathroom just when I was leaving for work, and said, "In India I spend all day in the bath. My servants do everything, I just lie in the bath."

Then the breakages began. She broke a sash-cord, and the electricity meter. Then she dropped the iron and broke the back shield so that all the wires were exposed. She said, "I will get it repaired," but after several forays into the local shops the repair proved to be a piece of sticking-plaster over the vacuum. "I have left it as I found it," she declared. "It was broken before I used it." When I pointed out the danger of electrocution, she said, "It was dangerous before I dropped it," and she refused to replace it. (I deducted the cost of a new iron from her deposit in the end.)

After that she took to staying *four* hours in the bathroom, and even had a shower in the middle of the night. A new word entered the English Language: I spoke of "being mahawalled" when I could not get into the bathroom, "to mahawal" meaning "to occupy egoistically for an indefinite period of time", with a secondary sense of "to be plain bloody awkward". The word could be abbreviated to "MW", as in "I've been MW-ed".

Mrs. Mahawal now spent the nights pacing her room above our bedroom, talking loudly to the Bhutanese until 3 or 4 a.m., often with the door open, and her husband sometimes rang her from New Delhi at 5.30 a.m. He seemed very surprised when I said, "She's asleep, I'm the only one in this house who's awake, you woke me up." Sometimes in the morning she left the front door wide open. Once when we were at work the front door was wide open for half an hour, with the empty house gaping invitingly, until my wife had a hunch that she should look back; and was able to close it. She dropped her front door key outside the front door; luckily I found it before any of the local burglars. Mrs. Mahawal never paid for her milk until I asked her three or four times.

She demanded to read the daily and Sunday papers before I had looked at them "because my course director says I must read the editorials". Eventually she decided "we will be paying rent weekly from now on, not four-weekly in advance", and was sulky for a few days when she did not get her way. One Saturday she announced: "I will be needing your front room tomorrow. I have a visitor who is calling and we do not wish to receive him in our room, so you will please use another room at 11 a.m. tomorrow." She thought it very unreasonable that my mother was visiting us at exactly 11 a.m.

By this time I had had as much as I could take of Mrs. Mahawal, and I was relieved when it was time for her to go. "We must be off at six a.m. on Saturday to catch our flight," she announced. "We do not know how to get our luggage to Tooting Bec station." I suggested a taxi to Heathrow, and rang two firms for quotations. Both said £12, which was "too much". So I agreed to get up at 5.45 a.m. after a hard week and drive them to the local station. "Then I will return to bed and sleep," I said.

That Friday night I went up to weigh her luggage on the bathroom scales, and was aghast at the confusion: clothes were strewn everywhere, one of her hold-alls had a broken zip which she ordered me to repair ("Get pincers and a screwdriver and mend this zip"), and despite her six degrees she seemed incapable of distributing the weight so that the two cases to be weighed came to no more than 25 kilos.

Eventually I escaped, and I tapped punctually on their door at 5.45 a.m. the next morning. The two women had still not packed, and Mrs. Mahawal was fiddling with her cases, having talked all night. I humped up the heaviest and crept down the darkened stairs with them and put them in the car boot, and at six Mrs. Mahawal announced, sitting at her table, "Now we are going to have breakfast."

"No," I said, "I've got up early to drive you to the station and I'm going back to bed. You said 'Off at six', and it's now gone six."

Ten minutes later, and with great reluctance, Mrs. Mahawal clumped noisily down the stairs, waking the children of course, and got into the car. I drove to Tooting Bec station and unloaded the luggage.

"We have changed our minds," Mrs. Mahawal declared without any reference to Nima, who did not seem to have changed *her* mind at all. "We have too much luggage, we want a taxi to Heathrow. Never mind the twelve pounds, order us a taxi."

I explained again, as she well knew, that a taxi could not be ordered from the street in this part of London at 6 a.m. any morning. It had to be telephoned for, and the telephone numbers were all at home. (I was not getting involved in phoning directory enquiries for local taxi firms from one of the perennially vandalised local telephone kiosks.)

"Ah," said Mrs. Mahawal, "you have a car, *you* can drive us to Heathrow."

I saw now where all her muddle had been leading, and why she had got me up at 5.45 a.m. after a hard week at work to drive her to the local station. Her egoism had a calculating, premeditated look about it now. She had cast me in the rôle of her chauffeur-servant, her car wallah. The Raj may have been reversed on the Indian subcontinent, but I was not going to be any national's wallah, and certainly not at 5.45 a.m. when, under the circumstances, I had already done more than I was required to do.

"No," I said, "I haven't got the map book in the car, I don't know the way. It's an hour or more to get there, and I would need to study the route. I'm not prepared, it's unplanned – "

"You can go home for your map book and study the way," Mrs. Mahawal said. "If we go by car we do not need to leave until eight o'clock. Now it is only just after six o'clock. There is plenty of time. We only had to set off at six o'clock if we were going by tube."

That did it. "No," I said, "I don't know the way, I should be in bed now. You have arranged to go by tube, and to change now will just cause confusion. There will be plenty of people to help you with these cases."

She treated everybody as her servant, she would have little difficulty in turning a passenger or two into her luggage wallahs. And, imagining how the traditional British imperialists in *A Passage to India* must surely be turning in their graves at the British rôle in this example of Indian-British relations, I carried the two heaviest cases to the top of the escalator and waited while the Bhutanese bought two tickets and Mrs. Mahawal trailed slowly down with one shoulder-bag.

The Bhutanese and I went down the escalator with the heavy cases and at the bottom we stopped and turned round. Mrs. Mahawal stood protestingly at the top, her shoulder-bag on the ground. "Come on," I called, beckoning her down with my arm. Mrs. Mahawal did not move. A train came in and left, and trains were not frequent at 6 a.m. Then a passing West Indian picked up Mrs. Mahawal's shoulder-bag and put it on the escalator, and Mrs. Mahawal herself reluctantly stepped forward and was borne down.

On the platform Mrs. Mahawal chattered non-stop about how she would not be able to cope. "We must change at Kennington and then at Ly-cester Square. We cannot manage. We need a taxi and there are no taxis. You have a car. You should take us to the airport." There were no thanks, there was no appreciation for the fact that I had left my Saturday lie-in to help them, and I half-wondered whether she would propose that I drove her all the way to New Delhi.

Another train trundled in, the doors opened. I put the luggage inside, waved the two women in, smiled goodbye to the Bhutanese girl and stepped back. Mrs. Mahawal stood inside the doors, protesting. The doors closed.

"By-ee", I waved.

The train jolted and pulled out of the station, and my last glimpse of Mrs. Mahawal suggested the affronted look of an Indian imperialist who had been cheeked by the local British wallah, or of an egoist who could not understand why her latest whim was not granted. She had given an order, and I had disobeyed her. No doubt she would be back as Indian Ambassadress to the Court of St. James, and would have more of a chance to enforce some of the orders she had such a need to give, but I could not help feeling that if she did become Indian Ambassadress, despite her six degrees and her diploma in Russian, Indian-British relations were destined to enter a period of unprecedented muddle and confusion.

AFTERNOONS LIKE CINDERS
(OR: BLACK ASHES ON A WHITE WICKET)

Bob White was a short man with a pointed nose and greased hair. He had bloodshot eyes and played cricket for the Hill. Between overs he used to crouch down, one knee of his white flannels on the grass, and put his thumb and nicotine-stained forefinger between his teeth. When someone was out he sat down, even though club cricket attracted a thousand spectators or more on a Saturday afternoon in those days.

He was a dashing left-hand opening bat. My brother and I used to go and watch him when we were boys – though we were more interested in his brother Bill who played for Essex – and I never dreamt that one day we would be in the same team and exchange comments from short leg to slip. He was sixteen years older than me, and I remember he said after my first innings for the club, when I scored 48 not out in a total of 116, "Well done, *young* man."

I never knew what he did for a living, but I knew it was not anything very much. "Work is just work, I live for my cricket at weekends," he told me once. I thought it was sad his life was so empty. I walked away from the team without any difficulty and explored foreign cultures and never returned, but he carried on playing. Later on the club changed grounds, and the "Top Ground" in the Forest was seldom used. But even when he went to South Africa and set up a business, he came back during the summer months and played cricket for the Hill.

One wintry day I read in the local paper that he had died. It did not say how, but I thought of his nicotine-stained fingers. At his own request, his ashes had been scattered on the pitch of the "Top Ground", the scene of his – and my – cricketing heyday.

I felt very sad. Somehow those ashes lying on that frosty pitch revealed the emptiness in his life, which I had always seen. He had dropped his guard and let it be publicly known that belonging to that club and its beery laughter and cheery applause was the most important thing in his life. He had admitted that his life was so empty that cricket was its centre, and I felt embarrassed for him.

Now I sometimes pass the "Top Ground", and I always say, "It wasn't safe for the buses to drive along square leg when *I* was batting there." For I always aimed my hook shots at the passing traffic, with the aggressive lack of care of early youth. Occasionally some low-level game is in progress. Not all the players are properly kitted out in white shirts and flannels, and there are no spectators. Sometimes I stop and watch for a few moments, and if a ball rears awkwardly off a length and a batsman jerks his head out of the way, I think "That pitch has been a graveyard for many a fine batsman", or more specifically, "That was because Bob White is strewn across the pitch." And I feel very sad that the slight figure in white on his haunches, one knee on the grass and fingers at his teeth, is, like those golden summer afternoons among the oak-trees, a few trodden black cinders on a neglected wicket.

A TIDE IN THE CELLAR
(OR: SEEPAGE FROM A BLOCKED DRAIN)

That morning I pondered the creative process: the images that appeared in my mind, uninvited, which I stared at as at a reflection in water. Then I smelt the whiff of drains from the cellar, and went down the dirty stairs to inspect the still pools among the coal. I remembered from my childhood the time there were frogs in the cellar. But this was different. This was a tide that came and went mysteriously when it rained, and though most walls were damp, there was no evidence of any leak from any pipe or grating.

I linked this secret tide with the upstairs loo, which did not flush well, and the smell of gas in our bedroom chimney vent. I tracked them all back to the main drain outside the back door. I lifted the cover, expecting to see a culvert running under the road, and only a few inches down floated foul-smelling, brown frothy scum. From this I deduced that water was seeping through the sides of the drain and welling up through the soft cellar floor, and that sewage that could not run away was making a foul stench up the bedroom vent.

I called in a company. A boy with tattooed arms rang the bell and sniffed unenthusiastically. He assembled green rods and ran them through scaffolding pipe and plunged them seven feet down while the stirred muck stank, and then bent on his pliable rods as if he was punting. He prodded and pushed and poked and rammed, but to no avail. So he put the rods away in his van and ran a machine with a coiled-wire drill. But after two long gos, he was unable to clear the blockage.

"It's the gate to the sewer that runs under the road," he said. "It's rusted up, the hinge is rusty because no water's been going through."

He went off to bring a more powerful machine, leaving the cover off the thick brown scum, on which lay several used pink things.

I stared at the foul mixture of brown excreta, bubbly urine and slime, and wondered at all the accumulated waste we expel from our bodies. These unwanted ejections from our limbs were like the immediate bits of experience that pour into our minds when we are creating as into a blocked drain, and seem unimportant, uninterpreted, forgotten images. I thought of the gate to the sewer which, if opened, would wash all these chaotic fragments away, and then I thought of the tide that mysteriously came and went in my mind, leaving pools of water among my unconscious bits of coal.

And then I realised that the seepage into my mind which became stories like this one would not happen if the everyday images were washed cleanly out through the gate, and I was relieved and grateful, before the boy with the tattoos returned and forced the gate open with one blast of his 1065 machine, that I had a permanently blocked drain on the outside of my senses: it accumulated all the transient things that most people flush away and forget, and allowed this mysterious tide of images to well up deep in my being.

A RUN-AWAY'S STONE AND A FOUR-KNIGHT DOOR (OR: COURAGE)

After Whitsun we went on a great swing round Thanet. We drove through Whitstable and stopped on the Swalecliff cliffs for tea, then lunched on Herne Bay beach in the sun while the two boys jumped on the trampoline, had rides on the roundabout and helter-skeltered down the helter-skelter. We sunbathed while sunlight leapt from the waves, then went on to Margate and sat on the sands by the old pier and rusty iron barge green with seaweed. The boys each held starfish.

We went on to Broadstairs and stood in Dickens' study with its sea-view and imagined him writing *David Copperfield* there, and then I walked in the garden with my six- and four-year olds and remembered September 1850 and Dickens' fun with Alfred and Sydney, his five- and three-year olds: "When he and Ally had run away, instead of running after them, we came into the garden, shut the gate and crouched down on the ground. Presently we heard them come back and say to each other in some alarm 'Why the gate's shut, and they're all gone!' Ally began in a dismayed way to cry out, but the phenomenon (Sydney) shouting 'Open the gate!' sent an enormous stone flying into the garden (among our heads) by way of alarming the establishment...." Leaving the ghost of this spirited child, we drove to Ramsgate, where we gathered pine-cones among some pines, and then went to Canterbury Cathedral, the centre for all Anglican mystics.

I had told the two boys the story of how Becket was murdered, and we immediately headed down the nave, and climbed the side steps to the choir (whose elevation suggests the Kabbalistic spiritual world) and then plunged down to where Becket stood on that fateful evening of 29th December 1170. "The four knights came through that door," I told them, "and Becket stood there, and

THE CLEAR, SHINING SUNLIGHT OF ETERNITY

they swung their swords at his head and killed him. See the picture above?"

Little Paul, who at four had one of those angelic Anglo-Saxon faces that spurred Gregory the Great to send Augustine to Ethelbert at Canterbury, and to murmur "Non Angli, sed angeli", asked: "But where are the knights now?"

"They're dead," I said, "it happened a long time ago."

"I think they are hiding in there," he said, going to a small shut door that seemed to lead up into the wall. He tried to push it open. "I will catch them and take their swords," he said, and some of the visitors smirked.

I took the two boys up to the mosaic which lay by the site of Becket's shrine and explained how some stones near it had been polished by the knees of millions of pilgrims, including Chaucer. I fell into conversation with a nearby priest in black, who reckoned the mosaic was brought from the Middle East in the time of the Crusades. I said that explained the four rings in it. They were the four worlds of the Kabbalah, which was very influential in the first quarter of the 13th century.

Then the priest took me to the Miracle windows and, while the two boys held hands beside me (and Paul tried to kiss a sculpture of a dead man to wake him from his tomb), showed me Becket with his mitre, and then three aghast figures who had just realised they had the plague, and then a man who had been sentenced to have his eyes gouged out, and then Becket healing his gouged eyes with the crook of his crozier. It was fascinating. Here on stained glass was the educational system of the Middle Ages, for the pictures taught the illiterate the scriptures and recent history and I could see Chaucer's Pardoner being instructed during his pilgrimage by such a priest as this. I craned my neck and screwed up my eyes to make out the details of these medieval visual aids, and then Simon said, "Daddy, Paul's not here. He went to find Mummy. That way."

I excused myself from the priest and with sinking heart crossed the choir to where I had just seen my wife and her mother. "Paul?" my wife said. "He's with you. I haven't seen him." And so we all separated to search the huge Cathedral, which was suddenly very crowded. I listened for a child's boo-hoos.

Several minutes later I arrived at the "well" where Becket was murdered. Paul was sitting on the step in front of the small shut door.

"They're in there," he said. "The knights. They can't get out. I've caught them. I will take their swords and kill them for killing that kind man in black."

Then I realised that somehow Paul had associated Becket with my priest, and I grasped how deeply and vividly he had felt and imagined the murder of Becket among the shadowy arches. I understood that though four year olds lack an adult's sense of time, though last week and last year are muddled in a small child's mind, and though in Paul's outlook eight hundred years were no different from eight minutes – nevertheless his mind was truly timeless, and therefore eternal. And so to him a past event had a present urgency and immediacy. He was nearer to the Kingdom than many bookish adults who knew all the implications of the murder of the Head of Church by the Head of State, and I grasped the courage that had led him to imprison the four knights in their hiding-place, at the risk of his own life.

And later, as I held him up to see the Black Prince's armour and the spikes on his knuckles, I was reminded of young Sydney Dickens in Bleak House. By talking to the priest I had in effect crouched down behind a gate, and little Paul had run off and sent an enormous stone flying in our direction, by way of alarming the establishment to the urgency of his brave stand for what was right.

LOUD VOICES AND THE LONG SILENCE OF CHRISTENDOM

I attended a conference on the Kabbalah at a country house near Tetbury (Prince Charles's retreat). After lunch on the Saturday I wanted to rest, but one of the members said, "A friend's offered a lift to Painswick, will you come?"

I looked at the leaflet and saw "Prinknash, 7 miles."

"Yes," I said, "if we go to the Benedictine monastery of Prinknash first."

So we went off in the car of a lean-faced, fluffy, middle-aged woman who drove jerkily and dangerously and talked about her experience in the morning meditation, when she saw a Byzantine Christ. "I don't understand it," she said, "I'm Jewish."

The conversation passed on to religion, and the two of them dominated from their egos. "See how much I know," they seemed to be saying. The Jewish driver was especially assertive. I had seen her return to her chair in the circle that morning, and finding it occupied, say "That's my chair", and when the offending woman flushed and pointed to the chair next to her, which was free, insist, "No *you* move."

The new abbey of Prinknash proved to be a hideous redbrick modern building by an enormous car-park and gift shop. I headed for the old St. Peter's Grange, now used as a retreat, while the two Jews sneered at the monastery, and then loudly discussed the architecture, insensitive to the silence of the retreatants and treading on dozens of daisies. I found the bas-relief of Henry VIII as a straight-haired boy. He had stayed there in 1535 when it was owned by the Abbot, and he dissolved it in 1540. I felt the long silence of Christendom, and regretted its weakening that had led to the garish feebleness of the car-park Abbey in 1972.

"Christendom has no tradition," the Jewish driver announced as she drove us jerkily on to Painswick. I objected and said it was the tradition from St. Augustine to Eliot that included St. John of the Cross and St. Teresa and many other mystics. "That's not Christendom," she said, and in the medieval Painswick church she talked noisily, oblivious of the silence, and incensed at the two Jews' disrespect for what they knew nothing about I hissed "Shhh, the silence is holy, don't pollute it with ego," and the Jewish driver looked as if I had slapped her round the face.

She left the church and noisily addressed a blackbird among the graves, "Are *you* a gentleman?" and then declared, "I want some tea, it's up the road."

"I want to look at a tomb with a skeleton carved on it," I said, finding the first excuse I could think of, "I'll see you at the car," and I wandered back round the church, relieved to be on my own, and sat and contemplated the beauty and the Idea the stones materialised for the next forty-five minutes while the Jews had tea. Outside the church wall there were stocks.

On the way back to the conference I was silent. The two Jews talked noisily and assertively, and the driver announced that she was a London solicitor. I could imagine her revelling in any situation in which she was called upon to express an opinion or give advice, and grasped that her rôle in her job was the greatest obstacle to her spiritual progress beyond her enormous ego.

Later the Jew who asked me to go knocked on my door as I was bathing a swollen toe and said, "I apologise for this afternoon, you wanted to stay behind and I persuaded you to come and you didn't enjoy it."

"It wasn't that," I said, "Jews should stick to their own religion and not knock Christendom, which they don't understand."

For the rest of that evening I demolished the arguments of the bearded Kabbalah teacher, another Jew. He was a magician who had formed us into a circle, he caused one girl to have the shakes. I had turned away from the Kabbalah and from the teacher's method of ransacking the unconscious for instant images which could be fantasies rather than archetypes, and then saying that anyone sceptical of his method was Luciferian.

I felt I was an advanced mystic among novices, like someone who had expected an 'A' level class and found a first year one. I, who had known Keter for ten years, had helped novices like the Jewish solicitor to taste it before they were properly ready, I had given but had not received. It was as if I had shared a map of the way to work with others who did not know how to get there, when I could walk it with my eyes closed. Those who knew did not speak, and those who did not know and were ruled by their egos asked all the questions and reported on their images first, as if to say 'Me first, look at what I saw.'

I was sick of the images the teacher said we had trawled up from the unconscious by sonic radar, instead of angling for them with a rod and line – to me they were no more unconscious than an image of my house and no more archetypal than a fantasy that could have found a place in a creative novel. I had turned away from everything that was not the long silence of Christendom. Mysticism is creedless, but I felt I was closer to being a Christian mystic than to any other tradition, and that Christian mysticism was the foremost of the traditions.

A POMPOUS FOOL AND RIVER JORDAN WATER
(OR: A BREACH IN A SOLICITOR'S VALUES)

We went to the christening of a nephew of mine. We arrived at the church early – the church where my father had his funeral – and sat at the back in the few enclosed pews round the font, on which stood what looked like a bottle of gin. My wife whispered "What's that?" and my hospital-aunt leaned forward and whispered, "I think he's going to be baptised in spirit." My solicitor-brother fussed around, curly-haired and with thick glasses and full of the solicitor's social values – a lifetime of evenings on other people's conveyances and contracts and wills – and another aunt, who had blue hair, whispered, unfairly I thought, "Pompous fool!"

The service passed off without incident. There were two hymns about the Light descending, which went with the altar inscription "Veni Creator Spiritus", and at one stage a candle was handed to the godparents, who included my solicitor-brother, who gave loud responses. The Devil did not trouble the baby unduly – though he did give a cry when the vicar held him for baptism – and the bottle that gulped out into the font so that the waters of Light could be scooped and sprinkled on the baby's curls turned out to contain water brought back from the River Jordan by a thoughtful churchwarden.

My hospital-aunt whispered, "I hope it's clean, the River Jordan isn't exactly pure, is it? I hope it hasn't got cholera in it."

Little Paul, my second son, whispered, "He's had a hairwash."

The reception proved a bit damp. The immaculately decorated house, polished parquet floor and lawns mowed in tramlines like Wembley stadium proclaimed how the baby's family spent their evenings, but no one seemed very interested in anyone else, and the conversation over champagne, salmon and strawberries was polite. My two brothers avoided me. There was an undeclared war between their values and self-image and mine, and their image of themselves could not be threatened if they ignored my search for truth and the meaning of life.

Then my solicitor-brother made a speech urging the baby's parents to make use of time, and I watched my two brothers standing side by side, and pondered the different reasons that had led us to forsake the angelic orders and choose the parents we had.

Later I took my solicitor-brother for a short walk down the lawn, and he opened up, spoke from behind the false front of his ego. "I'm not in the best of moods today," he said, "my best friend who ran a fruit-and-veg empire dropped dead on Friday, aged fifty-two. It's come as a great shock. He wanted to do so much. Just to think, it could happen at any time to anyone. It's made me think." It was a though he had been touched by something like the water that splashed from the little baby's head.

Then I saw the breach that had been made in his values and his doubt about the meaning of all his hard work in the office and at court and in the evenings, dictating letters and completing documents. And I said in consolation: "I once heard the Buddhist Judge, Christmas Humphreys, give an off-the-cuff lecture in which he said, 'When I look at the *Times* obituaries and read about someone I knew, I think "Old so-and-so's gone *again*."'" In other words, we have several lives, and perhaps we have been before and will come again. In which case we all have a purpose here, a mission, which we must achieve *now*. We must do what we have to do now, not defer it for ten years, for then it may be too late." He agreed.

Later, having seen the grief behind his "pompous" mask, I thought of the threat death brought to all materialists who lived for their houses and social functions. I knew how Beowulf felt when "wyrd" (fate) touched him, and I felt that some of the River Jordan water had splashed off on me and given me a new sense of urgency: time was short, I had spent whole years researching into other people's "isms" and mistakes and deferring my own important work, and now it was time to start it – I had to at all costs. But where would I find the time to channel eternity?

MR RUBIN'S FORTUNE

Mr Rubin was a handsome young man who was nicknamed Casanova. He made a pass at every girl who joined the staff. I knew he had been in the RAF, and when he was appointed Acting Head of House, he brought a toughness of outlook to his rôle. He left that school suddenly, telling everyone that his father, whom he had not seen for twenty years, had died and left him a lot of money, "a fortune" was how he described it to me. Out of this he bought himself a Mawgan sports car.

"I'll be in Sierre Leone next week," he told me, "and on the way back I'm going skiing."

"Why Sierre Leone, as opposed to the Bahamas or somewhere more fashionable?" I asked, puzzled. For Sierre Leone was rather off the beaten track, and was a run-down socialist country from what I had heard.

"Why not Sierre Leone?" he said.

In fact he did not go to Sierre Leone, nor did he go skiing, and a few months later he was a supply teacher in Greenwich, going from school to school.

"It doesn't add up," Mr Murdstone told me over lunch, "and so I

THE CLEAR, SHINING SUNLIGHT OF ETERNITY 311

checked him out. You know, of course, that he was really Rubinovitch, a Russian Jew? The name is the Russian form of Rubens. I've found out that the Russians got at him in the RAF. I know about these things, for Praeger, the man jailed for handing secrets to the Russians, was under me when I was in the RAF. I asked Rubin why he was slung out of the RAF and he said, 'That's classified.' The Russians sent him to the LSE where he was incredibly idle on paper and conned his way to a pass degree at interview. Then he was sent here.

"I have a hunch what the attraction here was, it was what brought me. You know his classes were in a mess? The Head's known for some time, there was a terrible lot of clearing-up to do, which I've done. He was conning the girls. Now, since I've arrived, they've removed him from here with that cock-and-bull story about the inheritance – it was only £10,000 they paid him and he spent half of it on his car – and now he's repaying it by recruiting for them in a part of London that's very Red in the schools, where education is in turmoil.

"They got him because he was a homosexual. Blackmailed him. You didn't know that? He was. All the womanising was a front, like his tough stance as Head of House. I bet you can't produce one lady teacher here who's actually been to bed with him. He may have propositioned them, but he never went any further. He was told to go to Sierre Leone, and then they changed their minds and told him not to go there – I know. They want him to be a peripatetic supply who visits all the schools and identifies targets for Russian recruitment. He's very unhappy in Greenwich, or so I understand."

Later that afternoon I thought of all the trips Mr Rubin had made to the north of Scotland with his friend, the Head of Music, who was pale and very handsome. They drank together every night and went about together at school, and slowly it dawned on me that possibly there was more to their relationship than even I had suspected. Then I thought of Mr Murdstone. How had he investigated Mr Rubin, "checked him out"? He often spoke of "MI5 or 6 and seven-eighths", and I wondered if an organisation had sent Mr Murdstone to my school.

"What *was* the attraction that brought you – and him – here?" I asked Mr Murdstone later, when I next ran into him.

He looked at me very shrewdly.

"You," was all he said. And suddenly I had a nightmare vision of Mr Rubin being sent from the LSE to monitor me, because I was a known opponent of Trotskyite education, and I saw Mr Murdstone as being sent to check Mr Rubin and frighten him into moving on – hence the sudden story of his father's fortune.

We were supposed to be living in a free country, but the freedom was thick with unexplained coincidences and relationships and mysterious happenings that were put down to Fate, and in both Mr Rubin and Mr Murdstone I saw a manifestation of the hidden, secret State that controls all our lives and has us all bugged and tape-recorded and computerised. Freedom was an illusion, and Mr Rubin had no fortune, as a Russian pawn he only had his Fate.

A RED IN THE SURGERY
(OR: LEFT-WINGER AGAINST PAIN)

I went to the doctors to show my infected toe and was seen early by the sallow-skinned, shock-haired, bespectacled Doctor who always saw me. I peeled off my plaster and showed my ingrowing toe-nail, and he disagreed with the doctor who had seen me while he was on holiday in Devon: "If you have a wedge-shaped section taken out of the nail, it will be extremely painful, and it has almost got better. I want to save you the pain."

He told me what to do and I admired the photographs he had taken of his young children, which were framed on the wall, and he commented on a file I had put down. "I'm just going before the Governors," I said, "it's public accountability. In a few years' time it will probably be *in* public, for you've probably heard, the ILEA has been taken over by young Marxists."

"Yes," he said, his eyes lighting up.

"We were supposed to go on the People's March," I continued, taking the interest in his eyes as delight that we had transcended the doctor-patient question-and-answer that must have been the basis of most of the talk in his surgery, "on full pay on Monday afternoon, but then these damn Marxists were told they'd have to pay our salaries out of their own pockets, so they changed their minds very speedily. Even so, a hundred teachers went, and they're trying to work out who should pay their salaries for that afternoon."

"What confusion," he said.

"Rumour has it you were an MP once," I continued.

"It's not rumour, it's a fact," he said. "I was MP for this area from 1964 to 1970, during the time of the Wilson government."

"Conservative?" I asked, thinking of his bow-tie and neat dress and rather disdainful air as he stalked through his surgery.

"Oh no," he said, "I was a neo-Marxist radical socialist. I've been Director of War on Want for over ten years."

I gasped, "Oh, er, I didn't mean to run down the Marxists."

"That's all right."

"You must be very interested in what's happening now," I went on, trying to extricate myself. "Foot and...." Normally I would have said 'Foot and mouth'. "Foot and Benn."

"Yes," he said, "I chuckle. They tease me at home. I saw it all coming."

Outside in the street I thought: I've got a Red boss and now I've got a Red doctor. I pondered why he was so interested in War on Want. It attracted BOSS as well as the liberation movements, both sides, and I wondered which side he was on.

Then I remembered he would not recommend an operation on my toe. I thought: all left-wingers try to eliminate pain because they only believe we have the physical, material body, hence the left-wing belief in welfare states and wage increases. Right-wingers on the other hand, believe that a certain amount of material discomfort is good for the growth of the soul.

No, his attitude to pain gave him away. He was a genuine left-winger all right. There weren't just Reds under the beds, there were Reds in the surgery. I felt a Revolution gathering round the corner like a wind.

GOVERNORS LIKE BOWLERS
(OR: UNTOUCHED JACK)

I duly reported to the Governors. I arrived before they turned up and indulged in awkward conversation about cricket with the two Deputies and School Secretary, and then greeted each Governor as they came in with a shake of the hand. In due course we all sat at square tables overlooking a game of bowls across the green fields outside in the evening June sun. White-hatted, shirt-sleeved men bowled at the jack.

I was introduced and identified the documents I had placed before them, and then I curved through the progress of my Department since the Inspection. It was the oldest trick in the book:

confuse them with a lot of papers, suggest that the answer to their questions is in the papers, and reduce them to silence. Eventually one of the Governors asked a question: "Are there any residual weaknesses and how will you improve them?"

From the word "residual" I guessed that the questioner was the Professor. It was like a bowl sailing towards me – a white jack that had stopped – and I watched it finish wide of the mark and gave my reply.

Then a local doctor asked, "How does one know what another teacher's methods are?"

That too curved wide of the mark. And it was over after two soft questions.

I withdrew and went downstairs, where I met the large Chairman of the Governors who had just arrived. "Phew," she gasped, "just pausing before I climb the stairs. Don't know why they've put us up there, because of the leaking staff-room roof I suppose. I'm afraid I'm late and missed you because – I don't know whether you heard – I've had a bereavement. Yes, an old friend died on Friday. She collapsed on Thursday evening and had a twelve-hour operation, and they kept her going until 8 p.m. on Friday. We were very close. It's thrown me, I can tell you."

Her eyes were slightly wet, and as I made sympathetic noises ("it must have been very distressing for you") I saw that she was at that moment a victim of her emotion and not the daunting Chairman of the Governors at all, and I realised that Governors were people who came out of their homes and problems to ask questions about the school just as the bowlers across the field had left behind their agonies to wheel their woods at the pure white, untouched jack.

ANOTHER PLACE

I heard that the son of Denis the schoolkeeper had been killed and seeing Denis pushing a trolley near the staff room, I stopped him to express my condolences.

"Oh," he said, short and stocky and smiling and creased and obliging as ever, "yeah, he was in the Army, killed in a car accident in Germany, twenty."

I said how terrible it was and how inadequate words were. "But," I said, "there is a possibility that we have lived before and will come again. I was speaking to Britain's leading brain physiologist the other day about mind and brain. He did an hour's television programme on BBC a couple of months ago, about epilepsy. He said that a year ago he thought it was fifty-fifty as to whether brain controls mind or mind controls brain, but now he reckons that mind controls brain, comes in from outside, lives in it, then leaves it. That means there's some sort of after-life."

He looked at me as if I were mad. "Oh, yeah," he said, as if I had said nothing out of the ordinary, and were somehow under the misapprehension that I *had*, "I believe that, I've never thought otherwise. I'm sure he's just gone to another place. I know I shall see him again. When I die, he'll be there, waiting for me in this other place. Oh yeah, he hasn't just disappeared. He's still himself somewhere."

After I left him I thought of the insight he had revealed. And immediately I had a mental picture of Denis's former colleague John, the schoolkeeper who died of a heart-attack. He used to rest on his broom and I used to say, "Don't work too hard" and he used to grin, and remembering his personality I was sure it had not disintegrated, and that it was in "another place".

I glanced back. Denis was pushing a trolley of provisions, and I looked at him with a new respect. He was wiser than many of the clever materialistic teachers who were higher up the social scale than he was. He belonged to another place in relation to the social heights of most of the rest of the school, and I wondered if we frequented a society-in-reverse, in which the true angels and leaders were beneath us, and those who were learning were in positions of authority and power. And for the next five minutes I walked through a nightmare in which the angels of Heaven appeared to defer to the demons of Hell.

A CANON IN HIS DREAM HOUSE
(OR: SILENCE AND WHITE BREAD)

I spent a weekend with a recently founded Order in a secluded house in the country. It had been reclaimed from thirteen years of dereliction by the dozen residents. A tree had actually been growing through the roof when they found it. I arrived on a Saturday morning and entered a yellow Edwardian house whose long room was full of sofas and easy chairs. Here the dozen visitors like me stood and chatted. The residents were mainly old ladies, and their guests fingered the books on display and made a pretence of studying the titles in the bookshelves.

Then the course on Mysticism began. We were addressed by the Canon, a charismatic figure of fifty-five who had hair that fell on both sides of his head. He had the aquiline, idealistic, ego-less, beautiful profile of a Gerard Manley Hopkins, and he spoke on the need for silence like a man fired by one idea. He was only interested in practice, and he had little time for the history of the mystical tradition. Practical mysticism, he said, could be taught like the Direct Method of learning a foreign language, and its starting-point was silence.

We were indeed silent for the rest of the day. We ate a silent lunch and walked in the grounds in silence and felt the deeper continuity return to our job-fragmented beings, and then we meditated in silence in an improvised chapel which was really just one room in the house. It had a painting of Ezekiel's vision in it. Then we dined and talked, and I heard from one of the more irreverent younger members of the community what it was like when the Canon was not there.

"Normally there's a prayer meeting every morning and a cassette-class in the afternoon," he said, "and everyone has jobs to do, like weeding, even though they're not paid – no one's paid, they just get full board free – but when the Canon's away on a speaking engagement, the jobs don't get done, they sunbathe on the grass and play Radio One." He was one of four teenagers there who had nothing beyond the clothes they were wearing – ragged jeans and frayed shirts – and it seemed to me that they were only there for the roof and meals, and that the Canon, seeing them as latter-day monks living lives of chosen poverty, did not realise it. That evening I studied the idealism of the Canon and wondered how much he grasped of the practical difficulties.

I spent that night in a house down the road. It was owned by the Canon's wife, an imperious nut-brown middle-aged woman who greeted me with: "You're in the wrong room. Of course I know, I live here." (I had been shown into the room by one of the teenagers from the community.) Next morning she served a parsimonious breakfast of muesli and *white* bread when all New Age communities served nothing but wholemeal brown bread, and as I chatted to the nun who had painted the vision of Ezekiel, the Canon's wife began to disagree.

"Those young boys," she said scornfully to the nun, "what do *they* know about mysticism?"

I described how an Archdeacon from New Zealand had played some of the Canon's cassettes in Wellington Cathedral.

"Yes," she said, "but how long can one go on saying the same thing? That's what I wonder." And I gathered that the Canon and his wife were not on the best of terms.

The Canon gave another talk about mysticism that morning. He rebutted the idea that it can take thirty years to purify oneself for the Light, a notion of the "Piscean mystics" of the "Old Age" which denied the sincerity of his four teenagers. Then we filed to the chapel and had a Eucharist in deep contemplation of the Light.

Later we had a social lunch, and I sat opposite the Canon, who seemed preoccupied. He was not interested in the chat around him, and I could see that he lived his philosophy of detachment and genuinely preferred silence.

"Do you feel tired after a course?" I asked.

"No," he said, "I feel resilient."

Soon afterwards he left the table. I continued eating the lunch, which had been picked from the garden, and I asked the elderly resident next to me, who had been prattling away about life in India, "Does the Canon's wife come up her?"

"Yes," she said, "yes," and there was a silence that signified that the subject was taboo. She just suddenly lost interest.

I persevered. "But the Canon lives here, has a room here?" I said.

"Yes," she said, "yes."

And then I grasped that the Canon had left his wife, and withdrawn from her censorious, disagreeing eyes into the silence and dream house he had always yearned for, which his course members kept going with their fees, donations and weeding. He was an evangelist, yes, but just as much he was a man who had changed one family for another one. There was something ruthless about this paterfamilias who ruled the teenagers and old ladies who depended on him.

SILK APPLE-BLOSSOM AND DRIED GREENGAGES (OR: CHAMPAGNE ROSES)

I ran into Mrs. Burns' actor-lover in a pub on Wandsworth Common. I looked in for change for a phone-box, and he was sitting at a table by himself. He said, "Hello, you were James's teacher, you sat next to me at his funeral. Tom Moody. Mina may have told you about me."

"You're an actor," I said.

"Sometimes," he said, "when I've got a part."

I sat down, and we talked about *Dr. Faustus*, in which he had a small part playing the "good angel", and death, and he said: "Yeats said there were only two things worth writing about: love and death. I've been aware of this all day. I've just spent the afternoon with Mina. She looks after a baby for an American film couple round the corner. I've just come from their house, looked in here for a quick pint before I go on to the theatre. There's something physical about Mina Burns," he said running his fingers through his dark, greying hair and sharing intimate details as though it was normal and appropriate to refer to them in conversation. "It may have been the pills she's on, for she's got an undiagnosable disease which I think is heartbreak, and various doctors are working on her hormones, but this afternoon she had a magnetic layer all round her. I lay back and felt my aura activate into a healthy magnetic field. I always manage to hold myself back and she said, "You've a won-derful sheen, you're so silky." Then I bit into her juicy apples and, in a scattering of blossom, we came together. She whispered, 'I feel you love me, I'm sure you don't but I feel you do,' and I said that when we were angels in Heaven again – she often speaks of James as being an angel in Heaven – we would look back on this time when our two bodies could get so close. 'It's so strange,' she said, 'I keep thinking of dear James. Love and death seem to go together.' She hasn't even heard of Yeats, but that's what she said. And I said, 'It's because we're all angels, he as well. We all met up before we came down to earth.'" I nodded.

"With her love and death do 'go together'. Not long ago the Americans were home and her daughter was home, so she waited for me by the grass sward, and as it was a Saturday we drove to the cemetery, at her request. It was open till eight, and it was not yet six, and there was no one about. It was a fine summer's evening, and I drove to the far side and parked among the bushes by the railway line and I turned round and looked at the long vista to the gates, and the thousands of still graves. She was hot for me – some guilt about James heightens her urge to abase herself in places that house the dead – and she caressed me and her cheeks went bright

THE CLEAR, SHINING SUNLIGHT OF ETERNITY 319

red as if a spirit from one of the graves had taken possession of her lungs. Although it was summer a condensation crept up the back window and I saw a boy with black hair enter the cemetery a long way off and head off among the graves, all misty like a truant angel returning to its lodging-place. I watched him in the mirror for he looked like James. Later she lay across my chest, red-cheeked, and looking out I saw a robin watching me on one side, and a squirrel watching me from the litter-bin on the other side, like two spirits from the graves who had put on form to get a better look. And entering their beings, I saw why they were curious. What a strange ritual was this passionate drinking that humans got so steamed up about before they joined the sleepers in the graves!

"This afternoon she reminisced about the day James got wet. She told me, 'James said "My teacher" – that's you – "let me go home and dry."' (He always spoke of you as 'his teacher'. He liked you so much. He worshipped you.) She told me, 'James said "When I'm old enough to go out to work, I'm going to wear a suit like my teacher's."' She said, 'I remember once Meg came round – she was always after James – and he asked "How's my teacher getting on at your school, because he's left mine and started there now. Have you seen him yet?" And he was so eager to talk about his teacher. And one day when he'd been sent to that horrible place after being bad, we saw his teacher. He was in his car and James said, "That's my teacher, don't let him see me, don't tell him I've been bad." His teacher was all that was good to him. I keep thinking of these things, they're like those flowers: everlasting silk apple-blossom.'"

Then I was back at that school on a hot summer day, telling off James. I looked at his parting in his black hair and his brown eyes, and the cut of his black blazer round his thin neck and the awkward long trousers, as though he were not ready for them. Then I was back in the day when Mr Dyack lent me his cane for safe-keeping, and I again walked among the desks and brandished it in fun, and once again James rose and naughtily turned his bottom and bent and jerked it out of the way as I flipped playfully in his direction, and sat down with his behind firmly on the chair. My impression of him was in the raw – there was no silk idealisation in the way I remembered him – but there was still something eternal about the image, and I was appalled at my ignorance of the terrible fate that awaited him that day, the awful blasting into pieces by the whoosh of an electric train that would hit him at sixty miles an hour. He was still there in front of my eyes, though his flesh had disintegrated, and the time that divided us was strangely unreal. It was like remembering seeing Bernadette Devlin in the Bunch of Grapes when I did not know she would be shot. It was like flying through the night air to the other side of the world and walking again in my Tokyo bungalow, leaving the kitchen-drawer with the scurrying cockroaches and the swing-door with the knot in it, and wandering to the tiled bath were I floated in water that came up to my neck.

"I went and washed," Tom murmured, "and in the bathroom I saw some dried greengages in a vase. They looked dead, their red lanterns hung to a bare stem like images from a summer long past, but they were still there, unfading and frail and tantalisingly hollow, one squeeze away from a pop.

"She came to the bathroom and saw me looking at them. 'I like them, *he* liked them,' she said. 'They're what he looked for in the garden we used to live in, but I still prefer my silk apple-blossom, that's truly everlasting. But most of all I remember the champagne roses – white with a bit of red on the edge of the petals – which James gave me just before he died, and which I carried to his funeral.'"

Later I watched him walk across the green common to catch a bus towards his theatre, and in the setting evening sun it seemed that all humans were insubstantial shadows beneath the dazzling light of eternity.

FROTHY WEIRS AND A RISING SUN
(OR: HEN-SQUAWKS AND A GUARDIAN ANGEL, OR: POW! ZAM!)

I went to Winchester to attend a conference for mystics and scientists. I drove down the M3 and booked in at the Rising Sun in Bridge Street around six, then drove out of town to King Alfred's College, and, having been given a yellow non-resident's badge, ate a vile vegetarian dinner overlooking wooded hills whose peace reminded me of Kita-Kamakura. The elderly woman next to me said, "I've been told that this is my last life if I do well."

Sir Thomas Roper, the organiser, held my hand in a gentle

healer's grasp. He looked like Albert Schweitzer with his now white hair and bushy white moustache, and he went into a trance while he tried to remember who I was. I said I was looking forward to hearing the biochemist, and he said, "Oh, he's in the Galapagos Islands, we've had to replace him." He strangely did not know who was doing the replacing, and hazarded the wrong name.

Sir Thomas Roper gave the first lecture. Typically he began, "This is a mo-MENtous occasion." The elderly woman whispered, "Sir Thomas is a bit like Moses, he's always looking for the Promised Land, but won't do anything to find it." We watched him in the yellow-badge hall on closed circuit television, for the main (white-badge) hall was full. I sat in a room darkened by curtains and looked at a curved screen which had yellow daffodils and white narcissi at the base.

A tousled-haired young physicist spoke next, about how subatomic physics had debunked materialism – he followed his book, which I had read – and then the leader of the Sufi sect spoke. He was disappointing; he looked like everyone's idea of a guru, with white swept-back Indian hair and a grey-white beard and swarthy skin, and his brown monk's cloak fastened at the front with a pin, but he did not so much as mention mysticism. He got lost in long words and in long analogies, and everything was "dynamic".

The physicist had said that scientific theories were "models"; so all language was an approximation to Reality that had no objective validity. There were too many words, and the mystic side was not presented and the conference was unbalanced. I went back to the Rising Sun and had a cider until closing time, and slept in a freezing room upstairs.

Next morning I had breakfast in the Pool Room near a log fire. Then I went out for the papers. I walked across the bridge and passed the old City Mill, 1744, in the sunshine. Two weirs converged under the Mill and frothed dynamically under the bridge, like the words in King Alfred's College.

That Saturday morning began with lectures by a psychic researcher, a Professor of Chemistry, and a biologist. There was a distinction between the mystic and the psychic, but there were no definitions. Again the words bubbled and foamed, but there was nothing about mysticism or the Light.

After a wretched vegetarian lunch I drove into Winchester, for we had the afternoon free. I saw the fourteenth century Round

Table of King Arthur, and then went to the Cathedral. I looked up at the mortuary chests which contain the bones of the Saxon kings, and of Canute, and I was bossed round the Cathedral Library by an elderly woman. I lingered in the Guardian Angels' Chapel and gazed at the eight round murals of winged angels on the medieval roof. I wandered off to the City Cross – where William the Conqueror's Royal Palace stood, and where children pulled strings from toy hens and made loud squawking noises – and I walked back through the churchyard, where two lovers embraced on a grave, and saw the house where Jane Austen died.

I returned for the 5 o'clock lecture. The author of a well-known book on parapsychology spoke against scepticism. He made one point, which might as well have been a clucking hen's squawk, and there was still nothing about the Light.

I could bear it no longer. I sought out the subatomic physicist and said we were still awaiting something on mysticism. He agreed and said he was very disappointed in the guru. We discussed how physics saw the cosmic rays that shower our atmosphere and what happens to the body in enlightenment while women came up and smiled and said, "Thank you for your lecture yesterday," as if to say, 'I'm yours if you want to take me.'

"Is the enlightened brain a mirror or a bulb?" I asked him. "What model do you opt for?"

"I incline to the mirror view," he said in his Viennese voice, leaning back in his brown velvet suit and flowered shirt, "bulbs are an aspect of materialism, of outmoded Newtonian physics. We polish our mirrors to reflect the Light. But I think you are taking enlightenment too literally. It is understanding, not light."

Then I knew that he was one who did not know. The guru had said, "There are four categories of people: those who do not know they do not know; those who know they do not know; those who do not know they know; and those who know they know." This physicist was one who did not know he did not know. "No," I corrected him, "the mystic sees the Light as actual Light."

"I know strange things happen," he said, "once I looked out of a window at midnight, and everything was lit up as bright as day."

Again I knew he did not know. I extricated myself from the conversation by saying, "In your terms, human beings are particles."

"Yes," he said, "maybe photons cause the Light, but....I do not

THE CLEAR, SHINING SUNLIGHT OF ETERNITY

know what causes the Light."

I saw he was speculating, and after another wretched vegetarian meal he gave a doctrinaire near-Marxist lecture at the end of which he said, "The whole cosmos is divine, and we relate personally to it, but there is no personal God in it. This is a Taoist or Buddhist view, and it is scientific."

I drove back over the bridge to the Rising Sun and thought of Omar Khayyam's words. In his youth he "did eagerly frequent/Doctor and Saint, and heard great argument/About it and about: but evermore/Came out by the same door as in I went". I had heard the subatomic Doctor and the guru-Saint, and all that had changed was that I had come out of the door in which I went.

That night the Rising Sun was filled with a drunken football team talking about the afternoon's game. Next morning I was up early as Sir Thomas Roper was leading a meditation in the white-badge hall. I jokingly said to the elderly woman whose last life this was, "The organisers know that the conference is unbalanced, so they're putting us all in a trance to outmanoeuvre our criticisms."

Some hundred people sat in the plush theatre seats. Soon I was feeling my breathing ("the ebb and flow of life" Sir Thomas Roper intoned), and the Light rose and kept threatening to send shafts up the sky of my dark being. I saw a revolving spiral in Light – a chakra? – and then POW! Zam! There was an explosion of Light and shock waves of Light radiated outwards like ripples as if an atom had been split in my head ("see the Light that casts no shadow," Sir Thomas Roper intoned, behind where I was on the space-time continuum). I was held down by gravity, but my spirit felt buoyant and wanted to soar into the upper reaches of the air, and then up I went, I was flying on air currents, the explosion had been the firing of my rocket engines, and then I was out in space and hurtling into the Light ("fall upwards into the Light," intoned Sir Thomas Roper), and I felt clean inside, washed through with Light. I basked in the risen sun until it was time to leave Eternity and change my observer's position and fall back into time and return to my body back on earth ("pull the cloak of Light around you," intoned Sir Thomas Roper).

When I came to, blinking for the electric light, back in the illusory world of phenomena, I looked at Sir Thomas Roper. He sat, pale and gaunt and sallow, his white hair and white moustache like Albert Schweitzer's or Einstein's, a strangely disembodied spirit, an ethereal Guardian Angel with yellow wings, and I marvelled that he had appeared not to know about the Light at the conference about the Essenes.

I tottered out of the white-badge hall and walked unsteadily back to my car. The sun shone, spring birds were twittering in clean fir-trees, there were daisies in the field. Reality was what I had just experienced, and this peace at being one with the cosmos, at sharing its electrons and photons, and somehow I had gone beyond language, with its scaffoldings, its approximations that could be dismantled when their work was done; I had gone beyond works of art, which were only models for interpreting our experience. I had existentially made contact with Reality, and the words could be dispensed with; unless they served to record the thing-ness for future reference.

Soon I was walking back over the bridge to the Rising Sun for a lone breakfast in the Pool Room. I felt light inside, buoyant, exhilarated. One ray of my rising sun was worth all the words that frothed like water under the Mill of the lectern.

THE CURTAIN PULLED ASIDE AND GAMMA RAYS

Later that morning the guru led us in meditation. I already had the Light in my mind. He was Indian-brown, white-haired and bearded, and he looked down from the tele-screen and asked us to "sit up straight so the gamma rays can reach the back" and then to breathe out and hold each exhalation as long as possible so that breathing in was no effort and we sank into relaxation. When we were relaxed he asked us to breathe in and hold each inspiration as long as possible, and to ascend on it, to fly.

The buoyancy came back, a levity which resists gravity, and as I began to soar he murmured, "You are little in a vast universe. The ant looks for the ant-nest." He directed our attention to the stars – "you are being in the cosmos" – and as I fell deeper up into space, he said, "Look down from a mountain top and see your whole life beneath you," and I saw why I sought out Japan and returned to the West so that I could pursue Eternity like this; I saw how my whole life was leading me to the beyond, that was why the material things had never meant much to me.

"You have no ego consciousness," he said, "be detached from it, see the divine intention." I went further and further away in a

THE CLEAR, SHINING SUNLIGHT OF ETERNITY

shadowy world of no-Light. Then the guru said, "You have transcended your body, you are in Eternity. The curtain has been pulled aside. Once that curtain has moved, nothing can be the same for you. Now slowly drop back into time. Now return to earth, to your body. Now move your fingers."

And I was back in the curtained hall thinking of something a college friend once said: "I have spent too long sitting in draughty drill-halls, waiting for messages from the Absolute."

Out in the grounds I told the guru about a written question I had submitted to the panel of speakers for the coming Question Time. "What 'model' do you envisage for the Light that streams from the cosmos into the body and the enlightened mind?" I suggested three possible models: the mind as a mirror, the mind as an electric light bulb and the Theosophical model of prana and chakras and rays. The guru nodded and said he would answer in the hall.

Yellow badges were allowed into the white-badge hall for this session, and I sat through a host of questions in my plush seat – and the Chairman did not ask my question. So when the Chairman had closed the session, I went up to the guru for my answer.

He immediately said with a conniving furtive look, "I have thought, and I can say this. Light descends from the Light of Lights, and energy becomes matter, waves become particles in accordance with the quantum theory. Light ascends from the person, matter becomes energy in the corona, the halo; electrons become photons. That is all I can say." A group of admirers had gathered round us, and I could not discuss the problem any further then.

I went out into the sun and pondered on his answer, and then I saw the guru walking up to his room, his brown monk's cloak dancing above the ground. I intercepted him and diverted him from a blonde authoress with bedroom eyes who had intimate things to ask. While she stood resentfully to one side, I recapitulated my view of enlightenment as one process which physics must be able to interpret.

"Yes," he said with a conniving, furtive glance over his shoulder – he spoke to me as if we both knew – "gamma rays come from the cosmos and enter the base of the spine. Their radiation can smash an atom. The Hiroshima bomb contained gamma rays and it smashed the atoms in the DNA of the chromosomes of the victims, and caused genetic variations. Gamma rays send the electrons spinning, and there is ionisation and the energy travels up the spine and becomes photons all over the body, and especially in the corona or halo. This is the same as the aura, the electro-magnetic field. It is all one. It is not a mirror. The Sufis used to say that the brain reflects God like a mirror because of the Moslems, they would get into trouble with the Moslems if they said that God could be known directly, God could therefore only be reflected. That is an outdated 'model'. Gamma rays are very dangerous in large doses, but they come to us through the atmosphere in small doses that are not dangerous."

And now I knew that when I had opened myself up to 'spirits' I was really feeling the shiver and surge that are felt when the gamma rays of Divine Love and intention are received from far beyond the stars.

The guru placed his hands together and bowed. I watched him head for his room with the girl in attendance, and I thought of his lecture, which had not mentioned mysticism and I thought of the Taoist text: 'He who knows does not speak, he who speaks does not know.' He knew and so he had not spoken of the Light at his lecture, but had pulled a dark curtain across his sunlit mind.

INDEX

A Bafflement like a Netted Fish 158
A Bird's Song and a Spreading Yew 232
A Bleary-Eyed Look and a Belly-Laugh 230
A Blind Will and a Blunder 37
A Boast and a Provoked Fate 229
A Body Fooled into Milk 160
A Bonfire and a Village 100
A Boutique behind a Mask 48
A Buzzing Bluebottle and a Frozen Fish 186
A Canon in his Dream House 315
A Castle like a Dazzling Girl 46
A Causeway of Light 255
A Chanted Introduction and a Dig 91
A Chauffeur for an Inspector 291
A Cherry-Blossomed Hell 76
A Chile Badge and a Lanced Boil 226
A Christ in Hell 103
A Clown and a Volcanic Eruption 203
A Cobweb Christ and a Feather Duster 177
A Colonel in Civvy Street 280
A Deathly White Boy and a Pact 149
A Deck-Chair in the Sea 88
A Destiny in Hebrew Letters 260
A Dotty Bard and a Cotton-Wool Ear 207
A Duchess in the Sun 18
A Feathered Witch-Doctor and a Stranded Crab 42
A Flash in the Chemistry Lab 216
A Gasman Conned 35
A Grandfather among Ras Tafarian Hats 194
A Hanged Man's Gift and a Mongol's Eyes 174
A Harbour Creek and a Tiger Cowrie 98
A Ladder and Quarrels at Church 102
A Late Boy in the Sea 82
A Light on Dead Anemones 284
A Mother in Action 69
A Mouse under the Counter 159
A Nice Day for the Match and a Bottle of Optrex 118
A Partridge in a Pear-tree 30
A Piggy-Eyed Broker and a Conniving Smile 239
A Poker Fork and a Bursting Bubble 234
A Pompous Fool and River Jordan Water 308

A Red in the Surgery 312
A Ring and Horizontal Bars 13
A Rolls Royce Day-Dream and a Naiad's Chipped Nose 245
A Run-Away's Stone and a Four-Knight Door 304
A Sandcastle and a Sun-Kite 181
A Shermozzle and a Freudian Slip 162
A Situation like Nerve Gas 121
A Smell of Leaves and Summer 1
A Smile and Violent Streets 278
A Speaker like a Hurricane 294
A Spoon-Feeding Bully and a Pacifist 206
A Standard like a Fluttering Pound 79
A Stumble and a Slammed Phone 212
A Tide in the Cellar 302
A Twelve-Year Dream and an Unsailed Boat 110
A Vision in Winsor and Newton 26
A Wag in Lyonesse 146
A Windmill and the Real Things 60
A Zoo of Buffers 161
Across the Frontier 251
Afternoons like Cinders 301
Alison Bush, Eighteen, Wants Proof 242
An Alternative Girl 9
An Archangel and Personal Responsibility 201
An Eagle and a Basking Shark 179
An Exile in Noyna Road 223
An Imperial Egoist and a Car Wallah 296
An Imperious Neo-Platonist, and a Genius's Volume of Verse 209
An Old Lady and a £40 Sack 82
An Orgy in the Churchyard 164
Anarchic Laughter in the System 222
Another Place 314
April Fools and the Thirteenth Stream 140
As Spanish as Lasagne 16
Baby Belling 75
Beehive and a Dahlia Horn 27
Bonhomie like an Oxbridge Smile 154
Breaths like Waves 73
Caravan People and a Fun-Hat 184
Cardboard instead of Bread 28
Castles in the Air 5
Chairman's Action and a Red-Eyed Comedy 204

INDEX

Christmas-Tree Patterns on the Lunatic Fringe 281
Clubbing with Donald 22
Crabbe under Shingle 58
Crying Eyes and a Nearly Perfect Rose 119
Decca and Blue Flowers 19
Doorhandle for a Slammed Door 258
Earth in the Way 139
Edward Thomas and the Swimming Gala 86
Eternity beside the Traffic Jam 157
First Mate in the Coliseum 293
Flicking Fingers and Frayed Cloth 64
Folks Stoned 33
French Howlers and Spilt Wine 236
Friendship like a Potato Crisp 72
Frothy Weirs and a Rising Sun 320
Governors like Bowlers 313
Heart and Burning Night 25
Hoi Mate and the Water Music 74
Horses like Elves and Goblins 14
Irish Fishing and a Hurried Grave 220
Lad's Love 192
Laughter in the Dark 211
Like a Burst Water-Main 78
Like a Fish in a Storm-Tossed Sea 110
Like Bricks on Sand 196
Like the Smell of Fresh Beans 270
Lost Glasses and Clanging Seats 115
Loud Voices and the Long Silence of Christendom 306
Loyalty like a Company Label 272
Marinated Pilchards and Silver Lead 101
Mean Time 94
Mixed Metaphors and a Diamond Light 268
Mr Rubin's Fortune 310
Mulled Empire and a Hymn-Singing Flag-Planter 290
Nemesis at the Extraordinary General Meeting 55
08.15 Horas and Fresh Fish 62
Of the Cannibalism of Mice and Shrews and Voles 51
One of God's Chosen 235
People Like Us and a Sash-Cord 200
Pinned Butterflies and African Carvings 257
Politeness like a Split Canvas Chair 80
Providence like a Retribution 267
Radiator in the Snow 7
Rôles like Fancy Dress 265
Shahites in our Road 262
Shout to the Lord 116
Silk Apple-Blossom and Dried Greengages 317
Soda Water and a Scallop Shell 199
Solitaire and a Nudge 96
Spirits up the Spine and a Bucketful of Stones 171
Stagnant Eyes and a Vein 276
Stone Cottages and a Teeming Sea 99
Stone Lions and Marble Veins 285
Subtle Bodies 247
Tattered Walls and a Gorgon's Scream 142
The Buses was Late 72
The Clear, Shining Sunlight of Eternity 152
The Cold Heat of Alpha 288
The Curtain Pulled Aside and Gamma Rays 324
The Director is an Idiot 66
The Little Life and a Mirroring High Self 190
The Manageress and the Pigeons 20
The Mystery of the Great Pyramid 249
The Ordinary in Pearly King Clothes 237
The Sweet Smell of Decay 263
The Waters of the Ocean, the Upper Reaches of the Air 183
This is the Way the Term Ends 11
Three Cowherd Angels and a Cattle-Branding 125
Three Pure Chrysanthemums, or Faded Petals 132
Toy Planes and Doggies, and a Merry-Go-Round 188
Twinkling Hubert and a Hypocrite 45
Two Burps and Three Cheers 283
Two Smiling Buddhas and He Who Speaks 164
Tyranny and Bad Luck 52
Waves across the Hedge 15
White Cars, Black Hands 227
White Globes and a Blood-Red Sun 275
Woodcutter's Hut and Dolphin Square 20
Yes Please to a Peeling House 224